For Six Good Reasons

Lin Stepp

Books by Lin Stepp

Novels:
The Foster Girls
Tell Me About Orchard Hollow
For Six Good Reasons
Delia's Place
Second Hand Rose
Down by the River
Makin' Miracles
Saving Laurel Springs
Welcome Back
Daddy's Girl
Lost Inheritance
The Interlude
Happy Valley

The Edisto Trilogy:
Claire at Edisto
Return to Edisto

Christmas Novella:
A Smoky Mountain Gift
In *When the Snow Falls*

Regional Guidebooks
Co-Authored with J.L. Stepp:
The Afternoon Hiker
Discovering Tennessee State Parks

For Six Good Reasons

A SMOKY MOUNTAIN NOVEL

LIN STEPP

MOUNTAIN HILL PRESS

This is a work of fiction. Although numerous elements of historical and geographic
accuracy are utilized in this and other novels in the Smoky Mountain series, many other
specific environs, place names, characters, and incidents are the product of the author's
imagination or used fictitiously.

Scripture used in this book, whether quoted or paraphrased by the characters, is taken
from the King James Version of the Bible.

Cover design: Katherine Stepp
Interior design: J. L. Stepp, Mountain Hill Press
Editor: Sandra Horton
Map design: Lin M. Stepp

Library of Congress Cataloging-in-Publication Data

Stepp, Lin
For Six Good Reasons: A Smoky Mountain Mountain novel / Lin Stepp
        p. cm – (The Smoky Mountain series)
ISBN: 978-1-7343883-8-1
First Mountain Hill Press Trade Paperback Printing: December 2020

eISBN: 978-1-7343883-9-8
First Mountain Hill Press Electronic Edition: December 2020

1. Women—Southern States—Fiction   2. Mountain life—Great Smoky Mountains
Region (NC and TN)—Fiction. 3. Contemporary Romance—Inspirational—Fiction.
I. Title

Library of Congress Control Number: 2020922978

Cover Art

The beautiful works of art, featured on past Smoky Mountain novels and gracing the front cover of this book, were painted by well-known regional artist Jim Gray. The painting on this book is entitled *Spring Ablaze*.

Jim Gray (1932-2019) is a nationally recognized artist who painted Smoky Mountain scenes and southern landscapes for over thirty years. In 1966, Gray and his family moved to East Tennessee so that Jim could explore and paint the beauty of the countryside surrounding the Great Smoky Mountains. He has sold over 2000 paintings and 125,000 prints to collectors in the United States and abroad. Jim is listed in *Who's Who In American Art* and has been featured in many publications including *National Geographic* and *Southern Living*.

Prints of *Spring Ablaze*, or other fine works of art, can be purchased at the Jim Gray Gallery, 670 Glades Road in Gatlinburg, TN, or ordered through Jim Gray's website at: http//www.jimgraygallery.com

Jim Gray Gallery business mailing address is:
GREENBRIAR INCORPORATED
P.O. Box 735, Gatlinburg, TN37738
Business Phone: (865) 436-8988

ACKNOWLEDGMENTS

Warm thanks and gratitude go to those who helped make this book a reality ...

... All the staff at Mountain Hill Press

... J.L. Stepp - Book Layout, Format, and Interior Design; who shares my writing journey, and is my tireless business manager, husband, loving friend, and the first reader of all my books.

... Katherine Stepp - Cover Designer, who creates and maintains my author's website and shares her expertise in computer graphics.

... Sandy Horton - Manuscript Editor

... And to the Lord, who continues to support and guide me in all I do.

DEDICATION

This book is dedicated to my mother, Joy Grigsby Mathews, who was 99 years young when this book originally published in 2011—but who has now gone on home to heaven. A gifted story teller, she introduced me to the love of words and stories at an early age, transporting me back in time to her days on the family farm with her eleven brothers and sisters. She read to me with animation and helped me memorize the beautiful words and rhythms in countless poems and songs. At her knee, my love and appreciation for the written word began.

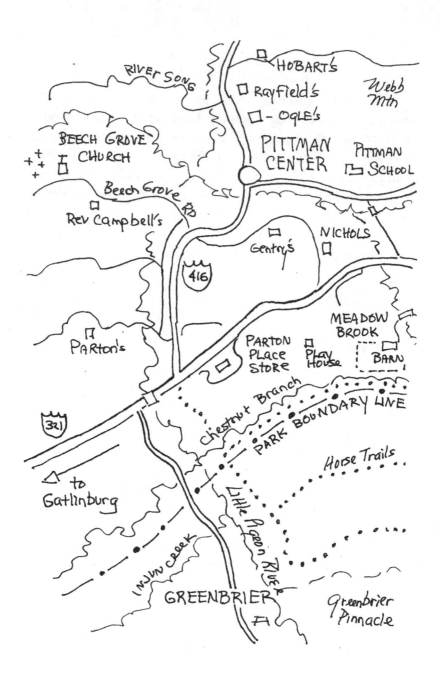

Map for Greenbrier Area
In *For Six Good Reasons*

CHAPTER 1

"Unbelievable. I'm having that dream again." The familiar scenes of it filtered into the edges of Alice's consciousness as she began to wake. Knowing it not quite time to get up, she rolled over and let the dream play on softly in her mind. She drifted, in half sleep, into the winter scene.

Alice stood in a fresh fall of snow on a narrow, arched bridge spanning a backwoods creek. A mountain range rose in misty layered beauty before her. Halfway up the mountain slope, a man, poised on a rocky cliff, looked down at her. The man, dressed like a cowboy, sat astride a black horse shrouded in a swirl of white snow. His lower face lay muffled in a woolen scarf wrapped around his neck to ward off the cold, and he wore a long, bulky tan jacket and a dark, weathered cowboy hat pulled low over his forehead. A stretch of distance separated the two of them, he high on the rocky point above and she on the bridge far below, but Alice could sense his eyes on her.

They'd locked eyes the minute they saw each other, and an intense drawing electrified the air between them. She couldn't actually see the man's eyes at this distance, but Alice felt she could see them just the same. She sensed them, focused on her, watching her intently, calling to her in some odd way.

Goosebumps ran up her arms, and her hands gripped the rails on the bridge, as she gazed at the man. A magnetic current bolted between the two of them, pulling them toward each other. Such a peculiar sensation. If the bridge railing and a mountain creek hadn't stood directly in front of her, Alice knew she'd simply start walking toward him. The pull felt that strong. Yet she didn't move.

Instead, the man started down the mountainside toward her, reining his horse around and starting to ride down a side trail from the cliff. Alice followed his progress with her eyes at first, watching with fascination as he began moving towards her. Then, with a shiver, her good sense kicked in.

"For heaven's sake, Alice," she whispered. "You're out here in the country by yourself, looking at rural property for sale. There's probably not another soul around for miles." She shivered and wrapped her coat tighter around her. "Be sensible, would you? It's cold and snowing and some strange man is riding down the mountain towards you."

Her heartbeat and breathing escalated and her initial attraction turned to an icy edge of fear. Adrenalin pumping, Alice turned quickly away and fled to her car, driving off before the man could ride down to her.

Most of the time the dream ended here, as it did this morning. No further images played across the screen of Alice's mind as she pulled the covers around her neck, beginning to wake more fully. Yet, Alice knew the story possessed other endings. Frequently she dreamed romantic and even passionate final chapters to the fantasy—where she waited on the bridge until the stranger galloped down to her. She woke up feeling foolish, and somewhat embarrassed, after these episodes, depending on how far the romantic events progressed. Admittedly, she also felt a little stirred after the dream's more Harlequin endings.

She stretched, knowing she should get up. "It's an odd dream to experience over and over again. A Freudian psychoanalyst would have a heyday with it, especially since the event actually happened." She shivered. "I stood on that bridge in February, saw the cowboy on the hill, and fled in a panic when he started down the mountain. The dream played out this morning exactly as it happened. No frills and romantic endings this time. I drove away sensibly as a prudent woman should, and just like I *did* that cold, wintry day."

With the bedside alarm humming now, Alice flipped back the covers, climbed out of bed, and padded into the bathroom to start her day.

"Honestly, Alice Graham," she told herself in the bathroom mirror, sighing. "You *really* need to get more of a life."

Later in the same day, Alice couldn't help remembering the morning's latest dream sequel as she scanned the roadside for the sign to the same country property once again. She discovered this mountain house and land in February, not quite ready to consider a major move yet. Now ready, she'd come back to look at the property in earnest and meet with the realtor.

"There's the sign," Alice said, spotting Jamison Realty's For Sale sign to her left. She turned off the highway and down a wooded lane.

Remembering her last visit here, Alice's heartbeat quickened and she felt goose bumps run up her arms as before. She shook her head and frowned at the memory. "Get a grip, Alice. You experienced an odd event with a man on the mountain that winter day before. So what? In actuality, it's more unusual you even noticed a For Sale sign with all that snow coming down."

She slowed her SUV over a bump in the rural lane. "That's what you should remember most, Alice—that you even saw a For Sale sign in an incoming blizzard and that you were nutty enough to stop. You know how dangerous the mountain roads get in the backwoods of the Smokies. but you had one of those crazy witnesses to turn off. Snow or no snow, it's a wonder you got back home safely at all."

She laughed at her impulsiveness now. "Oh, well. Despite what happened in February, this time I know I'm here for practical and well-thought-out reasons."

A logical and sensible woman by nature, these last words comforted her. However, she'd learned not to discount inner leadings or to laugh at the idea of fate either.

"Perhaps all of these quirky happenings helped get me to the house I need to consider." She smiled at the thought. "Grandmother

Beryl would say everything that's happened is simply a part of the Lord's leading and guidance. Who knows? I've certainly prayed enough over this decision."

Focusing on the road now, Alice watched the driveway curve to the right through a stand of trees, before opening out to reveal a sprawling, two-storied white house set on a green expanse of lawn. The rural home, charming in appearance, sported weathered grey roofing, neat black shutters, and a welcoming shiny, black front door.

A long porch wrapped invitingly across the front and around one side of the house, connecting to a two-storied garage wing nestled among a cluster of dogwoods. Crisp, white Victorian arches curved decoratively across the length of the front porch above fanciful, ornate railings. A row of white-painted rockers lined the porch with graceful ferns hanging between the arches above them. It made Alice think of a country bed and breakfast she once stayed in with her family in rural Virginia.

Back in February, the house appeared stark in its snowy setting among bare, black-trunked trees and snow-blanketed shrubs. Now, in May, the yard looked lush and green. Shrubs bloomed in colorful array around the property and old climbing roses and clematis sprawled over sections of fencing along the roadside. Iris, in shades of blue and yellow, nestled against the foundation of the house among an array of purple phlox, sweet William, early yellow coreopsis, and old-fashioned daisies.

Alice smiled and hugged herself in delight. "I knew this place would be pretty in spring. But it's even more beautiful than I imagined."

She parked her car where the realtor would see it when she arrived and got out to walk around. She'd come early to explore.

Hanging on the lamppost beside the front sidewalk swung a wrought-iron sign that read *Meadowbrook*. Alice walked over to rest her hand on it. "The realtor said the past owners, Carl and Dora Newland, gave the house this name thirty years ago when they built it. They raised their family here and now they've gone to live full-time on the Florida panhandle near their children."

She looked around the property thoughtfully. "If the house sat closer to towns and stores, it probably would have sold before now. But property in a rural area like this sells slower."

The Meadowbrook property lay far out Tennessee Highway 321 between Gatlinburg and Cosby in a rural area called the Greenbrier community. It took some seeking to even find the few municipal buildings and small township of nearby Pittman Center. However, Alice wanted a rural, country place with land and a big house like she'd grown up in. Meadowbrook appeared a sizeable house, but Alice had good reasons for needing a lot of space right now.

She wandered up on the porch to peep in the windows and then walked around to the back of the house. Here, a deep, screened porch looked out over the lawn and down to a whitewashed horse barn at the back end of the property. Several horses grazed contentedly in the field around the barn.

"Someone must be using the barn and keeping up the property. Everything looks neat and immacutely kept."

Strolling through the back yard, Alice enjoyed the green shade trees and the scattered beds of spring flowers in bloom. She smiled when she spotted a little playhouse peeking out between two shady maple trees.

Midway down the acreage of the back yard, Alice paused on a small rise. There, to her left, a mountain creek tumbled along, forming a crooked boundary line. An arched log bridge led across the creek. Alice walked up onto the bridge to look back toward the mountains. The Greenbrier Pinnacle rose beyond the lower ridges with the mountain peaks of the Smokies ranges peeking out behind.

Alice's eyes automatically searched upward to locate the rocky ridge top on the mountainside. She knew she looked for the man again, the man she saw that first snowy day.

She shrugged and smiled at her foolishness. "You idiot," she said. "You know it's silly to even look for that man again. It's not as though you know him. He could be anyone, and it's doubtful he's around now. He rode horseback—probably passing through. He might even be a criminal or dangerous."

He'd felt dangerous, despite his attraction.

Alice shivered as she looked up at the rocky cliff. "You know you felt afraid as you watched him riding down the mountainside," she reminded herself. "You panicked and fled, too. That should tell you something."

Despite her continuing lectures to herself, she knew she wouldn't easily forget the man. He'd faded in and out of her dreams for months now – making her feel young and foolish, waking her up with odd yearnings she hadn't felt since before she married David.

"Yoo-hoo!" a voice called from behind Alice, interrupting her thoughts. "Is that you, dear?"

Alice smiled. Her realtor, Stella Jamison, always so bubbly and delightful to be around, had arrived to take her through the house.

Alice waved and started back up the path to greet her warmly.

"How good it is to see you again, dear." Stella swooped Alice into a big hug as soon as she could. "You look absolutely marvelous—blond and pretty, like one of those graceful ballerinas twirling around on a music box. You know, if I hadn't just married off my last boy Scott to Vivian Delaney, I'd be matchmaking to get him to meet you." She laughed. "At least you caught the bridal bouquet!"

Alice rolled her eyes over that memory as she returned Stella's hug. "It's good to see you again, too, Stella. Thanks for taking the time to come show me around the house today yourself."

"I wouldn't have let anyone else come, Alice. I'm sure you heard Scott and Vivian adopted little Sarah Taylor. We're all grateful for your help with that." She took Alice's arm companionably in hers as they started back toward the front of the house.

Stella looked impeccably dressed, as usual, in a tailored slacks set, her short blond hair immaculate and her makeup perfect.

She raised her eyebrows in question to Alice. "Is it true that you've taken Loren and Richard Stuart's children in with you for a while?"

"It is, Stella, and that's why I'm here looking at this big house.

I've had the Stuart children with me in my little Sevierville house for almost a year now—a tight fit, believe me. We're all ready for some more space. Loren and Richard actually looked at country places with you or Franklin before they died, if you remember, wanting to make a move closer to the mountains. They loved it so much up here. I think they considered this house once."

"I'll check on that." Stella made a tut-tutting sound. "I was simply shocked when they died. How long has it been now, a year and a half?" She shook her head as she talked. "I remember I couldn't believe it when I learned both of them had been killed coming back from that conference up north. Icy roads can be so dangerous. They were such fine people and such a credit to our community, too, running that counseling center and serving on many committees in Sevierville – many with Franklin and me. We liked them so much."

Alice nodded, hating to remember that unhappy time and the sad memories it conjured up.

Stella gave her a questioning look. "You often worked with Lauren and Richard, didn't you, Alice?"

"I did." Alice smiled. "Our Sevierville branch office of the Wayside Agency shared space in their counseling center off Middle Creek Drive. The Stuarts included me in nearly everything at their clinic, like another staff member. They often helped me and my agency director, Dorothy Eaton, with our family and child counseling problems, too."

"You've placed so many children in foster homes around the area as a social worker with the Wayside Agency. Is that how you got involved with the Stuart children after Loren and Richard's death?"

"Yes, in a way," Alice acknowledged. "I always promised Loren and Richard I would help to see their children placed happily if something happened to them. They worried because they had so little family."

"Six children are never easy to place together, as you well know." Stella turned her eyes to look at Alice thoughtfully. "Are you sure you know what you're doing, dear, taking on such a huge undertaking? Surely, there is some family connection that would take the children to raise or some couple the Stuarts knew that would take them in." Her voice drifted off on that.

Alice shook her head. "Believe me, Stella, I searched in every capacity possible the first six months after the Stuarts died. Loren's elderly father, Lloyd Ingles—in his eighties and with poor health— came up from his retirement community in lower Georgia to help out. The kids, grieving and upset, proved a handful for him alone. It wasn't easy for him. I stopped over to lend a hand whenever I could that spring, and then Lloyd fell down the stairs and broke his leg. Somehow, before I knew it, I practically moved in at the Stuart's house to help. I got more and more involved after that."

"How very good of you, dear," Stella observed.

"Actually, as a social worker, it was not good, Stella. We're not supposed to get involved with children we work with in a foster capacity. It's a definite no-no in the field—but the rules got bent with children of good friends. At first, I didn't funnel the kids through the agency but merely tried to help Lloyd. Like you, I felt sure family or friends of the Stuarts would step up."

"But no one did?" Stella looked amazed.

Alice spread her hands. "No. Loren, an only child and a late child, had a small family circle. Her mother died young and, as I told you, her father Lloyd came to help temporarily, even with congestive heart failure and several other health conditions. Richard's parents are both deceased, and he only has only one brother, Nate. Nate's a recovering alcoholic with a rather troubled past. He owns a little boat dock up on Norris Lake, lives on a battered houseboat nearby, and is a little eccentric. A court would hardly grant Nate custody of the children, and he acted scared to death of the idea, anyway, with all his problems. He wants to stay in touch with the kids, of course, but that's about as far as that would go."

Alice shrugged before continuing. "Some distant family and friends considered the idea of taking one or more of the children, but none would even consider taking all six. They acted shocked

I would even ask such a thing and offered an array of sensible excuses as to why it wouldn't work. That's when our Wayside director, Dorothy Eaton, started helping me through the agency, but we never got anywhere with any potential foster parents once they heard the magic number six."

Stella examined a nail. "Six children are a lot to raise in this world today, Alice. Are you sure it's something you should do, dear? You're young and attractive. To be quite frank, it may be hard to ever get a young man to consider marriage to you with six young children to consider in the package."

Alice smiled at that. "Stella, when the Stuarts first died, the thought of actually taking the kids never crossed my mind. I sort of fell into it backwards."

She paused beside a forsythia bush bursting with yellow blooms. "After staying with the children, the thoughts of fostering them just gradually evolved. By then, of course, they wanted to stay with me and began to ask if they could. They've been wonderful, all of them, helping to make this work. Hoping to stay together as a family."

Stella, watching Alice's face, smiled. "It's evident you've become involved with them and truly fond of them. Children have a way of working their way into your affections, don't they?"

"They do." Alice smoothed back a stray hair. "They feel like part of my own family now."

"I can't imagine that any children of Loren and Richard Stuart's wouldn't be wonderful children." She picked off a bell-shaped blossom from the forsythia to examine it in her hand. "What are their ages now, Alice? I can't seem to remember. I think most of them should be in school by now."

"They are, Stella." Alice warmed to this subject. "Hannah, the oldest, is twelve and finishing the sixth grade. She's a good help, responsible, thoughtful, and a lot like her mother, Loren. Megan is two years behind her at ten. She makes me think of Richard, serious, practical, and a nature-lover. Stacey at eight, is outgoing and feisty while Rachel, only a year younger is her opposite, shy and sweet. The twins, Thomas and Tildy, at five, are simply a handful—always into something, incredibly inquisitive and adventurous. I don't know where they find such energy. I get tired simply watching them."

Stella gave Alice's arm a squeeze as they walked on. "I know that little house you live in on Collier Street very well because our agency sold it to you when you moved to Sevierville. It's a cute little place, Alice, but I honestly don't know how in the world you've packed all six of those children into that small home. You certainly need a bigger house and this is exactly the sort of place you need."

She paused to give Alice a considering look as they rounded the corner of the house, heading for the front door. "I guess you know this is not a very modestly priced property, Alice. If it's too much for your budget with all the children to think of, I'll help you find something more affordable."

Alice smiled. "Fortunately, I'm a woman of some means now. I got a large military settlement when my husband David lost his life in Saudi five years ago and I invested wisely. Then I inherited some money from my Grandmother Duncan when she died and put that away, too. I have enough to pay cash for the house if my offer is accepted. My accountant says property is a good investment, and, believe me, I'm ready to have some space to spread out in—for myself and the kids."

They started up the porch steps then, ready to explore.

"Now, this is a big fourteen room house, Alice." Stella moved into her professional mode as she unlocked the door into the broad entry hall. "I'd need to look at my specs for the square footage, but the house is definitely spacious. It has six rooms downstairs. To the right of the main hall is a living room, dining room, a kitchen and separate eat-in area. A half bath sits off the entry, and then to the left of the main hall is a study, a parlor, and a master bedroom with its own bath. Upstairs are a small den, five more bedrooms and two full baths, and, above the garage wing, there is a bonus room and a sixth bedroom and bath."

Alice grinned. "All that space certainly sounds like heaven to me right now. In my little Collier Street cape cod, I only have a living room, an eat-in kitchen, one bedroom, and a small office downstairs. Upstairs, the children are packed three to a room in the two bedrooms under the eaves."

Stella commiserated with Alice over this as she led her through the entry hall and into a wide arched doorway on the right. "Here's the living and dining area," Stella gestured with a sweep of her hand.

"It's lovely." Alice looked around the spacious area. "I can easily envision Loren and Richard's formal furniture in these rooms. It's in storage now. The children's grandfather, Lloyd, wanted the children to have something to bring to a new home later, so he put all the family furniture in storage when the Stuart's house sold last summer. With their furniture and mine, there shouldn't be much I need to buy."

Alice and Stella talked and visited as they made their way through the first floor of the house. Alice especially loved the big, country kitchen on the back, it's eating area looking onto a shady, screened porch and then across the back lawn. She also liked the roomy master bedroom, bath, and nearby study with its built-in shelves that would be perfect for a home office.

Returning to the front entry, Stella next led Alice up the broad stairway leading to the upper floor.

"You may not like all the colors in the bedrooms upstairs," Stella told her as they walked upstairs. "There is a lot of wallpaper in this house, but I know someone who can take it down and paint it for you reasonably. The children probably have their own furnishings and toys they want to bring to the house and you'll need to coordinate to suit that. I'm sure, after so many transitions, it will make them feel more at home to have the things they know and like around them again."

"That's true," Alice agreed. "It will be nice for the children to have their own bedrooms here, too."

Stella paused on the stairs. "How are you going to continue managing your work out here in the country with all these children, dear? Who keeps them while you work now?"

"I've had help from their old sitter and housekeeper, Martha Pike, since the Stuarts died." She ran a hand along the smooth wood banister. "As for my continuing to work, Lauren and Richard always worked, Stella. My working doesn't seem that different to the Stuart children. Fortunately, I found a sitter and housekeeper, a widow that lives here in Pittman Center - who's agreed to help me if the house works out. I already know her because she's worked occasionally as a foster parent for Wayside when we needed a temporary place for some of our children. She's easy-going, wonderful with kids, a good cook, and has raised a large family of her own. I couldn't even consider this house if I hadn't lined up someone to help me. Her name is Odell McKee."

"What a small world." Stella's laugh tinkled out gaily. "I know Odell McKee. She and I went to school together when we were girls. She's a peach, Alice. You must tell her I said hello. I haven't seen her for an age."

Stella chatted on gaily after that, sharing memories about Odell, and then asked, "Will you continue to work full time, Alice?"

"Actually, our director at the Wayside Agency is letting me cut back to a part-time status here in Sevier County," Alice confided. "I already dropped my old Blount County workload, which another social worker took on. I can do much of my work at my home now and will only need to spend a few days in the field traveling and doing my home visits every week. Also, having the Stuart children set up as foster children in my care gives me a monthly income to help cover their expenses."

"That sounds like a sensible arrangement." Stella stopped at the top of the stairs. "Now let's look at these bedrooms and see what you think."

The upstairs rooms proved spacious with big windows to let in the sunshine. Alice liked the aged floral and striped wallpapers in many of the bedrooms and baths and believed the colors would work nicely for the family with only a few changes.

"It's absolutely perfect in every way," Alice told Stella after they finished touring the house. "I know you're not supposed to sound overly enthusiastic to your realtor, but I'm simply too pleased to hide my feelings."

They sat outside on the front porch now, comfortably settled in two of the house's weathered rocking chairs. Their view looked across the rolling front lawn and down the winding drive leading towards the main road.

Stella crossed her leg. "I'm glad you like the house, Alice. It does seem to be perfect for your large family." She looked at her notes. "The former owners, the Newlands, had five children of their own. I think they'd be pleased to think a new family of children would grow up here at Meadowbrook."

She patted Alice's hand then. "Here's the figure I think you should offer for the Newland's house, dear." She scribbled a number down on a worksheet she'd taken out. "Do you have that much put away?"

"Yes, I do." Alice studied Stella's figure with pleasure. "Do you think the Newlands will take this offer—so far below their asking price?"

"I think they'll agree to this price, or at least a counter offer very near it." She waved a hand dismissively. "Besides, this is a reasonable offer. The house is large and the property lovely, but the place is a little isolated. That's why it's been on the market for over two years and hasn't sold."

She paused. "You do know there's only a K-8 school here in Pittman Center and no middle schools or junior high schools. That has put a lot of families off that considered this place, even though the high school nearer Gatlinburg is an excellent one."

Alice rocked with contentment in the old chair. "I studied the school situation and have already visited the elementary school at Pittman Center. It isn't far from here, only a mile or two away—a small school, but a fine one with a good reputation. Actually new research shows smaller, community K-8 schools are better for children's intellectual and social development than the larger mega schools being built now."

"Is that right?" Stella raised an eyebrow with interest. "Well, leave it to you to know about useful things like that, dear, as a social worker." She waved a hand again. "I just wanted to be sure you knew everything pertinent before you sign the contract."

Alice smiled at Stella then. "You know, I think I know all I need to know to sign today, Stella."

"One never knows all there is to know about a place until one moves in, dear." Stella gave Alice a conspiratorial glance. "You don't know any of the gossip about the neighbors or even who your neighbors are yet. But I'll try to find out about that for you before I see you the next time. We don't want you moving in without knowing all the scoop."

She dropped her voice. "For example, the man that lives next door to you to the east—Harrison Ramsey, I think his name is—I heard his young bride-to-be stood him up at the alter years ago when they were about to be married. Took off right before she walked down the aisle. You know, you think all those stories are only in books or movies, but they happen in real life, too."

"How sad that must have been for him." Alice frowned.

"Perhaps, or maybe the problem is with him. I hear he's never talked about it to anyone." Stella leaned forward and lifted her eyebrows for emphasis. "My sister Mary told me the year before, his little fiancé just up and left the area overnight, sending him his ring back through the mail. Can you imagine? She was one of those nice Reagan girls, too. It's all very odd, dear. I'll bet there's a story there if you could ferret it out."

"I'll be too busy with my own life, Stella, to worry about old tales about my neighbors." Alice hoped to fend off future gossip with this comment. She didn't like engaging in idle chatter about other people's personal business.

Alice studied her watch then. "You know, Stella, I'd better start back to Sevierville so Martha Pike can leave for the day." She sat forward. "I try to get home before the children come in from school when I can."

Stella took a sales contract out of the folder on her lap and began to fill in pertinent information. "As soon as you sign this contract in a few places, Alice, we'll get you right on your way." She looked up with a smile. "I'll call you as soon as I hear from the Newlands to let you know if they accept the offer."

CHAPTER 2

Not far away, Harrison Ramsey reined in his horse Bishop on the mountain ridge above his property. He looked, with satisfaction, over his house and land in the valley below and then swept his gaze across the Newland place and beyond to where Webb Mountain rose in the distance. From this high perch, he could see a deep swath of the Greenbrier valley winding along the tumbling Pigeon River and curling beside rural Highway 321—a fine view he never tired of.

Since his father died, he'd worked hard to keep up the family land and to expand their properties and businesses. In addition to the Ramsey Riding Stables, in the family for over a generation, he owned the W. T. Market and Gas Station his grandfather started on the highway seventy years ago and the apple orchard behind it his great grandfather planted in the 1800s.

On his own initiative, Harrison had developed the rental cabins near Redwine Falls four years ago, before his father passed, and finished them shortly after. Today, six rental cabins clustered amid the scenic setting by Webb Creek and brought in a nice profit— since being paid out—as did the old rental house behind the market. Harrison held almost 1000 acres of Greenbrier land now and cherished all of it.

He let his eyes seek out the little bridge between his place and the Newlands, the one that crossed over Timothy Creek at a narrow point in the stream. He knew he thought about that girl when his eyes sought the arched bridge over the creek, but he indulged himself for a moment. That had been an odd experience seeing her there this winter. How long had it been now? Months? And the memory continued to play through his mind. Shoot, if he dealt honest with himself, he needed to admit he dreamed about that girl sometimes at night.

It snowed the February day he saw her. He'd stopped at the ridge point on his way down the trail, pausing to watch the soft snow drift down on the valley below, and he'd seen her. Just like that. A spot of red in a white landscape. He guessed she wore a red coat that day. Her blond hair gleamed in the sun, and she stood in the middle of the bridge, her arms propped on the rails. He knew the moment she looked his way because something strange happened. Their gazes locked and a drawing arced between them Harrison couldn't explain.

He felt an urgency to go to her and started down the hillside after only a short hesitation. She watched him come at first, but then panicked and bolted. He'd never understood why she did that—left so suddenly with such a powerful pull between them. Curiosity alone should have made her want to stay. Or, at least, that's how Harrison saw it. It frustrated him to get to the bottom of the valley and find her gone. Only tire tracks in the Newland's driveway told him she'd ever been there at all.

"Dang girl." His unexpected voice caused Bishop to jerk and prick his ears. "I haven't experienced any real attraction for a woman for a long time. Mostly tune them out." He leaned forward to pat the horse's neck. "Women generally turn out to be more trouble that they're worth, Bishop. Oh, I had my young years of being interested enough. Of chasing skirts, as Deke calls it. Now I keep my interest banked. There's enough to deal with in this life without worrying over the flightiness and fussiness of women. I can live contented enough without them. A good horse and dog are more reliable company and both better friends."

The bay gelding nickered as if in agreement.

Harrison shifted in the saddle, knowing despite his words that he wondered about the girl from time to time. Today he'd found himself drawn all day to come up here and look for her.

"Dang foolishness. Probably a tourist passing through the mountains, likely back out in Minnesota, Wyoming, or someplace by this time." He scowled in irritation. "It's been four months since that snowy day, and I keep mooning over that girl like a dumb kid. Bunch of nonsense."

He gave Bishop his head and let him lead the way back down the mountain. The familiar side-trail soon connected to the well-traveled riding trail winding down from Redwine Ridge. Bishop splashed through a shallow stretch of Chestnut Branch at the bottom of the mountain and then trotted along the creek path at the backside of the Ramsey farm. From there, a short, half-mile ride led to the wider trail curling into the back of the stables.

Hobart Rayfield sat in front of the barn, leaning back in his usual, worn chair whittling on a piece of wood, his battered cowboy hat shading his weathered face. Hobart's old beagle, Skeeter, lifted his head sleepily to greet Harrison and Bishop as they rode up. Harrison noted the group of riding horses, always saddled and ready for the trail, weren't tied up inside the fence now.

Hobart followed Harrison's glance there.

"Deke took a group of girl scouts out on a trail ride. Twelve of them—plus their leader—working on some sort of horseback riding badge." He grinned, showing one gold tooth. "It got all ten of our regular horses out at once today, and we had to saddle up Tinker and Cleo from over at the Newland barn and get Hollywood from our barn here to ride the tail. Deke and I gave them scouts a group rate, but we made good money with so many of 'em riding out."

Harrison looked up the horse trail leading into the woods. "That's a large group of kids for Deke to look after alone. Who's riding the tail on Hollywood to keep an eye on all those kids from behind?"

"I reckon I could have." Hobart frowned. "The girls were of a right good age though and appeared to be a pretty responsible bunch. Their scout leader assured us she rode well herself. We settled her on Hollywood to watch the rear, and we put the less experienced girls on the easier horses in the middle. All of those girls had ridden on horses before, Harrison. We thought it'd be okay."

Hobart paused, considering the issue for a moment. "You think I should have saddled up Beaumont, too, and gone along with them, Harrison?"

"No. Sounds like you did right, Hobart," Harrison assured him. "You and Deke can read a situation with riders better than anyone I know."

Hobart grinned. "Shoot fire, I been at this since you was a pint-sized kid underfoot, you know."

"Heck, you've been at this since before I was born, Hobart Rayfield." Harrison dismounted and tied Bishop's reins over the fence rail. "Daddy told me you drove mother to the hospital when her time came to deliver me."

"Whew, I almost forgot that one." He shook his head. "Probably wanted to forget it. Your mother Mozella got madder than a wet hen 'cause I took her to the hospital. She said W.T. had no business riding off to check trails with her due a baby any time."

Harrison scowled. "Daddy was only seeing to business. What did she expect him to do anyway? Just sit around and watch her all day long?"

"You know your mother," Hobart drawled, shrugging and grinning. "Speaking of which, she's been over here looking for you. Said to tell you she was going over to the house to dig up some vinca from around the front porch to take over to her and the preacher's place. Been over there about twenty minutes, I'd say."

"What did she want with me?" Harrison asked cautiously, looking over toward the short road leading through the trees to the old home place.

"She didn't see fit to tell me." Hobart turned over the stick he'd been whittling, examining his handiwork. "But then you know she ain't too fond of me anyway. Says I'm too much like your daddy, W.T. Shame she wasn't more fond of him than she was. Dang good man, your father."

"Yeah, I know." Another scowl creased Harrison's forehead.

"You know," Hobart mused. "Mozella told me once she thought I influenced your daddy to leave all his land and the house to you when he died, instead of leaving it to her as she thought proper."

Harrison kicked at an old bucket by the fence. "She'd have sold it all off the minute he died and Daddy knew it. You know that, Hobart." He frowned. "It had nothing to do with you. Daddy did what he needed to do to protect the family land."

"Yeah, well that's rightly so ... but that woman has always been able to word things so as to make a man feel guilty even when he ain't done nothin' wrong." He scratched his head thoughtfully.

"Tell me about it," Harrison agreed, frowning again. "She thinks I worked against her, too. Calls it Daddy's Grand Conspiracy."

Hobart reached over to scratch the beagle's head. "Funny thing, she never acted put out W.T. didn't leave nothing to your sisters, though. I always thought that right odd."

"Mother got what she wanted for the girls, Hobart. She wanted them all to marry well and get out of the valley. They all did. Only Wanda stayed anywhere around the area, over in Knoxville. She's the one died of cancer a few years back."

"Where are them other three girls now?" Hobart interrupted. "Seems they keep moving around so's I can't keep up with 'em."

"I'm surprised mother didn't catch you up on them when she stopped by here." Harrison propped a booted foot up on the fence rail. "She and the preacher recently took a little vacation visiting them all. Yvonne's up at Norfolk, Virginia. She's on her second husband, has three kids, teaches piano. Roberta's in Columbia, South Carolina, and has two boys. Her husband is stationed at the army base there—Fort Jackson—but she's traveled everywhere. Pauline's down at Seagrove Beach on the Panhandle in Florida. She and her husband run a motel on the coast. Mother loves to go down there. Pauline has two little girls, and Mother likes Pauline's girls."

"She always favored girls," Hobart remembered. "Didn't wanted another little 'un when you came along, Harrison. She felt real satisfied with her four daughters. It was your daddy got real excited when you showed up. He told me the odds finally turned around in his favor." Hobart laughed and slapped his knee.

"Lord, that man loved you." Hobart grinned, slipping off into old memories. "Carried you around everywhere and took care of you almost from the very first. You know, your ma fell sick a lot right after you got born."

"I don't remember that." Harrison flexed his fingers. "But she's told me often enough, and with bitterness, that Daddy loved me more than any of them."

"Now that ain't true, Harrison, and you know it." Hobart made a fist and shook it for emphasis. "Your Daddy loved your Mama and those girls and he took real good care of them all. It's only that there was always a special father-son bond between the two of you. You came out to be the spittin' image of your Daddy, too, and exactly like him in personality."

Harrison grinned at Hobart fondly. "I see that as a fine compliment, Hobart, though Mother certainly wouldn't. She wanted me to be a city gentleman, get a college degree, work in an office in a three-piece suit. Be different from Daddy."

"You did get the degree," Hobart drawled, grinning back. "You simply didn't care for the suit."

They laughed amiably over this.

Harrison looked toward the direction of the farmhouse. "I guess I'd better get on over there and see what she wants. She doesn't like to be kept waiting long."

He swung back into the saddle, tipping his hat to Hobart as he kicked Bishop into a brisk trot. Only a half-mile separated the stable from the farmhouse, the distance even shorter on horseback. After he talked to his mother, he'd take Bishop on over to the barn at Meadowbrook.

Harrison kept Bishop, like a few other of his horses, in the Newland's horse barn, an arrangement he started with Dora and Carl Newland about eight years ago. The riding stable barn pushed capacity with the trail horses it housed and the old Ramsey farm barn needed remodeling.

The arrangement with the Newlands evolved easily in the past, with Aunt Dora Newland his father's only sister. Harrison spent many happy days at the Newland's house growing up, playing with his best friend and cousin Carter. Even through Carter now practiced as a veterinarian in Nashville they stayed in close touch.

Harrison thought about the Newlands as he rode down the well-worn road to the farmhouse. "I miss Dora and Carl," he told the horse, slowing their pace to an easy walk. "It was a happy day for me when they moved to the valley. It always vexed Mother for some reason when they built next door. I never understood that, nor why she and Aunt Dora never got along."

He shifted in the saddle. "My daddy and Aunt Dora were the only two children of my grandparents still living. We moved into the big home place after Grandma's passing. Ma was tickled pink to inherit all that new space."

The Ramsey farmhouse, a typical rural farmhouse in plan, settled comfortably in the midst of a grove of old trees with cleared fields spreading out around it. W.T. always said Mozella ruined the house when they moved in – putting fussy furniture, chintz, bric-a-brac, and doilies everywhere. Harrison didn't remember this, but he remembered his four older sisters quickly laying claim to the two large bedrooms upstairs, while he got the smallest bedroom downstairs. He slept back in that room again now, in the same room he'd grown up in.

Oh, he moved out when he grew up, of course. Couldn't wait to. In fact, he moved over to the old rental house behind the market, where his grandfather once lived, right after he graduated from high school.

"I found it hard living with Mozella," he said, thinking out loud. "A critical woman with set ideas about how things should be done and how people should act – based mostly on how she acted and what she thought right. A person couldn't act or think much different from Mozella in any way of significance without being labeled as wrong." He shook his head. "Of course, that made me wrong about one-hundred percent of the time."

He clucked at Bishop to keep him moving along. "She criticized Aunt Dora and Uncle Carl all the time, too. Never could figure that one, with Dora warm, friendly, and loving to everyone. As I grew older I realized much of Mother's dislike of Dora was simple jealousy. Everyone liked Dora, and she married into a wealthy Gatlinburg family that made a fortune in land and real estate sales. Carl Newland met her one summer working at one of his family's candy shops and called her too sweet to pass up."

Harrison chuckled over the memory.

"They made a happy couple, Dora and Carl. Dora loved my daddy and our grandad, too. She took care of Grandad Will when he got older." He adjusted his grip on the reins. "I reckon that formed another bone of contention between Mozella and Dora. Will Ramsey never had much use for his daughter-in-law, Mozella Trent Ramsey, and although he had every right to give his own daughter, Dora, some property to build a home on, Mozella resented that, too, even when she and Daddy got all the rest of the Ramsey property and land."

Harrison blew out a breath, causing Bishop to snort back in answer. "It's hard to figure how Ma sees things, Bishop, but Daddy said she always resented the fact Dora built a finer house than hers right next door." He grinned. "Ma complained Dora 'put on airs' and built a big fancy place to show off all her money. But I reckon it just jealousy, pure and simple."

He leaned over to pat Bishop's neck, grateful for the horse's easy acceptance of him and lack of criticism. That was the best thing about horses and dogs.

"Ma didn't like any of the Newlands and despised Dora's two daughters, constantly comparing them unfavorably to my sisters. You know, I can't remember a time when Mother didn't pick apart those two Newland girls in some way or other, even keeping it up after they moved away."

It never helped Harrison's relationship with his mother that he loved all the Newland family and spent most of his free time there. To be honest, Harrison nearly idolized the two older Newland boys, Russell and Doyle, when small. He and Carter trailed them around whenever they could. He always liked the Newland girls, too, Patricia and Joanne. In fact, he liked them better than his own sisters, who took after their mother, fussy and critical in nature. They teased and picked on him mercilessly in childhood and made Harrison's home life a misery.

"Yeah, I miss the Newland's," he said again, swatting at a horsefly buzzing around Bishop's ears.

Harrison spotted his mother ahead, sitting in the glider on the front porch of the old farmhouse. He could see a box of vinca at her feet that she'd dug up from one of the flowerbeds around the porch.

She called out to him crossly as he rode up. "I'd have let myself in to get some iced tea, if I was still allowed a key to my own house."

Harrison bit back a reply. "I'll unsaddle and wipe down Bishop, Ma, and then I'll get us both something cool to drink."

"Always horses before people," he heard her mutter.

He came back quickly and then went into the kitchen to get his mother some tea. She followed him in, naturally, versus simply waiting out on the porch.

"You sure have turned this house into a stark man's place since I moved out," she complained. "I would hardly know the place it's so different."

It echoed the type of negative comment she usually made every time she dropped by. She'd stayed in the farmhouse for two years on her own after Harrison's daddy, W.T., died, and then married the minister of the Beech Grove Baptist Church. The Reverend Henry Campbell was a good man, a widower for a number of years himself. It seemed kind of natural to everyone that Mozella and Henry got together like they did. Mozella played the piano at the church and the two had known each other for years.

Harrison felt sorry for Henry Campbell when he first heard he planned to marry his mother. But Henry and Mozella's relationship appeared different than the one his daddy and Mozella had. Henry, sociable and outgoing, liked visiting and traveling, enjoyed music and shows. He couldn't ride a horse without falling off and didn't know a fig about gardening, except how to trim the shrubs around his new brick rancher beside the church, but he and Mozella suited well. Mozella acted sweet to him in a way Harrison never saw her act toward his father. She hung on Henry's arm, bragged about him to others, and acted genuinely pleased with him.

His mother's words interrupted his thoughts. "Why'd you have to go change everything around so much in this house?"

"Partly because you took most of the furniture and household items with you over to Henry's or gave it away to the girls," Harrison replied, knowing he purposely goaded her. "I didn't have a lot to work with."

"I had a right to something," she snapped back. "Since your daddy left the house and everything else to you."

Harrison busied himself fixing the tea. "I didn't say I minded you took what you did, Ma, but I had to get some new things to fill up the space when I moved in here."

She crossed her arms irritably. "You didn't have to make it all browns and beige. Or buy all these stark pieces and this black furniture." She looked around in displeasure. "Whoever heard of black furniture in a house? You've got black chairs in your kitchen and a black breakfront."

"It's supposed to be fashionable now, Ma. The lady at the furniture store called these colors good ones to choose." He smiled to himself. He picked what he liked as soon as she moved out, happy to say goodbye to all the fussy brocades, velvets, bric-a-brac, and lace. What furnishings Mozella left behind, Harrison recovered, refinished, or simply gave away.

She sniffed. "I suppose you can't expect a single man to know what's nice or know how to select things to make a place homey."

Harrison ignored her comments and led her back to the front porch to sit with their drinks.

"I see you got your vinca." He nodded at the plants, crowded into a cardboard box on the porch floor.

"I hope you didn't mind I took some," she challenged. "I tended them here for long enough."

"There's plenty, Ma. The beds needed thinning out. Take all you want." He sat back in his chair and crossed an ankle lazily over his knee.

She lifted her chin. "I wanted to put some plants around the back patio behind the house. There are some bare spots there. You'd know the place I'm speaking about if you ever came over to see me."

Harrison sighed. "I work hard, Ma. I come by when I can, and I see you every Sunday at church."

"When you even bother to get to church," she put in sarcastically. "It's embarrassing that my own family isn't there every Sunday. Especially now that I'm married to the minister. What do you suppose people think, Harrison?"

He gazed out over the pasture. "Everybody here has known me since I was a kid, Ma. I think they know me about as well as they could by now. They'll think what they will. I often have to work on Sunday."

"It's wrong to work on Sunday." Mozella sat forward. "It's the Sabbath and a day of rest...."

Harrison sensed Mozella gettin' worked up for one of her sermons, so he quickly put a spoke in her wheel. "You know, Ma, you don't seem to worry about all those folks working at the restaurant where you and Henry always go to eat for Sunday dinner after church. And you don't seem concerned about the guy that takes your money at the gas station on Sunday mornings...Or the girl that runs that little market where you pick up your Sunday donuts."

Mozella pursed her lips. "That's about enough, Harrison Owen Ramsey. You know well enough what I meant even though you're trying to twist things around to annoy me." She paused. "Besides, I had a reason for coming over here today. Some news I thought you ought to know."

She pushed the old glider back and forth rhythmically with her foot while she talked. Mozella possessed a restless nature, and Harrison's remembered her from childhood as always in motion— pacing around the kitchen while she talked, rocking in her old rocking chair, pushing herself back and forth on the glider, or smoking nervously for more years than he cared to recall. At least she'd quit that.

Harrison studied his mother, a tall, thin woman, with a long face and red-brown hair, tinted even redder by her hairdresser, Bernice. A pretty woman in her youth, she continued to fuss over her appearance. Harrison remembered it took his mother and sisters hours to get ready to go anywhere. They obsessed about their appearance, putting so much importance on every little detail. Even today, when Mozella came to dig up plants, she'd dressed for show in a flowery, patterned pants-set, red pumps, and her usual array of costume jewelry. A smart straw hat lay on the seat beside her, alongside a bright floral purse, loaded and bulging.

"Harrison, are you listening to me?" his mother asked. "You have that spaced out look, like your mind's wandering off. I just told you I'd run into Odell McKee at the pharmacy and found out the Newland place sold."

Harrison looked up in surprise.

His mother cocked her head and smiled. "There, I thought that might get your attention. If you're anything like your father, you probably spent hours trying to figure out a way to buy that place yourself to keep the land in the family."

Harrison frowned. "I thought about buying it, Ma. But like I told you before, there's a big house on the property and only a small amount of usable land. The value of the house upped the cost of the place considerably. It didn't seem like a good investment for me."

"Hummph." She tossed her head. "You might be changing your tune and wishing differently after this new family moves in there. I hear they've got six kids—all of them under twelve. They'll probably traipse all over your farm property, pester the horses at your stables, and steal apples from your orchard, showing no respect. Kids today are not like they used to be, you know. Parents are not raising them right. Women go off to work and leave them in those day cares. Teach no discipline or manners in the home."

"Where'd you hear about the house being sold?" Harrison interrupted, cutting off one of his mother's familiar spiels about the state of today's children.

"I told you." She frowned at a broken nail. "Over at the pharmacy. I heard Odell McKee telling her son about it. She plans to work for them, to help out with the family and the housework."

Harrison considered this. "I haven't heard anything about a sale from Aunt Dora and Uncle Carl yet," he said. "I'm sure they'd call me if they sold the property. They know I keep some of my horses at their barn."

"And you're keeping up their property in return for that," his mother put in. "Which means *they're* getting more out of that deal than you. There's a lot of acreage in that place."

He tried to ignore the barb. "Yes, and most of their land is wooded, natural and doesn't need any maintenance. I'm not being taken advantage of by Aunt Dora and Uncle Carl, Ma."

"Hummph. Not that *you'd* see it if the fact bit you." She put a hand on her hip. "You always did nourish a blind spot about Dora Ramsey Newland. Even though you didn't want your Daddy to leave me this house or any of his land, thinking I might sell it, you never offered a single criticism about Dora putting her place up for sale. It's Ramsey land, too."

"She gave me first option." Harrison took a long drink of his tea. "I may pick up the place later on if I want it. Right now I don't. I have my money tied up in other investments."

Mozella looked to her left in the direction of the Newland's place. "I can see why you wouldn't want to live in such a big place as Dora and Carl built anyway. It's too big for the valley here. Pretentious, I always said."

Harrison rolled his eyes.

His mother pursed her lips. "You know, I never could figure

out how dumpy Dora got a man like Carl Newland to marry her, anyway. It's one of life's great mysteries. She's made no effort to keep her figure over time, either - gotten herself as fat as mud."

He frowned. "Aunt Dora's a little plump, Ma, but she's not fat. Go easy."

Mozella's eyes flashed. "You always defend her and stand up for her over me and your sisters. I still remember the time her daughter Patricia snaked that Briley Gentry right away from your sister Yvonne. You took Patricia and Dora's side in it. Sided with them against your own sister."

Harrison shook his head wearily. "Ma, Briley Gentry saw Yvonne necking with Sam Allen in his car at the drive-in when she was supposed to be going steady with him. He broke up with Yvonne because she cheated on him. He asked Patricia out weeks later. There is nothing wrong with that."

"Hummph. Briley asked Patricia to the senior prom, Harrison. To the senior prom." She waved a finger at him in emphasis. "He cancelled his date with Yvonne. Yvonne already bought her dress and shoes, and then didn't get to go to the prom at all because Briley took Patricia Newland." She narrowed her eyes at him. "Yvonne said she and Sam Allen only kissed a little and Briley took it all too seriously. I say Patricia simply took advantage of the situation and Dora Newland encouraged her in it."

Harrison blew out a long breath of exasperation. "Ma, that happened over twenty years ago. What does it have to do with anything now?"

She crossed her arms. "It's one of the many examples of how you always stood on the Newlands' side instead of your own family's. I never did understand why you spent so much time over there, Harrison. Hardly ever at home."

"I lived at home, Ma. Until I turned eighteen." He banked his irritation, keeping his voice calm. "I spent a lot of time at the Newland's house because they had three boys and I liked to play with Russell, Doyle, and Carter."

"Hummph. I hardly ever saw Russell, Doyle and Carter at *our* house."

Harrison shook his head wearily. "You didn't like boys in the house, Ma. Said they broke things and got your house dirty. Also, my sisters acted silly around Russell and Doyle whenever they came over and always teased Carter. The Newland boys didn't like to come over much."

She leaned towards him and shook her finger at him once more. "Now you listen to me, Harrison Ramsey. Your way of remembering your childhood shows very little resemblance to the way it actually happened." She sat back in the glider primly. "You know perfectly well I always acted gracious and welcoming to all of your friends and to the girls' friends. You ask anyone."

The fact that most people in the valley remembered all too readily how Mozella never liked to entertain other people's children in her home hardly seemed a point Harrison wanted to bring up at this junction.

"How's Henry?" he asked instead, trying to change the subject.

"Fit and sassy," she replied, actually smiling. "We had a real good time on our trip, too." She sent a critical gaze his way. "You haven't even asked me about our trip or about how your sisters are ..."

Harrison listened then as his mother gave him a detailed description of their recent travels to see his sisters. Told him all the news of their families.

He listened, admittedly, with half an ear.

She stopped the glider to study him. "I've got all my children married and settled now except for you, Harrison."

He squared his shoulders. "I'm settled, Ma. I've simply chosen to be single instead of married."

"Hummph. It's hardly *choosing* to be single when two women walked out on you, Harrison. But that doesn't mean you can't keep looking around." She paused thoughtfully. "There's a new couple in our church with a girl about your age. She's coming for a visit soon. I told her mother Helen we might get the two of you together when she comes. Have dinner or something."

Harrison's mouth hardened while she rattled on. As usual, she never noticed his discomfort as he stood up to look out over the porch rails.

"You know, I think I need to see to Bishop, Ma," he said when he could finally get a word in edgewise. "I only gave him a quick rub-down earlier and put him in the corral. I need to take him on over to the Newland barn. Besides, you should take your vinca home if you expect to put it out today. It's getting on toward four o'clock."

"I suppose." She looked at her watch. "I did want to put a chicken pot pie in the oven for Henry's dinner before he gets home. You can come over and eat with us if you like, Harrison. Henry would be right glad to visit with you, even though you don't talk as much as Pauline's husband, Stanley." A wistful smile touched her lips. "Henry always enjoys Stanley when we go to their place on the Gulf. Now, there's a sociable man. We do enjoy our time with Stanley and Pauline."

Harrison blew out another breath and inwardly counted slowly to ten. He knew he'd hit the end of all the innuendos and subtle criticisms he could take from his mother today. With never a compliment along the way.

Mozella got up and gathered her hat and bag while Harrison loaded her box of vinca in the floorboard of the car.

She presented her cheek to him. "Well, give your mother a kiss," she said.

Harrison complied, eager to get her on her way.

She climbed in the car, pulling a fancy key ring out of her purse. "Harrison, you call me when you talk to Dora or Carl and learn who's moving into their place. Maybe you should give them a call tonight." She tossed her head. "You'd think they'd keep in better touch with their family than they do. I guess they're forgetting all of us, flitting around down in Florida with their rich, new friends."

Harrison bit back a reply, shut his mother's door, and stepped back as she started the car. When she finally drove away, he let out a deep sigh, savoring the peace and quiet around him as he put the empty glasses back in the house and ambled toward the corral. He saddled Bishop again and started down the old wagon road toward the Newlands' barn.

"Don't ever get married," he told the horse. "You'll never know a moment's peace if you do or ever feel like you've amounted to anything worthwhile. Just nag, nag, nag—that'sall you'll get every day."

Bishop nickered in response, as if in agreement, and Harrison patted the gelding's neck congenially.

CHAPTER 3

Within a few days, Alice learned the Newlands accepted her offer and in another two weeks, the house closed. Today, she worked at Meadowbrook getting things ready for the move in June. Stella's friends, Clive and Aldon Barker, had painted throughout the house, cleaned and refinished the hardwood floors, and completed the list of small repairs Alice compiled. Local movers hauled over the Stuart's furniture and household items from out of storage earlier in the week, and although Alice told the movers where to place all the big items, she'd made minor rearrangements and unpacked boxes for days since—hung pictures, put up curtains, and started setting up the kitchen and the baths.

What she hadn't done was tell the children about the move yet. Alice hoped it didn't prove a mistake. She decided to keep the move a surprise and use this time in May, while the Stuart children finished their school year, to get as much work done at Meadowbrook as she possibly could.

Dorothy Eaton, Alice's director at Wayside suggested the idea. "I'd wait to tell them," she said as they talked after a planning meeting. "They'll be so excited they won't focus on their schoolwork at the end of the term—want to be at the house every minute they can, which will keep you from having the time you need to get the house ready for them." She shook her head. "It's no asset to have six children running helter-skelter around with painters and workers in a house, Alice. Think about it. I know you're eager to share with the children, but there will be time enough to tell them closer to the moving date when school is almost out."

Alice chewed on her lip considering this. "You don't think they'll be hurt I didn't tell them sooner?"

"Not if you don't act like you should have," Dorothy assured her. "Make it sound like a wonderful surprise, Alice. Tell them you wanted it to all suddenly appear—poof—like a fairy godmother did it."

Alice grinned at Dorothy. "That's a good idea."

Dorothy reached over to pat Alice's hand fondly. "Take some time off from work, too, Alice, to make this happen more easily. You're due vacation time, anyway. We can cover for you on days you need to be at the new house."

Odell McKee agreed with Dorothy. Alice visited her to finalize their childcare plans and to see if Odell might like to help set up the house after the movers came.

Odell pressed a cold glass of lemonade in Alice's hand and sat down in a chintz chair across from her. "I totally agree with Dorothy," she confided, pushing her round glasses up on her nose. "You keep those children out of this as long as you can, Alice. They're likely to argue about who gets what room or what color of paint their room is going to be. Or they're likely to get into the paint and track it all over your newly cleaned hardwood floors. Wouldn't that be a mess?"

She chuckled and shook her head, barely disturbing the soft grey curls that covered it. "No sirree, you and I will do a lot better setting up as much of that house as we can before those children come. God bless them. They'll understand when you tell them you wanted it to be a grand surprise."

Alice hoped so. She played a pretend game with the children one night, titled, "What if we had a new house", trying to get some of their input. She gave them blank paper and told them to write or draw their ideas about the sort of house they thought she should look for and what they wanted their rooms to be like. Then they shared their ideas.

"What did they say?" Odell asked as they set up the kitchen one day at Meadowbrook.

Alice paused, remembering. "They actually offered some very creative ideas. Especially Hannah and Megan."

"They're the oldest girls, right?" Odell scratched her head. "I'm trying to get them all straightened out in my mind, you know."

"Yes, Hannah and Megan are the oldest at twelve and ten. Stacey is next, then Rachel and, last, the twins. I hope you're ready to be busy, Odell." Alice laughed.

"I can't wait, darlin'." She smiled. "It's been too long since I had children to take care of. They keep you young, you know. Make every day interesting."

Alice smiled back at her. She liked Odell—a pleasingly plump, warm-faced, congenial woman in her early sixties.

Odell lifted a box of dishes to the counter. "You know what my favorite thing is you've done in this house?"

"What?"

"Put those cute little wooden name plaques on each of the children's doors. I love those." She slit the box open with a kitchen knife.

Alice laughed. "Thomas's idea, Odell. He said if we got a big house we should write everybody's name on their door so they wouldn't get lost."

"That's cute." Odell chuckled, taking a stack of plates from the box. "Remind me of that other thing you told me yesterday, about every one of them having a special color?"

"A tradition Lauren started. When each of her children got old enough to decide, she let them pick a special color, mainly for their dish color in the Fiestaware Lauren collected."

"That's what I'm puttin' away right now." Odell held up a bright green plate, her eyes scanning the multi-colored dinnerware all around her. "Pretty colorful dishes, aren't they? Make the kitchen and dining real bright and cheery."

Alice picked up a yellow plate and turned it around in her own hand. "You'll learn quickly, Odell, that the Stuart children are very serious about their colors. It carries over from dishes to linens, towels, sheets, and favorite clothes." She grinned as she shelved the plate in the cabinet. "I will say it made decorating their rooms easier. They each wanted their special color prominent in their bedroom color scheme."

Odell straightened the old, calico apron she wore. "You know, that's actually a good idea to use for a big family. I wish I'd thought of that with the five I raised." She put the green plate in the cabinet. "Is that one of those psychologist kind of things the doctors taught in their clinic?"

"Loren and Richard definitely believed creative organization made any household run smoother," she answered, sitting down on a kitchen stool. "I listened to their parent group lectures on that subject often enough, and they did train their own children in the principles they believed in. You'll find the Stuart children to be very organized, resourceful, and efficient. More so than most children. They work better cooperatively together than most siblings do, too."

Odell studied the stack of colorful Fiestaware plates on the counter. "Did you decorate their bedrooms in their special colors?"

"I certainly did." She pointed to plates as she answered. "Peach for Hannah, yellow for Megan, purple for Stacey, green for Rachel, blue for Thomas, and pink for Tildy." Alice laughed. "I painted Hannah's room apricot, gave Megan the yellow-striped bedroom, and put Stacey and Rachel in the big front bedroom with the sweet violets all over the wallpaper. They wanted to share a room together."

She sighed. "I found gorgeous Laura Ashley twin spreads to coordinate for their room, too. Even though I'm using the children's old bedroom furniture, I did buy new spreads, rugs, and a lot of cute accessories."

Odell smiled at her. "You show a real gift for decorating from what I've seen. Where'd you put those little ones?"

"I put Thomas in the bedroom bordered with sailboats and Tildy across the hall in the room with the pink checked wallpaper."

Odell interrupted. "That's the little bedroom with all the

ballerinas on the bed quilts. I saw that upstairs cleaning—a darling room with all that white furniture you painted up, Alice. You even found a dollhouse and play table to put in there."

"I found many things at used furniture stores and flea markets—and paint can easily brighten anything up." Alice tucked her feet under the kitchen stool. "Because I put the twins old maple furniture in Thomas' room, that left me with no furniture at all for Tildy's room. Painting all those used pieces I found in white made a nice room for her."

She propped her chin on her hands. "I didn't have to buy much, except beds for the twins' rooms. They had little youth beds before that they'd outgrown. I gave those to one of my foster parents." She smiled. "I think the twins will both be excited to have their own separate rooms. They shared before."

Odell leaned against the kitchen counter. "You did a real nice job with everything, Alice. Dora Newland and I held a long time friendship and I know she'd be pleased with how you fixed things up here—but kept some things the same".

Alice stood and scanned the kitchen to see what else needed to be done. She smiled at Odell. "Most of the house is clean and set up now, Odell, thanks to your help. It's hard to tell exactly how everything will look until the rest of the furniture arrives from my Sevierville house, but I think it's coming along nicely, don't you?"

Odell patted her arm fondly. "It looks wonderful and I know the children will love it."

She sat down on the stool Alice vacated. "Do you think it's hard for little Thomas, being the only boy with five older sisters?"

Alice considered this. "I guess it has to be sometimes. Especially with his father gone."

"It's too bad about that." Odell shook her head. "But I'm sure Thomas will find himself some boys around here to play with soon enough."

She looked around the kitchen with satisfaction. "You know, I can finish what little is left here, Alice. Why don't you go sweep out that little playhouse in the yard while I unpack this last box of dishes, and then I'll put together some lunch for us? Those children will high-tail-it straight out to that cute little playhouse the minute they spot it, and I don't want them getting' into dirt and spiders when they start exploring."

"Good idea." Alice grinned, looking out the window toward the playhouse. "It's gorgeous out today. I'll enjoy getting outdoors." She paused, smiling. "You know, I can't get used to the pure pleasure of looking up at the mountains behind our property every day. It's incredibly beautiful."

Odell glanced out the kitchen window with a smile. "You won't need to worry about commerce messing up your view at this place. The back boundary of the Newland farm meets the Smokies park boundary a short ways up Redwine Ridge. You'll see the fencing and park signs when you go walking that way later on."

She made a shooing motion to Alice. "For now, you run on outdoors in the sunshine and sweep out that playhouse. I'll call you later when I finish and fix us a bite to eat."

Alice located a broom and a few cleaning supplies in the spacious pantry off the kitchen and headed out into the May sunshine. The big Meadowbrook house looked more like a home every day, making Alice feel encouraged about her life ahead.

She sang to herself while she cleaned the playhouse, and, then, since Odell hadn't called her about lunch yet, she walked down to look at the horses in the corral by the barn. At the closing, Carl and Dora Newland told Alice their nephew, the owner of a nearby riding stable, housed several horses in the barn. In return, one of his employees maintained the Meadowbrook property—mowing the yard, trimming the shrubs, running the weed-eater. The Newlands suggested Alice might want to continue this agreement. Another neighbor paid board to keep two of their horses in the barn, and Dora also asked if Alice might allow them to continue that arrangement, at least for a time.

Alice hadn't met either the nephew or the neighbor yet, but she thought it sounded practical for the horses to stay in the barn for the time being. She wanted the horse barn utilized. In fact, she planned to bring her own horse Elsa over from Murfreesboro now that she owned a place to stable her. The barn sported nine stalls and a tack room, with only six horses currently stabled. Plenty of space existed and Elsa, a sociable animal, would enjoy other horses in the barn with her.

Alice grew up around walking horses in Murfreesboro and traveled to horseshows with her grandparents and family for as long as she could remember. Although she seldom found time to ride anymore unless she went home to Murfreesboro, Alice looked forward to doing so again. She'd noticed several trails behind the barn and looked forward to riding and exploring these later on. She hoped the children could learn to ride at the nearby stables, too. She'd seen a sign for it about a mile down the highway.

She rested her arms on the fence railing to watch the horses now. One of the mares came over to study her tentatively. Alice talked to her and soon had the little bay nuzzling her hand and letting her pet her neck.

Hearing another nicker off to her left, Alice turned to see a man riding up from the trail behind the barn. Her heart caught in her chest as soon as she spotted him. It was the man from the ridge top!

As he saw her, he reined in his dark horse to stare intently at her. The drama played almost like before, except that he stood much closer. The man wore a cowboy hat again, but he wasn't swathed in a heavy coat and scarf this time. Alice could see his face and eyes clearly, and she watched his gaze lock quickly to hers like it had the other time.

The man, tall and comfortable in the saddle, wore faded jeans, a black cowboy hat, and an old denim shirt rolled up to the elbows. Dark, wavy hair showed beneath his hat above a long face, his eyes a steely grey under dark brows

She couldn't seem to do anything but stare at him. That strong magnetism crackled between them like before—freezing Alice in place and robbing her of speech. The man did no better to break the moment than she, studying her as intently as she did him.

Clearly, he remembered her, too.

Alice watched a muscle twitch in his jaw and a bit of a dimple flash in his chin. She'd always loved a man with a dimple in his chin, and the dimple softened his tough, rugged appearance. She smiled at it despite herself.

He noticed her smile and walked his horse forward until he stood closer to her. Leaning over, he reached down to touch her cheek gently, but then drew abruptly back.

Alice shivered at his touch.

"Why did you leave before?" he asked huskily, breaking the silence.

"It was snowing. I didn't know who you were and I was out here alone," Alice answered softly, telling him the truth.

His eyes probed hers. "Why are you back now?"

"I'm going to be living here." She tried to smile.

He shook his head, clearly confused. "I heard a family with six children were moving in at Meadowbrook. Do you know them? Are you going to be living with them?"

Before she could frame an answer, Odell hollered from midway down the yard. "Yoo-hoo, Alice, I've got our lunch ready!"

Coming closer now, Odell spotted the man.

"Well, if isn't Harrison Ramsey," she exclaimed with warmth, walking swiftly toward them. "I haven't seen you in a month of Sundays. How are you, son?"

Harrison tipped his hat. "I'm fine, ma'am. And you?"

"Just as fit as can be. When are you going to come by my house and sample some more of my apple pie?"

Harrison chuckled in reply, a deep, warm sound that gave Alice a sweep of goosebumps up her arms again.

Odell turned her gaze towards Alice. "Harrison here brings me apples from his orchard. As a thank you I make him an apple pie now and again."

"You make one fine apple pie," said Harrison, his mouth turning up slightly at one corner.

Odell smoothed down her apron. "It's nice to have a handsome man come by my house once in a while." She paused thoughtfully "You know, you look more like your father, W.T., every day, Harrison. He stood a fine looking man, too. Why don't you get yourself down off that big horse and come up and have a bite of lunch with Alice Graham and me?   She's going to be your new neighbor, and it's high time the two of you became acquainted."

"I'll do that," Harrison drawled, surprising Alice. "I'll go wipe Bishop down and put him in the barn and then I'll be right up. You two go on to the house. You know I know the way, Odell."

"Lord, yes," she answered, grinning. "Harrison practically got raised in this house, Alice—here all the time playing with his cousin Carter, the same age. By the way, Harrison, how's that Newland boy doing these days?"

"He's a vet near Nashville, but he gets over this way now and again to visit."

"You tell him the next time he comes that Odell McKee would like to see him. I took care of him often enough as a boy, and I'd like to see how he turned out. You tell him that, okay?"

Alice pasted a smile on her face, and, somehow, got her wobbly legs to carry her up the path toward the house behind Odell. However, her mind and emotions felt ragged and stirred.

"Good heavens," she muttered to herself softly. "That man is going to be my next-door neighbor!"

She remembered his touch on her cheek and a small shiver ran up her spine. She touched her cheek thoughtfully. Alice hadn't reacted to the presence of a man in this way since before she'd met her husband David. She'd almost forgotten how it felt. But her next thought proved a more sobering one. She had six children now. She wasn't a free and single woman anymore. Wasn't life the oddest thing?

CHAPTER 4

Harrison stopped to scrape his boots before he opened the back door of the Newlands' screen porch. The old metal boot-scraper huddled in a clump of mint by the porch step where it had stood for as long as he could remember. It helped settle him to notice that—his nerves jittery from seeing the woman again. Alice Graham, Odell called her. A nice name for her, he thought. She looked like an Alice.

It shocked him to see her again when he rode around the side of the barn—so unexpected and close this time. The reaction between them hit just like before. The two of them gawked at each other like a couple of young kids discovering the opposite sex. A downright embarrassing situation.

Harrison imagined scenes where he encountered this girl again, admittedly, but in all of them he held more control. Handled things smoothly. Acted cool and confidant, took charge of the situation. Kept his distance like he always did. Instead, he let this woman see how she affected him today. He leaned over and touched her. Established intimacy. Fortunately, Odell appeared when she did or he might have done something even more foolish. He'd been focusing on her mouth about that time, on those flushed cheeks of hers, that darkening of her eyes when he touched her. He'd probably have gotten off his horse and kissed her if Odell hadn't interrupted.

He shook his head. She planned to live at Meadowbrook. He needed to get himself in hand. He'd calmed down seeing to

Bishop, gotten over his initial shock of running into her again. He felt better ready to face her again. Ready to find out who she was, what she was doing here.

"She's beautiful. I admit that." He scowled. "Blond-haired, blue eyed. Creamy skin. Only a touch of makeup. Full soft mouth." Yeah, he remembered that mouth.

Harrison let the picture of her slide into his mind. "Only a touch of makeup. Doesn't do artificial stuff with her hair. Pretty hair, honey-streaked. Loose and free. Nice eyes. Good shape, too. Graceful in the way she moves, with something pretty about the bone structure around her neck and shoulders."

Harrison kicked at the boot-scraper. "Figures I'd notice bone structure from examining horses all these years." He smiled at the thought. "I'd enjoy running my hands over her to check her out, like I would a horse I considered buying."

He shook his head to clear it, annoyed at the direction of his thoughts. "It would help matters if the woman hadn't been much to look at. Instead she's one of those types a man daydreams about. Dang woman."

Straightening his shoulders to deal with the inevitable, Harrison opened the back door. "I'll simply have to deal with it, because there's no way I'm allowing myself to get involved with a woman again."

He walked through the screen porch and let himself in the back door to the big dining area adjoining the kitchen. Along the way, he noted furniture already in place, comfortably worn wicker pieces, little tables scattered around.

Harrison braced himself for the changes he expected to see inside. He'd seen painting and cleaning crews parked in the driveway, watched the moving van bringing furniture one day. All more reasons to avoid coming over. Not all change proved positive, and Harrison held fond memories about this old house he hated to let go of.

With interest, he found the kitchen and family eating area didn't look much different from when the Newlands lived at

Meadowbrook. The rooms hadn't become modernized with stainless steel and granite counter-tops. The soft cream wallpaper with the little apples across it rose above the chair-railing and kitchen countertops just as he remembered. The old, built-in cupboards lined the dining room wall as before, their weathered red paint still in tact.

Harrison sighed with relief and immediately felt more comfortable. The biggest difference he saw was the bright array of multi-colored dishes stacked in the cupboard and set out on the long family-sized table, replacing the old stoneware Aunt Dora used.

"Looks good in here," Harrison commented.

Odell turned around from the stove and gave him a welcoming smile. "That it does, Harrison, and I'm real glad to see the old place coming back to life again and getting itself another family. It needed that."

Harrison noticed Odell, too, looked pretty much the same— short and sturdy with her shock of curly, grey hair and the same familiar wire glasses propped on her nose.

With Alice nowhere in sight, Harrison asked, "Who's the girl, Odell?"

"The girl's Alice Graham. I told you that." She pushed her glasses up her nose. "She's a social worker with the Wayside Agency out of Knoxville. They work with placing foster kids with families in several counties around this area. Alice works in Sevier County, although she used to handle Blount County, too. I've known Alice for a lot of years through that work. You might recall I kept foster children now and then for short term until more permanent places could be found for them. I'm what you might call a temporary foster parent. But now I'm going to work over here for Alice with her children."

Harrison's mouth dropped open. "You mean all those children moving in are Alice's children? She can't be over thirty years old, Odell. And where's her husband?"

Odell studied Harrison thoughtfully for a minute. "I can see you noticed our Alice is a looker," she commented dryly. "You're about right in guessing her age, too. She ain't even turned thirty yet. She's twenty-nine, told me so yesterday."

She put some more dishes on the table before she spoke again. "Alice is a widow, Harrison, and you better be real nice to her or you'll answer to me for it. She lost her husband, David, over in that Saudi war. Been on her own for five years. Works hard and is a fine woman."

"Are those six kids all hers?" Harrison asked, incredulous at the thought. "She seems too young to have that many children."

"I had five kids up in school by the time I was her age."

He watched a smirk pass subtly across Odell's face. She toyed with him for some reason. Probably had picked up on a little reaction going on between he and Alice earlier. Odell didn't miss much.

"Sit down, Harrison," she said at last. "And relax. You'll learn soon enough Alice is fostering these kids. They're not her own natural born children, although they look like they could be hers from their pictures, all of them blond and blue-eyed. They're the Stuarts' children, belonged to those two psychologist doctors killed in a car crash about a year and a half ago. The ones who owned that clinic over by the hospital on Middle Creek Road outside Sevierville. Good people. Alice worked with them, became friends with them. She helped to see about the kids after the Stuarts' deaths and ended up getting involved when no family or friends would take them in."

She took a hot casserole from the oven. "It's not everyone that will take six kids on, Harrison. But she's decided to foster the children herself. You gotta' admire her for that."

"Or count her a dang fool," Harrison murmured.

"Watch your mouth, Harrison Ramsey, lest you start sounding like your sharp-tongued mother." Odell chastised him. "I'm real admiring of what Alice is doing and I won't have a critical word said against her."

"Ouch. That was a low insult, Odell." Harrison slumped into a kitchen chair. "You must admit anybody would wonder about a young girl alone taking on six children to raise."

"Well, I'm sensitive on her account." Odell wiped her hands on her apron. "I've heard too much unkind criticism among the gossips already to suit me. It's got my dander up."

Odell opened the side door leading out of the kitchen and hollered up the stairs. "Alice!" she called. "Harrison's come and lunch is on the table."

She walked back into the kitchen, picking up two potholders and heading for the stove. "Alice went upstairs to set up the guestroom while I kept lunch warm for you," she explained. "I made one of my hot casseroles, and I think it turned out real tasty, even if I do say so myself. I popped some rolls in the oven, too, when I knew you were coming up. Alice watches her carbs, so I don't bother much with extras when it's only me and her to eat. But I know how you like your bread."

She carried over a basket of rolls with pride. "You know, Harrison, I'm looking forward to doing some real cooking when the children move here in June."

Alice walked around the corner then, flushed rosy from exertion. Harrison's breath caught in his lungs. He thought he'd steeled himself not to have an emotional reaction when he saw her— obviously a wrong assumption. She affected him like a powerful punch in the gut.

If she felt the same, she hid it this time, and busied herself helping Odell bring glasses of tea and a tray of relishes, with celery, carrots, and pickles to the table. They sat down together and Odell asked Harrison to say the grace.

It had been a while since he prayed aloud, but the words came back, and he offered up a short blessing without stumbling.

Odell smiled her approval. "Alice, I started telling Harrison how you came to have the Stuart children before you came downstairs," Odell said, starting to dish casserole onto their plates. "Maybe you can tell him about the children individually, since I didn't come to that part yet."

Alice glanced up and smiled, a sweet, easy smile that flashed naturally, crinkling her eyes and lighting up her face, giving Harrison another jolt to his middle. He focused on his food, trying to get used to the reactions she caused in him.

Her voice filled the room like soft honey. "There are five girls and one boy in the Stuart family. Hannah is the oldest at twelve, Megan is next at ten. Then come Stacey eight, Rachel seven, and the twins, Tildy and Thomas who are five."

"Just one boy?" Harrison raised his eyes. "Kind of tough on him being the only guy among five females. Probably gets teased and razed all the time."

Alice bristled and frowned. "Thomas is fine. And the girls are not like that."

Odell waved a hand. "Oh, Harrison's remembering how his four older sisters always gave him the devil of a time." She passed him a disapproving look. "Not all families are like yours, Harrison."

"Thank the heavens for that," he conceded. "In social work terms, you might classify my family as somewhat dysfunctional."

They chatted about this and that throughout the lunch meal. Getting acquainted talk—Harrison called it. However, Alice wasn't overly talkative, and he caught her watching him every now and then. Once or twice their eyes connected, and a slight flush on her neck and cheeks let him know she hadn't moved totally past their awareness of each other any more than he had. He felt grateful for Odell's presence, filling in the gaps around their awkwardness with each other.

Harrison cleared his throat. "Odell, will you be at Meadowbrook every day once the children come?" He hoped the answer would be yes. He needed a buffer around until he got more comfortable with this woman.

She smiled. "With summer coming and all the settling-in going on, I guess I'll be here almost every day. Of course, once school starts next fall, I won't need to be come quite as often, but for now, with Alice working, I'll be here a lot."

Harrison looked up at Alice in surprise. "You're going to keep working an outside job with all these children?"

She gave him a frosty look. "Women do that today," she said simply.

"I know that." Her patronizing tone rankled him. "But you do have six children. Won't they need you at home? Isn't this where you ought to be?"

A chill settled around Alice's eyes. "I like my job, Mr. Ramsey. It's important to me, and I feel I make a vital contribution through my work. I have no intention of giving up my career, nor do I feel women need to do that today when they have children. That's what the women's movement was all about, Mr. Ramsey. It gave women choices. It made all those choices acceptable according to what each woman needs and wants in her own life. The children's mother Dr. Lauren Ingles-Stuart never stepped out of her career even though she birthed and raised all six of these children. I see no reason why I should be any different."

Whew! Harrison thought. A women's libber. And he'd stepped right into it like putting his foot in a ripe horse pile.

"I did cut back my schedule by choice." She straightened her shoulders. "Although I could continue to carry my full workload and responsibility for two counties if I wanted to. However, I chose to make some changes I think will work better for myself and the children at this time. I'm setting up a home office at Meadowbrook, and I'll use the central office in Knoxville when I need to conduct parent-training sessions or have parent meetings that require a more professional setting. Dr. Eaton and I let our old Sevier County office space go when the Stuart's clinic sold to a new medical group. My director and I believe this new arrangement will work out very well for Wayside."

"I'm sure it will," Harrison said, attempting a smile and trying to gain back the ground he'd lost. He also wanted to remove that frown he saw on Odell's face.

He offered them both a slight smile. "I know you couldn't find better help than Odell McKee," he added, working to gain back points with her. "I can guarantee you Odell will keep your house in order and see that your children are fed better than any children in the Greenbrier area."

Alice's smile hadn't quite returned, but Odell's face lit up at that.

"If you're lucky, you can come and take some meals with us, Harrison," she offered. "I always cook too much, and there's always plenty to share."

She looked over at Alice and shook her head. "Out here in the country, Alice, men haven't caught up with the times about women's choices. Most of them don't think women have any. Not many of them know how to cook worth anything, either, even though you see all those male chefs on TV now. It's not the way the men around this area got raised up. So, you might as well expect to get a smattering of old-fashioned comments about women's roles and women's place out here in the country yet."

Harrison felt irked at her general critique about men. "Odell, I remember you stayed home and raised your family."

She lifted her chin. "That I did, but there wasn't any choice to it in my generation, Harrison," she returned. "I got married at only seventeen. Worked to help see my husband Leland through pharmaceutical school. We came back to Greenbrier then, opened the McKee Pharmacy, started having children. I only worked occasionally after that at the store—ordered gift items and toiletries, put out stock, helped with the account books, filled in when staff got sick. Those were different times. Some folks around here had a thing or two to say about my working at the pharmacy even the few times I did."

Alice looked up with interest. "Is that the drug store you said your son runs?"

"Yes, you'll find the McKee Pharmacy right up the highway on the way to Cosby. My oldest boy, Mason, runs the store and my youngest girl, Sheila, is the pharmacist. Sheila and her husband, Kenny, have three children, too. See how times are changing, Harrison? When I was a girl they wouldn't even let women in those pharmacy schools. But now women can do all sorts of things."

"I guess I've got some catching up to do in my thinking,"

Harrison acknowledged, wondering if he believed his own words. He assumed a woman who could afford the Newland place could devote her time totally to her kids. He wondered if this was one of Mozella's indoctrinations implanted in his mind or if his thoughts were his own. He figured he'd ponder on it a bit more later.

Over their general lunch conversation, they established Dora Newland as Harrison's aunt and talked about Harrison continuing to stable a few of his horses in the Meadowbrook barn.

"I keep twelve trail horses in the Ramsey stable barn—one of those a lead trail horse and another a good tail to follow. Not all horses can lead competently, and some are better to follow up the line," Harrison explained, buttering up another roll while he talked. "I have four other horses I keep at your barn." He looked toward Alice. "One I personally ride, and three extra we use on the trail if we need them. There is a work barn on my farm property next door, but it's full of equipment at this time—horse trailers, mowers, a bailer—and some chickens and little chicks."

"I'm coming over to see those baby chicks," Odell said.

Harrison grinned, spooning out another helping of casserole. "I plan to renovate an older barn across the highway by a rental house I own to give me more storage for farm equipment. When it's complete, I can renovate the farm barn for additional stable space." He hesitated. "But I haven't gotten around to it yet. Right now, the farm barn isn't secure for horses and the roof leaks."

He stopped to eat before continuing. "I can begin work on both barns this fall after the stable business drops back. But it's going to take time." He lifted his eyes to Alice's again. "I appreciate you letting me keep my horses at your barn until I can make these changes. My men will continue to keep your property up in exchange. That should help you, too."

"It will," Alice agreed. "At this point, I don't see any reason why keeping your horses in our barn will be any problem." She looked thoughtful. "Who's the other neighbor who uses the barn for their horses?"

He pushed back his plate, beginning to feel satisfied. "That's the

Nichols' family. Vick and Donna Nichols plan to talk with you about continuing to stable their horses, also. I told them they could use space in my barn later when it's finished, but for now, they'd need to ask around the valley if they can't stable their girls' two saddle horses with you."

Odell got up to start clearing off the plates. "The Nichols are good people, Alice," she put in. "You'll enjoy them and I think you'll especially like Donna Nichols. They only live a short distance away—across the highway and a block or two up Beech Grove Road. Their girls, Deidre and Rhoda, can safely walk to the barn, which is nice for them, and they have easy access to all the riding trails behind the stable and up the mountainside without crossing the main highway."

Harrison handed Odell his plate. "The Nichols pay Dora and Carl board money for using the barn," he said. "However, Dora and Carl wouldn't let them pay much because they were neighbors."

"Why did they build such a large horse barn?" Alice asked.

"They built it when their five kids were young and when they owned a lot of horses themselves. After the kids grew up and moved away, they sold their horses and the barn sat empty."

Alice nodded. "I see no reason for the barn not to be put to use," she commented. "It's a good horse barn, and when a barn's not used, it starts to run down and the vermin take over."

He raised his eyebrows with interest at her comment.

Alice sent him a challenging look in return. "I was raised around horses outside Murfreesboro, Tennessee, Mr. Ramsey. I know a little about barns."

She was an observant and discerning little thing, Harrison thought. A real opposite of his mother, who possessed no gift for reading others. Mozella always babbled on endlessly, never seeming to notice the effect her words had.

"Were you raised around Tennessee walking horses?" Harrison asked curiously. "Or around pleasure horses?"

"Walking horses." She smiled a bright smile that lit her whole face and took Harrison's breath away. "The Beryl family, my grandparents on my mother's side, raise and show Tennessee Walking horses. Murfreesboro is not far from Shelbyville, the walking horse capital of the world, you know."

"Do you ride?" he asked, banking down his emotions.

She leaned her chin on her hands. "Since I grew old enough to sit on horseback," she replied, smiling again. "I own a Tennessee Walking horse in Murfreesboro I want to bring over when I can arrange transportation."

He scratched his chin. "I don't know how a fancy walker will fit in around here."

"Elsa fits in anywhere." Alice frowned at him.

His jaw tightened. "I just mean we don't have any training areas or fields for working out a walking horse in Greenbrier. This isn't much of an area for fancy horses."

Alice gave him another of those patient, considering looks and then lifted her eyebrows. "Elsa doesn't show anymore, Mr. Ramsey. She didn't display the right temperament. She was too personable, didn't know how to keep her mind on business. Elsa preferred meeting and greeting people to keeping her mind focused on the show ring. That put her gaits off; it made her performance unreliable in serious competition. Grampa Beryl considered selling her, but I talked him into letting me keep her, so I could ride her for pleasure. That's what Elsa is best at, simply being a pet and being loved. It will be nice to bring her to Meadowbrook where I can see and ride her more."

"I'm sure you know best," he conceded, hoping he sounded like he meant it. He wasn't sure how a purebred, high-strung walking horse would get along in the mountains around a bunch of trail horses.

Harrison dug into the chocolate pie Odell put before him.

"Elsa's name is Bea Elsa Fairmont Duncan's Pride, out of Fairmont Dream and Duncan's Pride," Alice continued. "She's solid white with some gold flecks in her coat and mane. A pretty horse."

"You ride English or American saddle on her?" Harrison asked.

"I can ride either," Alice said, giving Harrison that considering look of hers again. It made him feel uncomfortable every time she sent it his way, made him feel weighed and analyzed.

"Elsa's very easy going," she continued, after a minute. "She doesn't care what kind of saddle is used on her. She'll ride as easily with a western saddle as with an English or an American saddle." She lifted an eyebrow. "I guess western saddles are what you use for your trail horses, right?"

He nodded, wolfing down the last of the pie.

Odell pushed back her chair. "It sounds like you two got all that business worked out about the horses now." She started toward the kitchen, carrying the last of the plates from the table with her. "Alice, why don't you take Harrison and show him around the house, let him see all you've done while I clean up in the kitchen."

"That would be nice, but I need to get on back to the stable." Harrison stood and pushed in his chair. "We stay busy this time of year and I have other work to do." He knew his statements weren't completely the truth, but he didn't want to chance being alone with Alice while walking through the house with her. He needed more time before an intimacy like that.

He found his hat on the table by the door and twisted it in his hands. "I'll come back later and let you and the children show me around," he said to Alice, making an effort to sound cordial.

"I'll look forward to it," she said politely, her look telling him she understood exactly why he declined the offer. "It was nice meeting you, Mr. Ramsey."

"It's Harrison." He edged toward the door. "There's no need to call me Mr. Ramsey. That's too formal for neighbors."

"Harrison," she repeated quietly. His nerves tingled at the sound.

He pulled on his cowboy hat, offered his goodbyes, and made his escape while he could. He felt certain his afternoon would include a lot of hard physical labor. He needed it to clear his mind.

CHAPTER 5

Alice had precious little time to think too much about her meeting with Harrison Ramsey over the next weeks because her life spiraled into a frenzy of activity with the move. Okay, in all honesty, thoughts of him played through her mind in odd moments. It did seem incredible, after all, that she'd actually met the man she felt so drawn to that snowy day in February—and and experienced the same reactions again when she did.

Grudgingly, she also admitted she often thought of Harrison's touch on her cheek late at night. Remembered the way he looked at her when they first saw each other again. On the other hand, Alice recalled many of the man's narrow and judgmental comments over lunch, too. Those memories helped skim some of the prince charming finish off Alice's previous image of Mr. Dream Man.

It appeared patently obvious to Alice that Harrison Ramsey made excuses to leave quickly after lunch that day—all too eager to put space between them. Hadn't she expected that? He'd learned by then about her six foster children. He acted appalled, too, like so many others, that she chose willingly to take six kids on.

She smiled. But then, of course, he didn't know the children yet. Alice could remember she thought the idea inconceivable, too. She shrugged. What did it matter? She doubted she would see much more of Harrison Ramsey, and when she did, he'd have his initial attraction carefully in check. Probably just as well. She had no more time for him than he did for her. A busy summer lay ahead.

A week after Alice met Harrison Ramsey, she held a family

meeting to tell the children about the new house—an accepted weekly event in the Stuart-Graham household. Richard and Loren always held these meetings to talk about family events, air grievances, and discuss needed plans for the future. Alice kept the meetings up, like many other Stuart traditions.

She looked with fondness at the six Stuart children as they settled into the sofas and chairs around the living room. Alice watched Hannah and Megan take charge of the younger ones. Always responsible girls, they'd taken on a more maternal role since their parents died. Hannah roomed with Stacey and Rachel in one bedroom upstairs in Alice's house, while Megan roomed in the other with the twins. They divided their parental responsibilities in caring for their siblings the same way.

Alice noticed Hannah starting to show signs of puberty at twelve. A pale blond with fair skin and a sweet softness to her looks, Hannah could be orderly and conscientious to a fault. She zealously worked to see her family didn't forget their parents and often overstressed to her siblings what she termed "the way Mother and Daddy would have wanted us to behave." Alice understood it as her way to hold her parents close in heart.

Megan, more laid back and easy-going than Hannah, displayed energetic and tomboyish tendencies. She had her father's fascination with nature and outdoor life and possessed Richard's easy sense of humor. Her hair appeared darker, her features stronger, and she usually wore her hair in casual braids, twisted off with rubber bands.

Stacey and Rachel, only a year apart in age and unusually close for sisters, displayed polar opposites in personality. Words like impulsive, out-spoken and strong-willed best defined Stacey. With long, wavy, golden blond hair, big blue eyes, and perfect features, she already drew attention as a budding beauty. Stacey also exhibited a mature confidence and natural leadership somewhat unusual for her age.

Perhaps that explained another reason she and Rachel got along so comfortably, since most people described Rachel as timid and shy. An ash blond with a rosy complexion and fragile features, Rachel possessed a tenderhearted and emotionally sensitive nature. She displayed a sweet prettiness along with very loving and thoughtful ways, and she adored animals. It was generally Rachel that Sophie, the family's black and white English Spaniel, followed around faithfully. The family got Sophie as a puppy after Rachel's birth, and the dog gravitated to her right from the start. Sophie usually slept at the foot of Rachel's bed at night when not in her dog bed.

According to Richard, the twins, Thomas and Tildy, never originally figured in the Stuarts' game plan. As twins not of the same sex, Tildy and Thomas weren't identical, but their looks bore striking similarities. They both possessed cherubic faces, bright eyes, light blond hair, and infectious smiles. Both also had the same boundless energy and sense of adventure. Alice smiled. The two of them, like Megan, charged into life—always on the go and full of new ideas.

Alice knew the children tried hard to be cooperative in her home. They promised her to work hard and not to cause her any problems if she kept them. She almost teared up remembering the pleas and promises they offered, desperate to stay together as a family, wanting so much to live with her. She admired the way they'd handled being crowded into her small house this year with such good spirits.

"School's out in two and a half more days," Stacey announced excitedly, as they settled down in the living room. "I hope we're going to talk about summer plans at our meeting." She squeezed into a spot on the sofa by Rachel. "I hope we get to go to camp again. Usually every summer we go two weeks to Buckeye Knob Camp."

"Hush, Stacey," prompted Hannah, giving her a chiding look. "We probably can't afford to go to camp anymore."

Stacey stuck out her lip. "We went last summer."

"Grampa paid for it," Hannah explained to her. "We can't ask Alice to do that."

Alice reined her own thoughts in to catch that comment. "You know, I'd completely forgotten about camp," she acknowledged. "You should have said something about it earlier. I do remember now you all went last summer. Perhaps I can call and make arrangements today."

"Tildy and I didn't go," said Thomas. "We weren't old enough to go to camp."

"I didn't get to go either because I hadn't turned seven yet," put in Rachel softly. "But I'd like to go this year for the first time if I can be in Stacey's tent."

Megan leaned forward in her chair. "Alice do you know if Mrs. Pike's daughter, Teresa, will stay with us again this summer? I liked her. She's nice. She took us to the swimming pool, to the movies, and even hiking once or twice."

The Stuarts employed a sitter to stay with the children in the summers, and last summer Lloyd Ingles hired their housekeeper's college-aged daughter, Teresa. Since Teresa's mother, Martha, worked in the Stuart's house daily, doing the regular cleaning and much of the cooking, it proved a good arrangement.

Having Teresa helped tremendously last summer—especially when Grampa Lloyd broke his leg. Later, when the Stuarts' house sold, Teresa and Martha graciously continued helping with the children when Alice moved them to her place on Collier Street. Grampa Lloyd, his congestive heart failure giving him problems again and his leg weak from the fall, returned to his assisted living community in southern Georgia.

"Is Grampa coming up this summer? I miss Grampa," said Tildy, sighing.

Megan giggled. "I don't know where Grampa would sleep if he did come. We'd need to build a wing on this house if he came."

Catching her cue, Alice took control of the floor. "Actually, that's what I wanted to talk to you about at this meeting," she said. "We won't need to add on a room for Grampa Lloyd if he wants to come visit this summer, because we're going to be moving to a new house."

Megan's eyes grew wide. "Did you find us a house, Alice? You said you planned to start looking."

Alice smiled. "Yes, I found a house I think will be perfect for us. In fact, it's one your mother and father looked at near the mountains."

"You mean the country place?" asked Rachel wistfully. "The one Mommy and Daddy said would be nice for us?"

"The realtor, Mrs. Jamison, said your mother and father seriously considered this house, Rachel. Perhaps it's the very same one."

The questions hit then. "Where is it? ... When do we get to go see it? ... How big is it? ... Will we move before school starts again?"

Alice finally had to raise her arm like a schoolteacher to get their attention. "Shhhh. If you'll listen, I'll tell you about it and show you pictures of it."

To Alice's surprise, Rachel started to cry.

"Whatever's the matter Rachel?" Alice reached a hand over to smooth her hair.

The child looked up with tears dripping down her face. "Does this mean you might keep us forever now, Alice, and not send us away?"

Alice felt her mouth drop open in surprise. "Why Rachel, you know we all decided a long time ago to stay together. I had no idea you continued to worry over that."

"We've all worried about that, Alice," Hannah answered candidly, going over to give Rachel a consoling hug. "There are six of us and we know it's a huge thing for you to decide to care for all of us."

Thomas nodded. "Yeah, we thought you might change your mind. Especially because we're not always good."

"My teacher said it's too much for a single girl like you to take care of six children." Stacey crossed her leg. "She told Mrs. Hardesty she bet you'd change your mind after you kept us for a while. She said no one would ever marry you if you took us, either. I heard them talking in the hall."

"I don't want you to never get married, Alice," five-year old Tildy said, coming over to climb on Alice's lap. "Because you're nice." She sniffed loudly and wrapped her arms around Alice's neck. "But we love you, Alice, and we don't want you to leave us or send us away."

"Now, listen," Alice insisted, surprised at this turn of events. "You all know I married before and you know my husband David got killed in Saudi Arabia while in the military. I didn't think I'd ever have a family after losing David, and now I have all of you. I think that's very nice for me and very nice for you, too. Don't you agree?"

"Maybe." Rachel came over to curl up beside Alice on the sofa. "But we've been scared, Alice. Megan said we'd all get split up if you didn't keep us, and she said you couldn't find anybody else that wanted us."

Megan looked at Alice sheepishly. "I heard you and Dorothy Eaton talking one time," she confessed. "I heard her say she couldn't find anyone who would take all six of us together. She said some people might take one or two of us but that's all."

"That would be awful," Thomas declared, crossing his arms. "I told Megan I'd run away."

"Listen, all of you, I want each of you to gather around right now and put your hands on top of mine on the coffee table." Alice waited until they did.

"This is a serious moment and we're going to take a vow," she said. "Do you know what that is?"

"It's a promise you make that you'll keep forever," Hannah answered.

Alice nodded. "Hannah's right, and we're going to make a vow together tonight that we all promise to keep."

"If you break your vow you have to walk the plank," Thomas put in, causing everyone to giggle.

Alice looked around at each face. "Our vow is going to be like a wedding vow. We're each going to promise to love and care for each other from this day forth. I don't want to be moving into a new house if we're not all committed to being together as a family from now on."

"You mean like in sickness and in health and till death do us part, just like in the movies?" asked Stacey.

"Yes, we're going to say all of those vows to each other and mean them with all our hearts. Then we'll be a real family. Okay?"

Six solemn sets of eyes met Alice's. She led them, after that, through a set of commitment vows, improvised from the wedding vows she recalled from the last ceremony she attended.

"What do we do now?" Megan turned wide eyes to Alice. "Do we have to sign anything?"

"No, it's signed in our hearts," answered Alice, making a little x across her heart. The children followed suit and did the same.

She smiled. "All we need to do now is to quit worrying and start planning our move to our new home."

"Are you honestly buying a house for us?" Hannah asked as Alice sorted through her briefcase to locate the pictures of Meadowbrook to show them. "Houses are expensive, Alice. You don't have to do that. We can keep living here on Collier Street."

Alice smiled. "That's very thoughtful of you, Hannah. But this house is too small for us, and I have some money put away to pay for the house."

"You get money for fostering us, too," put in Stacey. "I heard Mrs. Eaton say so. You can use some of that for the house, can't you?"

"Pooh, there's not enough of that to buy any kind of house," Megan countered. "It helps Alice feed us and buy us school clothes and stuff."

"Believe me, I'm grateful for that money, Megan. And I will keep getting that even when we move to our house."

Hannah looked around at her siblings. "You know, I think we should look at the pictures and stop worrying like Alice said," she suggested practically. "We're *maybe* going to get a new house before the fall—and a move to the country—like Mother and Daddy always wanted."

Alice smiled at her then, a cat that swallowed the canary smile.

"There's no maybe about it, Hannah. I already bought the house, and we're moving in this weekend after school is out."

Six stunned faces stared at her. Alice wished she had her camera ready to capture their expressions.

Finally, Thomas broke the silence, jumping up from his seat. "Whoopee! We've got a house! I hope I get my own room with *no* pink stuff and *no* baby dolls."

Everyone laughed after that, and Alice began to show the children the realtor's pictures of Meadowbrook. Excitement soon filled the room, and Alice waged a struggle settling the children down to talk about moving plans and getting ready for the van coming Thursday.

Stacey held one of the pictures of the house to her chest and hugged it dramatically. "When do we get to go see the new house, Alice?" she asked. "Tomorrow after school?"

Alice took a breath. "This venture has been my big fairy-godmother surprise for all of you. I had a wonderful time getting everything ready so it would be like a magic moment when you all come to the house for the first time. So-o-o-o." She paused to enhance the suspense. "Because of that I want you to wait to see the house until the very day we move in when everything's complete. Then it will become a magical, special day you'll always remember forever."

"Like a fairy story," whispered Rachel.

"Yes, just like a fairy story," Alice agreed, smiling. "I hope you can all wait a few more days until everything will be moved in and absolutely perfect. Martha Pike is letting you spend the night at her house after school Thursday while the movers are packing our things. On Friday, I'll come get you and take you to the new house as soon as the movers finish unpacking and everything is ready. Is that okay?"

The children fell quiet thinking about this. She could see them battling their eagerness to see the house with her plan to wait.

Hannah finally spoke. Alice, will our old things be moved to the new house, too? Grampa put them in storage in case we ever got a bigger house."

"There're already there," Alice told her, watching Hannah's face light up at her reply. "Everything's except the furniture and things at this house."

Tildy sighed. "Is it going to be just wonderful, Alice?"

"I certainly hope so," said Alice, hugging her.

A moment or two more of quiet followed, and Alice wondered if the children would argue—push to see the house sooner when so excited.

"We can wait," Hannah declared, speaking as the eldest for all of them like she often did. "Can't we, Stuarts?" She looked around at her siblings, waiting to see their nods of agreement.

"You know, Alice," she added. "I think it's incredible you've done this for us. Thank you. It's all starting to sink in, that we're actually going to have a new home. I think I'm going to cry, I'm so happy."

The rest of the evening, and the next few days after, rushed by in a flurry of packing and planning. Now, on Friday afternoon, Alice drove the Stuart clan out to Meadowbrook for the first time. The movers finished packing everything in the Collier Street house late Thursday afternoon, and Alice made her way wearily to Meadowbrook to catch some sleep after before the van arrived the next morning to unload.

Odell McKee arrived bright and early Friday to help Alice direct the movers and finish setting up the house. The two worked rapidly, stopping only for a quick sandwich at lunch. They made beds, unpacked boxes, shelved books, and put kitchen and bathroom items in place. By three o'clock, they decided the house as ready as they could make it in a day. Odell headed home and Alice left to get the children.

With the big moment finally here, Alice found herself feeling anxious as she drove her van down the winding road leading to their new house. What if the children didn't like it? What if they were disappointed?

Hannah, as expected, took charge as they pulled up to the house.

"I think we should do everything in an orderly manner." She

crossed her arms. "Mother and Daddy would want that. There should be no running around or acting silly. We'll stay together and let Alice take us through the house and show us everything. Like a special, magic tour."

Megan pushed open the door of the van. "And *then* we can explore the yard," she said eagerly. "Look, it's huge and there is a mountain behind it!"

"Oh, it's a wonderful house, Alice," Rachel whispered, starry-eyed. "I just know it's the one Mommy and Daddy wanted for us."

"Let's go inside and look at it," she told them. "It's not just a *house* any more, you know, this is *our house.*"

Alice led her wide-eyed tour group chattering noisily into Meadowbrook. Each babbled with plans about exploring and playing on the big front porch and in the country yard.

Inside the front door, they stopped to greet Sophie the dog, whom Alice had brought over last night. Then Alice directed the children to the right of the broad entry hall to see the living and dining rooms.

"This is the furniture from your old house. It should look familiar to all of you." She gestured around.

"Oh, look! It's our things!" exclaimed Stacey. "It looks wonderful!"

The living and dining rooms did look striking, especially the living area with its deep maroon sofas, navy and floral brocade chairs, and dark floral rugs.

"You've arranged everything beautifully." Hannah walked around touching old, familiar pieces. "Mother would love it."

"Look! The dining room isn't crowded anymore." Megan headed on eagerly. "All the leaves are in the table, too. We can all fit together around it and even have company now."

"Let's go see the rest." Thomas danced up and down impatiently, even though Megan tried to shush him for hurrying them.

Alice took them through the dining room door and into the kitchen—which got only a quick look from the children who were immediately attracted to the long screened porch and its views out over their new back yard. And, of course, Thomas and Tildy had to try out the porch swing.

As they came back through the eating area off the kitchen, Megan stopped to locate her chair around the large family dining table.

"I know this is my chair." She grinned at Alice. "Because Daddy said I chewed out these little places on the back of it when I started teething."

"I'm glad we get to have our old dishes back." Thomas pointed at the colorful stacks of Fiestaware in the built-in cupboard. "Alice only had white dishes at her house. I like our colored ones better."

Rachel sighed wistfully. "We can have our own colors again when we eat."

Going through nearly every room downstairs and upstairs proved a continual rediscovery adventure to the children. They opened every door and closet, familiarizing themselves with the new layout, and they bubbled with old memories seeing all their familiar possessions stored away for almost a year.

The furnishings in Alice's bedroom and the front parlor looked the most familiar since they came from Alice's Collier Street house. Her antique living room furniture graced the parlor and her dark cherry bedroom suite and king-size bed, from her earlier married years, settled comfortably into the master bedroom.

"Children, this study is my home office," Alice explained as they checked the front room out. "It is off limits just like at the Collier house. I keep important records and papers here that relate to my work with Wayside."

"And your computer," said Hannah on a long wistful sigh.

Alice grinned. "Actually, your father's old computer is in the upstairs den now. You can use it anytime, plus I put your mother's laptop from her office in the bonus room. Both will be good to help with homework, do research, and play games on."

Enthusiastic hurrahs greeted this announcement and the children eagerly headed upstairs next to see the bedrooms.

Alice led the way. "Everyone has their own room now, except for Stacy and Rachel, who asked to stay together." She paused. "I think we'll look at the rooms by age, Hannah first, because she's the oldest."

Megan spotted the name plaques on the closed bedroom doors. "Here's Hannah's room," she cried, pointing to Hannah's plaque with excitement.

"That was my idea." Thomas stuck out his chest proudly.

Tildy pushed open Hannah's door eagerly. "Look, it's all peach, like your special color." She clapped her hands. "How pretty! I hope my room is pink like my color."

Hannah, overcome, could hardly speak. She simply walked around touching things she hadn't seen in a long time—the familiar brass twin beds, the antique hand-painted dresser and chest of drawers, her old stereo/CD cabinet and bedside tables. Knowing she had a sentimental, romantic side, Alice put eyelet valances on each of the twin beds and then used quilts with clusters of peach nosegays on the top. Feminine pillows tumbled across the beds and lay tucked in the cozy side chair Alice upholstered for Hannah to dream and read in.

"Oh, Hannah," Megan blurted out, coming over to hug her sister. "It's so you. Look at all the flowers everywhere and at the straw hats with ribbon streamers Alice hung on the wall. It's wonderful."

Hannah started to cry. "I didn't think I'd ever have a nice room again. I don't know what to say."

Thomas wrinkled his nose, confused. "How come you're crying if you like it?"

Megan ruffled his hair playfully. "Oh, sometimes girls cry when they're happy."

He made a face. "Girls sure do a lot of dumb things," he muttered.

"Let's go see everyone else's room," Hannah offered graciously.

They went to Megan's next—a room totally different from Hannah's. Not fussy or feminine. Just simple and bright, with yellow-striped wallpaper, casual maple furniture pieces from the Collier Street house, and botanical prints Alice framed, knowing how much Megan would like them.

"Look, your quilt's got stars sewed on it." Stacey pointed. "And your old rock collection is on the bookshelf with all your books."

"It's exactly what I said I wanted." Megan grinned.

Stacey and Rachel found their room next.

"Wow. Your room is huge," commented Thomas, as they walked in.

Alice leaned in the doorway, enjoying watching the girls' reactions. "I gave Stacey and Rachel the biggest room upstairs because they're sharing."

"I like having the biggest room." Stacey lifted her chin. "And, look Rachel, it's got wallpaper with both our colors, little purple violets and green leaves. Plus we got *new* bedspreads!" She went over to touch them.

"All our things are back," whispered Rachel, the more sentimental of the two. "Our white furniture and our beds. Our dolls and books and toys we didn't have room for at Alice's." And, of course, Rachel being Rachel, she sniffled and cried while she hugged old dolls and stuffed animals.

"I'm next! I'm next!" Thomas reminded them impatiently. "Let's go see my room, okay?"

"Mine, too," said Tildy, bouncing up and down.

They explored the twins' bedrooms next, Thomas' room bordered in sailboats and decorated in blue and red, and Tildy's room papered in pink checks with its ballerina spreads and framed prints.

Thomas spotted his new beds the minute he walked in his room. "Bunk beds!" he cried, running across the room to climb the ladder to the top bunk. "Just what I asked for!" He soon looked down at them from the top bunk grinning. "I have cars and boats and cool stuff everywhere and *no* pink and *no* dolls!"

Tildy gladly welcomed the pinks and the dolls. She loved the white-painted furniture and the big doll's house filled with her old stuffed animals, dolls, and toys.

"You remembered the ballerinas and the little tea table I wanted," she squealed, running to check them out and then racing back to hug Alice's legs. "I love it all, Alice. Thank you."

They cut through to the bonus room above the garage wing now, filled with the brown leather sofas, chairs, and furniture pieces from the Stuart's former family room. Against the walls sat their piano, a big television, a stereo/CD player, the family computers, and Alice's oak kitchen table from the Collier house, perfect for homework and games.

The guest room behind the bonus room held Loren and Richard's old furniture, but Alice added new spreads and accessories to keep it from looking too familiar and upsetting to the children.

"I'm glad you could use Mommy and Daddy's furniture," Hannah assured Alice, tracing her finger across her mother's dresser with a sigh. "It will be nice for Grandpa Lloyd when he comes. He stayed in it before."

They paused for a solemn moment then, but Thomas soon hurried them on, eager to see the rest so he could go outside. They checked out a small sitting room at the top of the stairs—the shelves filled with the children's books.

Then Stacey looked up and down the hall. "Have we missed anything?"

"Yes, the bathrooms," said Thomas, holding himself. "I need to go, too."

They found the closest bathroom for Thomas while Alice pointed out the second bathroom near the children's bedrooms.

"I assigned one bath to Megan, Thomas, and Tildy and the other to Hannah, Megan, and Stacey. I did florals or stripes to use all those colorful towels you have." Tildy pulled on Alice's hand to get her attention. "Mommy bought our towels in our special colors, Alice. Remember? That's so we can know which towels are ours."

"I kept them exactly that way." Alice smiled at her.

The doorbell rang suddenly, followed by excited barks from Sophie, and the Stuart children raced down the stairs to welcome their first houseguests. Odell McKee and the Nichols family had brought dinner for them all. With Vick and Donna Nichols came their two girls, Deidre, nicknamed DeeDee, about Hannah's age, and Rhoda, who recently turned ten like Megan.

To Alice's surprise, Harrison Ramsey walked up the steps behind them, carrying a serving dish of his own and two bottles of wine for the adults. Following introductions, a happy get-acquainted time ensued as everyone gathered to fill a plate to take to the dining room, porch, or kitchen tables.

After supper, the children dragged everyone back through the house to see every room all over again and then went outside to explore with the Nichols' girls. Alice sat on the screened porch visiting with Odell, Vick and Donna Nichols, and Harrison. Despite an initial weak-kneed reaction Alice felt when Harrison first arrived, she found the tumult of the children and other guests kept her from overreacting to his appearance today. However, at odd moments her nerves tingled with awareness of him and it made Alice feel gauche and foolish. She could only hope in time she'd stop having silly physical reactions to her neighbor every time he dropped by. He'd clearly banked any romantic emotions he held about her—if he ever entertained any at all.

CHAPTER 6

Harrison knew it would seem churlish of him not to go to the welcome party Odell put together for Alice and the children. After all, he and the Nichols were the closest neighbors. It would look bad to make excuses or refuse to go. At least, with safety in numbers, a large group gathering would allow him no time alone with Alice Graham. Harrison didn't want to risk that yet. Not until he leashed his emotions under better check.

"I hope you can come," Odell said when she called him with the idea. "Vick says he's bringing one of those special chef dishes he makes at his restaurant in Gatlinburg and Donna and I are making side dishes."

"I'll be there," he said. "Free food is hard to turn down for a bachelor who lives alone and cooks predominantly chuck wagon recipes."

Walking up to the Newland porch later, he hoped Alice might not affect him the same way this second time. But he felt immediately shaken as soon as he saw her. Dang woman. Even dressed in old denim shorts and a T-shirt with strands of hair slipping out of a clip, she looked beautiful. As Harrison passed her in the doorway, he got a whiff of a scent like summer lilacs that made him itch to lean closer.

A friendly, black and white English setter helped him shelve the moment by coming to nudge him with her nose. Behind the setter waved a sea of young faces. The Stuart children were all blond and blue-eyed, just as Odell had said, and looked enough like Alice to easily be mistaken for her own family.

Introductions quickly made, everyone filed back to the kitchen with their food contributions to set up for supper. The women chattered and got out plates and silverware, while Harrison and Vick leaned in a doorway and caught up on political news and football scores.

After dinner and a tour through the house, Harrison settled down on the screen porch to visit with the adults while the kids played out in the back yard. He selected a spot for himself at a distance from Alice, where he could watch her but avoid eye contact with her any more than necessary. He hated how she made him uncomfortable in his own skin.

Tuning in to the conversation, he heard Donna telling Alice about their move to Greenbrier eight years ago. "Vick and I rented near Gatlinburg when Vick first got the job at the restaurant." She leaned toward Alice. "While house-hunting, we spotted a dilapidated old farmhouse over on Beech Grove Road for sale. It looked pitiful on the outside, peeling paint and a scraggledy yard, but we loved it and thought we could fix it up. A contractor examined it and pronounced it structurally sound, and that's all we needed to hear to take the plunge."

"It looks real cute now," Odell put in. "It belonged to one of the descendants of the Abe McCarter family originally, but the house got neglected and run down over the years. All of us counted it a blessing when Vick and Donna bought the old place—a real eyesore in the community—and started to repair it. They brought it back to life, restored all the gingerbread trim, painted it a nice shade of yellow, spruced up the property. Alice, you and the children will have to go see it."

"You can walk over easily," Donna told her. "Beech Grove is the street almost directly across from your driveway on the other side of the highway. It's a quiet country road, but be careful the children watch for traffic going across the main road. Once you're on Beech Grove, it's only two blocks to our house on the right."

Harrison watched how effortlessly Donna put Alice at ease and made her feel welcome. She'd always been a natural with people. In appearance, Donna made a stark contrast to Alice, tall, full-figured, and comfortably attractive with sleek black hair from her Cherokee ancestry. Rhoda looked a lot like her, while DeeDee looked more like Vick, with reddish brown hair and fairer skin.

"Both our girls learned to ride at Harrison's stable." Vick shifted the conversation. "That's when the horse-bug bit them hard, and they started begging to have their own horses. We held out a few years, but finally gave in when Dora and Carl said we could stable the girls' horses at Meadowbrook. We don't have a barn at our place, and the riding trails are all on this side of the highway."

"There are a few trails on your side of the road, Vick," Harrison said. "One nice one is behind the apple orchard along Webb Creek. It leads down to Redwine Falls then under Reagan Bridge and along the edge of the woods to my stable. You can ride under the bridge without crossing the highway there. I use that trail often to check my rental cabins near the falls, and Bishop likes a good run in that flat stretch of land behind the orchard."

Odell came out the screen door carrying a big pitcher of lemonade. "Harrison knows every nook and cranny around this region, Alice. He grew up here and has explored these hills all his life."

Alice nodded, contented in herself, curled back in an old wicker sofa enjoying listening to everyone talk. She looked relaxed, one foot curled up under her leg, an easy smile often brightening her face. It annoyed Harrison that she appeared so comfortable when he felt profoundly uncomfortable, his awareness of her almost painful. She was a very distracting woman. He caught himself noticing every time she moved, every instance she smiled or gestured, and he found it oddly touching how loving and attentive she acted toward the children.

"Alice, guess what?" Stacey called excitedly at that moment, running up to the screened porch where Alice could hear her. "There's a playhouse down in the back yard. You can only barely see it from here but it's almost like a real house." She pointed in the direction of the house. "It has a big room inside and a window with real shutters. Do you think we can fix it up and find some old furniture to put in it?"

"I'm sure we can." She smiled easily at the child. "We'll go to some garage sales and thrift stores to look for furnishings. You and Rachel think about what the house needs and we'll shop for it next week when I have a day off. Possibly Friday or Saturday when we can hit the yard sales."

"Cool! Thanks! I'll tell Rachel!" Stacey ran off to tell her.

Harrison heard Alice laugh softly to herself.

Twilight had started to fall, and the lightning bugs started twinkling in the darkness. The little boy, Thomas, came tromping noisily up on the porch holding a lightning bug cupped in his hand.

"Look, Alice, I caught one! And it keeps lighting up and everything."

"It's beautiful," Alice said, peering inside his hand. "But hold it loosely, Thomas. It's tender, and if you hold too tight you'll hurt it."

"Can I keep it?" he asked, wide-eyed. "Put it in a jar in my room?"

"No, Thomas, its world is meant to be outside." She patted his hand. "The lightning bug would be sad in a jar, cooped up and not free to fly where it wanted to go anymore. It might die, too. Remember our story about the nightingale and how it stopped singing beautifully after it became caged?"

She put an arm around him and gave him a quick hug. "You enjoy the lightning bug for a little while in your hand, Thomas, and then let it go and watch it fly away happy and free. Another night you might see it again."

Harrison marveled at her. She never acted irritated when the children came up to interrupt her with the adults—behaving so patiently with them, actually listening to what they had to say. It was nothing like his own mother had acted with him or his sisters. She always resented any interruption they presented her and made them feel foolish for asking childish questions.

Her voice echoed in his mind. "Harrison Owen Ramsey, can't

you see I'm visiting right now? That you're interrupting? Go play and quit coming to ask me a bunch of foolish questions."

When his father tried to listen more patiently to him, she snapped at him. "W.T., you indulge him too much, and you give a lot more time and attention to him than you do your own wife. Children should stay out of sight and out of mind. Haven't you heard that old saying?"

His daddy would whisper a few words to him, telling Harrison to come talk to him about it tomorrow at the barn. Harrison always did. His father always made time for him, but his mother never did. For years, he struggled hard to please Mozella and then simply gave up trying.

The twins ran up, clutching a mass of scraggly dandelions in their hands. "Look what we picked for you, Alice." Thomas presented her the handful of dandelions with a bright smile.

Tildy chimed in. "Aren't they pretty, Alice? We remembered to pick them in the yard like you told us and not in the flowerbed, too."

"They're very beautiful," she told them. "I love dandelions. I'm going to go put them in a jar on the table right now where we can all see them again over breakfast."

Surprisingly, she got up and walked with them into the kitchen to find a jar, politely excusing herself from the adults.

Harrison simply couldn't believe her. His mother would have said, "Get those weeds out of here, Harrison Owen Ramsey, before we all set up to sneezing."

He shook his head to clear the memories rising up. Odd how the contrasts slipped into his mind watching Alice tonight. After all, it wasn't as though he didn't spend time around kids at the stable or visiting with friends. He knew well enough his mother came down harder on her children than most parents did.

Perhaps sitting here at Meadowbrook brought the memories out. Aunt Dora always helped heal his wounded heart with later kindnesses when his mother lashed out harshly at him. Harrison realized Alice reminded him of Dora in some ways, although

Dora stayed home with children. He remembered his and Alice's conversation about this and frowned. Admittedly, she did all right with the Stuarts, even though she worked. Harrison knew Donna worked, too—a part-time job at Parton's Place craft store, the one his aunt Millie Parton owned.

Donna started talking about that now. "You'll have to come see the store one day," she said to Alice. "It's about a mile down the highway toward Gatlinburg. I work there three or four days a week, usually during the girls' school hours. In the summer, Mrs. Gentry next door watches the girls when I work."

"I think I've seen that store." Alice said. "Isn't it the long grey building with the flowers across the front porch?"

"That's the one." Donna smiled. "Millie opened it years ago and worked full-time herself for a long time. Since she's gotten older, she doesn't like to come in the store as much, but I love retail and talking with all the people that come by."

"Donna's real good to help with the store displays and the buying, too," Odell added. "Millie told me she didn't know what she'd do without Donna to help her."

"Millie is Harrison's aunt besides being Donna's boss," Vick added, for Alice's benefit. "If I remember, Millie Trent Parton is your mother's sister, right Harrison?"

"That's right," Harrison answered. "The youngest of the eight Trent kids."

"There sure did used to be big families around this area back then," commented Odell. "I guess it won't seem too different to most folks to see you with six children around Greenbrier, Alice."

Alice laughed. "Oh, I think people will always notice six children anywhere today. The current national average is less than two children per family. Large families are a rarity in our world now."

The evening waned on with small talk. The adults drank coffee or Odell's lemonade after finishing off the wine. Vick had brought his special beef tenderloin with grilled mushrooms on the side and a big plate of stir-fried vegetables. A heaping bowl of mashed potatoes and green beans came from Odell, along with chocolate cake that proved a big hit with the children.

By eight, with night creeping in, the adults began to gather up their things to leave. Harrison made sure he left with the others, but then slipped down to the barn to check on his horses before walking home. All in all, he thought he handled the evening pretty well.

Once at the barn, Harrison spent time cleaning and putting feed out for the horses. He whistled while he worked, by habit, and talked to the horses as he went about his chores. He was never more comfortable than in the stables.

He stopped to let Cleo nuzzle his neck. She nickered at him for fun—a playful mare and friendly.

"She obviously likes you," said a voice from the door of the barn. Harrison didn't need to turn around to know who spoke.

"What are you doing here?" he challenged, without turning around.

"You left your casserole dish," Alice offered pleasantly. "I sent the kids upstairs to get baths and settle in, and when I started cleaning the kitchen I found it. I saw the lights on in the barn and guessed you stopped by to check your horses. So I thought I'd bring your dish to you before you walked back home." She paused. "Apparently everyone liked your baked beans. Little more than a scrap remained in the bowl. Not enough to save."

Harrison had turned around as she talked. She stood in the light from the tack room, the light beams casting a soft glow around her. Making her skin and hair shine softly. Playing over her with little shadows. He found himself totally at a loss for words again.

"Listen," she continued, putting the dish down on a feed barrel, and walking closer to him. "I wanted you to know I don't think anything about what happened the other day when we met. I know it came as a shock for both of us. That day in the snow was a peculiar time, and I guess it surprised both of us to see each other again. Now, of course, you know who I am and about my responsibilities, and I want you to know I don't expect any sort of romantic interest from you." She rushed her words now.

"You needn't try to avoid me, if you know what I mean. I thought it would be easier if I cleared the air about that. So it wouldn't concern you."

"Is that right?" he finally got out. The barn hovered dark and intimate, and his blood pumped. His logic and control drifted hazily into a blur at the nearness of her. He could smell her scent of lilacs again and the aroma floated across to him sweet and sultry, like the lilac fragrances of his childhood wafting on the breeze of a summer's night.

"Yes, I think so," she answered softly. "We experienced an odd incident, one hard to analyze logically. But I think we can move past it and be friends, don't you?"

He made a sound in his throat he knew sounded like a death rattle. He couldn't seem to get his voice to create any coherent words again.

She moved a few steps closer to study him. "Are you all right?" she asked, laying a hand softly on his chest and looking up at him.

"No, I'm not," he ground out, just before he grabbed her and kissed her.

There had been no forethought about his action. When she touched him and looked up at him like that, he simply slipped past good sense.

He thought she would pull back immediately, possibly slap him, but, instead, she sighed a soft sound and let herself drift into the moment.

Harrison reveled in her then, deepening the kiss, letting his hands slip up to cup her face and then slide around her neck into her hair. He'd wanted to put his hands into her hair all night long, wanted to see how those pretty bones felt on her shoulders. He moved his mouth down to kiss the nape of her neck and taste the skin across her shoulder blades above her shirt. The rich lilac smell swirled all around him now, along with the fresh smell of her skin and hair. Always sensitive to smells and the feelings they invoked, she intoxicated him.

She lingered in the moment with him for a while, letting her soft hands slip into his hair and then play exploratively down his back. When he pulled her tighter, she responded warmly, snuggling up against him like a kitten might. Her head almost nestled under his chin, but when she lifted her head, it was only a sweet reach to her mouth again.

"Oh, my," she said in a whispery voice, pulling back reluctantly to gaze at him, her eyes cloudy. "I guess I shouldn't have come down here. It seems there's still something of that hum between us ..."

Her voice trailed off at that, and Harrison smiled a little despite himself. It took all of his strength to back away from her then, to pull himself under control.

"Despite your good analysis about our meeting," he drawled finally, his own voice still husky. "I think I showed better sense than you by avoiding time alone with you. We'd better be watchful in the future about having more intimate little times together like this, Alice Graham. You don't strike me as the kind of woman interested in a tumble, and I'll be candid and tell you that I'm not the sort of man interested in settling down and setting up house."

She jerked back from him, her eyes growing steely.

"You may be quite sure, Mr. Ramsey, that *settling* wasn't in my mind," she replied testily. "I can't even explain my behavior, and perhaps I should apologize for it. I don't know what came over me ...."

She blushed and backed away further from him, while he watched her.

"But I will *not* be intimidated by you." She straightened and lifted her chin. "You had as much to do with this as I did. And you had no better control than I. You know perfectly well, too, that I came to assure you specifically that I had no romantic designs for you. That is still quite true. As for the rest, I guess we'll just have to learn to deal with it."

She turned on her heel and stalked royally out of the barn, never turning once to look back. Harrison had to give her credit for a good exit.

He shook his head. "There's no fool like an old fool," he told Bishop, giving the horse a final pat before going around to finish his barn chores.

As Harrison walked home through the dark later, carrying his clean casserole dish, he smelled a whiff of lilac on the breeze from the old shrub in his side yard. He figured it Mother Nature's way of taunting him.

CHAPTER 7

It took Alice several days to get over her anger with Harrison, and even then, an undercurrent of resentment lingered. When she found his casserole dish and saw the light in the barn through the kitchen window, it seemed a nice thing to do to clean the dish and run it down to him. While walking down to the barn she decided to try to clear the air between them, set things on a new level. But everything backfired.

"Why did he have to act like that? And I can't believe I responded like I did." Alice sat at the desk in her office, trying to focus on reports she needed to complete, but memory swamped her instead. She'd let him kiss her thoroughly and kissed him back eagerly, too. Got lost in the sensations of his hands on her. Enjoyed touching him. She couldn't deny—even now when angry and embarrassed—that it felt wonderful.

"He certainly saw you were no green girl in matters of love." Alice groaned. "Surely he knows I've been married though—and I'm not sixteen anymore. I knew my share of boyfriends and steadies in earlier years. This isn't the first time I've been kissed." But she knew no kiss had ever felt as volatile as this with Harrison.

Alice groaned. "I can't understand it. It isn't reasonable or sensible. I should have better control." She stood up to pace the room. "What a mess. It's like getting caught in the undertow at the beach, tossed around by something forceful and unexpected, or like an impish cupid is having a hey-day with the two of us."

She walked over to the window to look out. "Harrison is angry about it, too. That's why he lashed out at me the way he did. He meant to hurt me. Meant to warn me away. He wants no relationship with me no matter what the feelings."

Alice sat back down at her desk, pulling her paperwork toward her again. "I refuse to entertain silly, romantic dreams over this. I have the children to think of and I'm not husband hunting. David was a good and sweet husband, and I hated losing him. It feels disloyal feeling passion or attraction for someone else after what we shared together."

She tapped her pencil in irritation on her desk. "David's and my relationship built slowly, gradually deepening and intensifying, like a relationship is supposed to. It didn't sweep over us." She wrinkled her nose. "I hardly know Harrison Ramsey and I don't know if I even like him."

Yet the man drifted through her mind all too often. Like today when she should be filling out her reports. She sighed, realizing she was getting nowhere with the task.

"I'll go check on the children again," she said, getting up. "See how the playhouse is coming along."

Earlier this Friday morning, Alice took the children en masse to a couple of garage sales and thrift stores where they found furnishings for the playhouse. At last check they all played happily with the Nichols girls fixing up the house. The yard boundaries had been fully explored and noted, and the children knew to stay within their set limits unless they obtained permission to go elsewhere. Since the property of Meadowbrook spread over a large acreage, this gave them a lot of scope.

Alice felt pleased to see how quickly Hannah bonded with DeeDee Nichols. DeeDee's vivaciousness made a nice contrast to Hannah's serious nature. Megan and Rhonda had developed a quick friendship, too, both similar in personality and interests. Alice wanted her two oldest girls to lighten up, have more fun, and feel less need to act too adult and responsible.

Alice could hear girlish giggling before she got to the playhouse. However, before she drew closer, she saw Harrison out of the corner of her eye coming across the bridge over the creek. He carried something. A prickle of premonition touched her before she heard Tildy's voice and saw her race out from behind Harrison.

"Alice! Alice!" she called. "It's Thomas. He's been hurted."

Alice set off in a flash in their direction, realizing now it was Thomas that Harrison carried in his arms.

"He got kicked by a horse at our stable," Harrison told her, as she drew near. "He was lucky. He didn't get hurt much. Just a kick in the bread basket." He shifted the boy in his arms. "It knocked the wind out of him and flipped him over. But there are no broken bones. Jasper's hooves didn't touch his head, thank God."

She'd drawn close enough to flutter over Thomas then. To check him and pet him.

"Let's get him into the house and up to his room," Harrison said. "He's fine, Alice. Just shaken up. He may be a bit sore tomorrow in his tummy and around his lower ribs. But there's nothing broken that I can tell."

"Do we need to take him to the doctor?" Alice asked, alarm threading her voice.

Harrison shook his head. "No, I don't think that's necessary, and I'd readily suggest it if I thought so. Deke and I checked him out and patched him up pretty good. The boy got a cut on his knee when he fell and he scraped his chin. We cleaned his cuts and scrapes."

Alice's eyes shifted to Tildy, now clinging to her leg. "Tildy, what about you? Are you all right?" she asked, reaching down to pick the child up. Tildy buried her head against Alice's shoulder and started to cry.

"The horsey didn't kick me, Alice. Only Thomas. But it was scary."

"She's been about as upset as Thomas," Harrison added. "But she's okay. I think they both could benefit from some rest and a little quiet time."

Thomas opened his eyes and looked at Alice. "Can I have one of those asprits?" he asked, sniffling. "Harrison said I could ask you for one. He said it would make me better."

At Alice's confused look, Harrison got the edge of a grin on his face. "I mentioned that he could probably take an *aspirin* when he got home, that it might make him feel better. Take the edge off the pain."

"Oh, of course." Alice smiled at Thomas. "I'll get one as soon as we get in."

They carried the children up the stairs to their rooms then. Harrison settled Thomas onto the lower bunk of his bed, while Alice took Tildy across the hall to her own room.

She helped Tildy take off her shoes and tucked her up under a quilt on the bed. "You lie down and take a short rest now," she told her, leaning over to kiss her forehead. "Thomas will be fine. Later, you can help me make him some cookies."

"The chocolate chips kind that are his favorites?" she asked.

"Absolutely." Alice walked over to draw the blinds.

She looked at Tildy then more seriously. "What were you and Thomas doing over at Harrison's stables? That's a long way out of our yard."

Tildy hung her head. "Thomas and me wanted to see the cowboys and the horses. We heard Rhoda Nichols say all you needed to do was follow the trail behind our barn to the stables. She kept talking about it and it sounded neat." She dropped her eyes. "The big girls got busy doing stuff we couldn't help with in the playhouse, because we were too little, so me and Thomas decided to see if we could find the trail. We did and we walked over."

"I think we'll talk about this later," Alice said firmly. "I need to see to Thomas now."

"I'm sorry we were bad," whispered Tildy. "Megan says when you're bad that bad things happen. And so Thomas got hurt."

"We'll talk about that thought later, too," advised Alice. "For now, you rest a little while."

Alice slipped out of Tildy's room then to cross the hall. At the door she stopped, hearing Harrison talking to Thomas.

"This used to be my best friend Carter's room. We enjoyed many adventures and good times here. When you're better, if you look at the baseboard in the back corner of your closet, you might find our names carved there. If it hasn't been painted out through the years."

"Did the room have sailboats then like it does now?" Thomas asked.

"Nah. It had cowboy stuff. That's what we were into back then."

Thomas gathered his stuffed dog into his arms while Harrison spread a blanket over him. "I'm sorry I got behind the horsey and made him get mad."

"You've got a thing or two to learn about horses, and that's a fact," Harrison told him. "One of those things you'll never forget now is to never walk right behind a horse. They can't see you then, and it makes them jumpy. They might kick out."

"And they have big feet when they kick," Thomas added solemnly. "They can kick real hard, too."

Alice heard a low chuckle from Harrison. "That they do," he agreed. "You were real lucky ole Jasper is used to kids and kicked less hard than most horses. Or you could be needing a lot more than an aspirin now."

Thomas put his small hand over Harrison's large one. "Harrison, even if I see a whole quarter laying on the ground behind a horsey again, I won't lean over behind him to get it."

"Good plan," Harrison added, as Alice came into the room.

He stood up then, from where he'd been sitting on the bunk beside Thomas.

"Just keeping him company until you could get here," he explained.

"Thank you," she said, sitting down on the bed beside Thomas herself to give him a kiss and to tuck him in.

"We did a bad thing," Thomas confessed to Alice.

"I know. Tildy already told me," Alice said. "We'll talk about it after you both take a short nap. I'm sorry you got hurt, Thomas. But I think Harrison is right that you're going to be fine and only have a little soreness later. So you rest now."

After more soothing and tucking in, Alice followed Harrison back down the stairs to see him out.

"I owe you for being kind enough to bring Thomas home," she began, once they'd walked through the house to stand on the screen porch by the back door.

Harrison turned to look at her then with hard eyes. "You owe a higher power than me some big thanks that boy wasn't seriously injured. What the heck were those two kids doing all the way over at my stables? And where the dickens were you that you didn't even know they'd gone missing until you saw me coming across that bridge?"

"I thought they were in the yard playing with the other children—fixing up the little playhouse. I checked on them earlier." Alice pulled back from him, crossing her arms defensively. "We went scavenging for furniture this morning, and they were having a good time making a playhouse."

He leaned toward her. "And what were you doing while all this was going on?" he pressed.

A lump filled her throat. "I was in my office catching up on work and filling out reports…"

Harrison interrupted her harshly "While you sat working instead of mothering, you almost risked that child's life. Deke and I were bailing hay around the side of the barn, and our blood ran cold when we heard those children scream. We ran around the barn to find that boy crumpled on the ground. Do you know he and Tildy had crawled under the fence into the corral and were walking along right behind our row of trail horses? And I do mean right behind them. Not having a clue about how to act and where to walk and not walk around a horse. The boy leaned over to try to pick up a quarter he saw under Jasper's hooves. He leaned right in under that horse's ass. Jasper did what any normal horse would do and kicked out. We're lucky those hooves didn't hit the boy's head, concuss him or worse."

"I'm truly sorry," she whispered, fighting tears now. "I never imagined they would leave the yard without asking me … or go so far alone."

"Why wouldn't you imagine that?" His voice snapped. "Didn't *you* ever sneak off from your mother? Or do something you weren't supposed to do when no one was watching? You gotta keep an eye on little kids. They don't have good sense yet."

"You're right, of course," she admitted. "They are my responsibility and by letting them get out of my sight, they caused you a difficult time. I can understand why you're upset. It would have been terrible for you if Thomas got injured seriously on your property—and for me."

He looked at her for a moment, scowling, perhaps waiting to see if she would say something more.

Alice lifted her chin, beginning to feel annoyed at his attitude. "Why were you not watching your horses better?" she challenged, anger flaring in her eyes. "What if other people came up to the barn that didn't know much about horses? Someone other than Tildy or Thomas?"

He glared at her. "We have a swing gate at the road coming up to the stable," he said, his tone steely. "If anyone opens it or walks around it, a buzzer sounds. There's another sensor partway up the driveway as a backup. Deke and I knew we'd hear the buzzers if anyone started to come up the drive. As an additional precaution, the horses stay saddled and tied up inside of the corral, not outside it. Most people would hesitate to crawl up under another person's corral fence and walk around inside it behind his horses. Most people, that is. I didn't say all people."

Alice felt a slow blush crawling up her face.

"You've a right to feel embarrassed," Harrison added mercilessly, watching her flushed face. "I thought you said you were a horsewoman? How come you haven't taught these kids anything about horses? About horse safety? There's a dang barn right here in your own back yard, Alice Graham. I guarantee you, if one of those little kids gets into a stall with Bishop or irritates Beaumont, they'll respond much more harshly than ole Jasper did. They're both spirited animals and not as gentle as our trail horses. Furthermore,

Tinker bites easily if provoked. Did you know that? And Cleo bucks if something upsets her. That's why we use them less on the trail. These four horses are staying in your own backyard."

She crossed her arms defensively against herself. "We've lived here less than a week, Harrison. There has been a lot to do and talk about. But, you're right, a talk about being around horses is overdue and apparently needs to be done right away."

"I certainly hope you give that little talk better than the way you watch your kids," he countered harshly. "There are a lot of rules at our stable we go by, and I expect all your kids to know them and to abide by them since they're going to live nearby now.

Alice felt a seethe of anger roll over in her mind. She banked it with effort and smiled at Harrison sweetly instead. "You present a very good point, Harrison," she said.

"I'll tell you what." She paused and took a deep breath. "You come over at the end of your day at about six o'clock. I want *you* to tell the children your rules about the stable and what your expectations are. I'm sure I could never handle it as competently as you. Then you'll be sure the children have it explained to them correctly."

She opened the screened door for him. "I'll have all the children sitting around the table and ready to listen to you. You can tell them everything they need to know about your stable. While you're here, you can take them down to our barn and explain any other facts they need to know about the barn and the horses there. You know all the horses better than I do, and you know more about horses in general than I do, I'm sure. Better you than me to give the little talk that's needed."

Alice maliciously enjoyed seeing how Harrison looked absolutely flabbergasted at this turn of events.

He frowned. "Well, I don't think it will be necessary for me to … uh … come over and … uh … do that." He stumbled over the words. "I mean surely …uh."

She presented him a bright smile. "Oh, but it was an excellent idea. I'm glad you thought of it, and if you make your rules and expectations clear to the children yourself, they will be much more likely to remember them. The guidelines will also be more accurate, as you say."

Alice relished his unease. She prodded him out the back door and waved a goodbye.

"You go on back to work now." She forced a congenial tone. "We've taken enough of your day with this problem already. I need to check on Thomas and Tildy to be sure they're sleeping and then check on the girls outside. After this little episode, I'll not be so quick to assume the children are always where they're supposed to be."

Flashing another brilliant smile at him. Alice turned back into the house, not letting out a deep sign until she saw him heading across the back yard again.

"Arrogant devil." She spit out the words as she sank onto the nearest chair, her hands starting to shake now. "Bossy, opinionated, and always right. I don't know how he stands himself. Going on and on about my responsibilities. Picking and criticizing. Making me feel like a dog when surely he knows I already felt horrible about what happened. And, of course, making it perfectly clear he would never have been in my position. Because, naturally, he is too perfect to ever make an honest mistake."

She got up to pace to the window, watching his retreating back move out of sight, across the creek and onto his own property now.

"That man would certainly be a failure at my job." She scowled. "I can't count how many times a concerned parent has called me, worried over an accident with a child, blaming themselves, questioning their parenting abilities over a mistake. Do I further chastise them? Make them feel even worse than they already do? No. I reassure them. Let them know children will be children. That accidents happen in the best of families. I soothe them and build up their flagging confidence as parents. Try to heal the situation. Then encourage a good family talk when everyone has calmed down."

Alice started up the stairs to check on Tildy and Thomas. She found them sleeping, and then went down to her room to indulge in a few moments alone along with a good cry. Gracious, she'd felt terrified when Harrison came across that bridge with Thomas. He looked so small and motionless at first. When Harrison pronounced him all right, she'd been intensely relieved.

Harrison behaved with kindness at the beginning, consoling her, telling her everything was all right and being very gentle with the children. She remembered how her heart warmed toward him when she heard him talking companionably to Thomas in his room, making him feel comfortable.

Then, he turned on her like a viper when she tried to thank him. His words stung like darts when she already felt so guilty and upset.

Alice wasn't sure where she got the inner strength amidst his tirade to step out of the picture and look at it objectively—to see his anger and upset and remember him the type to attack when upset. Arguing or exchanging barbs would only escalate his anger. Like throwing gasoline on a fire. No. She needed to disarm him.

Agreeing with him versus arguing with him might deflate and defuse him. After all, he had right on his side in several points. Even though he made a muck expressing it and used absolutely no diplomacy.

In truth, the children did need lessons about working with horses and needed riding lessons, too. Perhaps, she'd just let "Mr. Likes To Be In Control" and "Mr. Know It All" do the lessons himself. He'd never expect her to offer that, more used to arguing and blasting his way through any problem. Perhaps she'd show him another military tactic. There were more artful maneuvers than aggressive ones for winning in escalated conflicts.

She blew out a breath and almost smiled as she considered it. "Let him think about that one," she said to herself.

CHAPTER 8

Deke Olds strolled out to meet Harrison as he walked up to the barn a short time later. Younger than Harrison and in his twenties, Deke worked at the Ramsey Stables to supplement his woodworking business. Between trail rides and barn chores, he caned chairs or refinished furniture pieces in a lean-to shed beside the barn. Deke had good hands with wood, as he did with horses, and the man could fix practically anything.

"How's that little kid?" he asked, eager for news.

"He's fine and tucked up in his bed taking a rest now." Harrison sat down on a battered chair in the shade by the barn and pulled a bottle of water out of a rusty cooler. "Any business?"

"The resort down the road is bringing over a van of tourists that want to ride." Deke dug out another bottle from the cooler and settled on another old chair to join him. "Andy said there'd be about eight of them, mostly adults and a few teens. I'll take them around when they show up. It'll do Jasper good to ride after that little incident. It got him sorta spooked and jumpy."

"It got me sorta jumpy, too," mumbled Harrison.

"How'd the woman take it?" Deke took a deep swig of cold water. "Hobart says she's got six kids over there."

He raised an eyebrow at Harrison. "You know Hobart went over there the other day on some pretext of checking out the barn and met her." Deke grinned. "Said the woman was a real looker. He got acquainted, managed to weasel Odell into feeding him lunch, and took a look around. You know Hobart--likes to stay in the know on everything."

"Yeah, he told me he went over there." Harrison picked up a stick Hobart had been whittling to study it. "Alice Graham is the woman's name, Deke, but the kids are all Stuarts. She's fostering them—and trying to work at the same time. While those kids wandered around the countryside, she sat filling out reports in her office." He snapped the stick in half.

"Don't be too hard on her," Deke put in sympathetically. "It ain't far over here, you know. And all kids find their way to a stable if there's one near their house. It's only natural. I used to hike three miles to get here to be around the horses. You remember? My mama used to get madder than spit at me for running over to the stable all the time and leaving my chores undone at home."

Harrison snorted in reply. "She ought to keep a better watch on those kids."

Deke gave Harrison a sideways glance. "You didn't go blessing her out or anything, her being a woman on her own, did you?"

He bristled. "I simply talked to her about needing to watch out for the kids better and advised her to teach them more about being around horses."

Deke gave Harrison a considering look.

"I was diplomatic," Harrison insisted. He picked up an old lead rope to run it through his hands.

Deke shook his head. "Shoot, Harrison. You haven't got a diplomatic bone in your body, especially when you're all riled up."

Harrison's eyes narrowed. "I can be diplomatic when I need to be, Deke. I'm diplomatic with my mother."

"No, you're *resigned* with Mozella. There's a big difference." Deke punched his arm companionably. "You know, it wouldn't hurt you to learn to be sweeter with the ladies. Hobart said that girl acted real nice. I'll bet she got upset enough, when you showed up carrying her boy in your arms, without you reading her the riot act."

Harrison's hands tightened on the lead rope. "I think she handled what I told her without a problem."

"How do you figure that?" Deke raised an unbelieving eyebrow at Harrison.

"She's havin' me come after work to talk to the kids about rules at our stable and how to act around horses. I'm going to tell them, too, about the horses we keep down at Meadowbrook." He took off his hat and laid it on a nearby bench. "Somebody needs to talk to those kids and tell them what's what. Might as well be me, I guess."

"There's a surprise," Deke replied, looking puzzled.

Harrison smiled back smugly.

"Hey," Deke said, recovering quickly. "Why don't you suggest those kids come over to the stable and learn how to ride and work around horses?" He grinned. "We did that with the Nichols girls when they first moved here." He scratched his chin thoughtfully. "I'd like to see those kids become good riders and comfortable around horses if they're going to live close."

He paused to tilt his chair back against the barn wall. "Hobart and I can teach them," he offered. "You can tell 'em to come every weekday about ten o'clock—starting this Monday, if you want. We don't get busy until afternoons on the weekdays. I can start with a trail ride to get them comfortable in the saddle, and then Hobart and I can work with them individually in the corral, and later out in the pasture, until they get easy on a horse. Learn to handle the reins, know the gaits." He gave Harrison a wink. "It'll give me something to do. I like kids."

"Maybe," Harrison replied. But I want them knowing how to care for the horses, too. How to walk them, wipe them down, curry and brush. How to feed and water. Clean out the stable. I'll tell them they get riding lessons for chores. You and Hobart make sure they each have some work to do every day. It's not good for kids to get something for nothing. It's better for them to feel like they earn their way."

"You sound like your daddy," Deke shot back, grinning again. "That's what he made me do. Made me work so I could ride. He made me feel like a real cowboy, too. Lord, I loved that man. He bought me my first cowboy hat."

Harrison smiled at the memory.

Deke's eyes dropped to Harrison's well-worn Stetson on the bench. "Maybe we can get the little Stuart kid a hat. Make him feel like a real cowboy, too. Seems like he could use some men in his life, anyway, with all them women around. You and me know what it's like, having as many sisters as we did."

Harrison frowned. "You had nice sisters." He finished the last of his water and tossed the bottle into the trashcan.

"Nice to you," Deke agreed, grinning. "They all had big-time crushes on you."

"Here comes the resort van now," Harrison interrupted, hearing the gate buzzer sound in the barn behind them. "I'll help you mount everyone up, and we'll hope there's an experienced rider in the group to tail since Hobart went to town this morning. I'll mind the barn until you get back. I need to get some ordering done and check supplies."

Deke got to his feet. "Is Hobart bringing that grandson of his to help on the weekends again this summer?" he asked. "It's nice having that boy as an extra when we're busy."

"Yeah, I'm letting him work weekends all summer, I guess, and any time else we need him for special things. He's only thirteen and glad to get some summer work. Not old enough for much else, yet."

The afternoon passed quickly. Hobart returned from town, and Harrison left the stables to move on to other things. There was always work to do with the Ramsey businesses. Short a staff member today, Harrison mowed the field behind the W. T. Market and then looked at accounts in the market with Bud and Hazel Jenkins, grabbing a sandwich at the deli while there. After finishing at the store, he drove over to check in the youth group arriving to rent the Redwine Cabins for the weekend and then went to Sevierville to pick up a list of supplies.

He barely had time for a quick shower at home before he walked over to Meadowbrook about six that evening. Tired and hungry, he hoped he wouldn't be tied up long with the Stuart children and

Alice. He'd felt less affected by Alice during the little emergency earlier. Probably because his hormones redirected into adrenaline. He frowned at the thought. He didn't want to push his luck by having private time with Alice Graham. He knew he spoke harshly to her that night in the barn. But he wanted to be sure she understood how things stood with them. He squared his shoulders. Just because he felt attracted to her didn't mean he planned on dangling after her with rings and flowers.

Thomas, watching for him at the back door, came flying out to meet him as soon as he crossed the bridge into Meadowbrook property.

He skipped along beside Harrison to the house. "I'm okay now except for my band aid." He pointed to a colorful, Superhero Band-Aid on his knee.

"I'm glad to hear that." Harrison put a hand on the boy's shoulder, following him into the kitchen through the back porch.

He found the children setting plates out at the big family table.

"You're just in time for supper," Alice called from the kitchen. "I hope you haven't eaten. I meant to feed the children earlier, but Donna Nichols stopped by to pick up her girls and stayed to talk so I'm running late." She sent him one of those sunny smiles that appeared slightly contrived. "You can join us to eat and then talk with the children after dinner."

Harrison paused inside the door. "Look, maybe I should come back," he began.

Alice turned from her task in the kitchen to catch his eyes. "I may not be as good a cook as Odell, but I manage. Have you eaten dinner yet?"

He took off his hat, turning it in his hands. "Well, no but ..."

"Good. Then it's all settled." She turned back to her tasks in the kitchen. "Hannah, set Harrison a place at the table, would you? Down at the head, I think."

A pretty blond near pre-teen years looked up from setting the table to smile at him "What's your favorite color, Mr. Ramsey?"

Harrison looked confused at her question.

"Give him black," replied Alice. "He rides a black horse and wears a black hat."

She turned to grin at Harrison. "The Stuarts entertain a color tradition with dishes," she explained. "Everyone has their own particular color for tableware."

Harrison looked down the long family table to see plates in blue, green, yellow, pink, and a variety of other bright colors.

He hung up his hat by the door. "Who started that tradition? You?"

"No, their mother. She collected vintage Fiestaware—those colorful dishes you see." She gestured to a side cabinet overflowing with bright dinnerware. "I assume the idea evolved from the collection."

"What's your color?" he asked, interested in her reply.

"Alice's color is aqua blue," Hannah pointed toward the other end of the table. "It's almost like the teal blue she likes and has in her bedroom."

Harrison joined the children as they all began to take their seats.

"Alice makes great meatloaf so you picked a good night to eat with us," Thomas said, pleased to be sitting beside him.

"We're having potatoes with the cheese in them, too," Tildy added.

"Those are called scalloped potatoes," Hannah corrected, helping Alice to bring in other serving dishes heaped with food now.

"Hannah and Megan made the potatoes," said Tildy proudly. "But Thomas and me helped with the cookies this afternoon."

"It's Thomas and I," corrected Hannah.

One of the children offered a short blessing, and then a noisy, happy dinner began—as one might expect with six children around a table. It made Harrison remember meals he enjoyed long ago in this same room with Aunt Dora, Uncle Carl, and their large family. He helped himself to meatloaf, potatoes, salad, and pinto beans, glad to get a home-cooked dinner after a long day.

As the meal progressed, Harrison realized the children's table manners were very polite and correct. They made an effort to include him in the conversation and to ask him questions, obviously very nicely taught in how to entertain guests.

As they cleaned up the last of the ice cream and cookies for dessert, Hannah sighed deeply and looked his way. "Mr. Ramsey, Megan and I both owe you a true apology."

He lifted a brow in surprise.

Megan continued the thought. "Yes, we were supposed to be watching after the twins in the playhouse, but we got to playing and decorating in the house and let them get out of our sight." She shook her head regretfully.

"We were fixing up the playhouse," Hannah explained. "And we decided to paint the inside with some leftover house paint. We sent the twins away to play so they wouldn't get in the paint."

"They're not good with paint," put in Stacey, a little beauty with drifts of golden hair down her back. "They get it in their hair and on their clothes and everything."

Megan frowned at her. "You did, too, when you were little."

Hannah redirected the conversation. "The twins were Megan's and my responsibility and we handled it poorly. We got busy in the playhouse, and we simply forgot to check on them. We felt terrible when we learned the twins went to your stable and that Thomas got hurt. I want you to know we are truly sorry for what happened, Mr. Ramsey."

Harrison looked at the girls' contrite faces and felt a surge of anger instead of compassion. "It's hardly *two little girls* responsibility to look after their younger siblings." His eyes moved down the table to rest on Alice. "I'm sure that's Alice's responsibility."

"Oh, no, that's not true," disagreed Hannah and Megan almost simultaneously.

Hannah leaned forward intently. "If it wasn't for Alice we wouldn't even be together, Mr. Ramsey. We all help to make our family function well. Everybody has their assigned parts in that."

Harrison lifted his brows at such unusually adult reasoning from a child.

Megan cleared her throat. "The twins are my responsibility." She twisted one of her hair braids as she talked. "Stacey and Rachel are Hannah's responsibility. That's how mother trained us. To watch out for each other."

Thomas waved a cookie in the air for attention. "But me and Tildy were bad," he added. "We knew we were supposed to stay in the yard, and we knew we did wrong to wade across the creek to keep following the trail. The creek is our boundary." He dropped his eyes. "It's against the rules to cross the creek without asking."

Tildy shook her head solemnly. "Sometimes me and Thomas are not always good," she said, looking contrite.

With a nod from Megan, Thomas continued. "Tildy and me jumped the creek on some big rocks and then walked up the trail and saw the stable." His eyes lit up at the memory. "We could see it was a real stable with all the horsies lined up. Just like in the movies."

He paused and frowned, dropping his eyes to his plate. "Then we acted more bad, Harrison. We went inside your fence."

"You should never go in anyone's fence without their permission," parroted Tildy. "We did bad and so a bad thing happened. We're sorry, Mr. Ramsey."

"Yeah," said Thomas. He rubbed his arm where another bright, Superhero Band-Aid covered a scratch. "Alice says I need to say thank you for taking care of me when I got hurted and for bringing me home." He paused and frowned. "You acted real nice after you quit hollering."

Harrison saw Alice bite down on a smile.

He cleared his throat at that point, drawing their attention. "Actually, it's to avoid any more accidents like the one today that Alice asked me to come here tonight." He'd decided to take the floor now.

Looking around at the children, he thought how to begin. "All of you have moved from a city environment to a more country one. There are new ways you need to be more careful about in the country—along with new freedoms. I run a horse stable, have a small grocery store and rental cabins across the highway, as well as an apple orchard." He paused. "Because my stable is right next door to you, it's important that you know our stable rules. Also, because horses stay in the barn behind your house, it's important that you all learn more about horses than you seem to know. Horses are large animals and they can be dangerous."

"They kick big," put in Thomas. "You can get hurted."

"And really scared," added Tildy.

Harrison suppressed a smile. "Let me talk to you first about horses and what they are like." He launched off then into one of his favorite topics.

Surprisingly, he acquired a captive audience as he told them about horses in general and then about his stables and the barn at Meadowbrook. Alice even pulled out a pen and paper and took notes of several things he said while he talked.

After telling them most of the basics he intended to cover, he remembered Deke's idea and cleared his throat to catch their attention again. "Since you're going to live close to horses, I think all of you should have lessons in riding and taking care of horses properly. Starting on Monday, if it's all right with Alice, I want you to come every weekday at ten o'clock to the stables. Deke and Hobart will teach you to ride."

A whoop went up from the group.

"Oh, can we?" Megan put her hands together in a prayer gesture and turned toward Alice. "Rhoda learned to ride at the Ramsey Stable and she rides good, Alice."

Thomas could hardly sit in his seat. "Can I learn, too, Harrison— even if I made your horsey mad?"

"I want all of you to learn to ride and to learn stable and horse safety, but there's one stipulation." Harrison paused. "In return for lessons, you each have to do chores at the stable."

He saw Alice's lips twitch in the ghost of a smile.

Stacey leaned forward suspiciously. "What kind of chores?"

"Whatever needs doing you're asked to help with," he explained. "That could include walking a horse after a ride to cool it down, helping to curry or brush the stable horses as needed. Learning to put on and take off saddles and bridles. Putting out feed and water. Baling hay. Putting straw in stalls. Sweeping out the tack room or shed."

He looked around him at the sea of wide eyes. "With only Deke and Hobart at the stable most days, there's always extra work that needs to be done. I think if Deke and Hobart are willing to give their time to teach you to ride, you should be willing to give your time to help them with their chores."

"Is that all right?" Hannah turned hopeful eyes to Alice. "Could we do it?"

"It's the way I learned," Alice replied matter-of-factly. "My granddaddy Beryl made all of us work at the stable to earn the privilege to ride."

Megan's face lit up. "You mean we can say yes?"

"I have one extra condition," Alice added. "I will be working away from the home office some weekdays and Odell will be here. You will each *have* to be responsible to put on old clothes and get to the stable on time every day. For Hannah and Megan, that means you will have to help the younger ones. There's no other way this can work. You must all cooperate with Deke and Hobart and do whatever they ask you to do, with the horses and with the chores, with no problems or arguing." She paused dramatically. "If any complaints from Harrison or his staff come to my attention, the lessons will stop. Can you accept those terms?"

A chorus of 'yeses' ensued.

Her blue eyes moved to Harrison's, giving him a catch in his middle. "This is kind of you and your staff, Mr. Ramsey. What can we do for you in return?"

"Well." He scratched his head, trying to consider the matter fairly. He knew Alice didn't want to be overly obliged to him.

He nodded as an idea came to him. "Once the children learn how to take care of horses properly, perhaps they could help me with the barn at Meadowbrook. It's a lot of extra work for my staff to come clean this extra barn and exercise the horses I keep here."

His eyes found Hannah's and Megan's. "The older girls might

help with that. Hannah could exercise Cleo and Megan could take care of Beaumont. They could ride with the Nichols girls when they take their horses out. The younger children could look after Tinker and help to exercise the trail horses at the Ramsey Stable when we don't get many clients. That would help out a lot. Horses must be exercised and they need to be ridden or they begin to get wild."

The older girls drew in an excited breath.

"Bishop, I'll have to see to myself," he added. "You children should keep your distance from him. He's spirited and can be unpredictable."

Hannah leaned forward, her eyes shining. "Mr. Ramsey could eat dinner with us occasionally, so he doesn't have to eat alone." She turned her eyes to Alice for approval of her idea. "Or we could take him a dinner over sometimes."

"Hannah and I could come help you clean your house, too," put in Megan, eager to find a way to give back.

Tildy grinned widely, showing the gap in her front teeth where she'd recently lost a tooth. "Me and Thomas can bring you cookies sometime. We make good cookies and you like them. You ate five."

Harrison saw Alice drop her eyes, trying not to giggle at that.

He ran a hand through his hair. "Not all those gestures will be necessary, but they sound like fine neighborly offers. I'll certainly keep them in mind."

Quiet little Rachel, who'd hardly said a word all evening, got up and came around to his chair. "You're nice," she said, smiling sweetly up at him and laying a small soft hand on his arm. "I like you."

Harrison, looking down into her soft grey eyes, felt his heart turn over.

Thomas pushed his way up to Harrison now, too. "We're going to play Bingo after dinner because it's Friday." He jumped up and down with enthusiasm. "Will you stay and play? You can win real prizes. Alice always gets prizes for Friday night Bingo."

"We'll I'm not sure if …" he began.

Tildy interrupted, coming to crowd in beside him. "You can sit by me, Harrison," she said, giving him a winsome smile. "I'll show you what to do if you don't know how to play."

Megan, starting to clear the dessert dishes from the table, shook her head at the little girl. "Pooh, Tildy. I have to help *you* play because you don't remember all your letters and numbers. You can hardly help Harrison."

Tildy gave Harrison a small frown. "Sixty-three is hard," she confided. She brightened and stood up straighter. "But I know the numbers six and three all by myself except *when* they're not mixed up."

Alice busied herself cleaning off the table and didn't echo the children's invitation.

"Can I choose my own Bingo prize?" he said, catching her eye across the table. He'd come with business on his mind, but with that concluded, he found his awareness of Alice beginning to heighten. Funny how that suddenly slipped up on him.

He watched her across the room and saw a slight flush run up her neck when she saw his eyes roam over her. She felt the pull, too, he realized. Wasn't that the dangdest thing?

When he grinned at Alice, she gave him a steely look of warning. "The prizes are already wrapped and in a basket, Mr. Ramsey. However, I'm sure Bingo is too tame for you. You must have other things you'd rather spend your time with tonight."

"No." He drawled the word out slowly just to annoy her. "I can't think of anything I'd rather do than stay and play a game of Bingo with you and the kids. I might even win a prize."

She frowned at him but then shrugged. "Very well. Hannah, let's get the table cleared off to get ready to play."

Harrison watched Alice lazily while she and the children set up the game. He studied her legs in those little white shorts she wore, watched the way she walked and brushed back her hair. He noticed the way her striped top fitted smoothly over her figure, accentuating her small waist. Harrison grinned. What the heck? He saw no harm in watching, he thought—and six kids in the room provided a nice safety net.

Funny how feelings kicked in between he and this woman—like someone impishly turned on two magnets between them. Never knew quite when it might hit, either. Earlier in the evening he hadn't been aware of her in this way, but now the attraction jolted like someone suddenly turned on the power. Might as well enjoy it for a spell, he decided. As Hobart said, Alice was a real looker.

CHAPTER 9

Several weeks slipped by quickly after Harrison came to give his little talk at Meadowbrook. Alice realized a pattern had developed in their days. He came to Meadowbrook often, but they were never alone.

The children quickly grew fond of Harrison. Alice prepped the children for his first visit in a short family meeting. She primed them for his arrival, encouraged them to invite him to eat, hinted he might let them ride at the stable if they behaved politely.

Alice thought she set Harrison up rather cleverly, but the tables reversed on her. Harrison turned out to be a natural leader with the children and an excellent speaker. He made what could have been a tedious, boring lecture on horse care and stable safety turn into an interesting and informative teaching. The man had obviously been in his element. He interlaced his talk with personal experiences, humorous stories, and witty little descriptions about his horses that gave each of them a definitive personality.

Alice grumbled about it to herself as she sat answering email in her office. "Annoying man. I work hard to keep the children on focus during an important discussion and he waltzes in here and does it effortlessly. Simply clears his throat or gives the children a pointed look to bring them into line—even Stacey and the twins, usually the most outspoken and disruptive."

Her eyes slid away from the computer screen. "I hold the social work degree. I thought Harrison, with his background, would be awkward with the children. I expected him to be harsh and critical, like with me."

Alice frowned. "I thought he'd gain a new appreciation for me and all I do to keep up with and manage six children. Instead, he marshaled those kids with ease and grace. Does every time he comes over. I don't get it. He's heavily authoritarian, while I'm democratic, but the children don't seem to mind."

She chewed on a pencil. "When he comes for bingo nights, he plays with obvious enthusiasm, tells jokes, dramatizes the play and enhances the fun." Alice shook her head remembering. "When the man wins a Bingo game he's as exuberant as the children. He played with that dime-store snow globe prize Friday like he'd never received a better gift in his life. I never thought he'd be like this."

Now the children had begun luring him over for more dinners and games. She knew he filled the spot in their lives left vacant by their father, and that fact worried Alice. She wondered if Harrison fully understood the situation or realized how hungrily the children yearned for a father figure in their lives at this time.

Odell acted as bad as the children in encouraging Harrison's visits. She often invited him for lunch and frequently sent food to the stables when the children went for their lessons. She also sent treats to Deke and Hobart.

"It bothers me for all those men to be living on their own," she told Alice one day while they sat on the screened porch, Odell mending and Alice reviewing paperwork. "Harrison lives in that big farmhouse by himself, Deke in that little rental house behind the market, and Hobart bangs around alone in his old home place on Laurel Creek Road."

She paused in thought for a minute. "You may not know it but Hobart lost his wife back when his kids were young. He took to drink for a time, with his grief so bad. Not that I'm saying he behaved right, but it happened. Grammie Rayfield, his sister, helped with his children during that time, and, eventually, he got straightened out. Last year, his daughter Lucy, and her husband and boys, built a house down the street from Hobart. I know that helps, having them near. But Hobart rattles around in that big house by himself all too often and hasn't ever gotten married again."

She said the latter statement somewhat wistfully, Alice noted.

"Now Deke Olds, he's found himself a girlfriend now, named Julie Brady." Odell rethreaded her needle. "She works in a shop in Gatlinburg. A real nice girl. I'm feeling right hopeful for Deke."

"So you think everyone should be married?" Alice asked, teasingly.

"Pairing is nature's way," answered Odell, matter-of-factly. "There's some animal species that live alone, and perhaps a few folks would be better off living alone—but not many. I'm a big believer that we need other folk in our lives to rise to our best. I believe there's something about a good pairing between a man and woman that brings out their best." She looked up from her mending. "You've been married before. Didn't you find that to be true?"

Alice smiled in memory. "Perhaps. I lived very happily with David."

Odell laid her mending down. "What was he like, your David, if you don't mind me asking?"

"David and I met in college, at the University of Tennessee in Knoxville, in our second year of school." Alice tilted her head, remembering. "We always found ourselves going to the same plays and shows in those days. One night, two of our friends introduced us at intermission. After that, whenever we attended a symphony or a show and were both alone, we began to sit together or go for coffee afterwards. Soon, we started to date."

She smiled at Odell. "The next summer we married. I moved into David's apartment and we finished college together. A happy time for us. David studied logistics and transportation—loved system design and transportation problems. He liked detail work and the challenge of fixing things."

Alice laughed softly in memory. "He played the violin a little. That love for music drew him to the symphony and the shows where we met." She set her papers aside on the table beside her chair. "During those years, David participated in the Army ROTC program at UT to pay his way through college, so, of course, when we graduated, David had to give the military his requisite years. I moved with him to South Carolina where he was first stationed, and I worked on my masters' degree in Social Work at the university while David served his duty. The Army sent David to Saudi in the early 1990s when problems escalated there. I stayed behind, of course, finishing school and waiting for David to come back home."

She felt a catch in her voice. "Only David never came back home. He got killed in Saudi."

"You poor thing," commiserated Odell, reaching over to lay a hand over Alice's knee. "That must have been an awful time for you. Just awful."

"I remember it felt unreal for a long time." She sighed deeply. "I kept thinking it a mistake. That someone would come to the door and tell me it hadn't actually happened." She bit her lip. "That's how the Stuart children felt at first, too. I understood their emotions. They went through all the same grieving stages I did, the early denial stage and sense of unreality, followed by anger, depression, and eventually to the acceptance they needed to go on."

Odell picked up her mending again. "Hannah told me you were real good to them through that hard time. Said you knew all the right things to do. She also told me their Grampa Lloyd didn't do so good. Said he snapped at them, wasn't very understanding."

Alice shook her head. "He was grieving the loss of his only child, battling his own sorrows. A parent always thinks they will outlive their children. Lloyd lost his wife when Lauren was only a little girl and they grew unusually close afterwards. He waged his own inner wars during that time."

"I don't think the children hold a grudge against him for that time—even if there were problems." She studied a line of stitching.

"No, they remember mostly that he came. Held their hands. Cried with them. Grieved as much as each of them did. They developed a deep bond going through that time together. I hope Lloyd's health will enable him to come to Meadowbrook this summer or fall for a visit. He wants to come, and the children would love to see him again."

Odell laid aside the shirt she'd been mending and picked up a pair of shorts sporting a small tear on one side. "We'll make him feel right to home if he does come," she promised.

Alice found herself getting into more and more intimate conversations like these with Odell. She'd become a lot like a second mother to Alice, and Odell loved the children and dealt with them with warmth and patience.

Talking about David with Odell had, surprisingly, made Alice compare him to Harrison. She hated herself for that, felt disloyal to David for her thoughts to drift to Harrison after talking of how she and David met and married. It shamed her for Harrison's face to slip into her dreams instead of David's, to wake up thinking of Harrison instead of wishing David alive and lying in bed beside her.

While wrestling these thoughts, Alice heard Megan crying as she checked the children before bed one night. She slipped into Megan's room and sat down on her bed to comfort her. It was unusual for Megan, a stalwart, independent type of child, to cry over anything.

"What's the matter, Megan?" Alice asked her softly, brushing her hair back from her face.

"I can hardly see their faces anymore," Megan whispered. "And I don't want to forget Mommy and Daddy." She buried her face in the pillow for more tears.

Alice chose her words carefully. "I don't always see David's face as much as I used to in my mind and in my dreams anymore either." She rubbed Megan's back gently as she talked. "I know that doesn't mean I don't love David with all my heart. My Grandmother Beryl called it God's way of helping me move on. David is with God now, but I still need to live out my life here. If I always saw David's face in my mind and thought of him too often, I would be sad too much of the time. Grandmother Beryl said David would always be near in my heart, but that time would gradually diminish his presence in my mind. It's the way it's meant to be."

Megan turned her face up to look at Alice. "Then you don't think it's bad?" she asked. "I wouldn't want Mommy and Daddy to look down and think I was forgetting them and to feel sad and disappointed in me."

"They would never think that," Alice assured her, leaning over to give her a kiss on the cheek. "I think they want very much for you to heal, to go on and be happy. I believe it's like Grandmother Beryl said. I think it's God's way and plan for helping us when we've lost someone we love—that we need to forget a little."

Megan had felt comforted, and Alice comforted herself with the same thoughts afterwards. Five years had passed since David died. It wouldn't be healthy for her to continue to entertain overly intimate memories of David anymore. Those thoughts and feelings needed to slip away. But it felt wrong seeing Harrison show up in her intimate imaginings and dreams. She didn't want him there. Granted, she liked him better now because of how good he was with the children. But she stayed secretly annoyed and provoked with him for how he made her feel.

She got up from her office desk and went to look out the front window. "I know Harrison toys with me," she said to herself, hoping talking it out would clarify her thoughts. "I think he actually gets a kick out of the emotions that flare between us. When that magnetic attraction whips us and surfaces like a sudden unexpected gust of wind, he revels in it. He passes me that slightly quirky smile of his as if to say: There it is again. He thinks it's humorous and he thinks my discomfort is amusing. I hate that."

Alice crossed her arms in annoyance. "It started that night when he stayed for Bingo and watched me all through the game, and it's been going on ever since." She sat down at her desk again. "I keep assuming with time that the pull between us will diminish. After all, we haven't been acting on it and we're spending more time together and getting to know each other better. Any romantic attraction should, by all right, have dwindled out by now."

She picked up a pen and played with it idly. "The worst of it is that it's becoming intermittent. It might not show up for a day or two, and then it hits again."

Those shattering little explosions of attraction always dazzled her when they hit. Made her weak in the knees. Played with her senses. Highlighted Harrison in a way that seemed unnatural. Where she might have been casually talking to him across the table before, suddenly she'd become aware of his mouth, his muscled arms below his shirtsleeves, his strong hands. She'd find herself locking eyes with him, aware that he'd suddenly started watching her in the same way, too. It felt simply humiliating.

Giving up on getting any more work done, Alice decided to go down to the barn to take Elsa out for a ride. With Odell cleaning house and the children busy at the riding stable, it was a good time. Alice's uncle brought Elsa over to Meadowbrook a few days ago, and Alice had tried to take time to ride her whenever she could. To help acclimate her to her new surroundings.

As Alice drew near the door of the barn, she could hear Harrison talking to the horses. Or more precisely, talking to Elsa.

"There now, pretty girl," he said, petting her behind the ears. "You know I couldn't leave without noticing you." Elsa gave him an affectionate little push with her nose in response.

"I see you've met my Elsa," Alice stated, coming into the barn.

"Elsa sees to it that you notice her," Harrison replied with one of his half smiles that made the dimple in his chin noticeable. "You pegged it right about her being an affectionate animal—and beautiful, too." He ran his hand down Elsa's neck with appreciation.

Despite her awkward feelings about Harrison, it pleased Alice that he liked Elsa. Looking forward to her ride now, she went into the tack room to find a saddle and bridle.

"Going riding?" Harrison asked.

"Yes." Alice draped the saddle over her arm. "I've taken Elsa on short rides, but today I thought I'd venture further out. It's a gorgeous day, and my work schedule is light. The outdoors called and I couldn't resist."

"I know how that is," replied Harrison affably. "How about you and Elsa riding along with Bishop and me today? I know you've ridden several of the stable trails with the girls a few times, but I thought you might like to explore the trail following west down Chestnut Branch. There's a section on it where Elsa and Bishop can enjoy a good run before the trail winds into the national park along the Little Pigeon River. It's pretty there and good to first explore new areas with someone who knows the way."

Alice hesitated. It would seem womanish and emotional to refuse. He'd only made a friendly offer to ride with her, after all.

"That would be nice," she said at last.

They saddled up and soon crossed Chestnut Branch at the back of the property to follow west on a broad path weaving into the woods. The shallow stream splashed merrily beside them on the right and the sunshine filtered in happy rays between the branches of the trees overhead. Harrison rode quietly, and Alice felt content to be quiet, too, enjoying the peace and the simple sights and sounds of nature. After approximately a mile, the trail curled out of the woods and broadened into a smooth stretch that had once been an old farm road.

Harrison kicked Bishop into a gallop, and Alice followed, giving Elsa her head. They enjoyed a good half-mile run before the road came to a junction. At that point, Harrison turned left onto a narrower trail.

"If you continued to the right on the broader path, you'd meet the highway a half mile east of the Pittman Center Road." He leaned around in the saddle to point behind them. "A path along the highway leads past Parton Place, where Donna Nichols works, and then back to the front of your property. This trail takes you into the national park."

They rode single file now, the trail narrower but well worn and easy to follow. Alice soon saw the markers for the national park boundary.

Harrison turned in the saddle. "If you stay on maintained trails in the park like this, whether you're riding or walking, you're more likely to stay safe and not get lost," he said. "Also, if you ride in the park, it's a good idea to carry a hiking map showing the trails designated for horseback riding. A map will help you with direction if you ever get lost, too."

He ducked under a low branch. "The best thing to do until you learn the area is to ride on main trails and roadways you know and can follow clearly. That's what I told the children. I hope you don't mind, but I gave each of them restrictions about where they can ride and how far. There is nothing more frightening and dangerous for a child than getting lost in the mountains. And it's totally unnecessary."

Alice started to thank him again for all he, Hobart, and Deke had done to help the children learn to ride and be comfortable around their new home. However, she changed her mind before voicing the words and decided to simply enjoy the quiet and the ride. Her life churned at such a hectic pace these days that a precious hour or two of peace and quiet felt beautifully welcome.

She rode contentedly up the mountain trail behind Harrison. Elsa had no difficulty as a follower, enjoying her new exploration, and on the trail, Alice found it easy to be with Harrison. All she saw was his broad back, shifting occasionally as Bishop stepped over a tree root or a rock. There were no looks and undercurrents to worry about. Only the quiet to enjoy.

The trail soon angled right to follow along a wide stream. It looked huge compared to the little streams around Meadowbrook, more like a river in size.

"This is the Little Pigeon River." Harrison slowed their pace. "I'd advise never letting the children come to the river alone. It's swift and deep in many places and has strong currents and rushing cascades. But it's beautiful, too. You can always see more of the Little Pigeon by driving up the Greenbrier Road into the park alongside it."

He pointed ahead to where the trail rose rapidly. "These are the lower ridges of the Copeland Divide we're riding near now. You can see the mountain ascending ahead. If we kept riding all day, and took the right trail connections, we'd climb all the way to the

Appalachian Trail. If you watch as we ride today, you'll be able to see glimpses of the Smoky Mountain ranges now and again through the trees."

They rode about a mile further, and then Harrison turned down a side trail leading directly to the stream bank.

"This is a favorite spot of mine," he explained. "Let's stop for a minute and give the horses a breather before we start back. Can you hear the cascade? There's a falls nearby where a side stream runs into the Little Pigeon River."

He swung easily off Bishop and tied him to a tree by the stream, where the horse could bend his head to drink in a side eddy. Alice followed suit, and guided Elsa into the same area. When she climbed down from her horse, she found Harrison had already started rock hopping out into the stream.

"Come on out." He waved to her. "There are some great rocks to rest on, and this spot has a great view of the falls. You can't see anything from there."

After tying up Elsa, Alice worked her way out over the rocks, watching her step as she jumped from one rock to another over swirling cascades and pools. Harrison hadn't helped her off her horse or offered her a hand across the rocks, but Alice found herself glad for that. Contact and touching often proved an issue for them, and she didn't want to see the day spoiled.

Alice saw Harrison ahead, sitting on a boulder and leaning back comfortably against a rock. He looked happy, relaxed and was actually smiling—his smile one of comfortable joy. Alice couldn't remember ever seeing that before.

When she reached the boulder he sat on, he patted a spot beside him, encouraging her to sit down. "See?" he said, pointing ahead of him as she did. "There's the falls. Carter and I used to call this Hideaway Falls, because you can't see it unless you rock hop out here into the stream. The falls is formed from a side stream spilling over that rocky ledge."

He pointed upward to where layers of white cascaded from the ledge in a long, sweeping show of rushing water.

She leaned forward in delight. "How did you ever find it?"

He grinned. "Actually, you can hear it as you come up the trail. Big waterfalls and cascades make a lot of noise. Carter and I started looking for what made all the noise one day, and we found the falls."

They sat quietly enjoying the tumbling display of water, the cool serenity of the stream, the sounds of birds and insects in the air.

Harrison pulled a water bottle out of his pocket and tossed it her way. "Help yourself. I didn't think to bring two, but you're welcome to share."

"Thanks," she said, glad to have a drink after the long ride.

He searched in another pocket. "I tucked some crackers in my saddlebag, too. Nothing fancy. Just a couple of packages of peanut butter ones from the market." He tossed one to her.

Alice tore into the crackers gladly. They ate without talking, soaking up the sun and the beauty of the day. Alice thought it one of the nicest times she'd ever had with Harrison Ramsey. She almost hated to mount and start up the trail again.

CHAPTER 10

Harrison didn't know what prompted him to ask Alice Graham to ride with him today—perhaps her comment about wanting to explore. She could get lost poking around the area by herself, and he had some concerns about how that pretty little walking horse of hers would handle the mountain trails. Whatever. Maybe he simply wanted to see how he handled her company, now that some time had passed.

He quickly saw his initial worries unfounded. Alice rode with ease, had a good seat, and Elsa took to the trails—and to the day—with enthusiasm. Obedient to Alice's hands on the reins, the little mare sprinted into a strong, eager run on the farm road. Elsa displayed quite a personality.

As Alice said earlier, the summer day called to a person to be out of doors. Harrison expected to be bombarded by chatter and questions from Alice, but found her content to simply ride and quietly enjoy the day. That was a wonder with a woman. Now and again, at a turning in the trail, he caught a glimpse of her and saw several happy smiles slip over her face with the pleasure of new discoveries. Her riding behind him didn't mean he wasn't conscious of her being there, but he handled her company better than usual today.

Alice wore well-worn boots and blue jeans to ride in, instead of the usual summer shorts and tennis shoes she favored for casual wear. You'd think the longer pants would keep Harrison's mind and eyes off her legs, but they didn't. She'd tucked a cardinal red

T-shirt into her jeans and pinned her hair up to keep it off her neck and out of her way. Now and then he heard her humming a snatch of some cheerful tune behind him. Or talking companionably to Elsa. Several times she slowed to look at something along the trail, like a clump of wildflowers or squawroot, but afterwards, she'd kick Elsa into a trot and catch up with him.

Within a mile—despite his awareness of her—Harrison started to relax. He found Alice easy to be with. Surprisingly so for a woman. He usually found most females annoying. Because of that, Harrison took Alice on a longer ride than he intended to— even took her to the hidden falls he and Carter discovered as boys. Surprisingly, she didn't complain about the length of the ride or ask constant questions about where they were going. When they got to the falls, she rock-hopped right out into the stream without a whine. Then she sat back and enjoyed the falls, without spoiling the moment with womanly gossip or silliness. He liked her for that. In his more honest moments, Harrison admitted he'd come to like and respect Alice Graham a lot.

They'd never shared many deep conversations, but he learned all the facts about her past life from Odell, the children, and Hobart. Harrison never could figure out how Hobart found out all the things he did about people. And Odell told Harrison anything else he wanted to know over morning coffee or lunch on the days Alice worked out of the house. Odell didn't miss much. Harrison assumed she told Alice about his life, and the rest Donna Nichols probably filled in. He figured she knew him better now, too.

Harrison took a different trail back to the barn after leaving the stream, one that rose up through a gap in the mountains above the river and then skirted across Redwine Ridge. A half-mile out on the ridge, he pulled Bishop up to a spot where a picturesque view opened out over the valley.

"You can look out over Pittman Center at this point," he told Alice, as she reined Elsa in to join him. "You can see some of the main roads and the streets in the valley. There's the steeple of the Baptist church on Beech Grove Road over there to the left."

Alice put a hand up to shield the sun. "Odell's wanting us to visit there. I told her we might go Sunday." She leaned forward in the saddle to look more closely. "Odell attends there, you know."

"Her and about half the valley." Harrison snorted in irritation.

She looked at him curiously. "Isn't your step-father the preacher at Beech Grove? And doesn't your mother play the piano for services?"

"Yeah."

"Do you go there to church?" she probed.

"Sometimes," he answered evasively. She didn't push him for more. They sat and enjoyed the view instead, and then Harrison reined Bishop back onto the trail again. She followed, and he soon heard her humming once more, an old hymn he recognized: *This Is My Father's World.* It surprisingly stirred him.

A mile further on, Bishop veered automatically down a side trail to another overlook Harrison always stopped to enjoy. Alice followed him to the rocky ledge where they could see down into the valley again.

"There's your house to the left." Harrison pointed. "There's my place and the stable on beyond it. This is the best view across the valley to my way of thinking. You can see across the highway and past the market. Those neat rows of trees are my apple orchard."

Alice had walked Elsa up to stand closely beside Bishop and Harrison. He turned to look across at her, and sensed an odd tension gathering.

"Isn't that the bridge beside my house?" she asked, her eyes focused intently toward the arched bridge over little Timothy Creek.

Harrison knew then why she'd tensed. He'd brought her to the ridge top where he first saw her on the bridge that snowy day.

He turned to look at her more closely, trying to think what to say, and then felt that overwhelmingly powerful draw start to surge. Harrison knew she felt it, too, because he saw her hands clench on the reins she held, saw her shiver involuntarily even in the summer heat. Harrison took a deep breath, suddenly washed in a sweep of memories. She wore a red shirt today, the sun shining on her golden hair—much like before.

She avoided his gaze, but finally she turned her eyes to his, and Harrison was glad he sat securely on Bishop. He felt weak, and found himself suddenly drowning in her eyes and becoming keenly aware of her. A light waft of lilac scent, mixed with womanly sweat, floated his way. He heard her breathing catch and deepen and watched her lick her lips nervously. Alice hadn't pulled her eyes away from his, and he smiled slowly at her then.

"Don't do that!" Her voice snapped into the silence.

"Don't smile?" he drawled.

She crossed her arms, spots of bright color coming into her cheeks. "Don't be amused at this ... don't be amused at me," she said in a pinched voice. "You've been doing that for weeks. Smiling and looking smug and amused whenever this happens. I hate it!"

Harrison raised his eyebrows in surprise. "What would you rather me do?" He scowled at her then. "Kiss you and put my hands on you in front of Odell and all those children? Just yield to this pull and follow it however it draws me?"

"Of course not." Her mouth formed a sulky line. "But you don't have to look like it's funny. And make me feel foolish and silly. Like it's only me that's feeling awkward. Or like it's some little joke you're enjoying."

Harrison's voice quieted. "It's not only you, Alice, and it's not some little joke. But it is an odd thing between us, and you have to admit there is an element of humor in the situation."

Her eyes flashed. "I don't see the humor in the situation at all," she spit back. "It's upsetting. I'd hoped all of this would stop with time. Especially after what you said in the barn that time. How you made me feel." She hugged her arms tighter against her. "Suggesting I tried to stalk you—plotted to get you involved with me. Like the whole thing was something I did or caused. It's not, you know. I'd stop it if I could."

He knew he lashed out harshly to her that night he kissed her in the barn, but he hadn't realized she might continue hurting over it. He cared enough about Alice now that he didn't want her to be hurting over something careless he said.

"I was hard on you then," he said softly, reaching across to touch her cheek. "My response to you affected me strongly but I didn't want to acknowledge it. Didn't want to look at it rationally. So I lashed out at you. I'm sorry if it hurt you. It's hard to know what to do with these emotions between us, Alice."

"You can say that again." She lifted her eyes to his, anger flashing in them. "Did you bring me here on purpose today, Harrison? To start something. To laugh at me?"

"No." He reined in his emotions to answer her quietly. "I always come here, out to the ridge top when I ride this way. Bishop turns off the side trail automatically. You saw that. I didn't think, Alice. I really didn't."

"You should have." She gripped the saddle horn in annoyance. "We were having a nice day, and now ..." Her voice trailed off.

"Now we're attracted again and it's changed the mood," he finished for her. A slow smile spread across his face, despite his better intentions.

"Why are you smiling like that?" she said nervously. "What are you thinking?"

He maneuvered Bishop closer to Elsa. "I'm thinking how nice it is there's no Odell and no six children watching us right now." He leaned from his saddle to brush his lips over hers.

"Oh, we shouldn't do this," she whispered against his mouth. "It will only make it worse. I'm sure it will."

"I'll risk it," he answered huskily, leaning over to kiss her more deeply. He put a hand on Elsa's saddle, to hold the little horse close to Bishop, while his other hand swept behind Alice's back to pull her closer to him.

He heard her sigh and felt her yield to him. "You always smell like leather and spice," she whispered.

Harrison chuckled softly. "That doesn't sound very appealing," he murmured against her neck.

"Oh, but it is," she said, burying her face up against his shirt.

"You just don't know."

He kissed her forehead and nuzzled his lips into her hair. "You always smell like lilacs." He drew in the heady scent. "Like summer lilacs on the night air."

"I wear the lilac perfume oil my grandmother Beryl always used." She looked up at him with those deep blue eyes. "I've always loved it."

He kissed her again, long enough this time that they both grew breathy.

"I guess we shouldn't have been alone again. Like you said." She traced her fingers down his cheek.

Harrison shook his head to disagree. "I was wrong," he said. "This is too nice not to enjoy now and again." He grinned. "And we're not going to get in trouble on horseback high on a ridge rock."

"Maybe you're right," she agreed on a sigh, after he kissed her once again. "We're both adults. Like you said, we both know this isn't going anywhere beyond a moment like this now and again. We both have busy lives, and we both know what we want and what we have time for in our lives."

It sounded absolutely sensible what she said. Harrison knew it exactly what he might have said himself. Yet, it rankled him somehow for her to say it to him. It made everything so final.

The horses got restless then from being pulled so close to each other on the ridge. Bishop stamped and blew with impatience, and Elsa shied. Their actions finished breaking the moment, and Harrison and Alice turned to start back down the trail.

Alice chatted more going home. Probably nervous and trying to cover it with talk, Harrison thought. He felt almost relieved when they returned to the bottom of the ridge and splashed through Chestnut Branch behind the Meadowbrook barn.

They found Stacey and Rachel there, sitting on the fence.

"We were waiting for you," said Stacey. "Odell said you went riding but should be back soon."

Rachel sighed. "Hannah's crying and upset about something."

Stacey nodded to affirm the words. "She's in her room crying and she's locked the door and won't come out." She climbed off the fence to hold Alice's horse while she dismounted. "Megan and Odell tried and tried to talk to her, but she won't let them in. Odell says she's going to make herself sick if she keeps it up."

"What happened?" Alice asked anxiously.

"No one knows." Stacey rolled her eyes dramatically. "She came in crying and ran straight to her room and locked the door."

"She won't let us be nice to her," Rachel added, sniffling and on the edge of tears now. "I don't like it when Hannah cries."

Harrison dismounted and took Elsa's reins from Stacey. "Alice, you better go up with the girls and see what's going on. I'll see to the horses and then I'll come up, too. In case she's hurt or something."

Alice nodded and started toward the house, holding Rachel's hand.

Fifteen minutes later, Harrison walked up to the house and let himself in the back door. Odell sat in the kitchen, stringing beans.

"Got the problem solved with Hannah yet?" he asked.

She shook her head. "No, the child won't let anybody in her room. She's got her door locked, and you can still hear her crying. Alice is up there trying to urge her to open up the door, but she's having no more luck than we did. I don't know what's upset that girl."

"Where had she been before this happened?" Harrison quizzed.

"Over to the stable to ride, and then across the street to the market for a treat before the children walked back. Alice lets them walk to the store to get a drink and a treat at W.T.'s after they finish their riding lesson and stable chores. It's what they do every day. Nothing different." Odell stopped to think. "I don't know what the matter is, Harrison. But I don't think I've ever seen Hannah this upset."

Knowing Hannah had been to the stable, Harrison decided to check to be sure what upset Hannah hadn't happened at the stable. He found Alice and Megan sitting on the floor outside Hannah's door, trying to talk to her.

"Hannah, please let us in," Megan pleaded. "Maybe we can help."

Megan was in tears herself now, and Alice looked close to it. The muffled sobs of Hannah filtered out from her bedroom. The girl sounded distraught.

Thomas came down the hall and put his hand into Harrison's. "What's wrong with Hannah?" he asked, with young fear in his eyes. "Do you think she got kicked by a horsey like me? We could give her an aspirit if she'd let us in."

His young anxiety brought back a spate of memories to Harrison of his days as the youngest with four sisters older than he. They were always upset and weeping over something, and he'd always been too young to know what to do. Well, no longer, he thought to himself. He wasn't having Thomas put through what he experienced so many times.

Harrison strode over to Hannah's door.

"Hannah Stuart," he ordered in a steely voice. "You come and open this door to me right this minute and let me in."

"I don't want anyone to come in," she wailed.

"Too bad. I'm coming in. Either you open the door to me or I will kick it down, and you can be sure I will do it. You have two minutes to get this door open. It's a nice door, and I hate to splinter it up, but I'll take it down if I have to."

Alice looked startled and started to protest, but then she heard Hannah's footsteps coming across the room.

She peeked out a small crack in the door, her face tear-stained. "I don't want everyone coming in, Harrison."

"Well, I'm coming in, because you've been at my stable before all this crying started," he said. "After you talk to me for a minute, I'll expect you to talk to Alice. That's respectful. Beyond that point, who you want to talk to and when is rightly up to you. But when an adult in charge of you asks you to open your door again in the future, you will do what they ask. Do you understand that, Hannah?"

Hannah sniffed and nodded. She let Harrison in, immediately locked the door again, and then ran across the room to throw herself across the bed to cry once more.

Harrison found himself feeling completely provoked. The girl clearly did not plan to sit down and tell him sensibly what was going on.

"Did you get hurt at the stable?" he asked. She shook her head.

"Did one of the other children say something and hurt your feelings?" She shook her head again.

Harrison searched back in his memory for some of the many reasons his sisters got into weeping sessions. And an old memory hit him. She'd turned twelve, after all.

"Did you start your period and don't want to tell anyone?"

Hannah sat up with a shocked face to stare at him, squeaked out a no and then returned her head to the pillow for more tears.

"It can't be boys yet," he mumbled to himself. "You're too young."

At his words, she suddenly wept more.

Catching the intensity of her weeping, he walked over to sit down on the edge of her bed. "So, it's a boy problem," he said. "Let's hear it, Hannah. I'm tired of hanging around and listening to you cry. Did some boy say something to you he shouldn't have? Did some boy visiting at the stable try something?"

"Not at the stable," she sobbed. "At the store."

Harrison's blood ran cold. A lot of local men and tourists came into the store. "Who was it?" he quizzed carefully. "Was it anyone I know, Hannah?"

She buried her head in the pillow. "Vance Palmer," she wailed.

Relief washed over him. Vance was a kid. "You mean Bud and Hazel Jenkins' grandson? That skinny, spiky-haired twelve-year-old kid?" He laid a hand on the girl's shoulder. "What did he do, Hannah?"

"He said he *liked* me," she cried, her head buried in her pillow. "Every time I go to the store, he *follows* me around and tells me he *likes* me. And he tries to give me things." She sniffed loudly. "He promised to tell *everyone* when we start school that we're sweethearts. DeeDee said he would, too. That he'd tell everybody whether I liked him back or not."

She rubbed a hand across her face, scrubbing at the tears. "Then today, when the other kids had gone outside, and I was at the coke machine in the back of the store, he *kissed* me. Right on my mouth, without my permission!" This brought on another sob. "He said he was going to tell *everyone* we kissed, too."

Harrison watched her young shoulders heave as she cried.

"Can you make him not tell everyone?" she asked Harrison from out of the pillow. "I'll just *die* if he does! I know I will."

Harrison shrugged and rolled his eyes. He felt like telling Hannah that all of this was no big deal, a silly kids' matter, that she simply needed to get over it. But watching four emotional, irrational older sisters grow up ahead of him taught him better.

Instead he said, "I'll think on it, Hannah. I might come up with a good idea for you. In the meantime, you need to know that no matter what Vance says, you have a say in this, too. All you need to do is stand up for yourself and stoutly deny anything that boy says at your school or anywhere else."

She turned to look up at him. "But no one *knows* me at that new school. What if they don't believe me?"

"DeeDee knows you. She'll support you." He patted her shoulder again in comfort. "Megan will, too. She's been outside the door sniffling and worrying about you all this time. You know you can count on her."

"Meggie's been crying?" Hannah asked, incredulously. "She *never* cries."

"You've gotten her close to it with worry. Alice, too, along with the other children. Seems to me you have a lot of voices to help defend you if Vance decides to spread some untruths about you."

Harrison heard the crying tapering off. "You know, Hannah, life is often going to have times when people cause you problems— lie about you, betray you, or hurt you. In those times you need to remember who you are. Keep your head. Respect yourself. Be strong and not fall apart. Neither anger or tears help much when it comes right down to it."

"What does?" she asked, looking up at him with serious eyes.

Caught off guard with the question, Harrison searched his memory for an answer, and heard his Aunt Dora's voice drift through his mind.

"My Aunt Dora always said the best answer to any problem was prayer. Because God is always eager to listen and always ready to comfort and help."

"That's nice." Hannah sighed. "Aunt Dora lived here before us, didn't she?"

"She did and she was a big believer in prayer. She had a prayer stump out back behind that big willow tree hanging over the creek."

Hannah looked thoughtful. "I know where that stump is."

"You remember to go try it next time you have a life problem. I can remember many a time seeing Aunt Dora there. She claimed her problem always got worked out to the good shortly after.'

Harrison saw a tentative smile on Hannah's face. "Rachel's right," she said softly. "You are nice."

"Well," Harrison grumbled. "Don't let that get around too much. It'll hurt my tough cowboy image."

Hannah giggled. "I won't tell," she promised.

"You ready to talk to those other upset women outside your door?" he asked, standing up to look down at her now.

She nodded and, surprisingly, got up to walk over to open the door herself.

Harrison took a smug satisfaction seeing the incredulous look on Alice's face.

"What did you say to her?" Alice whispered to him as he passed by her.

"Nothing special," he said, shrugging. "Remember, I had four older sisters."

However, Harrison liked the good feeling he had as he walked over to the stable to get back to work. He found Hobart and his beagle there in their usual spot.

"Where's Deke?" he asked, seeing the horses lined along the corral.

"Working on a new chest of drawers he's making over in the shed." Hobart pointed in that direction. "Is everything okay at Meadowbrook? I walked over to the store to get a sandwich and Bud said one of the Stuart girls ran off from his place crying over something."

Harrison frowned. "She's okay now. It wasn't much she got upset over."

He leaned against the fence and thought about the matter for a few minutes, while giving the horses closest to him, Hollywood and Blondie, some pats along their necks. Then an idea occurred to him and he smiled to himself.

"You think your grandson Josh might like to put in some extra work time this week?" he asked Hobart.

"Doing what?" Hobart gave him a questioning look.

Harrison shrugged. "Checking out the trails, riding them to look for sticks and such that might be in the path. Stuff like that."

"When do you expect he ought to do that?" Hobart asked, watching Harrison carefully now.

"I thought late in the mornings before it gets too busy at the stable." Harrison put a foot up on the fence rail casually. "I might send one of the Stuart girls along to help him. Maybe that oldest one. They could work on clearing the trails together. I'd like most all the trails checked. Not only just the main ones we use the most." He paused to think. "I expect it would take them a couple of weeks to get around to them all. Josh does know all our trails. I wouldn't want Hannah doing those trails alone, her not knowing the area or anything."

Hobart sent him a suspicious look. "What are you up to, boy?"

"You did say Josh would like to do extra work if I ever needed him, didn't you?" Harrison asked innocently.

"Yeah, I did." He kept his eye on Harrison. "But this seems a mite over planned for you."

Harrison could see Hobart considering the matter while he busied himself checking the horses' hooves for stones.

"How old is this oldest Stuart girl?" Hobart asked at last. "I can't quite seem to remember."

Harrison picked a stone out of Blondie's back hoof with his pocketknife. "Twelvish, I think," he replied.

"Hmmmm," said Hobart. "And Josh is about thirteen. Seems to me I remember you and Ava Reagan started doing a lot of riding and trail-checking about that same age." He grinned. "You came back looking right satisfied with yourself now and again. You thinking on doing a little matchmaking between my grandson Josh Sheldon and Hannah Stuart?"

"Hadn't thought of it," Harrison answered, digging a few more stones out of Blondie's hoof with his knife. "But it's not as if Hannah Stuart's not a pretty little thing. If Josh notices, it wouldn't do any harm, I guess. They're at about that age where boys and girls do start noticing each other."

Hobart grinned at Harrison. "Well, if I'm to cooperate in whatever this thing is you're cooking up, you need to fill me in more. I might be able to lend a helping hand if you put me in the know."

Harrison closed his knife and tucked it in his back pocket. "When I started showing interest in Ava Reagan as a kid—do you remember how it kind of ran off Morgan Spade's interest in her. You recall that?"

"I do now you mention it," replied Hobart. "And?"

"I thought it possible that someone showing an interest in Hannah might run off an un-mutual interest Vance Palmer is showing in her." He gave Hobart a candid look. "An interest that seems to be overly upsetting Hannah Stuart."

"Ahhh." Hobart nodded his head up and down knowingly. "I reckon that was behind Hannah crying after she visited the market," he said. "Something that skinny little Vance Palmer did." He scratched his head. "You know, I never liked that kid much. He's got a mean streak in him that likes to stir up trouble."

"So you'll help?" Harrison asked him.

"I reckon I might." Hobart crossed a booted foot over his knee. "You know, we could get ourselves in some big trouble if things went too far with this or if we got found out for meddling."

Harrison ran a slow hand down Blondie's neck. "I'm not planning to mention it to anyone," he said casually. "I hope you won't either."

The old man shook his head with a chuckle. "You can be dang sure I'm keeping my mouth shut, and that's a fact you can bank on. I like my meals over with Odell when she'll invite me, and I'd sure hate getting on her bad side. Or on Alice's." He picked up a stick to whittle on and studied it. "I'd say what happens jest happens with this. Or it don't. All we can do is put out the bait and see."

"That's kind of what I figured." Harrison gave Hobart a sideways grin.

Hobart smiled slyly back. "You know, that grandson of mine is a right nice looking boy." He pulled out his knife to start chipping the stick in his hand.

"I noticed that," Harrison said, grinning more broadly at him. "I thought it might be nice for our little Stuart girl—that's so upset— to get her mind turned to something more pleasant."

Hobart chuckled. "Heck, I think we might have ourselves some right good fun over the next weeks." He studied the stick in his hand, thinking. "You know, boy, it's me that usually decides on the chores for the kids. I can see that role taking on a whole new dimension. I sure can."

"Be subtle, old man," Harrison warned him.

He waved his stick in the air. "Oh, I'll be as sly as an old fox sneaking after a chicken in the hen house."

The two men grinned at each other conspiratorially—just before the barn buzzer interrupted them, announcing a new group of riders coming up the road to the stable.

CHAPTER 11

The weeks of summer drifted by, and Alice realized with surprise that school was only a short time away. They'd enjoyed a happy summer overall. The children had settled into their new home comfortably. Hannah and Meg developed new friendships with the Nichols girls, and Alice knew the other children would find friends outside the family when school began.

Alice sat today on the screen porch with Donna Nichols, talking about how quickly the summer slipped by. The younger children had some sort of imaginative game going in the playhouse, and Alice and Donna could keep an eye on them while they visited on the porch. The two oldest girls, Hannah and DeeDee, had walked over to the stables after poring over teen fashion magazines in Hannah's room earlier.

"I think the children are beginning to feel at home now," Donna said. "Don't you agree?"

"I do and it's nice to see that," answered Alice. "This has proved a good move for us. I hope school won't bring any new problems. Everything has gone so well."

Donna curled a leg under her in the chair. "Didn't you say the children were all good students?" she asked. "That will help, I'm sure."

"They are good students." Alice propped her own legs on a stool. "They did fine in school last year until after Richard and Lauren died. Small problems occurred after that time, of course. Some of their grades dropped after the accident. Stacey and the younger ones acted out at school. Rachel cried a lot, and I often had to pick her up from school early. However, by the time they moved in with me and started the next school year, things improved."

She picked up a glass of iced tea from the side table to take a cool drink. "The children made stronger grades this last year. Fortunately, Tildy and Thomas had exceptionally strong kindergarten readiness scores—coached so much by the older children."

"I'm sure if they did well in the Sevierville schools, they'll do well at Pittman Center," Donna assured her. "The school is small, but it's a good K-8 school. DeeDee and Rhoda love it and I like the teachers and administration. I could go with you to see the principal, Mr. McCarter, and get the children set up, if you like."

"I'm sure that won't be necessary." Alice turned her iced tea glass in her hand. "I got all the academic records needed from the other schools and updated their health information. The four older girls had to get physicals for camp this summer, and I scheduled appointments for the twins, too."

Donna laughed. "You know, my girls going to Buckeye Camp with yours started something. They're begging to go every summer now. I'm grateful you helped my girls get into the camp with yours."

"Scott Jamison, who runs the camp, is a friend." Alice smiled at Donna. "He and his wife Vivian adopted one of my foster children, Sarah Taylor. He took pleasure in finding a place for my girls, and yours, in one of his camp sessions, and he gave me a wonderful discount since I sent four children at once."

Donna picked up her own glass of tea to sip it. "You took the twins to Murfreesboro with you during that time, didn't you?"

"I did. I wanted them to have an adventure of their own to talk about," she said. "We stayed at Grandmother Beryl's and took in some of the sights around the Nashville and Murfreesboro area." Alice smiled at the memory. "The twins especially enjoyed the horses at my grandparents' stable. We even got to attend a walking horse show and sit in the Beryl box while there. Thomas and Tildy loved that."

"How well I know," Donna said, laughing. "They must have told me about that horse show a hundred times."

Alice giggled. "It must be something about being five," she said. "They like repetition. Tildy and Thomas come tell me the same jokes again and again, and I have to act like they're funny every time. Then they want their favorite books read over and over until I literally know all the words by memory."

As if on cue, the twins raced up to the porch to show Alice and Donna some drawings and papers they'd made.

"We're playing school," announced Tildy. "Megan and Rhoda are the teachers."

Thomas held up his paper proudly for them to see. "I got an A on my numbers 'cause I did one to ten all by myself."

"That's very good." Donna admired the paper.

He looked down at his paper with a frown. "I can't do to a hundred like Rachel, though."

"You're not supposed to be able to write numbers to a hundred yet," said Alice, tousling his hair. "It's good if kindergarteners can write numbers from one to ten before they start school. Your new teacher is going to be very pleased with you."

Thomas beamed at that, and after some more sharing of papers, he and Tildy scampered off to play more 'pretend-school' in the playhouse.

Donna went into the kitchen then to get more iced tea, and Alice sat looking out over the yard, thinking about how nice it was to have a female friend again.

Alice had always made friends easily throughout her life, but after David died, things became more awkward. Couples friends of theirs felt uncomfortable with Alice, and she found herself with less in common with them, or with the young singles she met. She'd been grieving, too, and few people understood that. She took a job with the Wayside Agency after graduation, moved to Sevierville, and then absorbed herself into her new work role. It left her precious little personal or social time. However, she found she continued drawing back from close relationships.

When she got involved with the Stuarts, she realized why that might be so. As Stacey said candidly to her, "What if we start to love you, Alice, and then you die, too?" Alice realized she'd felt reluctant to let her heart out to others since David died. She'd tried to protect herself from possible hurt by keeping people at a comfortable distance.

When Alice moved to Greenbrier, Donna so easily initiated, and then assumed, a friendship that it became difficult for Alice to close herself off as carefully as she usually did. She felt glad she hadn't. Donna had become a good friend now and an important part of her new life. They shared and talked about many things, big and small, and Alice found Donna a faithful confidant. With the Greenbrier area small, Alice enjoyed knowing that what she shared with Donna wouldn't soon find its way all over the neighborhood.

"Have DeeDee and Hannah come back from the stable yet?" Donna asked, returning from the kitchen with fresh glasses of ice tea for both of them.

"No. They would have stopped in here first." She took the tea from Donna and squeezed a lemon wedge into it.

"You know," she added thoughtfully, as Donna settled back into a wicker chair. "Hannah has spent a lot of time at the stables in the last months." She frowned. "I guess that's all right, but it's surprised me. Hobart has given her all sorts of projects and stable chores most of the other children aren't asked to do but Hannah seems to love to do them."

"Oh, I wouldn't worry about that." Donna waved a hand. "She's smitten with the horse bug. I remember DeeDee and Rhoda wanted to eat, sleep, and breathe horses when that first happened to them."

"I suppose," mused Alice. "But I often think it's actually Megan and Rhoda who are the most horse-crazy. They read horse books and magazines, sit and write lists of horse names by the hour."

"Goodness, don't I know." Donna laughed. "Rhoda comes and reads horse names to me while I'm cooking and asks me which ones I like the best."

They both giggled at that.

Donna turned a glance to her. "Did you ever get that problem worked out with the church?" she asked. "I hated that you experienced a problem when you visited at Beech Grove. You never did tell me the details of it."

Alice blew out a breath. "That was a real mess, Donna," she confessed. "And I didn't want to talk about it when the children could hear."

"Well they're not here now," encouraged Donna. "So tell. I'm dying to know."

Alice grinned at her. "Well," she began. "When Odell invited us to go to church with her she didn't warn me the church was sort of old-fashioned and traditional in its dress code. I let the older girls wear slacks and blouses like they would have worn in the church we went to at Sevierville. With the temperature in the nineties, Stacey, Rachel, and Tildy wore those cute little culotte shorts so popular today. I let Thomas wear shorts, too, with a clean shirt."

Donna put a finger to her mouth thoughtfully. "Wasn't it Harrison's mother that criticized you after church about how the children dressed inappropriately?"

"Yes, among other things." Alice made a face. "We stood outside visiting after the service and getting to know some of the church people," she recalled. "The church held one of those outdoor pot-luck picnics after church. That's another reason Odell thought it a good day for us to go visit. She knew the children would get to play outside and meet other children after the service and that I'd get to meet and socialize with some of the adults."

"What happened?"

"Everything." Alice sighed deeply. "Yet nothing really. It all started, I guess, when Thomas knocked a pitcher of red punch over on one of the serving tables. Of course, he didn't mean to, Donna. He got excited, and it was only an accident, but it made a nasty mess, and the punch rolled all over the tablecloth and got on some woman's white purse she'd put down on the cloth for a minute."

Alice paused, remembering. "Then Hannah tried on this teenage girl's lipstick, and it looked terribly red. Hannah wandered around wearing the stuff for quite a while before I even spotted her. Of course, Hannah felt horrified when I pulled out a mirror and showed her how loud the color appeared on her. It hadn't looked that way in the tube at all."

She paused to sip her tea and then continued. "Megan and Rachel decided to climb some of the big mimosa trees on the church property after that. I saw no problem with that, but evidently many of the church people thought the children shouldn't have done that." Alice wrinkled her nose. "Next Tildy found a frog in the lily pond behind the church and came to show it to me. I sat talking to Mozella then. It was a fine big, yellow frog, but Mozella shrieked to high heaven at the sight of it and Tildy, shocked by her outburst, let go of the frog and it jumped right onto Mozella's lap."

Donna shook with laugher by this point.

"Oh, Donna, it wasn't funny." Alice swatted at her, but she tried not to giggle herself. "Mozella got terribly upset and lit into me in a tirade. Loudly, too—right in front of everyone. She yelled that I dressed my girls trashy for church and let my older girl wear lipstick like some little streetwalker. She said my children showed terrible manners, spilling things, running around like hooligans, climbing trees, and digging into the church's nice pond without a single thought to what was decent. She claimed it probably came from me working outside the home instead of staying home and taking care of my children like a good Christian woman should. Furthermore, she claimed Thomas simply ruined Mrs. Riley's favorite church purse and that the nasty frog Tildy threw on her had made spots on her best, white, Sunday dress and probably ruined it. She was in a livid rage, Donna."

"Whatever did you do?" Donna asked, wide-eyed now.

"I think I stood there in shock at first. Then, Tildy started to sob and threw herself against my leg and the other children all ran over to see what was going on."

She stopped a moment to look at Donna and sigh.

"The Stuart children feel very protective about me, Donna.

Perhaps too much so. They will hardly let anyone say a harsh word about me without getting upset, and they are very defensive of one another, too. They probably overreacted at that point."

"And did what?" Donna pressed.

Alice winced, remembering the scene. "Hannah swooped up Tildy into her arms and told Mozella to quit hollering at her and scaring her, that Tildy was only a little girl. Then in a very mature, firm voice, much like her mother Lauren's, Hannah told Mozella she was 'acting uncharitably and creating an unnecessary scene'."

"Naturally, Mozella grew furious at that and actually started advancing toward Hannah, calling her rude and disrespectful to adults and wagging a finger at her angrily." Alice paused, shaking her head. "Stacey got protective then, seeing Mozella move aggressively toward Hannah and Tildy. She ran up and kicked Mozella in the shin and told her to stay away from her sisters. Naturally, Rachel started to cry at about that time. Thomas rushed to hug Rachel, and he called Mozella a mean old woman. It was awful."

Donna's mouth dropped open. "What a fiasco. What did you do, Alice?" she asked.

Alice lifted her shoulders. "Before I could do anything, Harrison suddenly appeared," she replied. "You should have seen his face, Donna. He looked so angry, but he spoke very calmly and firmly to the children and apologized for his mother's behavior. He told them she often forgot how to be nice to visitors and was, exactly as Thomas said, often a mean old woman."

Her lips twitched with amusement. "I felt so stunned I simply stood there gaping, but Harrison stayed calm and took charge. He told Hannah to take all the children straight to the car and that I would be taking them home immediately. He said he didn't think the children needed to hear any more of his mother's unchristian like criticisms for the day and he announced—right in front of everyone—that his mother had lost her temper and forgotten herself. As he herded the children off in Hannah's care, he told them they hadn't done anything wrong, and that he planned to take them all out for ice cream later in the afternoon to try to make up for his mother's misbehavior."

"Unbelievable. What happened next?" Donna leaned forward in her seat.

"You could have heard a pin drop in that church yard." Alice bit her lip remembering it. "Hannah, to my great surprise, marshaled the children straight off to the car as Harrison told her to do. I attempted to apologize to Mozella, but Harrison cut me off and told me it wasn't me that owed an apology in the matter."

"Good for Harrison!" applauded Donna. "What did his mother say then?"

"She spluttered a minute and then called it typical of him to always take someone else's side against her no matter what. She shook her finger at him and claimed she had every right as the minister's wife to speak to anyone at the church if they acted inappropriately. In a hissing voice she said, 'I guess you're keeping up your pattern of taking up for whatever fancy lady lives at Meadowbrook, just like you've always done.' Then she tossed her head, brushed off her dress, and said snippily she was going into the church to wash her hands and clean up. She stomped off with her head held high, right by everybody."

"What a nerve that woman has!" Donna exclaimed. "You know, I always heard Mozella could be outspoken, but that sounds mean-spirited and cruel. What did Odell do, Alice? I'll bet she got upset, having asked you to come and all."

"Of course she was upset but sweet, too. She came up and hugged me and told me to go on home with the children, that she'd get my dishes and bring them to the house later. She whispered to me not to worry about Mozella, that she often lost her temper. It was a horrible day, Donna. By the time we got back to the house, all the children started crying. Even Megan. They said they never wanted to go back to that church again."

Donna shook her head back and forth with disbelief. "Didn't anyone else talk to you before you left? Apologize or anything? Tell you they were sorry all that happened?"

"Oh, the pastor kind of fluttered after me, trying to make light of it all." Alice wrinkled her nose. "And the lady with the white purse came to tell me she thought her purse could probably be washed and not to worry about it. The teenage girl who gave Hannah the lipstick actually cried, she felt so bad. Then, over the next few days, a few people stopped by to visit and try to make amends. Like Millie Parton and her husband, who lead the singing at the church. I think everyone felt sorry about what happened on our first visit. Several people counseled us not to pay it any mind and to come back to visit again real soon."

Donna leaned forward, eyes wide. "Have you gone back?"

"No. The children were too upset." Alice dropped her legs from the stool. "They didn't want to go back and I admit I haven't pushed."

"Gracious," exclaimed Donna. "I had no idea all that happened. It's simply horrible, Alice."

"It was a pretty bad day," Alice agreed, shaking her head.

"I am glad to hear Millie and her husband, James, came to see you afterwards. You know, Millie is Mozella's sister, but I think she's nicer than Mozella. A couple of times I've seen her in a huff herself over something Mozella said or did."

Donna thought for a minute. "You know, you can come and visit at our church, Grace Episcopal," she offered. "I don't think you'd run into anything like that there."

"Thanks, Donna, but I'm trying to keep the children in the denomination they've been raised in. For the last few Sundays I've taken them back over to their old church in Sevierville. I thought they needed to go somewhere where they felt safe and loved for a while."

"I'll agree with that," Donna confided.

They sat quietly for a minute thinking and drinking their tea, the only sounds the voices of the children down at the playhouse and the creak of Alice's rocking chair.

"Did Harrison come and take the children for ice cream later?" Donna asked curiously.

"He did." Alice smiled at the memory. "He showed up about an hour after church, with the children still snuffling and pouting in their rooms. He took us all down to Gatlinburg to get ice cream and then to the aquarium. He drove our van since we couldn't all fit in his truck. It made a great ending to a bad day for the children. I felt grateful to him."

Donna sat her tea glass on the side table beside her. "Did Harrison buy the tickets?" she pressed.

"Oh, you know how he is," Alice said dismissively. "He insisted on making it his treat. Harrison has a way of taking charge of things before you know what's happening and the children follow him along like the pied piper. I can't figure out how he does that. He's very authoritarian. Nothing like their father Richard Stuart, who exemplified the totally group-council oriented, democratic man in all his methods."

"You know, Alice," said Donna thoughtfully. "That sounds very protective of Harrison to rush in and be your champion like that."

"I think he was protecting the children," Alice reasoned. "He's actually become rather fond of them, I think. From what Odell tells me, Harrison already has issues with his mother, too. They often argue—and have for years. Odell says Mozella has a sharp tongue on her and that one of these days it's going to get her into real trouble. However, it seems everybody in the valley is used to her, and her ways, and puts up with her no matter what she does."

"You're missing my point." Donna rolled her eyes. "What Harrison did then … and the way I see him acting around you a lot of times … may mean more than you realize, Alice. I think he's beginning to have feelings for you."

Alice's eyebrows shot up. "No," she countered quickly. "There is nothing romantic going on between Harrison Ramsey and me. Harrison made it very clear when I first moved here that he's a confirmed bachelor and means to stay that way. You might say he warned me off, Donna. Not that he needed to with six kids in tow, but he did anyway."

"Hmmm," said Donna, evidently not convinced.

Alice shook a finger at her. "Now, don't start matchmaking with

Harrison Ramsey and me, Donna," she warned. "Just because he's nice to the children does not mean I want there to be anything personal between us. He's our neighbor and that's all."

Donna got up to look toward the playhouse to check on the children. "Vick told me Harrison carries some real hurts from the past with women." She turned to look at Alice then. "Has he ever talked to you about that?"

Alice didn't like the direction this conversation headed. "Harrison and I don't share deep, intimate conversations, Donna. I told you, we're only neighbors. I know very little about his personal life."

"Pooh, no one can be around Odell McKee for long and not know about other people's personal lives." Donna sat down again in her chair with a flounce. "Not that it's like gossip with Odell. She's interested in everybody and enjoys getting everybody acquainted. It's simply her way."

"That's an interesting spin on it." Alice stifled a grin. "And complimentary to Odell for always knowing everybody's business." She laughed then, despite herself.

Donna giggled, too. "Well, has Odell told you about Harrison's past?"

"Here and there," Alice admitted. "But I first heard about Harrison from my realtor even before I bought the house."

Donna's eyes flashed. "You see, everyone knows all about the way Harrison got dumped by that Reagan girl and stood up at the alter the next year," she claimed. "Yet no one knows all the details. Even Vick hasn't dug the story out of Harrison, but Hobart told Vick some of what happened."

"What did Hobart say?" Alice asked, hating herself for her curiosity.

"Hobart described Harrison as a fine boy – from childhood through his teens. Straight as an arrow, he called him, and good, like his daddy, without an ounce of his mother's meanness."

She leaned toward Alice. "Hobart told Vick that Harrison never had too many sweethearts and wasn't a charmer with the ladies like some. Too busy working. Too serious. But when he started high school down at Gatlinburg High he met Ava Reagan. Hobart said they matched like two peas in a pod. Liked all the same things. Even looked a lot alike, both tall with dark hair, both horse crazy, both serious about their studies. Ava began coming to the stable. Got her older brother to bring her. She started taking lessons to learn to ride better. Before long, Harrison and Ava became an item."

Donna paused and took a drink of her tea. "Hobart claimed Harrison and Ava dated all through high school. Went to all the class dances and events together. By senior year, everybody naturally assumed they'd get married. Harrison even gave her an engagement ring when they graduated, but Ava wanted to wait a while before planning a wedding. Wanted time and space before settling down. She went to work in Gatlinburg at one of the big Reagan family hotels over the summer. Met a college boy whose family owned some posh resort out in Colorado. She took off with him at the end of summer when he left, married him, and made her life in Colorado." Her tone grew hushed. "She sent poor Harrison's engagement ring back through the mail with a letter."

"She must have known when she put off the wedding she wasn't sure." Alice frowned. "But it seems a cowardly how she chose to handle things with Harrison when she met someone else."

"I always thought so, too." Donna nodded in agreement. "She probably simply kept Harrison in reserve in case the new boyfriend didn't pop the question. Makes you not like her, doesn't it?"

"It does." Alice's jaw clenched. "I wonder what explanation she wrote to Harrison?"

"I don't know." Donna shrugged. "Whatever she wrote had to hurt him. They dated all through high school."

The two sat and thought about that for a minute.

Donna leaned toward Alice again. "I always thought it Harrison got involved with that prissy Patsy Ogle the next year on the rebound."

"Prissy Patsy?" Alice repeated with a giggle.

"The name ought to tell you a lot." Donna crossed her arms irritably. "I've met her and, believe me, the name fits. She's the opposite of Ava. Cute, perky, pom-pom squad type—more serious about her looks and having fun than anything else. Had a rich daddy and a fast convertible. She still attended high school when she latched on to Harrison. Hobart said she liked sporting an older man on her arm. He said Patsy's daddy liked Harrison a lot, too. Thought him a steady type – and knew he'd inherit property."

Alice wrinkled her nose. "She doesn't sound like a type Harrison would like," she said. "But, of course, he could have been different then."

"I don't think so. Hobart told Vick he thought Harrison felt flattered to have a pretty, popular, girl like Patsy interested in him after getting dumped by Ava. Made him feel manly again or something." Donna's voice grew softer, as if to make sure no one else could hear. "Hobart called Patsy's reputation no better than it should be, either. Probably another factor in the attraction." She made a face. "Sheesh, men are dumb that way sometimes."

"What happened?" Alice asked. She hated herself once more for asking and for wanting to know so much. But she did.

"Odell told me they got engaged real sudden and planned a quick wedding." She sat back in her chair. "Everyone assumed the obvious, that Patsy probably got pregnant, but a big crowd turned out for the wedding anyway. Patsy showed up in a fancy white dress with all the trimmings, but somebody saw Patsy and Harrison having a big fight outside the church before the ceremony, under a tree by Harrison's truck. Then when the time came for Patsy to come walking down the aisle, she didn't."

Her eyes grew huge. "Her bridesmaids said she told them she wanted a few minutes of time alone before the wedding march. When her daddy knocked for her—to walk her down the aisle— they found her gone. She climbed out the window, Hobart said, and drove off in her little white convertible."

Alice's heart turned over. "How dreadful for Harrison! He must have already been standing in the front of the church waiting for his bride to walk down to him." She shook her head sadly. "I can't understand how anyone could feel bad towards him for what happened. It wasn't like he refused to marry her or anything."

Donna lowered her voice. "Well, some rumors say Harrison wasn't happy about Patsy being pregnant, that he didn't like being forced into a wedding over a pregnancy. Some people say that's what they fought about. Patsy's daddy claimed Harrison threatened Patsy and caused her to run off that day. She left town, you know and didn't come back to the area for years."

Alice thought about that. "Did she have a baby with her when she came back?"

"Nope, and that sort of made it worse." Donna wagged a finger. "Made it look like she might have done away with it. Patsy never said."

Alice's mouth dropped open. "You mean she never said where she went or what happened?"

"Oh, she ran off with Cleton Spangler and married him. Everyone knows that now." Donna shrugged. "He came from a bad family— wild as the day runs long. Of course, the marriage didn't work out. Eventually Patsy's daddy went to bring her home. He claimed the fight with Harrison caused Patsy to run off with Cleton. Evidently, Patsy told him that. Cleton, always a mean type as the story goes, beat up on Patsy once they married. Patsy's daddy and family lay all that sorrow to Harrison's doorstep."

"And Patsy let them do that? Totally blame Harrison?" Alice's anger flared. "That's not fair."

"I guess she must have blamed him in some way, too, Alice." Donna frowned. "Anyway, you know everything Vick and I know now."

Alice's temper rose. "What happened to this Patsy girl? Does she live here?"

"Woman now. She's in her thirties," corrected Donna. "She got remarried, to one of her daddy's young business partners, Kent Rimmer. Lives down in Gatlinburg and works at a small gift shop her daddy bought for her. Cute store. Sells perfumes and stuff. *Scents and Treasures,* I think the store is called."

"I can certainly see why Harrison got turned off on women."

She shivered, thinking of all Harrison endured.

"Vick said between what happened to him and having Mozella Trent Ramsey for a mother, it's no wonder Harrison avoids women." Donna stopped to think. "Millie told me once Harrison's sisters were much like Mozella. She claimed Pauline, the youngest, the only one that didn't have a knife for a tongue."

They both giggled at that.

Alice made a face. "I feel like the biggest gossip after learning all this," she confided guiltily.

"You shouldn't," Donna countered defensively. "I don't think it's gossip for you to know about Harrison's life when he spends as much time with you and the children as he does." She stiffened in her seat. "He should have told you these things himself, you know. I'm sure Odell told him enough about you. It seems only fair for you to know about him."

She gave Alice a smug smile. "Especially because I think he's interested in you."

Alice shook her head. "You quit thinking that, Donna. I told you nothing will come of that."

"Maybe and maybe not." Donna tossed her head saucily. "Vick and I have seen how Harrison looks at you. Vick said it isn't a neighborly look. Perhaps *you* ought to pay more attention."

Hannah came running through the yard then, tears streaming down her face. She slammed through the screened porch and into the house before Alice and Donna could even get up from their seats. By the time they did, DeeDee pushed through the screen door behind her. Only she wasn't crying.

"What happened?" asked Donna, jumping up. "Did you two have a fight?"

"No, it's something else, Mom. She wouldn't tell me what." DeeDee, stopping to catch her breath, looked distraught. "I went over to take some old bridles to the old barn behind Harrison's house. Deke asked me to. Hannah was working in the barn or in the corral. I don't know which. But I think something happened. I saw her running by the Harrison's barn a minute ago crying real hard. I called to her and tried to stop her, but she kept crying, pulled away from me, and ran for home. Honest, Mom, I don't know what happened or why she's upset, but it wasn't anything I did, I swear."

Donna looked at Alice. "Do you want the girls and I to stay and try to help? Or do you think it would be best if we go on home?"

"It might be best if Hannah and I work this through on our own. But thanks for the offer, Donna," Alice said. "I appreciate it."

Alice patted DeeDee's shoulder, seeing she'd started crying now, too. "Don't worry, DeeDee. I'm sure it's nothing much. Probably someone hurt Hannah's feelings. Who else was at the barn?"

DeeDee wiped her face with her arm. "Only the guys that work there. Hannah and I helped with a trail ride earlier, but those kids left a long time now."

She paused to think. "You know, the only other thing I can remember that happened at the stable was that Hannah and I saw some horses mating out in the pasture earlier." She stopped to make a face. "It looked gross, but Harrison walked up and he explained it. Told us all the birds and bees stuff. You know." She rolled her eyes meaningfully. "Nothing you and dad haven't told me before, Mom. Hannah didn't seem upset about it at all. Harrison acted real nice." She wrinkled her nose. "It wasn't until later Hannah started crying, anyway. I don't think the horse mating thing got her upset, do you?"

Donna and Alice raised their eyebrows at each other.

"Hmmm," Donna said. "I think we'll talk about this when you and I get home, DeeDee. Why don't you get Rhoda and I'll meet both of you out front in a minute."

DeeDee took off out the back door then.

"Honestly," she spluttered as soon as DeeDee got out of earshot. "Whatever possessed Harrison Ramsey to give our girls a lecture about the facts of life – or to let them watch horses mating at his stable? The nerve." She turned to give Alice an exasperated look. "It might be that very discussion that upset Hannah. She's a more sensitive girl than DeeDee."

Alice considered this. "She is and I'll go talk to her about it."

She let Donna out the front door and then headed down the hallway to start up the stairs. Like Donna, she could have wrung Harrison Ramsey's neck at that moment.

CHAPTER 12

A short time later, Hobart looked up to see Alice Graham cutting over from the Ramsey farmhouse toward the stable.

"Looks like your pretty, little lady from Meadowbrook is paying us a visit," Hobart commented to Harrison.

As Alice got closer, even Hobart could see she had a stormy look on her face. "Hmmm. Think I'll mosey down to the back pasture, Harrison, and check on them horses we've got down there." He stood up and started around the barn.

"Coward," Harrison called after him.

He heard the old man chuckle.

"Looking for me?" Harrison let himself out of the corral as Alice arrived.

She stopped in front of him, crossed her arms with a huff, and glared at him. "Yes, I am, and I am angry at you, too."

He assessed her slowly, noting that she looked incredibly beautiful even when mad. A flush colored her cheeks a rosy pink and her blue eyes flashed.

Harrison tried a smile. "What do you figure I've done for you to be angry at me?" he asked casually, leaning up against a fence post.

"You told Hannah and DeeDee some birds and bees story about how horses mate." She leaned toward him. "It didn't upset DeeDee very much, Harrison, but Hannah has been in her room upset and crying ever since." Her lips formed an angry line. "Neither Donna nor I think it your place to educate our girls about such a personal subject."

Harrison rolled his eyes. "Maybe you've got a right to an opinion about this matter, but I've got a right to ask a few questions, too. First, I want to know *specifically* what Hannah told you I said and then why she said it upset her."

"Well, uh …" Alice hesitated, her face coloring. "That's beside the point. It's obvious what happened. Hannah came running back to the house crying and she's been in her room ever since with the door locked. We can't get her to open the door and even talk to us, she's so upset."

Harrison's mouth tightened. "I told her not to do that anymore."

"She did, anyway." She glowered at him. "It's upsetting the children, and me, and this is all your fault, you know. I want to know exactly what you told her, Harrison. I have that right, you know…"

His anger flared. "You don't have any rights that hold up here." He stepped toward her, feeling his fists clench at his side. "You haven't even talked to the girl yet. You don't even know whether what I said to her upset her at all. It could be something else entirely."

She put her hands on her hips. "What else could have upset her like this?"

"I can't rightly say." His eyes narrowed. "Last time she got upset that some little boy said he liked her and planned to tell everyone about it at school, if I recall."

Alice had the grace to blush. "Girls get upset about things like that."

"So they do." He pushed his hat back slightly. "It could be something like that again that's upset Hannah. You don't know it was my explanation about the horses that upset her at all. As you said, DeeDee wasn't troubled about it."

"Hannah is more sensitive." Alice lifted her chin.

Harrison raised his eyebrows at that. "I see. What did DeeDee say I told them that sounded so out of line to you? You might at least tell me that."

"Well, uh … she didn't exactly say what you said," Alice admitted, twisting at a button on her shirt now. "She said it was the only thing unusual she could think of that happened at the stable. And I just assumed ..."

"You assumed," Harrison repeated, very slowly. "Seems like you'd have learned not to assume quickly being a social worker and all. Especially since you deal with upset parents and children all the time."

"Harrison, it's different when ..."

He interrupted. "When it's your child? Is that what you started to say, Alice? Seems to me like it shouldn't be."

Alice sighed and raised her eyes to his. "What else can it be, Harrison? I ask you?"

"I have no idea," he answered her. "Growing up I never made much sense of what my four sisters or my mother stayed upset about half the time. Usually when I did find out the issue, it was never what I thought it might be at all." He met her gaze. "Didn't you have problems like that understanding your sisters?"

Alice looked away. "I had four brothers and only one sister," she answered. "My sister Margaret, the oldest, was seldom emotional. I remember her as always incredibly sensible and mature." She snorted. "She probably needed to be since my mother acted so twitty and brainless sometimes."

Harrison raised an eyebrow at that and gave her a sideways grin.

"I thought you knew all about my life." Alice's eyes flashed.

He gave her a long considering look. "You know, I can't recall you and I ever talking about our lives much."

She twisted uncomfortably. "Odell's probably told you everything about me already," she shot back.

"You think so?" He folded his arms over his chest. "Funny how everybody seems to know all about me without ever bothering to ask me a dang thing." He kicked at a stone irritably. "Like this thing with Hannah."

"Oh, all right," admitted Alice, blowing out a breath. "Perhaps I am a little upset and over-reacting." She made a visible effort to calm herself and walked over to sit down in Hobart's old chair in front of the barn.

She rubbed a tennis shoe over the ground and studied the design she made in the dirt. "I hate getting upset like this," she confessed at last. "It isn't professional; I know that. It's just that I'm not used to having all these children, Harrison. Often it's simply overwhelming."

"I'm sure it is," he said quietly, coming over to stand near her. He ran a hand gently down her cheek.

"Now don't be nice to me or I'll probably start to cry myself." She jerked away from his hand.

Alice drew in a deep breath. "Tell me what you said to those girls, Harrison. You'll notice I'm asking nicely now."

"I noticed, and I guess I'll tell you." He grinned at her. "Yesterday, Marlo Benson brought his big grey stallion, Biff, over for a few days to mate with Ginger, one of my little trail mares. Ginger's got a good temperament, and I thought it would be good to breed her. The foal ought to come by next summer. This morning, I stayed to keep an eye on things down at the pasture where we turned Biff and Ginger out together. From what went on, it looked like we picked the right time to mate those two. I stood watching, being protective of Ginger, when I happened to look up and see two little girls sitting on the fence rail, their eyes bugging out, taking it all in."

He looked down at Alice. "What would you have done, Alice?" he asked, with a half grin. "I'll bet you'd have done the same thing I did. I went over, told the girls a quick story about what they saw happening in as calm a way as I could, and then suggested they go back up to the barn. To me saying nothing in those circumstances, or getting angry at them for happening to drop by at an awkward time, would be worse than offering some understanding. These were animals, after all, and not people, Alice. I gave an explanation suited to horseflesh. From what I observed, neither of the girls acted particularly upset at the time. They listened politely and then went off giggling."

Alice heaved a deep sigh. "Then why is Hannah crying after

being over here, Harrison, if it isn't about what happened with the horses?"

"I can't say." He put a hand on her shoulder. "It seems to me like we better go over to your place and see if we can get an answer to that."

"Perhaps Hannah will let me in to talk with her by now." She gave him a prim reply as she stood up. "There's no reason for you to come back with me."

He dusted off his old Stetson and put it back on his head. "I disagree, ma'am. You've involved me now," he insisted. "I want to be sure it wasn't something I said or something one of my staff did that's upset Hannah. I'll drive us over in the truck. It will save time."

It took them only five minutes to drive to the house. They went upstairs and found most of the children gathered around the door, trying to get Hannah to open it.

Harrison frowned. "You children go outside and play now," he told them firmly. "And all of you stay in the yard and don't cause any trouble, you hear? Alice and I will handle this. Quit worrying and fretting. I'm sure Hannah will be fine and out to play with you soon."

The children immediately got up and started toward the stairs.

Stacey sighed dramatically before she left. "How come Hannah always gets upset and cries about everything now? She never used to."

"It's that magic age she's entered," answered Harrison. "Twelve going on thirteen and nearly a teenager."

Megan made a face. "I'm not going to cry all the time when I'm twelve," she told the children emphatically as they started down the stairs.

Alice smiled at Harrison in spite of herself.

"She probably won't either." He grinned.

Hearing the children heading outdoors now, Alice leaned against the wall. "How come those children always obey you instantly whenever you tell them to do something. It always happens when you're with them."

"Perhaps it's my natural air of authority," he teased, making her smile again.

Harrison felt pleased to see Alice calming down now. Dang kid, getting her all upset. As if Alice didn't have enough problems, seeing to the six of them day in and day out. Irritated at the thought, he strode over to Hannah's door.

"Hannah Stuart," he called out firmly. "I thought I made it clear to you not to lock this door against the adults that care for you. I seem to recall you promised you wouldn't do that again."

"But I don't want to see anyone," she wailed. "I have a right to be by myself if I want to be."

"No, you do not," he replied tersely. "Not without an explanation for your behavior you don't. Now you open this door immediately and let Alice and me in. You remember the last time I told you clearly I would break the door down if you didn't. I still mean that, and you know I'm strong enough to do it."

To Alice's surprise, she heard Hannah immediately padding across the room to open the door.

"Don't pet on her." Harrison sent a warning look to Alice. "She may be upset, but she's in the wrong how she handled this. Let me talk to her first if you would."

He saw Alice's mouth tighten at that suggestion, but she didn't argue.

Hannah let them in, but then made a beeline straight back to her bed to cry again.

Harrison motioned Alice to a striped armchair, and then pulled Hannah's desk chair close to the bed.

"Seems like the last time I sat in this spot, it concerned Vance Palmer." Harrison crossed a leg over his knee. "He been bothering you again, Hannah?"

"No, it's not Vance." Her words jerked out between sobs. "He hasn't bothered me for a long time."

"Well, is it Josh then?" Harrison picked up a paperweight from the bedside table to examine it.

Alice's eyebrows shot up. "Who's Josh?" she asked in surprise, without thinking, but stopped her question after a stern look from Harrison.

"You might say Josh Sheldon is Hannah's current boyfriend." Harrison turned the paperweight over in his hand, studying the design in it. "I figured she might have mentioned him to you."

"He's not my boyfriend." Hannah's voice caught. "We're only friends."

"Maybe, maybe not. Did you know your friend Josh punched Vance Palmer's lights out because he said you liked him?" Harrison sat the paperweight back down on the table. "Gave him a nice black eye, too. A real shiner. Hobart and I saw it."

Hannah pulled a head away from the pillow to look up in surprise. "He did?" she whispered, eyes big.

"Yeah, got real mad over Vance making little smart remarks about you when he walked over to the store one day. Plain lost his temper."

"Oh ..." said Hannah, her eyes growing wider.

Harrison pulled his hat off and draped it over his knee. "Is this boo-hooing scene over Josh? Did he do more than hold your hand or something?"

She shook her head and started crying in her pillow again.

"Okay, is this because I told you and DeeDee a few facts about horse-mating?" Harrison asked next. "Alice seems to think so. She came over to take me to task about it earlier."

"It's not that!" Hannah cried, but then buried her head back in the pillow.

Harrison sent a significant look Alice's way then.

"All right, Hannah." He felt his anger rising. "I'm not in the mood to play twenty questions here. It's not boys, you say. It's not my discussion on horse mating. And it's not because you had a fight with DeeDee, or so she said. What else is there?"

Only sniffling came back in answer.

"Hannah, I'm waiting." Harrison said the words slowly.

"It's something you said last time ..." she croaked, almost in a whisper. "And please, I don't want to talk about it."

Harrison racked his mind to recall what in the world he'd asked her about the last time he'd been here. Then suddenly he remembered. He looked at Hannah more closely.

"Looks to me like you've changed clothes since you came back from the stable," he said probingly. "Got on some different shorts now."

Hannah started to bawl even louder.

He got up then and motioned to Alice. She followed him over to the door as he directed.

He spoke to her softly. "This is a woman's issue, Alice. Hannah has started her time, if you know what I mean. That's why she changed her clothes. Now, I'm leaving you to talk to her about this on your own. It's a girls' thing, but you make sure she knows it's as healthy and normal as breathing. My mother told my sisters it was a curse for women, and that understanding never gave them a moment's comfort, I'll tell you."

Before Alice could offer a reply, Harrison left and went back to the stable.

Later that evening as dark settled over the valley, he sat out on the porch of his house, drinking a cup of coffee and thinking over his day, when he saw Alice coming up the path toward the house.

"Coming to pick a fight again?" he called into the darkness.

He heard her soft laugh float back over the night.

"No, I've come to make my apologies," she said, stepping up on the porch.

"You want to sit down?" He patted the seat on the glider beside him.

She nodded and sat down, putting a box on his lap.

"What's this?" He lifted an eyebrow.

"Peace offerings and bribes, in case I need them." She smiled.

Harrison flipped the cover off the bakery box to find a couple of pieces of pecan pie and about a dozen cookies piled inside.

"Nice bribe." He gave her a small smile. "You make all this?"

"No, Odell did. My day got too tied up for baking."

He chuckled. "Did you get all that problem straightened out with Hannah?"

"Yes, thanks to you," she said. "I owe you, Harrison. Thank you."

"Considering the problem, I figure she'd have gotten around to telling you sooner or later," he observed.

"You're probably right." She sighed softly. "But you helped it along considerably. Where did you learn to handle children with such ease, Harrison?"

"Been a surprise to you, huh?" He teased.

"Yes, I'll admit it has," she answered honestly, finding it easier to make confessions in the dark. "I thought you'd be the gruff cowboy type."

He chuckled again. "Alice, I've worked with groups of kids of all ages and types at Ramsey Stable every since I turned Thomas's age. It would be a sorry thing if I hadn't picked up a thing or two along the way."

"Possibly," she agreed. "But I think you possess a real insight about what to say and when and about how to handle things efficiently. In addition, you display an excellent leadership capacity with a gift for taking command and the ability to calm down a volatile situation."

He grinned at her. "You calling yourself a volatile situation, too?"

She giggled. "You know what I mean. Let me give you a well-deserved compliment, Harrison, when you've earned it."

"Hannah going to be all right?" He moved to a question, uncomfortable with responding to her praise. Not used to it.

"She's fine." Alice picked at a nail. "We had a good talk, one we should have shared before. She's watching the younger children right now. Said to tell you she's sorry she caused such trouble."

"Hmmm. Tell her she'd better not lock that door again."

Alice laughed. "I think she'll remember," she assured him. "Harrison, Hannah told me, like DeeDee did, that your talk about the horses was an appropriate one. I stepped out of line to criticize you for doing that. I called Donna and explained to her what happened. She said you did the right thing, too, talking to the girls after what they saw. We both over-reacted, Harrison."

He sat listening to her, liking the way her voice sounded on the night air.

"What's this business about your mother being twitty and brainless?' he asked, artfully changing the subject.

She dropped her eyes. "I shouldn't have said that," she murmured.

"Hey. I told everyone in the church yard I agreed with Thomas that my mother is downright mean." He grinned at her. "It's not like you topped me, you know, criticizing your mother a little."

She laughed softly at his words and shifted in her seat. As she did the scent of lilacs drifted through the night air and wafted across Harrison's senses.

Alice's turned to him. "Whatever happened after that event with your mother?" she asked him, concerned. "Is she still angry with you?"

"My mother has stayed angry with me since I took my first breath at the hospital." He shrugged. "It's nothing new for the two of us to have a run-in, although usually not one so public."

"Have you been back to church?"

"The very next Sunday." He looked at her in surprise. "Not to go back right away would be like falling off a horse and being afraid to get back on. You and the kids should go back, too. Not let Mozella score that situation as a win and have power over you."

She fell silent for a few minutes "If you can get the children to go, we'll go. You may have a point in what you say, Harrison. I like to think they could face their fears. It might be a good life lesson for them, whether we continued going to the church after that or not."

"I'll talk to them," he said, liking the idea of a challenge.

"How'd your mother act when you went back?" Alice asked.

"Like always. Perhaps more huffy than usual." His eyes turned to hers. "You know, most all the folks at Beech Grove felt real bad about what happened, Alice. Many came and spoke to me about it. Said they wished you'd come back." He paused. "Don't judge that whole church harshly based on Mozella. There's some fine folks there. It isn't their fault they have to church with Mozella. Heck, she's played the piano there since a girl. Has a natural gift with music and plays by ear. Now she's married their minister. What can they do except put up with her?"

"She does play the piano beautifully," Alice acknowledged.

He smiled slightly. "Everybody has their good points. Even a snake possesses some redeeming qualities, although you'd like to avoid its bite as much as you can and whenever you can."

He saw her mouth quirk in a smile. "Was it hard having Mozella as a mother?"

"It was for me." He leaned back in the glider, crossing his foot over his knee. "Not for my sisters. They had a better relationship with her. Ma always thought me much like my father. Even looked like him. I think she hoped I'd be different and that disappointed her."

"I understand how that feels," Alice empathized. "My mother, the charming socialite, wanted me to love frilly dresses, delight in boutiques and hairdressers, and love to gossip with her about all her friends and what went on in the neighborhood." Alice shrugged. "She wanted me to thrill over the next party and social event on the horizon, delight in making h'ordoeurves and planning lavish dinners. Instead, I never enjoyed any of those things—a big disappointment to her. Especially when I looked like her."

She smiled. "She birthed Margaret first, you see. Tall, redheaded, strong-willed, capable, and independent from the beginning. Exactly like daddy's mother, Grandmother Duncan. Not the least bit sweet and malleable. Then she had the four boys. Finally when I came, blond and blue-eyed like her, I think she expected I'd be more like her. None of the other children were. I did try hard to please her, Harrison, but nothing I did ever seemed enough." Her heard her draw in a small sigh. "I quickly became too much my own person and nothing like her."

"What did you enjoy when you were little?" Harrison asked softly.

She tilted her head thinking. "Horses, books, sitting in the oak tree dreaming, taking long walks, being with good friends more than going to social events, taking in strays, reading about what made people become the way they were. That interested me. I always liked matching things up, too. Colors, things, people. Helping people fit where they belonged. Encouraging their best. Being useful, feeling like I made the world a better place."

"Sounds like you got in the right line of work in social services." He draped an arm behind her along the back of the glider. "What does your mother do with herself?"

"Nothing much, although you'd think so by how busy she always says she is. She's always got something going. Some club meeting or project, somebody she needs to call or drop a note to. Some church event or shopping trip or philanthropic thing she's working on." She turned her eyes toward Harrison wistfully. "But she had very little real time for us children. For Margaret, Ray, Harper, Carson, Julian, and me. I think Margaret raised us more than anyone. Bless her heart—she and Grandmother Beryl."

"What did you want most from your mother?" asked Harrison into the dark.

She didn't hesitate. "Her time. To play with me or do something with me I enjoyed, for her to see the strengths I had that were different from hers. Possibly to celebrate them. To encourage me. Not just absently say 'isn't that nice, dear' when I told her things. That's silly, isn't it?"

"No." He took a deep breath. "With my mother, I wanted to not always be criticized, to not always be in the wrong. To be complimented once in a while for something. To be liked for who I was. Some of the same things."

"Parents have so much power," Alice said softly, shivering. "What if I don't do a good job with Richard and Lauren's children, Harrison? What if I make them feel unloved and unappreciated? What if I make them feel wrong or uncelebrated—try to push them into a pattern that's not right for them? Make them feel guilty for what they are?"

"I don't think you'll do that." Harrison slipped his arm around her shoulder without thinking. "You're doing fine from what I see.

Odell agrees, and anyone can tell the children love you."

They sat quietly for a minute, listening to the cicadas and creek frogs singing on the night air. Enjoying the evening.

"Do you miss your husband?" The question slipped out before he could stop himself.

"I did very much at first." She leaned back in the glider, closing her eyes and resting her head on her arm. "David was a fine person. It seemed deeply unfair he lost his life so young. I felt bitter and angry at the beginning. I took it hard, and I grieved for him. We'd only been married three years. But time passed, and time begins to heal loss. I gradually healed, like the Stuart children are healing from their loss."

"Were there other significant men in your life?" he quizzed her, and then could have bitten his tongue off for asking—knowing it none of his business.

"David was my first serious relationship. I had some early sweethearts, of course. I remember the first boy who kissed me, too." Her soft laugh floated over to him. "His name was Edward Vincent Reese, and he kissed me under a big willow tree out in our back yard. A furtive young kiss, but I thought it very romantic."

"What about you, Harrison?" She turned her head to give him a teasing smile. "When did you get your first kiss?"

"Up in the hayloft with Ava Reagan." He chuckled. "We were thirteen."

He heard Alice hesitate before speaking. "Didn't you almost marry Ava?"

"I almost married two women." His voice, snappish and harsh now, broke their harmonious mood. "Surely, you've heard enough stories about that around the valley. You have, haven't you, Alice?"

"Maybe a bit." She dropped her eyes. "But I'd rather you'd tell me."

"And I'd rather not." He withdrew his arm, stiffening. "Some things are best kept personal."

To Harrison's surprise, Alice let the matter drop, didn't press him further. She didn't seem overly upset with him for clamming up, as he thought she would.

"I respect your right to keep some things personal." She stretched, rubbing her neck. "Let's change the subject, okay. Perhaps you might tell me about your father. I've heard such fine things about him from everybody."

Glad to not have the evening ruined, Harrison told her a few memories about his father, a subject he liked to reminisce about anyway.

At a certain point, he stopped talking. He and Alice sat quietly in the gathering darkness then, Harrison pushing the glider gently back and forth with his foot. He loved these times, when they simply sat together, both content with themselves and content not to talk.

"I'm glad we became friends, Harrison," Alice whispered silkily, laying her head on his shoulder then.

A warmth ran up Harrison's spine. He could feel her hair against his neck and could smell the scents of her—lilac and some fragrant lotion on her skin. The old draw began to pull on him then. He tilted Alice's face up to his.

"Alice Graham, we will never be just friends," he whispered, his voice thickening. "Never slip into that illusion." He put his other arm around her and kissed her deeply.

For some reason this kiss seemed more passionate than any other they'd ever shared and more tender at the same time. As Harrison enjoyed the taste, scent, and feel of Alice, there in the dark on the old glider, he realized for the first time she'd touched him in a deep inward place he'd kept hidden for a long time. It made him shiver, along with her, in the chilly evening air. It frightened him a little, too.

CHAPTER 13

The next weeks brought a flurry of shopping trips for school clothes and school supplies. Alice took the children's records to their new school and toured the kids around the school building. While they played in the schoolyard afterwards, she visited briefly with the principal. Alice continued to smart over the principal and secretary's subtle remarks about adding more foster kids into the school system. That day marked an omen for the problems that soon began to develop.

"How are things going with the children at school?" Odell asked after Alice dropped them off one morning.

"Not as good as I'd hoped." She slumped into a chair at the kitchen table after pouring another cup of coffee.

"I've heard grumbling from some," Odell said, coming to sit across from her.

"From the younger ones, I'm sure." Alice sipped her hot coffee gratefully. "The older girls, Hannah and Megan, settled into school with no problems."

"You need to remember they had DeeDee and Rhoda Nichols to help them settle in. It benefits to have friends in a new place." Odell flipped through a woman's magazine while she talked.

"That's a good point, Odell." Alice nodded. "Megan's in Rhoda's class and DeeDee swept Hannah right into her group of seventh grade friends, making her adjustment easier."

Odell raised her eyebrows and wiggled them. "Of course, it don't hurt that Hannah has a beau, either. I hear Josh Sheldon got into a fight on the playground with Vance Palmer the second day of class over Hannah."

"I heard about that, too." Alice's eyes narrowed. "I don't believe physical fighting a way to handle problems, Odell, but I'm happy Hannah's adjusting well. Josh seems likes a nice boy, too."

"He is." She got up to bring Alice a refill for her coffee. "So what are the problems with the younger children?"

Alice gave Odell a despairing look. "All of them have problems, Odell, and my visits to the school haven't resolved anything. Stacey's teacher says she has 'social problems,' especially with a classmate named Laura Sue Palmer."

Odell interrupted. "That's Vance Palmer's sister."

"Yes, and probably where the problem started, but I don't know what to do about it. Seldom a day goes by when Stacey doesn't come home mad or angry about something that happened in class."

"She does go on." Odell leaned over to study a recipe in the magazine. "I'm sure things will sort out after a while, Alice. Try not to worry too much. "

Alice pushed her hair back behind her ear distractedly. "It's hard not to. Rachel has started to cry at school again like she did after her parents died. Rachel's teacher says she has 'personal problems'— hardly talks to the other children, sits and plays by herself, is making no friends. If anything upsets her, she cries. I've had to pick her up several times, and she often cries in the morning, not wanting to go to school."

Odell made a tut-tuting sound. "Poor little thing. She's got such a tender little soul. Takes everything seriously."

"It gets worse." Alice heaved a deep sigh. "In Miss Marley's kindergarten class, some bully is picking on the twins. He takes their ice cream money or special pencils. When the teacher isn't watching, he threatens them—and scares Tildy. He trips them or pushes them to cause them to fall. Afterwards, he claims he didn't do it or, if caught outright, calls it an accident. It's making both of them unhappy at school."

Odell reached over to pat her hand. "You've got a big load

right now, but raising kids ain't no picnic. I can remember some times with my own." She launched into several tales about school problems with her own children, but offered no useful answers other to suggest again the situation would work itself out in time.

Alice wondered about that. With four of the six children unhappy at Pittman Elementary, the strain and discord at home kept increasing. She felt near her wits end with the daily anger, tears, and upsets of the children.

To make matters worse, as fall settled in, Alice's workload doubled. She suddenly had a rash of placements in her county requiring many home visits to see how the children were getting along in their new environments. In one case she'd been forced to move a child unexpectedly—always hard for the foster parents and the child. With the Stuart children back in school, Dorothy Eaton scheduled Alice to conduct many of the agency's foster care inquiry meetings again and to do parent orientation classes. With classes held at the Knoxville office, it made for many longer days for Alice to drive back and forth into the city.

At one a.m. in the morning after a particularly trying day, Alice got a call about an abandoned child. Usually these calls went through Dorothy—currently out of town at a conference. The caller, a minister of a rural church, had received an anonymous phone call about a baby abandoned on the church porch. Of course, he dressed and drove quickly over, finding the baby by the front door. Because the pastor knew Dorothy, he called her agency instead of the county social services office.

Now, Alice needed to get up and dress, contact one of her emergency parents to agree to take the child short term, drive out in the country to get the baby, and then take it to her emergency parents' house. Odell had gone for a long weekend to her daughter's, and Alice simply couldn't think of whom she could call to come and stay with the children. She knew Donna was sick, battling a head cold all week, and Vick had to work early in the morning.

"What am I going to do?" she muttered as she looked for her clothes to dress.

Of course, she could wake all the children, get them dressed, and take them with her. But that meant they probably wouldn't get back in bed until four a.m.

On a tired sigh, she did the only other thing she could think of at the moment and called Harrison. He arrived by the time she finished dressing and punched in the number for the emergency foster parents.

"I'm terribly sorry to call you at night," she was saying to Bill Morgan on the telephone as Harrison let himself in the back door. "And I appreciate you and Harriet taking in this little child at such short notice. The minister says the baby girl is only about two months old—only a tiny thing."

"Poor little mite," Bill said.

"Do you have everything you need? I can bring you extra diapers or formula."

"We're fine, Alice. All prepared. You drive safe."

"Thanks. I'll probably be at your house with the baby within an hour. If you think of anything you or Harriet need, you call me on my cell phone. You know the number. I haven't changed it since the last time."

As Alice talked to Bill, she watched the quiet look of disapproval deepen on Harrison's face. She knew he struggled with the idea that she continued working while trying to parent the Stuart children. This situation certainly didn't make things better. Oh, well, she thought. She wouldn't have involved him at all if she had a better option.

"You know, Hobart might come stay with the children," Harrison said as she hung up. "Then I could drive you. It's late outside. I don't like to think of you out on country roads by yourself at night."

She smiled at him. "I've been going out on night calls like this for over five years, Harrison. I'm used to it. I have a good car for the back roads. Don't worry. It's nice weather now. I've headed out many times before with snow and ice on the ground. I'm a big girl, you know."

"But you *are* a girl." His mouth tightened. "That's the point. There are dangers I wouldn't face that you do."

"I lock my doors well and I know safety measures," she assured him quietly, hoping to avoid an argument with him. "Harrison, thank you for being willing to come. I know it's a terrible imposition. Most of the time there are other back-up people to call, but most of our main administrative staff went out of state to a conference, Odell is out of town at her daughter Shirley's in Atlanta for the weekend, and Donna is sick. This is simply one of those unexpected emergencies."

He frowned then. "Who would leave a baby on a porch step at night?"

"Probably a desperate mother or father," she replied. "Of course, they did call and tell the minister about leaving the baby. That means they probably watched from a point nearby to be sure the minister came before they left."

Needing to leave, Alice gave Harrison a few directions and her cell phone number.

"Go back in my room and get some sleep, Harrison." She put a hand on his arm. "There's a phone by the bed. I won't call unless there's a problem. You should be able to get several hours of sleep before I get back."

"What about you?" he growled.

"I'll get the children off tomorrow, make the calls I need to about the baby, and then catch some extra hours of sleep before the children come home from school. I'll be fine. Don't worry."

She gathered her things and slipped into her lightweight coat. "It's unlikely any of the children will wake up. If they do, they'll come to my room to find me, and you'll be there. Seldom anything but an occasional bad dream wakes them. They're sound sleepers. You get some rest." She headed toward the door, pulling her car keys out of her purse. "I'll be back long before the children get up in the morning."

She turned at the door. "Thank you again." She slipped out the door and left him standing there, glaring.

As it turned out, she got back to Meadowbrook before four am, exactly as she hoped. She'd been able to pick up the baby, thank pastor Carlson and his wife for their help, and take the baby to Bill and Harriet Morgan's without any additional problems or delays. But, admittedly, she was exhausted. It felt wonderful to slip back into the warm house and realize she could get almost three hours of sleep before the children got up. She dropped her attaché and purse on the kitchen table and took off her shoes before she padded back to her bedroom in her stocking feet.

She found Harrison sprawled across the bed, his boots on the floor, and her teal comforter pulled carelessly across him. It was kind of a sweet sight to see him curled up in sleep. She tiptoed past him toward the bathroom.

"You don't have to be so quiet." His voice startled her. "I'm not asleep."

"Well, I certainly want to be asleep soon," she replied, smothering a yawn. "Let me get into the bathroom so I can head that way."

She slipped into the bathroom and stripped out of her work clothes. She attended to her teeth and other necessities, washed her face, and climbed into a loose pair of knit pajamas. Then she unpinned her hair and headed out to her bed.

Alice had expected Harrison to get up while she visited the bathroom, to be back in his boots and ready to leave. Or to have already left for home.

Instead, he still lay on her bed, propped up against two pillows now.

"Alice, tell me about what happened before I go home," he said, patting the space on the bed beside him. "I wouldn't sleep without knowing."

She felt too tired to argue. She climbed under the sheets, and propped up on an extra pillow beside him.

"The little baby was precious." She stifled a yawn. "Good, too. Pastor Carlson and his wife were enjoying her so much I found it hard to get her away from them. She slept in the car on the way over to the Morgan's, and Bill and Harriet took her right up to get her settled in her room. They keep two bedrooms stocked and ready in the upstairs of their house for fosters, one for babies and one for children." She yawned. "They're lovely people."

"Who left this little baby on that porch?" His voice sounded angry.

"We don't know. I found a note in the baby's bag. A childish script saying the baby's name was Lydia. That they couldn't keep her. To please take care of her. Little else. Only the baby's clothes, bottles, diapers, a few toys stuffed in the bag. Nothing personal by which we might find the parents."

"Do you deal with this kind of thing a lot?" He ran a hand through his hair.

"Every case is different, Harrison," she replied, curling up on her pillow and yawning widely again. "But I felt glad I could help Lydia. Take her to a safe place. Give her to someone like the Morgans to love and protect her. You never know what she might have faced where she lived. Possibly neglect or abuse. Maybe drugs or alcohol or parents in trouble with the law. There are all sorts of things."

He frowned. "What will happen to Lydia?"

"We'll use all the resources of the system to try to find who left her at the church. We might get lucky. Then according to the situation we find, a decision will be made about her. Until then we keep her safe in foster homes. The Morgans will keep her temporarily, and then we'll find a more permanent foster home."

"She was such a sweet little thing," Alice added, yawning again. "It felt good to be able to help her. To see she had a safe family to go to right away. To know she would be cared for."

"This is what you do, isn't it?" Harrison asked softly, smoothing back her hair with his hand. "You help children find a safe and loving place to go to when life goes bad for them."

She loved the feel of his hand on her hair. So tender. "It's part of what I do," she told him. "And I do feel it's important."

His hand continued stroking her hair gently. "I'll sleep better knowing that baby got rescued tonight. That she's somewhere safe."

"You helped, too, you know," Alice told him, smiling up at him. "Again, I thank you for that."

He gave her that lopsided smile of his, and Alice saw that flash of dimple in his chin. She noticed his dark wavy hair looked mussed and that a wave of it had slipped down over his forehead. She reached up to smooth it back and saw his eyes darken.

"Did you get some sleep while I was gone?" she asked, trying to lighten the moment.

"No." His voice dropped to a honey drawl. "I kept worrying about you, and the sheets smelled like you. That wasn't conducive to getting any rest for me."

She smiled at him again. "You need to go home Harrison. I'm too tired for flirting tonight."

"It wasn't flirting I had in mind." He leaned over to look down at her with passion in his eyes.

She yawned heavily. "I'm too tired for that, too."

His breathing quickened and he bent to kiss her, but she put a hand up to his chest to stop him.

"No, Harrison," she warned. "This is not a good idea. Not only because I'm tired, but because I own very strong morals. It would test them for you to be closer now."

She traced her finger over his lips softly. "You look good to me, too," she whispered to him. "Altogether too good."

"You're making this harder," he countered in a husky voice, running his own fingers over her lips in return.

Alice pushed at him again. "Go now, and make it easier, Harrison. I've got to catch some sleep. The children get up at 7:00. I need to help them make breakfast, pack lunches, and take them to school before 8:30. Please. I need sleep. Several of the children are experiencing problems at school already; I don't want to make any more."

"What kind of problems?" Harrison sat up reluctantly.

She yawned and rolled over. "Oh for one, I don't think Principal McCarter or his administrative assistant feel very excited about having foster kids in their system."

He interrupted her. "How do you know that?"

"They told me," she murmured, her eyes getting heavy now.

"Is that all?" His voice sounded testy.

"No," she answered on another yawn. "Stacey's having social problems, according to her teacher. Mostly with some little girl named Laura Sue something or other. Rachel's crying again. Isn't making friends or adjusting, her teacher tells me. Has to occasionally come home from school, she gets so upset. And some little boy is threatening and bullying the twins in kindergarten. In kindergarten, of all places. Can you believe it? It especially upsets Thomas."

Alice curled up under the sheets, weariness washing over her.

"I'll tell you more about it tomorrow, if you want," she murmured in a slurred voice. "Now, I'm going to sleep."

She felt Harrison's kiss on her cheek before she drifted off, caught the scent of spice and leather that always lingered around him. She vaguely heard him putting on his boots and leaving, as she drifted into sleep.

The next morning, Alice woke to the alluring smell of morning coffee drifting on the air. She relished it at first, and then looked at her alarm clock in panic, shocked to see the time. Nearly eight o'clock! She couldn't remember hearing the alarm go off.

Alice rolled over and moaned, then got up and headed for the kitchen. As she padded into the kitchen doorway, she found all the children already there, sitting around the table, dressed for school, and finishing up the last of their breakfast. Harrison stood in the kitchen putting dishes in the dishwasher.

"Hi, Alice," called Thomas. "You're supposed to be sleeping in. Harrison came to help us get ready for school because you had a late night."

Hannah sent Alice a sweet smile. "Harrison told us you got called out in the middle of the night to rescue a baby girl and didn't get back until four this morning. He came and woke me us this morning and we made breakfast to let you sleep late."

"Harrison makes good pancakes." Tildy speared another syrup-coated bite with her fork. "It's been fun."

"Megan and I made the school lunches all by ourselves," Stacey bragged, pointing toward the counter.

Alice could see their lunchboxes lined up neatly across the pass-through.

"Go back to bed." Harrison shut the dishwasher and walked back into the dining area. "I'll take the kids over to their school. It's on my way to the post office, and I have to go out, anyway."

"You didn't need to do this," she protested. "In fact, you should not have done this, Harrison. It was enough you helped me out last night."

Hannah crossed her arms and frowned at Alice. "Harrison wanted this to be a nice surprise." She raised her chin. "I think it was very kind of him."

Alice shook her head in defeat.

"All right. You win." She made a haphazard attempt to straighten her hair. "But I'm setting my alarm for ten, you hear? Don't turn it off again. I must make some calls in regard to Lydia then. It's important follow-up."

"No problem." He raised a hand as if to promise. "I've got work of my own to do, too."

"Okay. Thanks again," she said grudgingly as she headed back to her room.

"Enjoy your extra sleep," he said, catching her eye. He actually smiled and winked at her then. Wonders never cease, she thought.

CHAPTER 14

Harrison drove Alice's van to take the children to school. It was either that or pile them all into the back of his pickup truck. When he pulled up to the school, he parked the van and walked the children in.

"You don't have to walk us in, you know," Stacey told him pointedly.

"Yeah, I know," he replied casually. "But I went to school here myself and I haven't stopped by for a long time. I thought I might walk around and visit some. Check who's still around I used to know. Maybe I'll come by your rooms. See where you spend your day."

"We're in Miss Marley's room." Thomas pulled on his hand eagerly. "I can show you where it is."

Harrison bussed his head. "I gotta go see Jack McCarter first. He's an old friend, but I'll come by your room before I leave."

The children scattered off down the hallways, and Harrison stopped to study the bulletins boards and look at the names and pictures of all the teachers before he went to find Jack.

Miss Kimble spotted Harrison the minute he walked in the main office and waved. An institution at Pittman, she'd worked as school secretary for as long as Harrison could remember. Her hair showed grey now in its neat knot on the back of her head, but she still had the same long face and black-framed glasses.

"Well, well. Harrison Ramsey," she exclaimed, getting up to reach across her desk to shake his hand. "You keep getting more handsome every time I see you. What brings you by today? I didn't think we had you scheduled for any talks with the school children."

Harrison gave school talks from time to time on areas he had knowledge and strength in. Jack liked to use the community resources.

Hearing Harrison's voice by then, Jack McCarter came out to offer his own greeting and handshake. Harrison and Jack went back a long way, and Jack's father Curtis McCarter and Harrison's father grew up together.

They two men did the usual back-slapping and made a few jokes to break the ice. Jack, older than Harrison, had taught in Newport at the high school before he finished his administrative degree and applied for the principal's job at Pittman Center. Harrison's father supported his appointment through the school board. Harrison knew, in an indirect way, that Jack owed him.

"Now, what's brought you my way today?" Jack asked.

"I just dropped off some of my favorite kids at the school."

Miss Kimble looked up with interest. "Some of your relatives?"

"No, the Stuart children." He caught their surprised expressions a brief minute before they shut them down and smiled.

He propped a hip on the corner of Miss Kimble's desk. "Do you know whose kids those are?" he asked Jack. "Those are Dr. Richard and Dr. Lauren Stuart's children—the doctors that owned that psychological counseling clinic over on Middle Creek Road. You remember. That's the clinic that always gave our underprivileged kids free evaluations when they needed them. Great people, the Stuarts. I recall Richard a good friend of the Sevier county superintendent of schools, too. He and Lauren gave money for every fund-raiser the school system ran. A real sorrow when they got killed in that tragic car wreck. Big loss to our community area."

Harrison took a slightly malicious pleasure in watching the emotions play over Jack and Miss Kimble's face as he talked.

"Astonishing." Miss Kimble shuffled a pile of papers nervously. "I had no idea those children belonged to Dr. Richard and Dr. Lauren Stuart."

"I find those children much like their parents." Harrison laid his hat on a nearby chair. "Smart, conscientious, resourceful, thoughtful. It's a real pleasure to have them living next door to me as neighbors."

"Nice kids, nice kids." Jack agreed, affably shaking his head up and down.

Harrison picked at a nail casually. "I brought the kids to school today to help Alice Graham out," he continued. "Do you know she went out in the middle of the night to rescue a baby someone simply left on pastor Carlson's church porch? Can you believe someone would do that?"

Miss Kimble clucked over this information.

"Alice Graham put in a long night seeing this two month old baby got safely to the home of one her foster parents. Didn't get in until four am. That's why I volunteered to come bring the children to school."

He toyed with a tape-dispenser on Miss Kimble's desk. "I can't tell you how I admire that woman for the work she does. Now she's taken in Richard and Lauren's children to raise. Only way the kids could stay together. Nobody else would take all of them. She's a real credit to our community, that woman."

More chit chat followed. Sports talk and community gossip. But Harrison knew he'd made his point.

"I promised the kids I'd visit their classrooms before I leave. Meet their teachers" He lifted his eyes to Jack's. "Will that be all right with you?"

"Sure, you know it is." Jack said. "Do you want me to go around with you?"

"No, I can find my way." Harrison stood and smiled. "Just let Miss Kimble give me a list of their teachers, a pass, and a few directions."

"I'll get right to it." She got up to march over to a file.

Five minutes later Harrison strolled down the hall looking for his first classroom and starting his mission. He didn't like learning the Stuart kids had problems at the school and he meant to find out the reasons why.

Oh, he'd heard sleepy snatches of the story about it from Alice last night and more from the children this morning after he asked a few subtle questions.

To be truthful, Harrison liked nothing better than fixing things, resolving problems, and taking on a challenge. Despite what Deke said, Harrison actually could be an artful diplomat when he wanted to. Right now, he wanted to fix this problem for Alice and take away those dark shadows from under her eyes.

Hannah told him how many times Alice had made appointments at the school trying to straighten things out. He knew she'd given her best, but in a small community, a person could ferret out information and get things done faster if not an outsider.

His first visit took him to the seventh and eighth grade wing where the older kids changed classes during the day. Hannah waved at him from a study group in Mrs. Dixon's class and it didn't take him long to learn she had no problems. He found the same thing true for Megan in her fifth grade class with Mrs. Raymond. He stayed around a few minutes in each class, talking about the stable and giving out discount passes for a group trail ride. He'd brought them along thinking they might come in handy today.

He presented the same stable talk to Stacey's third grade in Mrs. Zimmer's class and made a point to identify Laura Sue Palmer.

"I know you." He strolled over and put a hand on her head. "You're Bud and Hazel Jenkins' granddaughter and their daughter Trudi's little girl."

She smiled and tweened at him—a cute child with short brown hair and big grey eyes and a retinue of little girls hanging around her. A girl of charisma and power, Harrison thought.

"I know you, too." She gave him a saucy look. "You come to the market and to my Mama and Daddy's restaurant."

"Palmer Corner Grill." He smiled at her. "Right up the highway, and one of my favorite places to eat, especially for breakfast."

Harrison saw Stacey scowling over the attention he gave her protagonist, and when Harrison gave his attention to Stacey later, the reaction from Laura Sue scored about the same.

Drawing Mrs. Zimmer into the hall before he left, Harrison came straight to the point. "Why do you think Stacey is having trouble at Pittman, Mrs. Zimmer? I know she's strong-willed but, according to Alice, also a good student and popular with other students in the past."

Mrs. Zimmer pursed her lips in thought. "It's seems to be something between Laura Sue and Stacey that causes the most difficulties. I can't figure out why those two girls spar the way they do. Truly, I try to make peace between them, but something always seems to flare up again."

He thought about that while walking to Rachel's room. Her eyes brightened as he stopped at the door and she ran to hug him fiercely—too glad to see him, he thought.

"I don't know why that child is so quiet and shy," her teacher Mrs. Brown confided to him before he left. "You know, she's almost as quiet as the little Draco girl, Jedd and Pauline's youngest." She motioned to the child, sitting and reading, a long brown braid down her back. "Beth's a quiet one, too. Makes me think of Rachel. But Beth has made a friend or two over the years, having always lived here."

Harrison left Mrs. Brown almost grinning. He had two ideas already percolating. Now he only needed to check out the little bully Mason Trent who caused Tildy and Thomas daily trouble.

It didn't take him long to see what he wanted to see. Mason kinged it around the classroom—a cocky, chubby little kid— taller and bigger than most of his fellow kindergarteners, but not a seriously mean bully. Harrison smiled. He could be easily dealt with.

The rest of the day, as Harrison handled routine work and chores, he worked on his plan in his mind. By evening he had it finalized.

During the next week, Harrison didn't see Alice much, her workload heavy, according to Odell. Once or twice when Harrison did see Alice, he thought she eyed him thoughtfully. Probably remembering that night when she climbed into bed with him only dressed in those thin little pajamas. He knew he'd thought about it often enough.

Now tonight, two weeks later, he sat on his front porch, enjoying the early evening and listening to the sounds of the radio filtering out softly from the living room. He thought twilight his favorite time of day. Harrison liked watching the light gradually fade away, the shadows playing over the land. The old snowball bush by the barn always held the light for a short while, its balls of foliage looking like soft lanterns in the darkened yard.

He heard Alice coming down the path before he saw her.

"Nice evening," he said to her as she came nearer to the porch.

"Yes," she agreed, coming up the steps. "It is."

"Want some iced tea?" He stood up. "I'll bring the pitcher out and get another glass for you."

"That would be nice."

When he came back, he saw she'd settled herself in the old rocker across from the glider. Not on the glider beside him like he'd hoped.

He poured her a glass of sweet tea and tossed some fresh mint leaves in it. She sipped it, and they sat in the quiet for a while.

He pointed out the snowball bush to her, glowing in the receding light. Drew her attention to the lightning bugs starting to blink beyond the barn.

"Harrison," she said at last. "I need to be candid. You're interfering too much in the children's and my life. I know it's partly my fault, reaching out and drawing you in more times than I should. But you've moved over the boundaries of what is appropriate the last two weeks."

He chuckled and grinned at her. "What is it you think I've done?"

She gave him a steely no nonsense look that let him know teasing and jesting were out for tonight.

Harrison sighed heavily. "Guess you'd better spit it out, Alice. I'd rather not sit here trying to guess what's upsetting you."

"Don't play innocent with me on this, Harrison." Her eyes narrowed. "There are coincidences that draw people together and get people's lives intertwined inadvertently and then there are deliberate actions that create interference."

He waited for her to air out her thoughts, his foot pushing the glider gently back and forth.

"I think the worst was you getting Thomas to start a fight with that little bully in his class, Mason Trent." She put a hand on her hip. "You know how I feel about fighting as a way to resolve problems. And you deliberately encouraged Thomas to fight Mason. In fact, you and Deke actually gave him fighting tips. Taught him how to throw a punch, as he told me. He actually hit that little boy right in the belly. I had to come home from work and go to the office to see Jack McCarter."

Harrison frowned. "Jack give you some trouble?"

"He should have." Alice's eyes flashed. "But he kept letting it slip how humorous he saw it. Said it was probably time someone belted Mason Trent, but that he needed to call me in and talk about it anyway as principal."

Harrison quirked a smile.

"I saw that smile," Alice accused. "It's the same sort of grin Mr. McCarter kept trying to conceal. I tell you I was furious."

"How'd things turn out for Thomas?" He kept his tone casual.

"As if you didn't know!" She bit out the words. "Thomas gloated all week about how he finally took care of Mason Trent."

He shrugged. "Is Mason Trent giving Thomas and Tildy any trouble at school now?"

"Do stop playing the innocent, Harrison Ramsey." Alice stomped a foot in irritation. "You know perfectly well he's not. In fact, the table's almost turned. It seems Thomas has taken on the role of class leader. Miss Marley says it's quite a change."

"If it's a good change, what's the problem, Alice?"

"It's the fighting. And you coaching Thomas to fight and encouraging him to fight Mason without even consulting me."

He considered this. "You would have told Thomas not to do it."

"Yes, I would have. And that's the point." Her tone grew cross.

Annoyed, he answered back in kind. "No, the point is that

Mason Trent kept bullying Tildy and Thomas and no one could get it resolved in the usual ways. Sometimes the only way to stop a bully is to make a stand and fight back. Most bullies are more talk than action."

"What if that hadn't been true in this case?" protested Alice. "What if Thomas had been hurt?"

"I checked the Trent boy out." Harrison shrugged. "He was soft. I didn't think he'd pose a problem. I figured the odds before I encouraged Thomas to take him on, Alice."

"You figured the odds?" she sputtered. "You checked the boy out? See? That's exactly the sort of thing I'm talking about. It was not your place to do that."

"I care about Thomas and Tildy." Harrison felt stung by her criticism. "I didn't want to see them or any of the other children hurt by this bully. I don't think what I did wrong."

He heard Alice blow out a breath.

"What about this other plot you had?" She raised her eyes to his in challenge. "With Stacey? Do you have an explanation for that interference?"

He lifted a shoulder carelessly. "You told me yourself Stacey's teacher said she had social problems, especially with one girl," he replied. "I decided if a person could just figure out what lay at the root of the problem, then perhaps the problem could be resolved."

She leaned toward him. "You fabricated a plan to get those girls to go off with you one afternoon. Dumped them somewhere out in the middle of nowhere and told them you'd come back later. Stacey said you told them you expected them to talk out their problem with each other and get it resolved by the time you came back."

He felt annoyed. "It worked, didn't it? In my view, whether a plan has merit shows up in the aftermath, in whether it works or not. I'm a pragmatist, Alice."

"Hummph." She snorted. "What if Laura Sue and Stacey had gotten into a fight and hurt each other while you traipsed off somewhere? Or what if a stranger found them out there alone?

What if things hadn't worked out as you planned, Harrison Ramsey?"

"I wasn't far away, Alice. I only told them I would be." Harrison grinned. "See, I know that old campground in the mountains. There's another road into it. I drove out the main road and then sneaked around up the back one. I walked in through the woods to keep an eye on them quiet like."

Alice shook her head in exasperation.

"I figured maybe two things caused the trouble between those girls." He held up two fingers. "One, that Laura Sue was Vance Palmer's sister—the Vance that Hannah chose not to favor. You know, Laura Sue only has one older brother."

Alice's mouth dropped open. "You mean, you actually think that child took a dislike to Stacey simply because Hannah didn't want her brother Vance as a boyfriend?"

He shrugged. "Kids are funny in their reasoning," he explained. "Laura Sue admitted to Stacey that was the reason she didn't like her."

"Honestly." Alice crossed her arms in annoyance. "What was your second thought on what caused trouble between those girls?"

"Laura Sue's got a strong, snappy personality. Somewhat of a natural leader. She held the spot as ringleader of her classmates for some time. As one of the prettiest girls in her class, too. Then along came Stacey." He shrugged meaningfully.

"You're saying she saw Stacey as a rival?" Alice gasped.

"I'd say that formed a subconscious part of it. A queen bee doesn't like to share her throne."

"That's simply unbelievable," Alice retorted.

"How's Stacey getting along at school now?" Harrison kept his voice casual, refusing to be nettled further.

"As if you don't know that, too." She glared at him. "Those two girls came up with an idea to start a third grade club, to have secret names and meet in our playhouse. They said you promoted that idea, too."

"Sometimes kids need a little help to come up with good ideas."

He crossed his foot across his ankle. "Now you've got six third grade girls having a club in your little playhouse. Good use for it, I'd say."

She frowned. "They're using pig-latin names for code names—TaceySay for Stacey and AuraLay UeSay for Laura Sue. Evidently your idea, too."

"We always had fun with pig-latin at school as kids. About time for the idea to be resurrected."

He looked at Alice then. "Isn't the main point here that Laura Sue and Stacey are now friends and new conspirators in their own secret club versus antagonists? For Stacey, especially, that's a nice outcome."

"It's manipulative somehow, Harrison," Alice put in testily. "The children didn't actually solve their own problems. You did."

"No, you've got that all wrong, Alice." He leaned forward. "They did solve their own problems. I only orchestrated an environment in which to do it. I figure, if the good Lord gives you a good idea, it's your obligation to use it. You know the Bible talks about how the peacemaker is blessed. You seem to be turning this all around to make it look like I did something wrong instead of something good."

"Like you did with Rachel, too?" Her voice rose.

Harrison bristled. "Especially like I did with sweet little Rachel. No child needed a friend more than that little girl did. It broke my heart to think of her scared and shy in the classroom. Crying and not having someone to talk with or eat lunch with. It would take a callous man not to want to do something about it."

Alice crossed her arms, her eyes hardening.

She picked her words carefully then. "You came to our house Saturday morning and said you wanted Rachel to go with you to pick out a pretty gift for Odell."

"I did need a gift for Odell," he stated defensively. "Her birthday is coming up next week. I know she likes colorful pottery, especially cookware and vases for her flowers. Jedd Draco and his son Roper make about the prettiest pottery in this area."

Alice interrupted. "And Beth Draco, who is in Rachel's class, simply happens to be their daughter."

"Obviously, that's why I asked Rachel to go with me." Harrison ignored Alice's sarcasm. "Her teacher, Mrs. Brown, actually put the idea in my mind. Said Rachel reminded her of Beth Draco, shy and quiet, too. I know little Beth, you see, and I got to thinking how much those two little girls were alike. Thought if the girls got together outside of school, without the pressure of that environment, they might click."

He leaned back in the glider. "After we visited at the Draco's a short while, Beth's mother invited Rachel to stay for the day. Seems they had new kittens. Rachel got real excited about those kittens. Talked about them—and about Beth—all the way home after I picked her up." He caught Alice's eyes. "I think it would be right nice if you let her have one of those kittens, by the way. She already knows the one she likes best."

She stomped her foot on the porch again. "See? There you go again? Suggesting I let Rachel bring home a kitten. Encouraging her along that line. We own a dog already, Harrison."

"So? Sophie is easy natured; she won't bother a kitten."

"You don't see it, do you? That none of this is your place." She leaned forward toward him, her face flushed with anger now. "These are not your children, Harrison. You're a neighbor, and you're stepping over the line of neighborliness."

He watched her face. "Because I helped little Rachel, and Beth, find a new friend?" He picked at a clump of dirt on his boot. "Pauline says Beth hasn't been this happy in school for years--has her first best friend. What's so wrong with that, Alice?"

Alice got up in a huff, walking over to stand beside the porch railing, her back to him. Harrison observed her hands gripping the railing so tightly her knuckles turned white.

"What's rankling you, Alice? That I helped solve these children's problems instead of you—when this sort of thing is usually your job? Working things out for children. Making their lives happier. Can't anyone else have a go at it without you getting your back bowed up?"

"That's unfair, Harrison," she accused between clenched teeth. "You know I'm not like that at all."

"I used to think not." He studied her rigid posture. "But when you get yourself all whipped up and mad because your children are happier, just because you didn't personally orchestrate the events to make it happen, then I start to wonder."

He stood up and went to stand beside her now. "Yes, I did a little interfering and manipulating with the children. But for a good cause. For their happiness. Believe it or not, Alice, for yours, too. I didn't like the look of worry in your eyes. The dark circles underneath them. The edge of pain I heard in your voice when you tried to be cheerful but felt confused and upset."

"Do you always try to fix everything and everybody?" Her voice sounded tight. "Do you always feel it your place to take control? Just because it seems right? Didn't you ever think it might be good if you talked about all these plans you had with me first before you enacted them? I am the Stuarts' guardian, Harrison. I'm like their mother now. I have a right to be involved in what goes on in their lives. You're being unreasonable and stubborn not wanting to listen to what I'm trying to say to you."

"No, I think I get it, Alice." He moved away from her. "You want me to butt out of the kids' lives. Even if what I do makes their lives better. Because you're the one that's supposed to be in charge. You're the boss. Anyone else who wants to help your kids is a meddler."

"That is not what I said." She whirled around to face him, her face flushed now. "You're twisting my words."

"And you're twisting my actions," he countered harshly.

"I'm going home," she said, her voice breaking now, tears near the surface of her eyes.

But he wasn't moved this time. She'd hurt him. She criticized him and cut him when all he'd tried to do was help the children. When behind all his actions lay a deeper desire to help her because he'd started to care for her.

He saw that now. He'd begun to care. Too deeply. Harrison reined in his emotions, closing them down as the thought struck him.

"There's the path home," he told her curtly.

With that comment, he turned around and walked into his house without looking back.

CHAPTER 15

The weeks of September slipped by and October drifted in. Alice saw many of the trees starting to change color as she drove her rounds through Sevier County. Bright red sumacs threaded the hillsides and yellow tulip poplars marched in sunny profusion along the roadsides. Fall was Alice's favorite time of year, and she usually enjoyed it more.

She sighed heavily as she headed up Highway 321 from Gatlinburg toward her home. Her life lacked its usual balance and happiness.

Mainly because of Harrison. Their relationship altered drastically after their disagreement. She hated, even now, to use the word *fight*.

"I had every right to speak to him," she said to herself, drumming her fingers on the steering wheel. "I wanted Harrison to realize he should talk with me before he devised ways to help the children solve their problems. He interfered in the children's lives without consulting me and I think some of his methods extreme and inappropriate. Like giving Thomas fighting lessons and encouraging him to fight another five year-old at school! Honestly!"

She passed a slow moving car before continuing her thoughts. "I can't believe he dropped Stacey and Laura Sue Palmer at some isolated campground and told them to resolve their problems before he came back. For heavens sake!" Her brow wrinkled in a frown. "They're eight year-old girls."

Alice slowed the van around a curve in the highway. "I expected Harrison to be embarrassed about it when I confronted him. Realize he'd been interfering and manipulative in his ways. Simply apologize. But no!" Her anger flared.

"Instead he acted smug and proud of himself. Pointed to the success of all his actions as justification for doing them. What did he say that night?" She tried to remember. "Oh. That the value of an idea lay in how effectively it worked. He simply refused to see anything wrong with his behavior at all. Stubborn man!"

Alice blew out a breath. He behaved so unreasonably, his accusations and criticisms of her completely out of line. She hated they'd gotten into slinging words back and forth at the end. She knew it no way to reach a resolution, but Harrison acted closed to the idea of compromise.

She drove along quietly for several miles, realizing she didn't feel any better after venting her feelings. In fact, she felt worse.

Her voice quieted. "I hated that hard, stony look on his face at the end." She recalled, a little shame-facedly, that he said he tried to resolve all the children's problems mostly for her sake. He'd grown tender then, but she'd been too angry to acknowledge it, insistent on making her own point.

"Perhaps I made my point too strongly. After all, I was upset." She bit her lip remorsefully as she acknowledged the words. "The result is Harrison has stepped out of my and the children's life almost entirely, and the children miss him. They're beginning to notice his continuing absence."

She sighed and added softly," I miss him, too. Almost the only time I ever see him anymore is at church."

Harrison had talked to the children about giving church another try before the disagreement occurred. He promised Tildy he'd come to church with them if they visited again. She told him she'd be scared of his mother if he wasn't there.

Alice smiled at that remembrance.

They did visit again—and because of the heart-warming welcome they received—the children asked to go back the next Sunday, as long as Harrison came, that is. They attended every week now. They liked Reverend Campbell, a good preacher and very congenial, and they loved the gospel-flavored music led by

James Parton every Sunday. His quartet, the Parton Boys, came to services most Sundays and often tried out new songs they'd written on the congregation. The children thought it exciting the Parton Boys were recording artists in the gospel music industry with James Parton related to Dolly Parton in some remote way. As for Mozella, she'd acted polite and cordial, as though past events had never occurred.

"At least in other areas, life is good." Alice rolled down the window to let in a little fresh air. "My workload has settled down, I completed my fall teaching responsibilities at the agency, and I've had no crisis placements to deal with for some time. All my foster children are progressing happily in their placement homes and I actually helped place several children for adoption. That's always rewarding."

Her thoughts drifted to the Stuart children again. After the bad beginnings at school, all were doing better now and had even started getting involved in community activities and clubs—modern dance for Hannah, 4-H for Megan, Brownies for Stacey and Rachel, and Tildy and Thomas engrossed in a new kindergarten project, collecting different types of Tennessee rocks. Quite a collection now marched across the screen porch rails – quartz, copper, shale, limestone, slate, marble, sandstone, humps of coal, a few fossils and arrowheads. Their teacher, Miss Marley, an avid geologist, had passed on her enthusiasm to the kids. They spent hours looking for new rocks to take to school for show and tell.

Thinking about the twins' project, Alice turned into Parton's Place as she neared home. Donna said the store carried a pocketsize guidebook about rocks and minerals, and Alice wanted one for Tildy and Thomas.

A typical Smoky Mountain craft store, Parton's Place carried a nice mixture of mountain crafts and gifts, tourist interest items, and sweets. The rustic building, of weathered grey wood, sported benches and tables of the same color on the porch along with a potpourri of flowers. Inside, Millie and Donna had divided the store into thematic sections, making it more fun for browsing.

"Hi, Alice," Donna called from behind the counter, as Alice pushed open the front door. "Come and meet Millie's daughter, Ivey Parton."

Alice walked over to greet a young woman, garbed in what Alice would term hippy dress, her hair hanging down her back in a long, dark braid. She wore a tie-died skirt, peasant blouse, and a lightweight, fuchsia hand-woven jacket.

"Ivey, this is Alice Graham who lives at Meadowbrook now." Alice and Ivey exchanged hellos.

"Ivey is Beecher's wife—he's Millie and James Parton's youngest son, the one that's a forest ranger." Donna straightened a row of jellies near the counter. "Ivey is a weaver. She's wonderful, Alice. She made that gorgeous woven jacket she's wearing and supplies us with beautiful things to carry from her shop. She owns a small place down in the Glades."

The Glades was a local nickname for the Arts and Craft Community not far outside of Gatlinburg. Many local artists—potters, weavers, painters—had working studios and shops along the loop route. Alice's favorite, the Jim Gray Gallery, filled a historic, 100-year old church building on Glades Road.

The three women talked for a few minutes, and then Ivey left.

"The store's empty for a while." Donna's eyes scanned the aisles. "Let's go sit down at one of the tables in the sweets section and have a cola. I can watch the door from there in case anyone comes in."

Alice walked over to settle into a chair. "I want a bag of yogurt-covered raisins from the sales case, too, while you're getting my drink." She grinned. "I'm snack hungry."

Donna brought over their drinks and snacks and sat down with Alice, propping her elbows on the table. "Did you notice how pained Ivey looked when we talked about our children?" she asked. "Bless her heart. She and Beecher have tried to have a child for about four years now. Visited a fertility specialist and everything, Millie said, with no luck. It's a shame, because I think they'd both make wonderful parents."

Alice considered this thoughtfully. "Do you remember that baby girl left on the porch of the Carlson's church?"

Donna nodded, popping a yogurt raisin in her mouth.

"We received release from the family for the baby to be adopted." Alice leaned forward. "The mother is underage, unwed, and her family doesn't want to raise the child. The father was a pass-through, and much older. We haven't found a way to track him, and he won't desire to be found, anyway, with the girl underage. Usually in cases like this, the family keeps the baby, but in this instance, they think it best for the daughter to release the baby for adoption. She hid the pregnancy, and they want her to finish high school. Have a more normal teenage life."

"You mean you think Ivey and Beecher might have a chance to adopt this baby?" Donna's eyes widened with excitement. "Oh, Alice, they would be thrilled."

"I think it might be a possibility." Alice considered it. "The baby, Lydia, is staying at the Morgan's, one of our temporary homes. We just started the search for a more permanent foster home when we learned she might be adoptable. Bill and Harriet volunteered to keep her longer because of that. I think my director would like the idea of Lydia going to a local couple with a good background like Beecher and Ivey's, even though we have connections to an adoption agency in Knoxville. The baby is from a nice family, and there's even a bit of a resemblance between Ivey and the baby's mother. It's what gave me the idea, that and your comment about Ivey wanting a child so much."

"I'm tickled I said something." Donna grinned with pleasure. "I'll give you Ivey and Beecher's address and phone. They're in our store file. I'll be a reference, if needed. I've known Ivey and Beecher since I started working at Millie's." She paused. "Oh, Millie and James will be thrilled! It would be a grandchild for them."

Alice shook a cautionary finger at her. "Now don't you say anything to them, or to anyone else, until I do some checking, Donna. Beecher and Ivey should be the first to share news about a new baby if this works out."

"Mum's the word." Donna zipped her lips, smiling. She got up to answer the phone, and then came to sit back down.

"It's been quiet today for a Friday." Donna looked around the store. "But it will get busier with the leaves turning. The tourist traffic will pick up as the color starts to peak."

"Hey, Alice." Donna eyed her thoughtfully. "What's the story about you and Harrison having a fight?"

"Who told you that?"Alice twisted her hands.

"DeeDee, I think. Or possibly Odell. Both mentioned it. DeeDee heard Hobart tell Deke you and Harrison had a spat. Odell said she thought you had a falling out because she hadn't seen much of Harrison lately."

Noticing Alice looked upset, Donna grinned. "It's hard to keep any secrets around a small area like ours, Alice."

"We didn't exactly have a fight." Alice's shoulders sagged. "Only a small disagreement."

"What sort of disagreement?' Donna probed.

"Oh, one about the children." She hated to answer. "If tell you, but I don't want you repeating this, Donna."

"I promise not to." Donna made an X across her heart and then her mouth.

"Gracious, Donna, that's what the children do." Alice giggled, then munched a few raisings as she decided how to begin.

"Donna, do you remember when Harrison got involved in helping resolve the younger children's school problems?"

She nodded. "Yeah, I remember the kids talking about it."

"Harrison never discussed any of those ideas with me first, Donna." Alice lifted her chin. "He just decided to resolve things— and then did. I spoke to him and encouraged him to talk with me in future before he simply handled things like that with the children."

"You mean *that* was the fight?" She wrinkled her nose in confusion.

Yes."Alice laced her fingers. "Harrison didn't like the idea of checking with me about situations involving the kids."

"That can't be all the story." Donna looked skeptical. "That's not enough to constitute a fight or enough reason for Harrison to be avoiding you and the kids."

Alice sighed. "He behaved very stubbornly about the whole thing. Refused to admit he'd done a thing wrong in taking charge. In fact, he acted downright smug about how positively things turned out due to his intervention. He suggested I felt jealous because he resolved things effectively when I hadn't been able to."

"Harrison actually said that?" Donna's mouth opened in surprise.

"Not exactly in those words." Alice dropped her eyes. "But he did refuse to see any of my points about the ways he intervenes too freely. In the end, he simply got mad and said he'd butt out entirely in the future."

"Pride," Donna pronounced. "Men are so proud about their ways of handling and doing things. They hate to consider they can be wrong, and Harrison isn't much of a man to ask permission before doing what he thinks is the right thing at any time. He's kind of a man-of-action guy. A take-charge type."

"Donna, he took charge *too* much." Alice crossed her arms in exasperation.

Donna sipped her cola, thinking. "If you think about it, everything did work out for the best, Alice, and no harm done."

"You sound like Harrison!" exclaimed Alice. "Honestly, Donna, he taught little Thomas to fight. He and Deke coached him. They encouraged Thomas to confront Mason Trent at school. I got called to the principal's office after Thomas punched that boy in the stomach."

"Maybe that's what it takes to stop a bully." Donna spread her hands.

"I disagree." Alice frowned. "I don't think violence is ever the answer."

"You and Harrison had some different viewpoints." Donna shrugged. "That happens a lot between couples."

"Harrison and I are not a couple." Alice snapped out the words.

Donna lifted her shoulders again. "Whatever you say, Alice." She twirled her straw in her glass. "But I know the children will miss Harrison. Everyone has observed the bond that's developed between him and the Stuarts. I think it's kind of sweet, considering what an old-bachelor-to-himself Harrison had become before all of you came."

"Are you purposely playing protagonist?" Alice asked in irritation.

"No, I'm trying to be fair." Donna lifted a brow. "It doesn't seem to me like Harrison did anything terribly wrong. He has a lot of ties in the valley and through the school. And you're new here. He knew ways to resolve the problems the children had that you didn't. I think it nice of him to care and to try to help. Most men wouldn't do that. Alice, I remember you almost at your wits end with the upsets of the children at school, and now they're happy. Everything did work out for the best, even if you don't especially like the methods Harrison used."

"Nevertheless, I think Harrison owes me an apology." Alice hugged her arms to herself in annoyance. "He acted smug and arrogant instead of being understanding when I went to talk to him. He said some very ugly things to me."

Donna lifted an eyebrow. "Did you stay calm and sweet through all this and say nothing you regret?"

Alice gave her a dirty look.

Donna smiled. "I'm playing devil's advocate. That's the way my mother talks to me when Vick and I have a fight. She says no fight happens without both parties being involved."

"What else does your mother say?" Alice glared at her.

"To kiss and make up," Donna said teasingly, grinning at Alice. "Oh, come on, Alice, don't be mad at me. I simply hate to see you and Harrison fussing. You had a nice relationship going, and he did some sweet things for you and the children before this happened. Like coming and staying that night when you had to go out to rescue the baby, defending you against his own mother at that church incident, and giving all the kids riding lessons. He's been a good friend, Alice."

"What do you think I should do?" Alice stared at her angrily. "Go apologize to him?"

"Maybe you don't have to go that far." Donna offered an encouraging smile. "Just put out the olive branch of peace. You know, like the Bible says: 'Blessed are the peacemakers.'"

Alice frowned. "I'm not ready to put out an olive branch. And I don't think I asked anything unreasonable of Harrison—by simply suggesting he consult with me about actions he wants to take in relation to the children. I am their guardian, and it's my right to be involved."

"Oh, well." Donna lifted a shoulder. "Perhaps Harrison will take the first step with you. If he does, Alice, don't bite off his head."

A group of customers came in the store and Alice, rankled by the continuing conversation, decided it a good time to leave. She'd expected Donna to side fully with her in this situation. Hiding her annoyance, she bought her rocks guide, paid for her cola and yogurt-raisins, and said her goodbyes. She needed to get home before the children got home from school anyway.

Arriving home ahead of them, Alice decided to make lasagna for supper. Odell cooked most weekdays when Alice worked, but not on Friday. Alice always took off early on Fridays for family night.

After a happy dinner, she and the children cleared off the table for Friday night Bingo. Alice had wrapped the rocks guidebook and set it aside as a prize for one of the twins, in case either of them won a bingo game.

She saw Thomas on the screen porch peering out the door.

"Why don't you come in and give out the Bingo cards to everyone, Thomas?" she called. "I don't think you'll see any lightning bugs tonight. It's too late in the fall."

His face dropped as he came back in the kitchen. "I was looking for Harrison," he explained. "Me and Tildy asked him to dinner and game night. I thought he would come."

Alice kept her tone light. "Did he say he would come?"

"No." He gave her a troubled look. "He said he thought he would be busy. But I hoped maybe he'd change his mind."

He looked up at Alice then.

"Hobart told Deke you and Harrison were mad at each other. I heard them talking about it." He shuffled his feet. "Is it because I fought with Mason Trent at school? I know you said I shouldn't have fighted with him."

"It's not that," Alice reassured him.

"Are you sure?" Thomas mouth formed a pout. "Megan said you were real mad about it."

Megan shrugged when Alice sent a pointed glance her way. "You were mad about it. Odell called it sputtering mad." She tried not to snigger.

"Odell exaggerates." Alice tried to keep her voice from becoming testy.

Rachel sighed. "I miss Harrison," she said on a wistful note. "I don't want him to be mad at us. He helped me find Beth for a friend, and he said he'd like for me to have a kitty."

Alice rolled her eyes at that.

Stacey flounced into a chair at the table. "I think you're mad at Harrison because he took me and Laura Sue to that campsite," she pronounced. "You called it a wrong thing for him to do that. I bet you told him that and he didn't like it."

"You did go over to talk to him." Hannah came in from the kitchen to sit down. "I bet that's when you had the fight."

Alice bit down on her rising annoyance. "Listen, we didn't have a fight. We simply didn't totally agree about a few things. But it's nothing for you to worry about."

Thomas gave her a cross look. "It is if Harrison doesn't want to be our friend anymore. He was the only other man besides me, and I like him."

Tildy jumped in to agree with him. "I like him, too."

Hannah gave Alice a thoughtful look. "You know, Alice. I think Harrison only meant to help with the things he did, like the day he came and made breakfast when you'd been out late. He just wants to be a good friend to us."

Rachel started to cry at that point. "Do you think Harrison isn't going to be our friend anymore because he's mad at us?"

"He's not mad at us," clarified Stacey. "He's mad at Alice, because they had a fight."

Rachel turned wide eyes to Alice's. "Couldn't you just say you're sorry, Alice?" she asked. "That's what you tell us to do when we have fights."

"This isn't exactly the same thing." Alice tried to explain.

"It never is when adults are involved," Stacey declared saucily, passing the other children a significant look.

Alice took a deep breath. "Look, I'm sure Harrison is not angry at any of you, and even if we disagreed over a few points, I don't think he is angry at me. I'm sure he'll be back over to visit soon. Also, tomorrow is Saturday. You'll probably see him at the stable, plus you'll see him on Sunday at church."

"It's not the same." Thomas's voice sounded sorrowful. "He makes game night more fun."

They were all too quiet for a minute after that.

"You know, Harrison isn't a part of our family." Alice chose her words carefully. "He may have visited our game night a time or two to be a nice neighbor, but that doesn't mean he'll want to keep coming for that. He has his own life and friends—and probably has other things he'd rather do with his Friday nights."

Alice smiled at them. "But we're all here, and I think we should play Bingo like we always do. Are you all ready?"

The children rallied then. They played four games of Bingo and then Clue afterwards in teams. Alice saw, with relief, that their moods all lightened as they played and laughed over their games.

The next morning, the old familiar camaraderie at the breakfast table returned. After all, it was Saturday—and sunny and warm outside. All the children had plans for the day and they were gaily discussing them.

"Me and Thomas are going to look for rocks." Tildy chimed in. "And use the new rock book we won in Bingo." She beamed at Alice in gratitude.

Thomas mumbled something about how Harrison had promised to take them somewhere to look for pink quartz but got interrupted by Megan.

"Rhoda says there are arrowheads in that big mound across the street from her house." She loaded the last of the breakfast dishes into the dishwasher. "Her daddy said some of the locals believe the mound might be an Indian mound. You could go over there and look for arrowheads."

Both twins replied to this idea with enthusiasm

Alice stood up, looking at her watch. "Megan, we need to leave. I promised to pick up Rhoda to take her to the 4-H meeting with you." She smiled at the twins. "Maybe I can drop you two over at the Nichols to look for rocks in the mound. You can stay with Donna until I get back."

"Oh, boy." Thomas bounded out of his chair with Tildy soon right behind him.

Stacey waved her hand. "You have to take Rachel and me into Sevierville to pick up our Brownie uniforms, too. We have to try them on to be sure we get the right size."

"I forgot about that." She looked toward Thomas and Tildy's bright faces. "I'm sure the twins can stay with Donna while we go into town—or come back to the house to stay with Hannah until we get back."

Hannah looked up at mention of her name. "That would work. DeeDee and I are going riding this morning, but we're doing a homework project here all afternoon, a display on planets for our science presentation. Donna already got us the poster board and supplies yesterday."

"Good." Alice smiled. "I'll call Donna and see if that will be all right. If she's not real busy, I think I'll stop at the grocery on the way home, too. And hopefully at the shoe store sale to see if I can find Rachel and Stacey new shoes while I have them with me."

"I want black tennis shoes." Stacey flounced out of her chair. "Laura Sue got black ones, and they're awesome. Her mother says they don't get dirty very easily." She added this last comment as a sales point in her favor. Alice grinned. She often thought Stacey had the argumentative skills of a seasoned attorney.

Alice headed toward her bedroom to call Donna and get her

purse. "Everyone who's going with me go brush your teeth and get whatever you need to take with you. We'll meet at the car."

It wasn't until the end of that long, busy Saturday that Alice realized the twins were missing. Hannah thought they'd spent the day over at Donna's looking for rocks, but Donna claimed she walked the twins across the highway and down the drive shortly before lunch. She said the twins wanted to go home, play in the back yard and look for creek rocks. They'd had no luck finding any arrowheads in the mound.

No one panicked at first. They searched the house, the yard, and around the creeks near the house. Then they went calling and hunting across Harrison's property and checked at the stable. Hobart said they hadn't seen the twins all day. Next, because Alice remembered telling Tildy and Thomas she'd bought their rock guide at Parton's, she and Megan drove to the store to check to see if the twins might be there. But Millie hadn't seen them all day.

By the time Alice and Megan got back, it was suppertime. Hannah had made sloppy joes while everyone looked for the twins. They all sat down to eat a quick bite, thinking the twins would pop in any moment, realizing the time.

"Thomas has his watch now," offered Megan. "He knows how to tell time now. I taught him, and he and Tildy both know they're supposed to be home by dinner at 5:30 no matter what. I'll bet they'll show up any minute."

But they didn't show. By six everyone started to panic.

Hannah paced the kitchen, tears threatening in her eyes. "Is this my fault?" She wrung her hands. "Should I have checked at Donna's?"

"No, it's not your fault," Alice assured her, trying to stay unruffled for the children. "You know the twins often willfully take off and don't tell anyone where they're going. I've talked to them over and over about it, but it hasn't done any good. Let's stay calm and remember that we always find them."

"Maybe we should call the police," suggested Stacey, which immediately made Rachel tune up and start to cry.

"No, we need to go out and search again." Alice stopped to think. "Rachel and Stacey, you look around the yard one more time. Don't go further than that. If the twins come back, ring the big bell hanging in the back yard to let us know they're home. Hannah, you call DeeDee and see if she and Rhoda will go look around the mound again, in case the twins went back over there. After that, you and Megan go search all along the creek behind the house. Follow it down toward the Greenbrier Road and check the trails skirting off from it. Come back by seven. I don't want you out in the dark. I'm going over to Harrison's place to look and to check again at the Ramsey Stable. I'm sure the twins will turn up." She attempted a smile. "They'll probably offer a pile of explanations and apologies like they always do when we find them. Try not to worry."

But Alice was worried. She had a fight with herself as she walked over toward Harrison's place. She wanted to ask him to help and needed him to help. It created an inner turmoil for her. Finally, she marshaled her courage and went boldly to knock on his door, but found no one home. When she got to the stable, she found the gate locked and closed and no one there, either.

CHAPTER 16

Harrison felt oddly restless, as he had all day. Saturday proved a big day with all his businesses—packed with work and problems to deal with. Tourists checked in and out of the rental cabins in droves, and with the fall weather nice, the stables attracted riders throughout the day. Harrison started pickers working early in the day, with several varieties of apples ready at the orchard, and drew a brisk trade at the apple shed beside the highway. As an added aggravation, a pipe sprang a leak at the W.T. Market after lunch, but, luckily, he and Deke fixed it.

He'd avoided going to game night at Meadowbrook last night. Thomas' disappointed face, when he said he might be too busy to come, haunted him.

"But it's more fun with you," Thomas pleaded with the innocence of childhood. "You make the boy numbers better." He smiled engagingly then, almost turning Harrison's heart over.

"Can't you try to come?" He put his small hand in Harrison's. "Please?"

Harrison told the boy he'd try, even when he knew he had no intention of trying to come at all, still seriously avoiding Alice Graham.

It had been a long time since a woman drew close enough to Harrison to hurt him, and he remembered all too clearly the feeling. He didn't want any more of it. He'd walked that route twice before in his life already.

Harrison's caring for Alice Graham sneaked up on him. It had been easy for it to happen with all the mystery and chemistry between them and with him being around her all the time with the kids. But he had to back off now. She'd made it clear she wanted him to. And for his own sanity and safety, he needed to.

However, restless feelings haunted him—especially today. Hobart said he hadn't acted fit to live with for weeks, but Harrison knew he exaggerated. The old man always did, but Harrison knew he hadn't been the best of company. He missed Alice, and, dang, if he didn't miss the kids, too. They'd all sort of slipped into his life, so that now his old solitary life without them didn't seem as natural and easy anymore.

Harrison angled Bishop around a log across the trail, and swung left off Old Settler's Trail onto one of his own horse trails. He'd ridden up to old Backcountry Campsite #33 on the mountain this afternoon and out to Overlook Point, a longer ride than he usually took. He hoped to wear himself out so he'd sleep better than last night.

He thought about Alice as he rode down the trail toward home, about how angry she'd acted that night. Strange to see her angry when she usually behaved with such calm and control. The only other time he remembered seeing her temper flare was when he first kissed her in the barn a long time ago.

"I must have a certain sort of magic with women," he told Bishop bitterly. "They always seem to get provoked with me after a while. Tired of me. Guess I'm too ordinary a guy."

Looking back on that evening with Alice, Harrison still couldn't figure out why the woman had acted so upset. Heck, he'd thought she'd come to thank him for working out those problems for the kids—all unhappy and troubled at school. He'd resolved it all for her. It didn't make sense to Harrison why she felt put out about that. Oh, he knew a lot of women felt funny about men handling certain issues with their fists. Even when it proved the best way. He'd suspected Alice might be upset with him about that, but the rest he couldn't understand at all.

Harrison thought his idea for working out Stacey's problem close to brilliant, and he couldn't understand why she objected to him finding a little friend for Rachel. Everyone thought it sweet to watch she and Beth Draco play together now.

That was the point, of course. Harrison couldn't see he'd done anything but good. Oh, perhaps, he should have put Alice more in the loop with it all. But she didn't come from this area—didn't know the ins and outs like he did. He expected her to be grateful, not mad, about what he'd done.

Harrison scowled. He and Alice spoke a string of harsh words that evening, and she'd made no effort since to patch it up. She made it quite clear she wanted him out of their lives—called him manipulative. Said he interfered too much in her and the children's lives. She told him solidly it wasn't his place to help the kids, reminded him he was only a neighbor. That woke him up smartly to realize he'd started to think of himself as more than a neighbor in her life. Guess he'd gotten that wrong.

Halfway down the trail, Harrison paused at a trail intersection—not sure why. He usually rode straight downhill and across Chestnut Branch to the backside of the stable. Today, he felt a memory drift across his mind.

He'd told Thomas he might bring him to the old Ramsey cabin one day to look for pink quartz in the rocky ledge behind it. Perhaps he'd drop by a minute before heading home, see if he could find a couple of pieces of quartz for the boy. He glanced up toward the sky. It wasn't quite dark yet, and it might help make it up to the child that he couldn't come over often anymore.

So Harrison turned Bishop left along the Redwine Ridge trail instead of down the main horse trail. He could check the old family cabin, too. In the past, a few drifters had tried to settle in it from time to time.

Here in Greenbrier, as in many other areas of the Great Smoky Mountains National Park, old family cabins, churches, and schools still stood—looking much as they did in the 1800s. Although the park took a sizeable chunk of the original Ramsey lands, one of the old family cabins remained on the ridge. The park allowed the Ramsey family to help maintain the cabin, mostly because the family graveyard lay behind it. Although only a two-room cabin with a loft room above you couldn't get to without climbing a ladder, the place held a lot of memories.

When Harrison's grandfather started the Ramsey Stable in the 1940s, he capitalized on the location of the old cabin and plotted one of the shorter horse trails to ride past it. He found a few old furniture pieces to put in the house, so riders could stop get off their horses for a break at the cabin, look inside the rooms, and walk around back to see the family cemetery. With his father gone, it had become Harrison's responsibility to keep up the site and the family grave plots.

A favorite place since childhood, Harrison had explored the area extensively in boyish games. That's when he discovered the veins of pink quartz in a rocky area behind the cabin. Even if no quartz pieces lay on the ground today, he could loosen a pretty chunk or two for Thomas with his pocketknife.

As he rounded the corner to the cabin today, he heard an anguished voice calling him. Even before the identity of the voice registered, he saw Thomas running into the pathway toward him, grimy and soiled, with tears streaking down his face.

He reined Bishop in quickly, before the horse spooked, and then slid out of the saddle to put himself between the big horse and the small boy heading his way.

Thomas threw himself against Harrison's legs, grabbing his arm to pull him.

"Come quick." He raised frightened young eyes to Harrison's. "It's Tildy, and she's hurted. I got her into the old house to be safer, but she's hurted bad, Harrison."

Harrison quickly followed the little boy into the cabin, where he found Tildy huddled on an old bench against the back wall, her face grubby and tear-streaked, too.

She started a new spate of tears—of sheer relief—when she saw Harrison. "Thomas said he was praying for you to come," wept Tildy. "I'm hurted, Harrison."

He tried to gather her into his arms, but she winced right away and drew her arm up against herself in pain.

Harrison brushed her hair back and kissed her forehead.

"I know you bear some hurts, darlin', but you need to tell me where and let me look to check you out."

"My arm hurts bad and my leg, too." She looked from one to the other, sniffling.

"She couldn't walk on her foot," Thomas added, biting his lip with worry. "I had to carry her in here from out back all by myself."

Tildy rubbed her arm. "Thomas said he thought I was deaded cause I fainted," she explained.

Harrison smoothed his hands gently over Tildy, deciding she probably had a break in her arm and possibly a strain or another break in her ankle. He felt a rising knot on the back of her head, and saw angry scratches in several places on her face and arms.

"Tell me what happened," Harrison said to Thomas.

Thomas hung his head. "We went to Donna's to stay this morning. We looked for arrowheads in the mound while Alice shopped. There weren't any so we asked Donna to come back home and stay with Hannah 'til Alice came back."

"Donna walked us home, but we didn't go in the house and tell Hannah we came back," confessed Tildy, tears dripping out of her eyes. "We were bad. We wanted to find some pretty rocks to take to Miss Marley on Monday. Thomas remembered you said we might find some behind this old house. We walked up here to look."

"Tildy and I forgot it was real far." Thomas shook his head. "Usually we ride the horses when we come to the cabin. But we 'membered where to come. We thought we'd find some rocks and go back before Alice came home or anyone knew we were gone."

"But we had a problem," Tildy said with a small regretful sigh. "I fell."

Thomas began to explain. "We got hungry, and we saw apples in the tree behind the house." He paused to take a breath. "So we decided to climb up and get some. I got up pretty high, and Tildy climbed up behind me but her branch broke. She fell a long way down the tree. It looked real scary. I climbed down as quick as I could, but she wouldn't wake up then."

"She got knocked unconscious?" Harrison felt a shiver of alarm.

Thomas nodded. "She wouldn't wake up at first. I thought she was deaded. I got really, really scared. But then, she woke up and I carried her into the cabin."

"How long do you think she was out?" Harrison probed.

Thomas shrugged. "I don't know. A little while after she fell. I don't know how long. When she woke up, she cried, and I could tell she was hurted bad then. I had to try to carry her because she couldn't walk. It hurted her to try and her arm hurted. I thought about going to get some help, but she acted too scared for me to go."

"I didn't want Thomas to leave me," Tildy cried.

He nodded solemnly. "I felt scared to leave her, too," he confessed. "Because of her not waking up and because of her not being able to walk."

Tildy sucked in a deep breath and leaned against Harrison for comfort. "Something might have tried to get me, and I wouldn't be able to get away."

Thomas pulled on Harrison's sleeve to draw his attention. "Did I do the wrong thing, Harrison?" His young eyes held anguish now. Harrison rubbed his back. "No, Thomas. You did the right thing, and I think it very strong and brave of you to carry Tildy into the safety of the cabin all by yourself. I know that must have been hard."

He shook his head affirmatively.

"I'm real proud of you, son." He put a hand on the boy's shoulder. "You've taken real good care of Tildy. Now we've got to get her ready to ride down the mountain to get more help."

Harrison let Thomas stay with Tildy for a few minutes while he went outside to get some flat sticks he could shape quickly with his knife into temporary splints. These he wrapped securely with a bandana from his saddlebag around Tildy's arm to immobilize it for the ride back. Then with Tildy in front on Bishop, and Thomas behind her holding her steady, he began the walk back down the mountain leading his stallion.

"We're gonna be in big trouble," said Thomas after a little while, frowning.

"Probably," Harrison admitted.

"Will Tildy have to go to the hospital?"

"Probably," Harrison answered again.

He heard Tildy whimpering and turned to speak to her. "When you fall from a tree and hurt your bones, Tildy, a doctor has to look at you."

"Will I have to get a cast?" Her eyes grew wide.

"I would expect so," he answered her honestly. "Especially on your arm. I think there's a break in your bone there. But I don't think it's real bad. The doctor will want to look at your leg and at your head where you bumped it. The doctor and his staff will clean up all your scratches, too."

"Do you think Alice will send us away because we were real bad?" he heard Tildy whisper to Thomas.

Harrison stopped Bishop and walked around to look up at Tildy and hold the little girl's hand in his. "Alice would never send you away, Tildy. You must never think that. She loves you."

"She sent you away," Thomas muttered, his lower lip trembling.

"That's not true, Thomas," corrected Harrison. "And I'm not Alice's child, like you are. I'm her neighbor and your friend. It's different."

Tildy squeezed his hand, tearing blue eyes looking into his. "I love you, Harrison."

He felt a lump in his throat. "I'm mighty fond of you, too, young lady. And, don't you worry. You're going to be just fine. You'll see."

"I'm glad you came, Harrison," Thomas said softly, his eyes large. He patted the boy's leg. "So am I, Thomas. So am I."

About twenty minutes later, they came to the bottom of the mountain at last and cut through the back property of Meadowbrook alongside Timothy Creek. Darkness nearly shrouded them now, but Harrison heard Alice shrieking the twins' names even before he saw her running across the yard toward him in the fading light.

"Oh, Harrison, thank God you found them," she cried before she launched herself into his arms, nearly knocking him over. "I went to your house, you know. I looked for you to help me. Oh, Harrison, I'm sorry about what's happened between us. About all the things I said. I prayed I would find you so you could help me find Tildy and Thomas. And now you're here."

She babbled and cried all at the same time, but the words felt sweet to Harrison's ears. As did her arms wrapped around him.

"Tildy's hurt." Harrison pulled her arms gently away from him to look down in her face. "We're going to need to take her to the hospital. I think she's broken her arm. Possibly sprained or broken her ankle, too. She had a bad fall."

Alice broke away from him to rush to the twins then, soothing and comforting and asking questions all at the same time.

When they arrived at the house, the other children swarmed around them. And they all wanted to go to the hospital with Tildy.

"None of you are going." Alice stated this firmly. "This will be complicated and difficult enough. All of you need to stay at the house with Hannah. I'll call Odell to come over, too. I don't know how late it may be when we get back. Hospital emergency rooms are slow places. If we're very late, you can all go on to bed. Right now, I'm going to go pack a bag for Tildy with some fresh clothes and some of her things."

As she turned to go, Harrison stopped her gently. "I think Thomas and Megan should go with us," he told her firmly. "Thomas is a part of this and part of Tildy. And Megan is like their other mother. She needs to go."

Megan started weeping at that and threw her arms around Tildy.

Alice looked at Harrison, defiantly at first, ready to argue. Then, to Harrison's surprise, she said, "You're right, Harrison. Thomas and Megan should go. Megan, get some things for Thomas he might need. Some clean clothes and a few books for while we wait."

She pulled the van keys out of her purse and handed them to Harrison. "If you wouldn't mind, maybe you could bring the van around to the front? It will be easier for me to carry Tildy out if you do."

"I'll get the van." He held out his arms. "But let me take Tildy now, Alice, and settle her in the back seat of the van gently. I don't want us to move her any more than we have to. You go make your call to Odell and get what you'll need for the hospital."

Within forty-five minutes they'd checked into the emergency room at the Sevier Medical Center on Middle Creek Road. When they experienced a short hold-up in the emergency check-in area, Harrison made it a point to find someone on staff he knew and to tell them they were admitting Dr. Richard and Dr. Lauren Stuart's youngest child. The Stuarts' former clinic sat right across from the hospital, and within ten minutes, a doctor who'd worked with Richard and Lauren came to check on Tildy. Harrison encouraged Alice and Megan to stay with Tildy for her x-rays and checks, while he took Thomas out to the waiting room to stay with him.

Thomas explored the waiting area restlessly at first, asking about what might be happening with Tildy. Then as dark fell more fully outside, and the waiting room quieted, he came to sit beside Harrison on the sofa, leaning his head against his side.

"Harrison?" he asked quietly. "Do you think God really heard my prayer that you'd come and find us?"

Harrison considered this quietly for a minute. "Yeah, I'd say that's a real possibility," he answered finally, as honestly as he could. "While heading home down the main riding trail, I felt led to stop at the intersection of the Redwine Ridge trail. I don't usually stop there. Then in an odd way I remembered you wanted some of that pink quartz behind the cabin. I decided to ride over to look for some."

"And usually you wouldn't have?" Thomas asked, wide-eyed.

"No, not usually."

Thomas nodded thoughtfully at that.

They sat silently for a time then. The waiting room had grown quieter with only a few small groups of people waiting for news of their loved ones.

"Harrison?" Thomas leaned tighter against him. "Are you borned again?"

This one took Harrison by surprise. "Why do you ask?"

Thomas looked up at him with the candor only found in young children. "Cause when I thought Tildy was deaded I worried about it. Our Sunday School teacher said we all needed to be borned again so we could go and live with God someday. She said when we got older we could decide about that for ourselves." He frowned. "It seems to me like we need to decide sooner. Cause me and Tildy haven't decided yet, and she might have been deaded today and I might have been deaded, too, if no one found us in the woods. So I want to know why little kids can't be borned again."

"Well." Harrison paused, scratching his chin. "Perhaps some folks think little kids don't have the understanding to make a decision about being born again yet. But I'm not rightly sure I agree with that. I always figured God made a particular point in making it a real simple thing to do—for folks to make a decision to get in His family. Cause He's not the type that would want to leave anybody out."

"Are you borned again?" Thomas asked the question again.

"Yeah," Harrison told him, nodding. "I got that straightened out right early myself. Seems like I'd turned eight about that time."

"Is five too little?" Thomas inquired candidly. "I'd like to get it straightened out, too, before something else happens."

Harrison suppressed a grin, realizing the seriousness of the boy's question.

"Let me tell you a short story my daddy told me about this issue, and then you tell me what you think."

Thomas nodded affirmatively.

"You see once a long time ago, God created people down here on the earth to keep Him company and to take care of things. He made them a lot like himself, both a male and a female to start things out. He let them name all the animals, and He came and talked with them every day. They had a real close relationship."

"Then the snake messed things up." Thomas looked up at

Harrison with bright eyes. "Me and Tildy have that in our storybook."

"Yeah, the snake put out the temptation. But the man and woman took the bait."

"And did a bad thing." Thomas interrupted again. "They had to leave the garden and God got mad."

"I always figured God felt more sad and disappointed than mad," replied Harrison. "Because what happened broke their good fellowship apart. He set about right from the first planning a way to get it back. So the people He'd made could get back into the family of God if they wanted to. Since a bad decision broke fellowship in the beginning, God had to come up with a way for people to make a good decision to restore it. Or that's how my daddy explained it to me."

Harrison paused, thinking how to finish. "God asked his son Jesus if He would come down and live among the people on the earth, deal with the same sort of stuff they dealt with, but see if He could get the victory over all the temptations they faced."

Harrison looked down at Thomas. "See, if Jesus could do this, He could sort of make it up for what happened before. If He could die sinless, without doing anything bad, it would make a way to reverse the process."

"You mean Jesus never did anything bad in his whole life?" Thomas asked incredulously.

"No, he never did."

"Wow, that must have been real hard." Thomas shook his head.

"I'm sure it was hard," Harrison agreed, trying not to smile again. "But He did it to create a way back into fellowship with God. By Jesus dying without doing anything wrong, without what God calls sins, He kind of made up for what happened in the garden. Jesus became a sort of a bridge back into the family of God for people ever since."

"So being borned again gets you back into God's family?"

Harrison nodded.

"How do you do it?" Thomas asked candidly.

Harrison sighed. Who'd have ever thought he'd be preaching a salvation message to a five-year old in the hospital emergency room?

"First you have to believe in God and Jesus and in the story," he explained. "Then you pray a prayer and ask God to forgive you of the wrongs and bad things you've done. You ask Him to help you change your ways and be a better person. Finally, you ask Him to come into your life to do that, to make Himself a part of you. He can do that. That's what gets you back into the place of being right with God again."

"And into God's family so if you die you'll go to heaven?" Thomas lifted serious eyes up to Harrison's.

"Yeah, that's about it," Harrison answered.

Thomas nodded, considering this. "Harrison, how did you do it after you decided?" he asked. "How did you get borned again? Did you do it all by yourself?"

"In a way, I did." Harrison threaded a hand through his hair. "I thought about it on my own for a while. Sort of like you've been doing. That's a first important step. Then I walked down front at the end of church one Sunday and told the preacher I felt ready to make my decision."

"Like they do every Sunday at our church?" Thomas sat forward.

"Like they do at the church we go to," Harrison replied. "It's different ways at different kinds of churches. You can do it private like or you can do it public. I always felt kind of brave doing it in public. That wasn't easy when I was only eight. But my daddy walked down with me when I told him I wanted to go. That sort of helped."

Thomas face fell and his lower lip pumped out. "I don't have a daddy anymore." He dropped his eyes on a big sigh.

Harrison could have kicked himself for bringing that aspect into his story.

He chose his next words carefully. "You don't need anyone to go down with you when you're ready, Thomas. But if you want someone to walk down with you, you've got Alice. I know she would walk down with you if you asked her."

Thomas thought about that. "If I decide to go down one Sunday, would you walk down with me?" he asked. "I'll come get you where you sit if I decide I want to do it. You always sit on the end, anyway. You wouldn't even have to climb over anyone to get out or step on anybody's feet."

Harrison suppressed another grin.

"I tell you what, Thomas," he replied matter-of-factly. "If you ever decide to go down and get this thing settled, then I'd be privileged to walk down with you if you want."

"Thanks, Harrison," Thomas offered him a beaming smile. "Me and Tildy worried about this a whole lot in the cabin. I'm going to tell her your story, too."

Harrison nodded.

They spotted Megan then, looking for them. Harrison waved to her.

"Is Tildy all right?" Thomas asked right away, running to hug her. "She isn't deaded or anything, is she?"

"No, she's fine," Megan assured him. "They cleaned up all her scratches, and did x-rays on her arm and legs. She has a break in her arm. The doctor called it a simple fracture." She looked at Harrison with a question in her eyes.

"That means it's a clean simple break and will heal easily," he clarified.

Megan nodded. "There wasn't a break in her leg. The doctor called it a bad sprain. They wrapped her ankle up, and now they're putting a cast on her arm. I think it might hurt some, because the doctor told Alice they had to set her arm."

Harrison turned to Thomas. "The doctors do this to be sure the bone is in the right place before they put the cast on."

He turned back to Megan, remembering the bump and the blackout. "What about her head?"

"They did a test, but they don't think Tildy had a concussion." She looked at Harrison again, twisting a pigtail. "Is that the right word?"

"Yes."

She smiled. "The doctor said except for her losing consciousness for a few minutes, that she didn't show any other signs of having a concussion."

"What about that knot on her head?" Harrison asked.

"The nurse put an ice pack on it while we waited for tests and doctors." Megan replied. "Tildy said it felt good."

Thomas shuffled his feet and bit on his lower lip. "Is Alice mad?"

Megan made a face at him. "She's too busy being worried about Tildy now," she said honestly. "I guess she'll get around to being kind of mad later. You and Tildy shouldn't have run off like you did. You both know better."

Despite himself, Thomas started to sniffle then.

Harrison frowned at Megan. "There's time enough for lectures later," he said. "I guess Thomas feels about as bad as he could over what happened to Tildy. And for how scared they both were. I think he's going to think a lot more carefully in the future about going off without permission." He passed Thomas a significant look.

Thomas caught it gratefully. "Me and Tildy are going to ask from now on, Megan," he assured her. "We're going to stop being bad."

Harrison put a hand on Thomas's shoulder. "Sometimes boys are irresponsible for a while when they're little." He made eye contact with the child. "But when they start growing to be real men, they always think first before they act. They count the costs. They try to do the right thing. Especially when they have women with them to take care of."

Thomas nodded knowingly, but Megan frowned at Harrison for that last remark. "Mother would have called that a very sexist comment," she announced. "Both Thomas and Tildy need to stop running off without telling someone where they're going. They both need to think before they act."

"I'm going to take better care of Tildy," Thomas told Harrison, sticking up his chin and ignoring Megan's remark. "Cause I'm supposed to."

Megan rolled her eyes. "Well, anyway. Alice said I could come and get you two now. Tildy's asking for you, and they're almost ready to release her. Pretty soon we can all go home. I'll take you to where they have her now. It's in a room down this hallway." She pointed and turned to start in that direction.

Harrison nodded, and he and Thomas went with Megan to see about Tildy. He glanced at the clock as they started down the hall. Past midnight now. It had been a long day.

CHAPTER 17

After a difficult night or two, Tildy began to bounce back in the quick way young children do. She collected autographs on her cast and enjoyed the attention and gifts she received from friends and neighbors.

Harrison came by often, mostly at Tildy's insistence. Alice could hardly refuse.

Anyway, she felt glad to have her quarrel with Harrison patched up. She'd apologized in the heat of the moment, when she hadn't meant to, but Harrison had proved a wonderful help in a critical time.

"I could hardly be small-minded enough to regret being humble and grateful in the situation," she explained to Donna, who smiled smugly in return.

"I notice everyone seems to have fallen back into their old pattern," Donna said.

Alice agreed. "Yes. First, Harrison stopped by to check on Tildy, next Odell invited him to lunch, then the children begged him back to family night." She laughed. "Even the dog acts thrilled to have Harrison back. Sophie sleeps with her head on his boots whenever he visits and he knows just how to scratch her neck to make her happy."

Donna grinned. "How about you—is Harrison scratching your neck and making you happy?"

Alice swatted at her friend. "Don't romance this, Donna. It's friendship, and I'm glad to have harmony back with our neighbor."

Despite her denial to Donna, Alice couldn't deny to herself how Harrison continued to affect her. She could feel him come into a room, sense him when nearby. She watched for him without realizing it, listened for his voice. Studied him. A strength and calm power emanated from Harrison that Alice felt drawn to. She'd begun to realize Harrison took charge of situations and got everyone to cooperate because it was his nature, not because he meant to be overbearing and controlling.

Donna, seeming to pick up on her thoughts said, "I think you're simply going to have to accept, Alice, that Harrison Ramsey truly loves to fix things—everything from squeaky doors to work crises to dilemmas and difficulties with people." She laughed. "Haven't you noticed how many people call on Harrison when they have a problem and need help? I've heard people say, 'Oh call Harrison, he'll know just what to do', and he usually does."

Later in the week, on Thursday evening, Alice sat out on the back porch with Harrison, watching the children play and listening to the evening sounds. The twins had begged Harrison to stay for supper after he dropped by to deliver feed at the barn. Now he sat in his favorite chair, enjoying an after-dinner coffee.

They'd sat quietly now for ten minutes. Harrison was one of the few people Alice knew that could sit easily and comfortably in a situation without feeling a need to start up a conversation. He called it "just being", and said not enough people did it. She grinned at the thought.

"What are you thinking about?" Harrison asked, catching her grin.

She shook her head. Even when the man appeared totally preoccupied, he never missed a thing, she thought.

"Nothing much." She answered evasively, not wanting to acknowledge to him how much he played through her thoughts.

"Are the kids ready for our fall overnight tomorrow?" he asked, crossing a booted foot leisurely across his ankle.

After hearing Harrison's stories about overnight trail rides, the kids begged him to take them on an overnight. They'd chosen this coming weekend with school closed on Friday for a teacher in-service.

Alice turned to smile at him. "They are really excited. I'll probably never get them to sleep tonight. It's one reason I'm letting them run themselves silly playing night-tag outside. Hopefully, they'll be worn out and more likely to fall asleep."

He chuckled and then looked thoughtful. "I'll check everybody's saddlebag and gear before we leave tomorrow. Once we're out on the trail, it's too late to return for forgotten items."

She closed the magazine on her lap. "Remind me again where we're going, Harrison."

"We're riding up the main Ramsey riding trail to Old Settler's Trail, a maintained trail in the parkland." He gestured in the general direction of the trail. "There we swing east, passing by the park's Campsite 33. Old rock chimneys in this section will interest the children." He grinned slightly. "I've got some Ramsey family stories to tell, too. The Ramseys lived on that land before the national park came in."

He stopped to prop his feet on a nearby chair. "Following Old Settler's Trail, we'll skirt across the creek a few times. See a nice waterfall along the way. Then we climb up along the banks of Noisy Creek and head up Chestnut Ridge. More settler remains lie along this stretch—chimneys, rock walls. The trees will be colorful along the ridge top this time of year. We may get a few views across the mountains."

Alice sighed. "The trees look beautiful this time of year. I hope we see some gorgeous fall color."

"There should be some nice vistas off the ridge and we pass through a stretch of colorful hardwoods before catching up with Texas Creek. The children will enjoy the cascades and waterfalls there."

He paused to take a drink of his coffee before continuing. "At that point we move through the old Texas Settlement area where about a dozen mountain families once lived. That's the six mile point, a good place to stop for a break."

"Is that where we'll have lunch?"

He nodded. "We'll follow Webb Creek after lunch, climb Snag Mountain—probably get another nice view or two—then start down the mountain along Bender Creek to an old lodge a friend of mine owns. It's right on the park boundary line and sits alongside the stream."

No wonder she could never remember all that, Alice thought.

She gave Harrison a teasing look. "You know, the children complained when you told them we're spending the night in a lodge instead of sleeping outside in tents."

He snorted. "None of them will be wishing for tents once the sun falls and they see how dark and chilly it gets in the mountains in October." He crossed his arms across his chest. "That old lodge of Dexter Johnson's may not be the Ritz, but it's got a roof if it rains, a big fireplace for warmth, a working pump for water in the kitchen, and some rustic furniture. For the kids that means an old sofa or two and a big Indian rug to spread their sleeping bags on in front of the fireplace, and for you and me that means a couple of beds in the back bedroom. I already told the kids we had dibs on the beds. They may not be the best, Alice, but they sure beat sleeping on the floor any day."

Alice thought about that one bedroom idea and frowned thoughtfully.

Harrison suppressed a smile, as if reading her mind. "Those two beds stand well-distanced from each other, and you know for a fact we'll be leaving the door open because of the kids sleeping on the floor in the next room." He picked at a clump of dirt on one of his boots. "I'll be getting up through the night to check the fire. Or to take scardy cats to the outdoor latrine in the dark. This won't be a romantic atmosphere, Alice, so don't worry."

She lifted her chin. "I didn't say I had any concerns, Harrison."

"No, you didn't. But I saw that worried look travel over your face." He let his eyes trail down her.

Alice glared at him. "Now you think you can read my face without me even saying a word." She snapped the words out, annoyed at him.

He leaned over to trace a finger down her cheek. "I'm getting to where I can just about do that these days," he murmured, that mouth of his quirking into a partial smile.

Alice changed the subject quickly, reaching over to pick up her cup of coffee. "I saw you and Odell loading up food yesterday to take to the lodge. I gather there's a back road into the cabin for transporting the food there ahead of time."

"There's an unpaved road that winds up the mountain to the cabin." He leaned back in his chair again. "I already took up all the food we need for the one night. Nonperishables and basics. We won't have the luxury of a refrigerator so that changes the menu possibilities. To the kids, it will probably seem like roughing it."

"Harrison, it's wonderful of you to take them on this riding trip at all." Her eyes moved to the children playing tag in the twilight. "Do you think Tildy will do okay with her cast?"

"Yeah, she's a trooper. She'll be fine. Don't worry, Alice. I've been to this lodge many times, and the kids will have a real adventure there."

She looked toward the sky. "What if it rains or the weather is bad tomorrow?"

"It wouldn't dare," he replied, with a real grin now. "Not with six kids believing for a nice day."

As if daring to cross Harrison's positive forecast, the next day dawned fair and clear. The weather report projected an unseasonably warm October day and the sun shone brightly in a beautiful, blue sky as they set out. This made all the fall tree color simply glow, and Alice had to admit it couldn't have been a more perfect day.

The children were excited about the trip and eager to be cooperative with Harrison. He took the role of trail boss and tour guide, which left Alice the pleasure of enjoying the day without having to plan or be in charge. Where once it rankled her pride to let Harrison take charge, now she saw the benefits of letting him do it. It gave her a well-needed break.

Shortly after noon, they stopped for lunch along the creek in the old Texas Settlement area Harrison described the night before.

"See if you can find the rock walls and chimney remains of the settlers' cabins we talked about," Harrison said as the children dismounted.

He pointed downstream. "You'll find a cascade past that big boulder you see, too. Walk around and stretch your legs before we eat our lunch. Then we need to get back on the trail again."

Alice soon heard them whooping and hollering as they jumped boulders in the stream while she and Harrison put out their lunch.

By late afternoon, the caravan reached the lodge, a long, rough-hewn and picturesque building with a broad porch across the front. Inside a large, arched room spread in front of a huge rock fireplace, with a rough kitchen to one end and a low-ceilinged bedroom at the other. The restroom, as predicted, proved to be an outside latrine behind the lodge.

To the left of the main lodge stood a long, covered horse shed, similar to many in horse camps around the Smokies. The children settled their horses in the shed first, showing how competently they'd learned to care for their mounts after a long ride. Then, they carried in their sleeping bags and gear and explored the lodge.

Harrison soon sent them all off to gather kindling and to bring in firewood from the woodpile so they could start a fire before dark fell. They cleaned and swept the lodge next, Staccy and Rachel shrieking over spiders they discovered. Then they filled and lit the oil lamps in the lodge and helped to start preparations for dinner.

"What are we havin' to eat for supper?" Thomas peered into the boxes and bags in the kitchen.

"Harrison is making us his 'trail-ride stew'," Megan answered him. "And Odell sent us homemade bread, jars of homemade pickles and spiced apples, and her fudge brownies for dessert."

"We have snacks for later, too." Tildy added, bouncing around the kitchen and then running into the main room with the younger children to play.

Hannah looked around the kitchen frowning. "How can we get

our tea cold? There's no refrigerator here and no ice."

Harrison gestured toward a closed door. "Go look in that closet and get two of those big sun-tea jars with the lids. Make the tea in those, Hannah, and then go put them in the creek until time to eat. That will get them cold."

"Oh, good idea." Hannah smiled and headed for the closet.

Alice moved to help Harrison cut up fresh vegetables—potatoes, carrots, and celery—to add to the big cans of beef stew base he'd brought up. He drained canned corn, green beans, and mixed vegetables while she worked, tossing them into the big stewpot on the stove.

She leaned over to whisper, hoping the children couldn't hear her. "Do you actually think they'll eat all these vegetables mixed together, Harrison?"

He turned to grin at her while he stirred the ingredients. "By the time I'm through with this stew they definitely will. My secret ingredients make this stuff irresistible, and it smells great while it's cooking, too. Especially to kids who spent all day outside working up a big appetite."

He pulled spices and bottles from a shelf now, and Alice left him to it. She busied herself in the back bedroom making up the two double beds. Even though they felt lumpy, Alice agreed they'd be better to sleep on than the floor.

By the time dark fell, they'd polished off Harrison's trail stew and finished cleaning the kitchen. The children clustered on their sleeping bags on the big rug in front of the fire now, playing cards, dominoes, and Chinese checkers they'd found in a closet.

Seeing them happy and occupied, Alice slipped outside to find a rocker on the front porch. She settled down in the chair, pulling it forward so she could prop her feet up on the porch railing. The night air felt chillier with the sun down, but with her sweater on, Alice felt snug. The creek splashed and tumbled in the dark, the sound soothing her nerves after the long day.

Harrison let himself out the door and pulled up a rocker beside her.

"Good idea coming out on the porch for a break." He propped his feet up on the rail as well. "I'm ready for a rest."

"The stew tasted great." She sent him a smile. "Even the twins took seconds."

"Mountain air and hungry people helped a lot." He leaned back in the rocker, closing his eyes.

The peace and quiet of the night enveloped them, with only the sounds of cicadas and the tumbling of the nearby creek touching the air.

"I love listening to the creek," Alice said.

"I knew having the creek nearby would be a plus for the kids." Harrison turned to grin at her. "However, I hadn't counted on Thomas falling in it."

Alice laughed. "He asked me if I thought it would count for his baptism."

Harrison chuckled.

"You know." Alice pulled her sweater more closely about her. "I've been meaning to thank you about that."

"For fishing the boy out of the creek?" His lips twitched in amusement. "It was a mite cold to leave him in there."

"No, silly." She reached over to swat at him. "For talking to Thomas the way you did about getting saved. I had no idea he was interested. It surprised me the next Sunday we went to church when he and Tildy walked down front when the minister gave the invitation. I didn't know if they knew what they were doing at first, but then I saw them go to your pew so you could walk down with them. That was good of you, Harrison. Later, Thomas told me the story you shared with him."

He shifted in his chair. "It wasn't exactly the way I envisioned spending my evening in the emergency room, but the boy had questions. I guess his and Tildy's scare made them think about death a mite more seriously than they probably would have otherwise."

"You explained it to them in a wonderful way and they both understood the decision they made." She waved a gnat away from her face. "Reverend Campbell thought so, too."

They sat quietly for a minute.

"Do you know, even your mother got touched." Alice grinned at him.

"What makes you say that?" Harrison flared.

Alice put a hand on his arm. "She sits up front at the piano, Harrison, if you recall. I could see her face. She felt moved, and she wiped away a tear, too."

"Hummph. I doubt that." Harrison scowled.

"After the service she told Odell she thought those Stuart children might be having a good influence on you." Alice giggled. "She said you'd been at church every Sunday for two months, a record for you."

Harrison laughed despite himself.

"I think Mozella is actually more fond of you than you think," Alice pressed. "She simply doesn't know how to express it."

"Listen, little Miss Social Worker, don't go trying to make peace between me and my mama. We have a healthy but cautious hostility going. It's served us admirably for a long time now."

"I don't believe that." Alice crossed her arms. "I think there's more affection between the two of you than either of you let on. After all, you are your mother's only child that lives in this area. She naturally leans on you. She will more as she ages."

"Now, there's a scary thought." He whistled softly.

She gave him a playful push, but he caught her hand when she did and raised it to press his lips into her palm. Even in the dark, Alice could feel her pulse start to quicken. Her senses became quickly aroused, too, as he began to nibble on her fingers.

Alice tried to pull her hand away. "Harrison," she hissed. "Those children are all right inside."

"And they have no idea how attracted I am to their Alice," he whispered huskily. "Or how often the desire to touch her sweeps over me."

Alice caught her breath, surprised at his tender words.

"I've tried hard to avoid intimate little times with you in the dark." His voice slipped through the night air in a slow honey drawl.

"They're my particular downfall moments. Have you ever noticed the dark has a more compelling draw to it than the daylight?"

He traced his fingers up and down her arm while he talked, and Alice found her breath coming quicker by the moment.

"I know it's still there for you." His voice softened. "I can see it in your eyes. Feel it in the air. Just like at the first. Like it is now."

He started to lean toward her, but then the door swung open.

"Rachel needs to go to the latrine but she's scared to go by herself in the dark," Thomas announced. "Hannah says she'll take her, but Rachel says she wants you to go, Harrison, in case there are more spiders. She's scared of spiders."

Alice heard Harrison groan softly.

"Tell Rachel I'll go with her." She started to get up. "It isn't right for men to go with little girls to the toilet."

Harrison put a hand out to stop her as he stood up. She heard his commanding tone as he started into the house. "Rachel needs to remember our assigned buddy system for this trip. When she needs to go to the latrine or anywhere else, she goes with her buddy. We agreed on that deal before we came. Alice won't be getting up all night to troop to the latrine with Rachel—or with any of you. Nor will I. You all have your own flashlights. You go with your buddy if and when you need to go. That's the deal."

Alice sat back in her rocker, letting Harrison resolve things while she tried to collect her shaky feelings. She could remember times when Harrison acted strongly on his emotions, but seldom did he express any of his feelings to her. His tender words played in her mind and nudged at her heart, and the feelings welling up within scared Alice and offered her no comfort. It frightened her to think of falling in love with Harrison Ramsey. She hated to acknowledge, even to herself, how near the edge of that fall she stood. How very near the edge.

Perhaps that explained why it felt tortuous later when she and Harrison settled down for the night in the lodge bedroom. It had taken time to get all the children settled for sleep and, of course, the children kept begging Harrison for just one more final story.

Now although she and Harrison lay in two different beds, Alice could hear every time he turned in the bed across the room from her. Could hear him breathing. Heard him cough once. Stirred with awareness every time he got up to check the fire and the children.

As the hours passed, she drifted fitfully in and out of sleep, her dreams and thoughts a confusing jumble. She fanaticized Harrison's lips on hers, imagined what it would be like to hold him close, have him slip into bed with her. Then she rebuked herself for those thoughts, thinking guiltily of David. Remembering how he'd loved her, how she'd loved him. How could she want someone else at all? Especially a man who'd made it clear he had no interest in marriage.

Surely she couldn't be falling in love with Harrison Ramsey? Not after what he said to her. With what she knew about him. There could be no future in loving him. He might care for her but he'd never consider marriage to her with all these children. It was one thing to come to dinner or enjoy a night of games and fun with the children—but quite another to take on six children day in and day out for a lifetime. If he married any one, it would be someone younger. Someone he could build a young family with. Like she and David hoped to build before he'd been killed.

Weariness washed over Alice. She sighed, wondering if Harrison experienced trouble sleeping like she did—felt the draw and tension she did in the room. Probably not, she thought. His breathing sounded deep and regular. He probably slept soundly, not thinking another thought about the words he'd said on the porch. Or how they made her feel.

Sighing again, she rolled over to punch the pillow, trying to get into a more comfortable position. She said some prayers quietly to herself then, struggling to gain inner peace. Asking God to help her with the problems she faced with her emotions. Praying for His help and guidance with her life and for the children in her care.

Gradually, she slipped off into a fitful sleep. In her dreams, David and Harrison appeared and reappeared in one disjointed scene after another—her dreams growing increasingly more turbulent and disturbing.

Somewhere toward dawn, Alice drifted into a vivid nightmare, running in frenzied terror from a pursuer, unable to get away. Calling to someone to save her, help her. Calling David. Then Harrison. Needing them. As she rounded a corner, running, panting, she knew her pursuer gained on her. Felt a hand reaching out to touch her shoulder, and she gave a muffled scream. Began to fight. Knew she had to fight, to try to save herself, to get away.

The hands felt more solid now. They shook her. Alice struggled even as she saw her pursuer slip from view and heard her name spoken. Was it David? She called to him. Felt someone gathering her in his arms. David? Had he come back to save her?

"I'm not David," a voice said gruffly. "Alice, wake up. You're having a bad dream." She felt lips against her forehead now, trying to soothe her. Alice slipped out of the dream and into the edge of reality and saw Harrison. Felt Harrison. Felt safe.

"Oh, Harrison," She threw herself into his arms and started to cry. "I felt so scared. Something chased me and I didn't know what to do and then it started to attack me and ...."

"And you called for David," he said softly.

She looked up into his face and saw a sort of pain there.

"Just a bad dream," she tried to explain. "Dreams don't always make sense in reality you know..."

"I'm not David," he interrupted hoarsely.

"I know." She barely found her voice.

He continued to hold her tight against himself, and his warmth began to take the chill the dream brought. How good he felt. How warm and solid. Safe and strong. How she'd dreamed of holding him like this all night long.

She touched his face, hating that she might have hurt him in any way. "I'm glad you're here, Harrison," she whispered. "I'm glad it's you ..."

He gathered her closer then, lowered his lips to hers and kissed her. A deep and intimate kiss. A passionate kiss. The kind of kiss she'd yearned for through the darkness of the night.

With abandon, Alice gave back with all her heart. With all the depth of her pent-up feelings. The heat between them grew and all rational thought slipped away into the darkness. She slid her hands under his shirt and heard him groan as her hands touched his bare skin. His hands moved to explore, too, his fingers touching under the edges of her breasts through her nightshirt, and Alice's breath caught and quickened. As though in a slow dream, she felt him press her back onto the bed and felt his body cover hers. Felt passion flood her bloodstream.

And then a voice touched into the edge of the passion.

"Does this mean you're going to get married now?" Thomas asked.

Alice looked up in a burst of reality to see the children standing wide-eyed in the bedroom doorway.

The next moments moved in a hazy and blurred panic. To sit up and recover. To try to make light to six children the scene they'd witnessed.

CHAPTER 18

The next day riding back from the overnight proved not as pleasant as the day riding in. The Saturday began as another bright and brilliant day, the fall leaves shining in glorious color in the October sun, but Harrison's relationship with Alice appeared neither bright nor brilliant. It was strained. Oh, Alice put on a gay, false front before the children all day, but it didn't fool Harrison. She felt upset, and he didn't know what to do about it.

Both made a good effort to pacify the children about what they saw in the bedroom the night before. Alice had a bad dream, they explained to them. Harrison tried to wake her and comfort her. The kissing proved harder to justify, but they did their best to be casual about it. Alice tried to artfully present it as part of her dream she couldn't wake from, but Harrison could tell the children didn't totally buy the story. He wondered why she tried so hard to dismiss the attraction between them. After all, the kids watched television. They weren't ignorant about the facts of adult relationships.

Hannah and Megan, older and wiser, replaced their shocked and surprised expressions of the night before with considering ones today. Harrison saw them watching him and Alice carefully through the day, and they soon sensed Alice's discontent. They began giving Harrison pointed looks as the ride home lengthened and Alice's mood didn't improve. They clearly held him responsible for Alice's unhappiness.

The younger children, more oblivious to the undercurrents of adult emotions, seemed more caught up in the new fantasy of him and Alice being in love and with the idea of having him for a new daddy. Although Alice tried to quell these comments whenever they cropped up, the younger children held on to them fiercely. In their young minds, people who kissed and hugged with the intensity they witnessed the night before had to be in love and would soon marry.

Rachel assured Harrison she thought he'd be a nice daddy, and, of course, Thomas and Tildy waxed ecstatic about soon including Harrison permanently in their family mix. They asked questions and babbled childish speculations all day, ignoring all Alice's efforts to convince them she and Harrison were merely good friends.

Basically, Harrison stayed out of the ongoing discussions. He figured people had watched his and Alice's relationship becoming more than neighborly. It surprised him the children hadn't picked up on it before. He already knew Hobart, Odell, and others weren't ignorant of the interest flowing between him and Alice. They'd offered comments and looks often enough.

Earlier, Alice hissed at him quietly that she didn't want other people knowing about this. Knowing what happened the night before.

"It's bad enough the children saw this," she insisted. "But they'll accept we're only friends if we keep telling them that."

He shook his head at her naiveté. He knew it more likely the little ones would blab to one and all every detail. Harrison marveled Alice could be so naïve. Or that she hadn't considered the little ones would soon be telling tales about what they'd seen.

Before the week played out it appeared everybody in Greenbrier knew he and Alice were an item. Harrison found people he held only a nodding acquaintance with shaking his hand and congratulating him on his upcoming marriage.

Somehow it didn't surprise him to return to the farmhouse one evening to find his mother sitting on the porch waiting for him. She wore one of her usual bright outfits, this one patterned in a riot of orange and yellow flowers – but her expression spoke of dark disapproval.

"I guess you know why I've come." Her sharp, clipped words met him even before he started up the porch.

"No, Ma, but I'm sure you'll tell me." He sat down in a porch chair to face the inevitable.

"It's all over the valley how you've been carrying on with that Alice woman over at Meadowbrook." She waved a hand dramatically for emphasis. "Going over to her place in the night hours and sleeping with her in front of those innocent children at the lodge. I swear, Harrison, even I am shocked. I know your father, W. T., and I did not raise you to sanction adulterous relationships, and I thought even you to possess better judgment than to carry on with a woman in front of her little children."

She shook her finger at him. "Worse, you've come to the church with that woman and her children Sunday after Sunday—right in front of the whole community—acting respectable. It's a wonder you can sleep with your own conscience at night, Harrison Owen Ramsey. I'm sorely disappointed in you."

Harrison listened to her rant and rave a little longer, and then finally interrupted her. "Ma, you've certainly offered your view here, but would you be interested in hearing mine?"

She sniffed. "I'm sure you've got some justification figured out for your actions."

Harrison bit back his temper and took a deep breath. "What you're hearing is gossip blown all out of proportion." He sat on a chair across from her, taking off his hat. "Granted, there's an interest between Alice Graham and me. But *nothing* beyond a few kisses and some embraces happened between us. Even those incidences occurred infrequently because of the children and, quite frankly, because of Alice's strong moral code. I won't have you labeling her a fallen woman or calling her "that woman" in tones implying she's anything less than a fine parent and a good moral exemplar to those children."

"Hummph." His mother snorted.

"If there's anyone to blame here, it's me. Alice had a bad dream at the lodge. I took advantage of her when she woke up upset and fearful." He dropped his eyes to the old Stetson in his hands. "I'm not proud of it, Ma. I like to think I wouldn't have pressed the situation for more than kissing, but I couldn't swear on it. I was aroused and not thinking at my highest moral level. It's probably for the best the kids woke up when they did and stopped things."

His mother pinched her lips. "What were you doing in the same bedroom with that woman?" she asked, not satisfied.

He blew out a breath. "You know that old lodge only has one bedroom. I took one of the beds for the overnight and Alice took the other. The door to the bedroom hung wide open and all the kids lay spread out in sleeping bags on the floor right outside the doorway. It wasn't a romantic setup."

She shook her head in disapproval. "Harrison, you aren't stupid. Any time you sleep in the same room alone with an attractive woman you're giving the enemy an opportunity for temptation." Her eyes flashed. "Even if nothing happened at that lodge, you made a wrong decision just in that. You should have known those kids would blab it around you slept in the same bedroom with Alice Graham. Realized people would assume the worst no matter what occurred. You should have given thought to that woman's reputation even if you didn't have a romantic setup in mind."

Harrison hated realizing she was right. "Maybe I should have," he admitted with a grimace.

"You should have set up a tent outside rather than putting yourself inside with either Alice or those young girls." She crossed her arms in annoyance. "You've slept outdoors in tents in worse weather than this. Relished the experience as I remember." Her angry eyes found his. "Quite frankly, I find it hard to believe you didn't have some inappropriate thoughts in your head setting up that situation to begin with, and Alice Graham should have insisted you sleep somewhere else herself."

"She tried to do that." He shifted in his seat, uncomfortable now. "The idea worried her."

"Obviously not enough, but you're a stubborn man set on getting your own way—often without a thought to others." She glared at him. "I'm sure you pushed it with her. Your father was like that, too. Stubborn as the day is long."

Harrison sighed.

She leaned toward him with a hand on her hip. "What about this other story of you going over to Alice's house in the middle of the night? Is that true?"

"That happened a long time ago." He wondered how she knew about that. "Alice got a call to pick up a baby left on Pastor Carlson's church porch. With Odell out of town, Alice's boss at a conference, and Donna sick, Alice called me to stay with the children while she went to pick up the baby."

She gave him a knowing look. "I also heard you cooked breakfast and took the children to school while Alice padded around in her night clothes. Did you stay over there and sleep with her?"

Harrison's temper flared. "No. I stayed until she got back, went home, and then came back to make breakfast for the kids and help her out the next day. Alice stayed out half the night, Ma. I just meant to be a good neighbor."

"If you believe that, you're doing an admirable job of fooling your own self real good." Mozella shook her head back and forth slowly. "You've had neighbors around you for years, and I never recall you steppin' in with this kind of consideration before. It's obvious you acted again using your groin for a brain and without a thought to that woman's reputation."

Harrison winced. "Look, Ma, nobody thought anything about me helping Alice when she picked up that baby until this thing with the lodge came up."

"Pigeons come back to roost," she retorted. "And wrong things have a way of being remembered and piling up over time."

Harrison frowned. "Nothing wrong has happened here, Ma," he insisted again. "Alice doesn't deserve to be flayed by the local gossips."

"Maybe not." She crossed her arms again. "But what's out there is what's out there now, Harrison Ramsey. I want to know what you plan to do about it. Henry wanted to come with me this evening.

He is your and Alice's pastor, after all, and he's grown real fond of Alice and those children. He is not happy with this situation and neither am I."

"What does Rev Campbell think I ought to do?" His head came up. "Stand up in the church and explain everything to stop the gossip? I'll do it if you think it will help."

"No." She gave him a considering look. "Henry and I think you ought to marry the woman. She and those children have to live in the valley from now on, and you sullied her reputation. Slept in the same room with her. Laid on top of her in the same bed with both of you in nothing but your night clothes and skivvies." She sniffed and tossed her head. "It's the honorable thing to do, Harrison."

"I don't think that's what Alice wants." Harrison crossed his arms.

"Have you asked her?" Mozella challenged.

Seeing his expression, she nodded emphatically. "I thought not, Son. My guess is what Alice wants or needs is not your priority."

Harrison offered no comment.

Mozella's expression softened, her voice growing almost kind. "Do you love her, Son?"

"I don't know," he replied honestly, twisting his old Stetson in his hand. "I've been attracted to her from the first, with something strong in the air between us from the very beginning. I've come to care for her and the children. But marriage isn't something I've thought about."

Mozella shook her head regretfully. "I wish it had come to love with Alice. That would make it easier."

Harrison squirmed. "I'm not sure I'm cut out for love and marriage."

"I don't buy that." She shook a finger at him again. "You loved Ava Reagan. I watched that relationship blossom for years, and I know you'd have married her if she hadn't left like she did." She paused and made a face. "Now, I'm not sure you loved Patsy Ogle even if you proposed marriage to her. I always thought you formed that relationship on the rebound after Ava left. But I know you loved Ava. You won't deny that to me, will you?"

"That was a long time ago, Ma," he said quietly. "I was a kid."

Mozella tossed her head. "No more a kid than your father and me when we fell in love and got married."

Harrison looked across at her. "Did you ever love Daddy?" he asked candidly.

"Now, that's an ugly question." Mozella's eyes flashed. "Just because your father and I disagreed about a lot of matters doesn't mean I didn't love him. Or that I married him for any other reason than love."

Harrison shrugged and dropped his eyes.

"Don't be looking back at your father's and my relationship as some kind of reason to justify not settling down and getting married, either." She pushed the glider to move faster with one foot. "Not every marriage is the storybook type, and not every couple finds themselves as much alike as they thought after saying 'I do'."

"You're happier with Henry though, aren't you, Ma?" he asked, surprised at this candid moment opening up with his mother.

"Henry and I are more alike in many ways than your father and I were." Mozella spoke the words honestly. "We're good companionable partners."

She paused and looked at Harrison thoughtfully for a minute, smiling softly at her own thoughts. "But I'll tell you a passion flared between your father and me that might not have shown on the surface of our relationship. It's what drew us together and kept us together. I guess you're grown up enough to understand a thing like that now."

Harrison could hardly mask his surprise.

Mozella laughed. "Funny how kids think the only thing between their parents is what they see day to day over the breakfast table. You need to get over this long-held bitterness of yours that I didn't love your father. Or that he didn't love me. Oh, we fought a lot, that's true. But there was love."

She gave Harrison a pointed look. "One thing I can say is that

I didn't close myself off from the idea of loving again after your daddy died. Didn't stay content to live only in the past." She fiddled with her purse. "There's different kinds of love, Harrison, and I was open to having a second love. My concern is I think you've closed yourself off from the idea of love and marriage ever since you experienced those problems with Ava Reagan and Patsy Ogle. In fact, I think they might be getting in the way of you looking at your feelings about Alice Graham more closely."

"You sound like Hobart," grumbled Harrison.

Mozella nodded. "Hobart was around during those years you dated Ava," she said. "He knows, like I do, how hurt you felt about what happened. It was after that time you went off to college, actually left this place for a while."

Irritation flared. "That's what you wanted for me, wasn't it, Ma?" His eyes found hers." You wanted me to make a life away from Greenbrier like the girls did and to never come back."

She made a face and shook her head. "You sure cherish some twisted notions about me," she complained. "I only wanted you to have a chance to choose, Harrison. To not get locked into the farm and the stables, following in your daddy's footsteps without having a chance to look around. I wanted your horizons to be broadened. I never had that chance myself, you know."

This revelation surprised Harrison.

Surprised, he asked, "What did you want, Ma?"

"To go off and study music." She looked out across the field in a dreamy way. "But eight Trent kids lived in our dirt-poor family and none of us had the opportunity to even think about such options. Or to be encouraged in them. I got made fun of from an early age to even consider it. Called a foolish dreamer."

"You have a real gift at the piano, Ma," Harrison observed, caught unawares by her revelation.

"Thanks for saying so." She turned to look at him. "I think that's about the first real compliment you ever gave me."

The remark stunned Harrison. His own concerns about his mother's disapproval for him went back so far he'd never given a thought to whether she'd even been aware of his disapproval of her. It would be something to reflect on later.

"I'm not sure Alice Graham is the woman I'd pick to be a wife for you," Harrison heard his mother saying, plowing right on in her usual nonstop way before he had time to absorb her last remarks. "She's not from around here. She's a career woman, which might not be best for an agricultural man's wife. I doubt she'll offer much help to you with the farm, the land, or the orchards. She's right good with horses though. That's a plus. Perhaps she'll be a help with the stables. I hear the two of you ride together, so you do share that interest."

Mozella paused for a breath. "Quite honestly, I'd have liked to see you marry a woman without a ready-made family. To birth your own children and build your own family. Children that would be my blood kin. But none of that matters too much in the situation right now."

She stood up, brushing off her slacks. "You definitely need to marry the woman, Harrison. It's the honorable thing to do in the situation. It would be nice if you'd had more time to see if love would come before you offered for her, but you fixed it where you don't have more time now. I came to tell you that, Harrison, to let you know how Henry and I feel about this situation."

"She may not have me," Harrison admitted, looking up at her. "Even if I offer."

"She'd be a fool not to," his mother said. "A woman with six kids isn't likely to get a lot of marital offers."

Harrison scowled at her.

"Now, don't get your dander up." She picked up her purse, tucking it under her arm. "You're a right fine man, a good looking one to boot, and you've got a lot of strengths. She's a pretty woman, a kind-hearted and a talented one, too. It isn't a bad match for either of you. It's a better one for sure than the one with Patsy Ogle you considered. I never did like that girl. Fast and easy. All about herself. At least Alice is other-centered like a good Christian woman ought to be. She's already liked around the area, too."

She paused to give him a pointed look. "Maybe liked better than you right now."

Harrison almost grinned at this last comment—one more like what he usually received from his mother.

"You let Henry and me know what you decide to do," she said, starting down the porch stairs to her car.

"You mean I have a choice in this?" he said, getting up to see her to her car.

"You know you do." She gave him a stern look. "You're a grown man. But be sure your decision is the right one, Son."

After Mozella drove off, Harrison slumped back into his chair on the porch.

"What a mess," he mumbled to himself after a time, dropping his hat over his face to think.

He got interrupted before he could sink into a funk by a familiar voice. "Looks like your Ma's been visitin'," drawled Hobart. "That's usually the case when you start mumbling to yourself and hiding under your hat."

Harrison pushed his hat back to see Hobart coming up the porch steps, his old beagle, Skeeter, tagging along at his heels.

"I saw Mozella heading this way' bout the time I got ready to leave the stable," Hobart explained. "Figured she'd read you the riot act, what with all this talk about you and Alice Graham traveling around the gossip mill."

Hobart lowered himself into his favorite rocker and tossed Harrison a paper bag, keeping the other for himself.

"Brought you supper," he said. "Palmer's grill leftovers from the daily luncheon menu. Some sort of beef and noodle casserole, corn and pinto beans." He pulled out a Styrofoam container and opened it. "Looks right good. She put pie in for dessert, too. I planned to take food home jest for myself, but decided maybe you could use company this evening."

"Thanks," said Harrison, digging out the Styrofoam container he found in his sack.

"Coffee would be good with this," Hobart hinted.

Harrison grinned. "I'll go put some on to brew, Hobart, and pour us a glass of iced tea for now. Want to bring this in to the kitchen to eat?"

"Nah, I'm a porch sort of guy as long as the weather permits. Guess it's the old cowboy in me."

Harrison went in, started the coffee, and came back out with a couple of glasses of tea and extra napkins. He saw Hobart had spooned out a chunk of his casserole for the beagle and put it in a dish on the porch.

They worked on their food for a while in silence, enjoying watching the late shadows of the sun fall across the farmyard. Then ate their pie with a cup of coffee. The beagle poked around in the yard, and then found a sunny spot near Hobart's chair where he could spread out for a nap.

"That old chicken hatch her chicks yet?" Hobart asked.

"Yeah, and they're running all over the barn," Harrison leaned back in his chair, crossing a booted ankle across his knee.

"I could use a few if you don't want to keep them all." Hobart spooned out the last bite of chess pie. "Didn't get any the last time, and two of my old hens stopped laying. It's a real hunt now to find enough eggs for the table. I could use a few new layers."

"Sure." Harrison stuffed his trash back into the empty sack. "Come take your pick when they get a bit bigger. Probably won't be but a week or two more 'til time."

They sipped their coffee, relaxing after their meal.

"You gonna marry that girl?" Hobart asked then.

"I sure have heard that question a lot this week." Harrison sighed.

Hobart eyed him thoughtfully. "I guess that means you haven't rightly decided."

"There's that." Harrison frowned.

"Nice girl and nice kids," Hobart said.

"You come to put pressure on me, too?" His eyes narrowed.

No." Hobart shook his head. "Just come to be a friend in case you needed one. It's tough to be the target of gossip in this area when the tongues start wagging."

"You got that right." Harrison kicked at a pinecone on the porch floor.

"You gonna tell me what happened up at that lodge or are you gonna leave me speculating along with the rest?" he asked.

"I took the kids on a trail overnight." He propped a foot up on the porch rail. "We all spent the night in Dexter Johnson's old lodge. I thought it sensible for Alice and me to sleep in the two beds and to let the kids have the floor with sleeping bags. Didn't think of it as a situation to cause talk or a problem. Had the door open to the bedroom and six kids for chaperone." He paused. "But Alice had a bad dream in the night. I went to comfort her, hormones kicked in, and the kids saw us. Guess they didn't have sense enough, being little, to keep their mouths shut about witnessing a little kissing."

"That's all they saw?" Hobart lifted an eyebrow.

Harrison ran a hand through his hair. "Granted, it started escalating into more, but, yeah, that's all they saw."

"This the first time them hormones been kicking around?" Hobart gave him a speculative look.

"No, there have been a few other times."

"How long back?"

"About since the first."

Hobart scratched his neck. "You've kept it under the lid right good until now."

"We tried to," Harrison said. "Because of the children and all."

Hobart played with the coffee cup in his hand. "Do you love her?" He raised his eyes to Harrison's.

"I don't know." Harrison blew out a breath. "Sometimes I wonder if I do. Sometimes I think I don't."

"That makes things tougher." Hobart reached down to scratch the old beagle's head.

"Yeah, it does," Harrison admitted. "I hoped time would sort it all out, that and other differences. Now I'm not sure if I've got that time."

"You'll know what's right to do," Hobart said.

"Thanks for the vote of confidence in my ability to make a good decision." Harrison dropped his feet down from the porch rail. "Mozella already told me what she and Henry think I ought to do."

"She hard on you?"

"No more than usual, and in some ways less," he answered. "She got candid with me and told me a few things about herself and her relationship with my daddy. Gave me a different take on things."

"There's always more to people and relationships than what's seen on the surface." Hobart stuffed his trash into the bag with Harrison's.

"Apparently so," Harrison observed.

They sat companionably and watched the sun dropping behind the hills.

"I guess Skeeter and me better be getting on," Hobart said at last, the beagle pricking up his ears at his name. "We got chores yet to do at our place, and my daughter worries if she don't see my car pull in afore dark. Thinks I might have stopped by the bar and gone back to the drink, I guess. Old worries are hard to break."

"You got over that bad time with alcohol a long time ago." Harrison looked up in surprise. "Lucy was a little girl then. She's grown, married, and has two kids now."

Hobart shrugged. "Yeah, but kids have their own ways of thinking about and remembering things from their past. She got hurt during that time, lost some of her trust in me. It's hard to regain trust when it's lost with a child, you know."

He left then, and Harrison found Hobart's last remark lingering in his thoughts more than any other. The idea of losing the trust of a child. He wondered if Hobart tossed that comment in on purpose or if it had just been random.

CHAPTER 19

Friday arrived at last and Alice welcomed the beginning of the weekend. It had been a long week and a stressful one. The younger children had unfortunately voiced their hopes around the community that she and Harrison might marry, including too many details of why they thought that might happen. It opened a floodgate of area gossip. As the days went by, Alice started to feel like she wore a scarlet A embroidered across her chest. Like most repeated tales, this one grew beyond the truth—embellished on freely as it traveled around the Greenbrier area.

The first hint Alice had of things amiss occurred at church the day after they returned from the overnight. Alice caught many knowing smiles, frowns, and considering glances coming from people at the service. She didn't think much about it at first, her mind focused on the day's baptism of baby Lydia by Beecher and Ivey Parton.

Alice successfully worked out the arrangements for Beecher and Ivey to adopt Lydia over the past month. A small triumph but one that made her feel exceptionally good about her work. Beecher and Ivey, ecstatic, promised to be fine parents. Ivey had created the hand-smocked christening dress the baby wore today and it looked lovely. Naturally, all the Parton family and a big crowd of church members and friends turned out for the service and reception after, as did Donna and Vick Nichols and their girls.

At first, Alice thought the unusual attention directed her way related to the baptism. Beecher and Ivey felt deeply grateful to her for arranging the adoption, and had asked her to be baby Lydia's godmother. However, when Donna came over and spoke to her after the service, everything became clear.

She leaned close to whisper in Alice's ear. "I told you Harrison was interested in you. Vick and I are thrilled to hear you two plan to get married."

Before Alice could reply, a crush of people moved in and Millie dragged Alice off for memory pictures.

As the week progressed, and Alice began to deny to people that she and Harrison had set a date to marry, the disapproval began. Suddenly, she moved from being a woman congratulated to a woman disapproved of. The rumors gradually grew to insinuate she and Harrison carried on an illicit affair. No matter how often Alice explained things, she kept getting raised eyebrows and disbelieving looks.

Odell offered little sympathy as they talked after breakfast Monday morning. "Neither one of you showed good sense in this." She slammed a cabinet in irritation. "You both ought to have known better than to sleep in the same room around them kids. Children don't know what they ought or ought not to say. They just tell it like it is."

"I thought you might be on my side in this," Alice complained.

There's not any sides involved here, Alice." Odell banged a few pots in the kitchen. "Only facts. You and Harrison have obviously been attracted to each other for some time and then made the stupid decision to put yourself in a compromising situation bound to get out and about."

She put a hand on one hip and frowned at Alice. "Whatever were you thinking, sleeping in the same room with a single man? Surely, having been married, you're not ignorant of how little it takes to get a man in his prime whipped up? Simply seeing you sashaying around in night clothes would do it, without even considering the emotional feelings going on between the two of you."

Alice studied her coffee cup intently, willing the tears not to start.

"Now, now, there, there," Odell muttered, coming over to pet on her. "I guess it's Harrison Ramsey I'm mad at the most. He knows this valley area and how little it takes to spark up a fire of gossip. He should have been more careful in how he planned that overnight." She crossed her arms. "He *should* have been over at the house to offer marriage by now, too, with all this gossip running around."

Alice looked up in shock at that remark.

"I don't want Harrison offering to marry me to quell gossip," she exclaimed.

Odell studied her. "I wouldn't think that the only reason. I've watched the two of you around each other for a long time now. Seems to me like there's a good bit going on between you."

Alice stirred her coffee, avoiding Odell's knowing eyes.

"Do you love him, Alice?" She sat down in the kitchen chair beside Alice and put her hand over Alice's in motherly affection.

"I think so, heaven help me." Alice started to cry now. "But I'm not sure it's a good thing to fall in love with Harrison Ramsey. We have issues and differences, and I don't think my love is returned. Harrison made it clear from the start he isn't interested in marriage. It's not a happy idea to care for him."

Odell's mouth tightened. "Harrison has fought the idea of getting involved with any woman since all that business happened with Patsy Ogle and Ava Reagan in the past. It put him off women, made him distrust the whole lot of them. He's simply locked up his heart in a safe place, I think. A man don't like to be hurt and made a fool of once—much less twice. He's not eager to go up to bat a third time, and he's just hid himself off from danger."

"Why has he become involved with me then?" Alice asked, confused.

"Perhaps there's a higher hand involved." Odell smiled at her.

Alice smiled despite herself. "You sound like my Grandmother Beryl."

"God has peculiar ways sometimes, Alice. It could be He's had himself a real fine time orchestrating this romance between the two of you. Knowing you'd be good for each other."

Alice winced. "I'm not sure we would be good for each other. You know Harrison doesn't believe I should work, and I value my career. I wouldn't want to quit—even if he pressured me. Harrison is often overbearing and insistent on his own way, too. He isn't a man readily able to admit he's wrong when it's needed. I see a lot of potential relationship problems, Odell."

"Shucks, any couple can work out a few differences like those." She waved a hand dismissively. "I've already seen Harrison changing his mind about your work, anyway. He's right proud of what you do now. I've heard him say so."

Alice looked up in surprise.

"You've softened him up a lot, Alice." Odell got up to carry more dishes into the kitchen. "You've got the strength to stand up and be counted against his strong personality, too. He needs that. You wouldn't want a spineless man you could walk all over, anyway. You know that. I've heard you say you enjoyed the times Harrison took over with the children and gave you a rest. Besides, it would take a strong man to take on the raising of six children effectively, and there's not a much stronger and better man than Harrison Ramsey for the job, Alice. You know the children love him, and the affection he holds for them is genuine. I'd say the good Lord has done a right nice job bringing the two of you together."

Alice sighed. "I know you may be right in many ways, Odell, but I guess I'd like to have love in the mix, too. I don't think that's there with Harrison. Even if it's slipped up on me, I don't think it has on him."

"Oh, it probably has and he's too stubborn and bull-headed to know it." Odell stacked more dishes into the dishwasher. "He'll come around."

Alice left for work then, thinking over the things Odell said through her workday. She continued to weigh the situation over the next days but found no clear answer or direction. She hadn't seen Harrison all week, either. Probably avoiding her again. She could hardly blame him with everyone in the valley pushing him to marry her and make an honest woman of her.

To Alice's surprise, Harrison showed up Friday night for dinner and game night. He swung in the back door about the time they sat down to a spaghetti supper.

"Hope you've got enough of that to share," he ventured, offering one of his half grins with the comment. Harrison hung his hat on a peg by the door, sat down at his usual place at the head of the table, and nodded to Hannah. "Hannah Lauren, how about you fixing me a plate and a glass of tea."

Hannah did so, and Harrison and the children fell into their usual camaraderie of sharing dinner and talking over events of the week. The children, unaware of any tension in the air, chatted happily to Harrison about their activities. He'd previously started a game with them, wanting to see their best A school papers on Fridays, and they all raced to get those for him to look at after dinner.

Alice watched his easy repartee with the Stuart children and felt touched, as always, at the affection the children held for him and at how easily he handled them. If any quibbling started, he had a way of quelling it with simply a stern look in the perpetrator's direction.

He stayed for Bingo, playing a few games and then commandeered the role of caller for the last games. He got up to refill his iced tea a few times, looking over Alice's shoulder at her progress in the game.

When she won a Bingo game herself, and started to get up to select a prize from the prize basket, Harrison stopped her and asked her to wait.

"I decided Alice shouldn't always be the one to buy the prizes." He walked around to her end of the table while he announced this. "When she wins, she always knows what she'll get because she chose everything. I brought a prize for her tonight in case she won."

He pulled out a small box wrapped awkwardly in Sunday comic newsprint paper and tied with a string.

Stacey wrinkled her nose. "Your wrapping's not as pretty as Alice's," she said saucily.

"No, it's not," he agreed, offering his prize to Alice. "But it'll have to do."

"This was nice of you." And out of character, Alice thought, feeling uncomfortable.

"I've been coming for dinner and taking home my Bingo prizes for a long while." He lingered by her chair. "Figured it about time I gave something back."

Alice pulled off the paper and string to reveal a felt jewelry box. She hesitated then, a little chill of premonition rolling up her spine.

"This looks fancy," she said as she worked to open the box. Inside, she found a diamond ring, a beautiful square cut diamond glittering between two rich, blue sapphires. Her breath caught in her throat.

Harrison knelt down on one knee beside her chair.

"Alice Beryl Duncan Graham, I'd like to ask you to become my wedded wife and to take this ring to show our formal engagement." He looked up at her in all seriousness, his eyes dark and intense.

The children sat in a rapt hush, simply watching them.

"Why would you ask me this, Harrison?" she asked quietly, finding her voice at last.

He looked around the table. "Well, I can think of six good reasons for why," he answered softly. "These children need a father as well as a mother and I'm hoping I can fill the bill and do a right good job in helping to raise them."

She studied him, weighing his words, wishing for more.

Sensing her hesitation, he added, "I'd say there's a right good attraction between us, too, Alice Graham, that ought to start things off nicely." He offered that half grin of his, his dimple showing, and then gave her a deep lust-filled look that set her pulses throbbing.

He lifted the ring out of the box for her, took her hand and slipped it on her finger. The size fit perfect and the ring sparkled up at her invitingly.

"Odell helped me figure out the size to buy but not the idea of adding the stones around the diamond." He kissed her fingers. "I knew blue your favorite color and to me these sapphires look like the color of your eyes."

It was a dreadful moment for Alice, and she looked at the ring in agony while she considered what to do.

"Say yes!" Stacey blurted out into the silence—always the most impulsive one among the Stuart children to express herself.

Tildy clasped her hands and echoed the sentiment. "Please, please, say yes, Alice. We like Harrison."

"Then I won't be the only boy anymore," Thomas put in encouragingly.

"Hush." Hannah frowned at them. "This decision is Alice's to make."

Alice found her voice then. "Yes, it is, and it's one I'll need to think more about." She took the ring off and put it carefully back into the box.

Harrison's face fell and quickly hardened.

"It's a beautiful offer." She bit her lip. "I think I understand why you've made it just now when you did, Harrison, but I'd like to think about it a little longer if it's all right with you. Getting married is a big decision."

He stood up then, a shuttered expression over his eyes.

She reached out and took his hand. "It was good of you," she assured him candidly. "And I appreciate what you're doing."

The kids had started to grumble and talk among themselves in disappointment. Harrison gave them a pointed look to quell them and pulled Alice to her feet.

"Walk me out to say goodnight," he said to her.

He turned to the children. "You children put away the Bingo game and clean up the kitchen while I tell Alice goodnight. Don't you be giving Alice a hard time about this after I've gone, either. She has a right to think on a thing as serious as marrying an old cowboy like me."

They walked out onto the porch, and then Harrison urged her to walk further with him, out of sight of the house and away from nosy eyes and ears. He stopped and turned her to face him as they got to the bridge across Timothy Creek that separated their two properties.

Alice felt a shiver, remembering the first time she'd seen Harrison Ramsey from this bridge. She felt sure he remembered that day, too.

"It wasn't only to satisfy the gossips that I proposed," he told her quietly, looking down at her with serious eyes.

A sweep of intense feelings rolled over Alice and she found she couldn't find words to speak to him.

He ran his finger down her cheek and leaned to brush his lips gently across hers. Her heartbeat kicked up, and Harrison touched his fingers more boldly to her heart above her breast, putting her hand against his own heart in return.

"It's good between us, Alice," he whispered huskily. "I've thought on it and I don't think it would be a mistake."

She shook her head, not knowing how to say what tugged at her heart. Not knowing how to tell him what she wanted most to hear without causing him to say the words to please her without meaning them.

"I don't want you doing this under pressure." She pulled away from his touch. "I don't want to do this under pressure, either. I want time to think, and I want you to have time to think and to be sure."

Harrison looked annoyed at her words. "I'm not the kind of man to make a decision without being sure in myself of what I want, Alice."

She shook her head, dropping her eyes, not wanting to meet his. "Let's wait and see how you feel later on when all this gossip is past and gone." She tried to smile. "You've done what you were expected to do. I'll tell everyone you asked for me honorably, and that I wanted time to think on it. That's honest."

Alice watched him searching her face in the dark, trying to read her expression. "There's something else you're not telling me, Alice. Is it David?" His voice sounded pained.

She touched his face. "No," she answered him. "There will always be the memory of David in my heart. I was married to him and I did love him. But time has helped me past that loss. My feelings and decisions today are not affected by that."

Harrison ran his hands slowly down Alice's arms and another sweep of physical sensations rolled over her. He drew her into his arms again, the waves of attraction between them igniting and washing over them both.

He kissed her, and Alice let herself deepen the kiss herself this time, enjoying the thrill of it.

"I do want you, Alice." He murmured the words against her mouth before he kissed her again.

She knew his words true and heartfelt, but she didn't know how to explain that she wanted more.

"You'll think about it?" he asked, as he let her go at last She knew he struggled to let her go and step back. She struggled to let him go, too

"I'll think," she whispered, starting to walk back toward the house while she could, before her feelings took precedence over her reason and caused her to accept his proposal just to have him.

A short distance from the bridge, she hesitated and called out to him. "You cheated at Bingo so I could win, didn't you?"

She heard his laugh float back through the dark.

CHAPTER 20

Harrison slept fitfully the night he proposed to Alice. His mother guessed wrong that she'd say yes gratefully, glad to get a proposal simply because she fostered six kids. Clearly, Mozella didn't know Alice Graham.

The next day Harrison found it difficult to concentrate or keep his focus on his tasks. His dreams the night before, a tormenting mix of images of Alice and Ava Reagan, kept him tossing and turning fitfully. Ava had seldom crossed his thoughts the past years and he couldn't understand why she roamed through his mind this freely now. Other than Alice, she'd been the only woman he'd ever felt a real connection to—so possibly his issues with Alice had stirred up memories of Ava.

He worked hard all day trying to eradicate his pent-up feelings of both Alice and Ava. Women were a torment. That was a fact. He'd done admirably to stay clear of them all these years.

By afternoon, Harrison gave up the idea of getting any relief through his chores. He walked to Meadowbrook, saddled Bishop, and took off on a long ride to clear his head. He rode to Pinnacle Point, knowing he'd felt drawn there before he found himself heading up the shaley, hillside climb on the backside of the mountain.

The point lay on a flat rocky outcrop on the lower ridges of the Greenbrier Pinnacle – a difficult spot to reach. Harrison dismounted to lead Bishop carefully around narrow sheer drop-offs along the narrow path. Near the rough trail's end, Harrison tied Bishop in a sheltered spot and edged his way on foot over rocks and around a series of familiar ledges to climb out on Pinnacle Point. The view spanned before him as spectacular as he remembered—across the whole valley and for miles beyond. He recognized the rolling hills of Webb and English mountains, saw the soft blue Smokies ranges and the misty hills of the Cherokee National Forest to the east and west.

He hadn't stood on this spot for fifteen years and didn't know what drew him here today. In the rocky outcrops behind the point, he searched for and located the old cave, stretching only twelve feet into the mountain and barely high enough to stand up in. Harrison worked his way toward the back of the cave, the afternoon sun slanting just enough light into the opening for him to see his way. He easily found what he sought, his and Ava Reagan's names scratched inside a heart they'd carved with their pocketknives into the rock wall.

This pinnacle and cave had been their special place—where they shared their hearts, their bodies, and planned their lives. He hadn't come since Ava left. He looked around, finding nothing changed. That often happened in nature. Places could remain almost the same for centuries if people didn't come and tamper with them.

Harrison inched back out of the cave to sit against the rock ledge high on the face of the Pinnacle. From here he could soak up the peace of the view and wonder why Ava Reagan rode his mind.

"Ma spoke right saying I do know how to love. I fell in love with Ava Reagan when I turned thirteen. Loved her all through high school." He picked up a stick to turn in his hands, remembering her black hair swinging straight around her shoulders, her dark eyes and olive skin.

"We dreamed our future, like kids do, got engaged before we graduated." He spoke his thought out loud, needing to put voice to his feelings. "I gave her my grandmother Ida Belle's engagement ring. Couldn't afford a new one. Started fixing up the old rental house behind the W.T. market for us to live in—same place my folks lived after they married." He frowned. "Didn't think it odd

Ava wanted to plan the wedding after summer, to work down in Gatlinburg and make some money."

He snorted. "Guess I showed myself green and naïve. Never imagined she'd met someone else. Didn't even know she'd run off and married him until I got her letter and my ring in the mail one day." Harrison snapped the stick in half. "Drew Vernon Cawood—some preppy college graduate doing a hotel internship, getting ready to take the head job running one of his daddy's resort ranches in Colorado."

Harrison took a deep breath. "I couldn't admit it then but it tore my heart out. I had to get away a while and got admitted into the university down at Knoxville and into a dorm at the last minute before fall session started. Majored in Ag Econ and Business." He rolled the broken pieces of the stick in his hand. "College did me good. Matured me and smartened me up." He chuckled.

"Got cocky, though. Met Patsy Ogle when I came home for summer. Enjoyed her flirting and simpering after me. Calling me the big college man. Offering herself up like birthday cake." He shook his head. "I enjoyed dropping in and squiring her to a few dances and events over the year. Came home to take her to the senior prom—and found her pregnant. Like Thomas said, when you do bad things bad stuff happens to you."

He smiled at the memory. "Did the honorable thing though. Arranged to marry her but she ran off before she walked down the aisle. Lucky break for me but another disgrace to live down."

He flung one of the sticks far out over the ledge. "That time proved a turning point for me in gaining some good sense. Went back to school, moved in the Ag frat house, got straightened out with my faith. Changed my attitudes and morals, even worked in campus Christian work." He grinned. "I felt a real sense of gratitude for my escape from Patsy Ogle."

Harrison shifted against the rock and stretched his legs in front of him. "At twenty-two I graduated and came back home, ready to work on the land. I worked hand-in-hand with Daddy until he died three years ago. Moved from the little rental house to the Ramsey home place when Ma married the preacher."

He stood to his feet. "Kept women out of my life—and trouble out of my path—until Alice came along. Can't figure how that one sneaked up on me or why Ava has played through my mind like an old song I can't tune out." He kicked a stone in his path as he made his way to where Bishop stood tied. "Maybe it's like a Pandora's box. Once you crack it, all sorts of troubles fly out."

Seeing the shadows lengthening over the mountain, Harrison mounted Bishop and started back. "It's a funny thing." He patted the horse's neck fondly. "I finally worked myself up to proposing to another woman, and she refused me. Danged if I know whether to be sorry or glad."

Harrison was nearly down the riding trail back to the stable when he saw the snake on the trail ahead. A good-sized rattler, it lay coiled in a patch of late day sun by the side of the path. If walking, Harrison could have avoided it easily, but as it turned out, the noise of Bishop's hooves on the trail stirred up the snake. It reared its head in defense at the oncoming horse, and Bishop shied, bucked, and tossed Harrison clean out of the saddle in the process. The dang horse never had acted right around snakes.

As luck would have it, when Harrison fell, he landed right by the rattler, and it did it's snakely duty and fanged him neatly on the leg before it slithered off to safety and left him there. Harrison stayed as still as possible until the snake moved completely away so it wouldn't feel further threatened by him. Snakes didn't really like to bite people unless they felt threatened or provoked.

The bite hurt like the dickens though, and Harrison knew he needed to get down the trail to get it tended to. "Dadgumit," he muttered, retrieving his hat to slam it back on his head. "As if this day couldn't get any worse."

He checked the wound. "Not too deep, mostly a knick where one fang penetrated above my boot, but it probably means another trip to the hospital."

The problem was he found it a real difficult to walk on the leg, and Bishop had run off like a dang sissy and left him alone. To further complicate matters, the anti-venom kit Harrison always carried lay neatly packed in Bishop's saddlebag.

Annoyed, Harrison resorted to the old time incision-suction method for snakebites. He cut a long strip off his belt for a tourniquet, bound it around his leg below the knee and above the bite mark. Then with his pocketknife he made a short, shallow cut above the bite. Having no suction cup, Harrison resorted to sucking out some of the venom above the bite with his mouth and spitting it out. Since he had no breaks in his mouth tissue from the fall, he'd probably be okay with this method in a pinch.

Harrison hobbled off the trail to locate a branch to use for a walking stick and whittled off its excess limbs quickly. By holding on to the stick, he found he could make some slow progress walking. Few people died of snakebites if they got to help, but it figured unlikely he'd get any needed aid if he didn't get down the mountain.

"Lord, I got no trouble praying and hoping a late trail group might come this way." He inched a few more feet down the trail, wincing at each step with the pain. "I could certainly use a rescue about now."

About ten minutes later, Harrison looked up from a daze of dizziness and pain to see a rider heading his way. It was Alice riding Elsa and leading Bishop behind her.

"Thank God." He sent up a prayer of thanks as he muttered the words. He didn't know how much further he could have limped on.

"Harrison, what happened?" Alice exclaimed in alarm, as she slid off Elsa's back to run to him.

"A snake bit me," he told her. "Bishop threw me right on top of the danged thing. Horse never has shown good sense around snakes. Gets frantic; acts stupid."

"What kind of snake?" Alice put an arm around his waist to help support him. He felt glad for the support with dizziness making him unsteady on his feet and his vision starting to fuzz.

"Rattler. Nice big one, too."

He heard her sharp intake of breath.

"In Bishop's saddlebag is an anti-venom kit. Go get it. I used the cut and suction method already, but it's not as effective as the anti-venom injection to neutralize the poison." He spoke the words slowly, working to organize his thoughts.

She went briskly to get the kit after helping him to sit down on the pathway and stretch out his injured leg.

"Think you can handle a shot needle?" he asked when she returned. "I'm a bit dizzy and shaky now. I want to be sure the stuff gets in there and not on the ground."

"Tell me what to do and I'll do it," she said matter-of-factly.

She injected the serum like a pro and then got Harrison on Bishop to start the walk back.

"Keep a watch on me in case I get woozy and start to fall off," he advised her, his speech slurring now. "I've been out here a while. In case I don't have the presence of mind to tell you when we get down the mountain, you'll need to load me up and get me to the hospital as soon as we get there."

She tied a lead from Elsa's saddle to Bishop's and then quickly mounted the mare. "How fast should you ride?"

"A fast walk but not a canter," he told her. "It's not far back now, Alice. Try not to worry. It'll be all right."

Her white face told him she was already worrying.

He tried to smile at her. "Lucky for me most of the bite got my boot. Only one fang nicked me above the boot line."

"One fang is enough," returned Alice through tight lips. "Hold on to that saddle horn and we'll see how fast we can get you down this mountain."

"How'd you find me?" he thought to ask out of the blur.

"I was out riding and ran into Bishop heading down the path toward the barn without you in the saddle," she said. "I started backtracking up the trail looking for you."

"Did it scare you finding Bishop without a rider?" he asked teasingly.

"Shut up and hold on to that saddle horn," she answered testily.

"You'd better be glad I went out riding when I did."

They rode in silence. When the Meadowbrook barn came into view, Alice rode directly by it and up through the yard to the driveway where her car sat parked. She managed to get him into the car on the back seat with his leg propped up.

"You stay put while I run and get my keys," she told him.

"It's not likely I could go anywhere," he answered as she leaned over him to settle him.

"You feel good," he said, his speech sounding muzzy to him. He looked up into her concerned eyes. "You know I prayed someone would come, and then you came."

"Glad to know you're a man of prayer," she said candidly, heading off to the house.

She ran back in a few minutes, all the children following anxiously behind her.

"Hannah and Megan." She waved a hand toward them. "You girls put these horses up and be in charge until I get back with Harrison. Rachel, you stop that crying right this minute. Harrison is going to be fine and your crying isn't helping in any way. Thomas and Tildy, I'm counting on both of you not to be any trouble to Hannah and Megan until I get back from the hospital."

"What about me?" Stacey asked, realizing she'd been ignored in the run down.

Alice turned to her thoughtfully. "Stacey, you get in the backseat with Harrison and be sure both he and his leg stay steady until we get to the hospital in Sevierville. I can't belt him in back there."

"You want me to go with you?" Her eyes widened in genuine surprise.

"You have a cool head in an emergency even if you are only eight," she replied. "Do you think you can manage Harrison all right?"

"Yes, ma'am," she said with a touch of pride, climbing into the backseat. "I'll manage him just fine." The determined look in her eye let Harrison know she certainly would.

The rest of the evening passed in a blur to Harrison. The venom started to addle his senses, and the pain filled most of his conscious thoughts. Harrison thought he might have drifted in and out of consciousness on the car trip, and he knew he drifted out after they wheeled him into the hospital from the emergency room. As he heard later, the staff dealt with him quickly and efficiently, then put into a room for observation.

He napped, woke up feeling some better, and found Stacey sitting there watching him intently.

"Where's Alice?" he asked her.

"Down seeing about your paperwork and getting you checked out," Stacey told him. "They say you can go home shortly but you've got to rest."

The pain felt greatly eased in his leg. He could see below the sheet they'd wrapped some sort of gauze dressing around his leg and he wore one of those scanty hospital gowns, his clothes folded neatly over a nearby chair.

Noticing Stacey twisting around nervously on her seat, Harrison asked her, "Are you all right, Stacey?"

"It was scary when we brought you in," she answered in that honest and direct way she always had. "A lady in the emergency room said people can die of poisonous snake bites."

"They can if they don't get the right first aid and help." He shifted to try to get more comfortable. "But deaths actually occur in less than one bite in 5000 with snakes. I'm glad I got to the hospital when I did though. The quicker a person gets anti-venom treatment and medical help, the better it goes for them."

Two large blue eyes looked his way solemnly. "Then you were lucky Alice came and found you."

"Yes, I was," he replied, giving her a bit of a smile.

They sat quietly for a moment.

She sat forward in her chair. "You know you messed up with Alice when you proposed to her."

This took Harrison off guard, having nothing to do with snakebites.

"How do you figure that?" he asked curiously.

"You weren't romantical enough," she pronounced matter-of-factly.

He crossed his arms in irritation, piqued at a child critiquing his marriage proposal. "I knelt down, said a proper proposal, and had a nice ring."

"That part went pretty good," she acknowledged, shrugging. "But you didn't do enough romancing before that to get her all readied up to say yes."

Harrison suppressed a chuckle. "How should I have gotten her readied up?"

"You didn't even take her out on a date or anything." Stacey rolled her eyes in exasperation. "You didn't send her flowers or buy her candy and gifts. I'd expect that if someone wanted to marry me." She lifted her chin. "I'd want gifts and for someone to call me beautiful and say they couldn't live without me. Girls like that stuff, Harrison. All you did was say you could help her out with us kids, make things easier for her. We all decided later that's where you messed up. And why she didn't say yes."

"I see." He bit back a smile. "But you did like the ring, didn't you?"

"Yes, we all liked that." She crossed her legs. "Especially the part where you said the sapphires in the ring looked like her eyes. That was the only real romantical thing you said, Harrison. She got all misty-eyed for a minute over that. But as Thomas said, there wasn't enough of the mushy stuff girls like in your proposal to make her say yes."

She looked directly at Harrison then. "I guess this isn't the best of times to be telling you this, Harrison, but if a little kid like Thomas would know what girls like, it seems a grownup man like you would. Have you not dated much or anything?"

"No, I haven't dated much or anything." He frowned.

"Perhaps that explains it," she replied tactlessly, getting up to go and look out the door.

A flash of alarm crossed her face as she turned back toward him. "You won't tell Alice what I told you, will you?"

"No," he answered. Not a chance.

She sat back down with a flounce. "Maybe if you really want Alice to marry you, you might try again and be more romantical the next time. I think you could do good if you tried. You're real handsome and Alice looks at you sometimes all mushy-like. We think she might say yes another time if you do it better."

"Thanks." He grimaced. "I'll keep that in mind."

"Here comes Alice." She lowered her voice. "Talk about something else!"

He took the cue. "Why don't you get me my clothes off that chair, Stacey. I'd like to get dressed to get out of this place."

"Now, slow down Harrison," Alice said, coming in the door. "There's a doctor coming to check on you before you can get dressed."

She leaned over to kiss him on the forehead, and Harrison saw Stacey give him a thumbs-up sign behind her.

"How are you doing, cowboy?" she asked, smiling.

"I hear I'm doing fine and that you're getting ready to spring me," he answered. "Alice, thanks again for all you did."

"That's what neighbors are for," she answered. But he saw more in her eyes than that before she turned away from him.

About an hour later, Harrison talked the doctor into letting him go home. Normally patients with pit viper bites are observed for eight to ten hours in the emergency department. However, because Harrison's bite was graded mild and because he showed normal lab values, little swelling, and no signs of toxicity, the hospital agreed to release him after only half the time.

Harrison got chewed out royally by the doctor, though, for utilizing the old incision-suction method on the trail. The doctor reminded him that many people create more complications for themselves by trying that outdated method. However, he grudgingly admitted Harrison had handled all aspects of it admirably and was impressed Harrison always carried an anti-venom kit in his saddlebags. He said few people thought of that when they went into the mountains—said he wished more people did.

Finally, after Harrison assured the doctor he'd get someone to stay with him over night and return to the hospital if any unusual symptoms appeared, the doctor agreed to release him. Alice took Stacey by Meadowbrook on the way to Harrison's place, briefly checked on the other children, and then drove him to his farmhouse. The clock over the mantle read eleven o'clock by the time Alice helped him into the house.

He enjoyed leaning on her and breathing in her scent as she helped him walk back to his bedroom. "Are you going to take my clothes off and help me into bed?"

"No, Hobart is coming to do that." She helped him settle on the bed, propping an extra pillow behind his head. "I called him from the house a few minutes ago and asked if he would sleep over with you. I figured it wouldn't be a good time for me to stay after all the talk that's been going on. Hobart should arrive shortly."

"Too bad," he drawled. "I'd hoped to persuade you to stay over, me being injured and all."

Alice gave him an admonishing look. "Let's get your leg propped up and elevated like the doctor said."

"I'm doing okay, Alice." He watched the concern in her eyes as she settled him. "You can stop being so anxious now."

"And why shouldn't I be anxious?" She snapped out the words. "You know I was scared to death through all this. You could have died up there, Harrison Ramsey."

"Would that have troubled you?" he probed, wanting to hear her say yes.

"Don't be silly. You know it would." Tears glistened around the edges of her eyes now.

She shook her head to clear them. "I'm going out in the kitchen to see if I can find you some soup and milk. I think it would be good if you ate something."

He caught her hand. "Kiss me, Alice. I've been wanting you to all evening."

"You're sick," she argued with him. "You need to rest."

"I'll risk it," he said, pulling her down on the bed partway across him and finding her mouth. He felt her sigh against his mouth and give in. It felt more like coming home to kiss and hold her than it had to walk in his own front door.

Harrison's head and leg ached, but he wasn't immune to the sweep of new emotions he felt invading his heart. He cupped Alice's face, looked at her intently, but found it difficult to unearth the words he wanted to say. She looked so beautiful, her hair falling softly around her shoulders, her eyes deep and blue.

She smiled, leaning down to kiss him lightly on the forehead like she would one of the children.

"I'm glad you're all right, Harrison," she whispered. "I don't know what I'd have done if I lost you."

Harrison's heart thrummed in his chest, but again he couldn't seem to find any words to express how he felt. His feelings felt so strange and intense.

Alice pulled herself away from him then, hearing Hobart drive up in his old truck.

"I hear Hobart," she said, touching a hand to his cheek one last time. "I'll go let him in."

The moment slipped away, and the words Harrison yearned to say continued to evade him. A few minutes later, Hobart walked in, and the story about the snakebite had to be retold and talked about.

Later that night, it was Hobart who soothed Harrison when bad dreams haunted and he woke with his leg throbbing. He saw Alice's face in his dreams—Alice's and then Ava's—another confusing night.

The next day Harrison felt much better. Hobart insisted he lie around the house and rest for the day. Alice came by before she left for work and insisted he do the same.

"I'll come by in the evening with a plate of Odell's supper for you after I get home from work," she promised.

Over the day, Harrison decided he might try to work on some of Stacey's romancing tips for when Alice arrived later. He took a hot shower, dressed more carefully than normal, tidied up the kitchen and even put a couple of placemats and two candles on the table to spruce it up. He thought about driving out to get flowers but dismissed that idea, knowing he'd have to drive by Hobart and Deke at the stables and explain why he wasn't resting.

Bored with being inactive, he went out on the front porch, with a glass of tea and a new paperback, to enjoy the late afternoon. He sat there, with his injured leg propped on a stool, when the phone rang. He picked it up absently, his mind lost in the book.

"Harrison here," he answered.

"Harrison, it's Ava," said the voice on the line.

Shocked to hear her voice, he dropped the book to the porch.

"I've been thinking about you for two days," she said, as though only yesterday they last talked. "Haven't you felt it? I've sent you mental messages like we always used to do to see if you would get them."

She giggled then, but the laugh had an anguished sound to it. "Oh, this is a painful time, Harrison. Drew's been in a terrible accident, and they say he might die. I'm having to act so brave and strong with everyone. I needed badly to call someone I could talk to who'd understand I'm falling apart." He heard her draw in a deep breath. "I hope you don't mind, Harrison. I so wanted to hear your voice. The voice of my very best friend ever."

Ava started to cry raggedly then. "I'm sorry about meeting Drew and hurting you, Harrison. I want you to know I'll never stop loving you and thinking about you. But I found this different kind of love with Drew I never expected. Now I may be losing him." Her breath caught. "I know it sounds crazy but I couldn't stop thinking about you during all this. Wanting to simply talk to you. I've missed sharing my life with you. I wish we could have stayed friends."

She began sobbing again.

"Harrison, are you even still there?" she asked on a harsh sob.

"I'm here, Ava," he answered.

"Do you ever think of me at all?" she cried.

"I went to Pinnacle Point yesterday." He leaned over to pick up the book he dropped.

"Now there's a memory." Her voice softened. "I loved that place. I've never been since we went the last time."

He flexed his fingers. "Neither have I, but something drew me there yesterday."

"I was messaging you," Ava said. "And you got it. We're still connected. Oh, I'm so glad I called. It's been awful here."

"How are your boys handling this?" he asked, knowing she had two little boys now.

"They're at one of our friends' homes. I thought they were too young to sit hour after hour at the hospital. To try to understand about their daddy."

He eased his leg off the stool, wanting to shift positions. "Who's sitting with you through all this."

"No one—and that's sad, isn't it?" She sucked in a ragged breath. "Drew's father died a long time ago. His mother comes occasionally but all she does is cry and say how hard this is for her to bear. How difficult for her emotions. Then she goes home, and I'm almost relieved to be alone again."

Harrison stood up to walk over to the porch rail. "How long has he been there?"

"You mean Drew?" she asked.

"Yes," Harrison said, finding it hard to say the man's name.

"Three days. He's in ICU, and they keep saying they don't know if he will even make it. If he'll live." She stopped to suck in a sob. "How am I going to get through this, Harrison? What am I going to do if he dies?"

She burst into tears again, and something caught in Harrison's heart.

"I'll be there on the next plane I can get," he told her. "Tell me where you are and where to come."

It didn't make sense, but suddenly Harrison knew he had to go. He went into the house and found a pen to write down all the directions and phone numbers Ava gave him. Then he called the airlines, scheduled a flight, packed a bag—some meds and pain pills for his leg—and started the drive to the airport. Hobart and Deke had left the stables now, so Harrison only had to stop and open the outside security gate before leaving. He didn't have to deal with anyone trying to dissuade him from going.

He knew now why Ava played through his mind these last few days. They'd always had the ability to connect to each other when they needed to. It had been one of the hallmarks of their relationship. Harrison knew if it reasserted itself now, after all this time, that he needed to go to her.

He left a note for Alice taped on the front door, telling her where he'd gone and asking her to call and tell Hobart to look after things. He assured her he felt fine and not to worry. He couldn't think what else to say right then.

Within two hours, he'd left his truck at the airport, checked in and picked up his ticket at the airline counter, and sat buckled into a seatbelt on a flight to Colorado. Luckily, he'd gotten scheduled on the dinner flight.

CHAPTER 21

Alice walked over with Harrison's supper at six o'clock. Dark fell earlier now with the autumn days getting shorter. The sun, an orange ball to the west, cast long rays in glowing fingers across the country fields. Perhaps Harrison would feel strong enough to walk part way back with her. Possibly to the bridge. She smiled at that thought.

Something in his eyes last night made her think his feelings toward her were deepening. She watched him struggle for words that wouldn't come, and it gave Alice hope.

As she walked up on the porch, she saw a note taped to the door. She scanned it quickly, then put her supper plate on a table by the door and sat down on the glider to read it again. It said simply: *Alice ... Emergency situation. Ava's husband may be dying. Had to fly unexpectedly out to Colorado. She needed me. No time to call anyone. Tell Hobart, Deke, and Bud to cover for me with the businesses until I get back. I'll call Bud with some contact numbers when I get there. Leg feels okay now so don't worry. Thanks ... Harrison.*

Alice felt stunned. Harrison had packed and taken off to be with an old girlfriend that, as far as she knew, he hadn't seen or talked to in over fifteen years. Simply because she needed him. Because her husband might be dying. All he'd left behind for her was this brief, business-like note. As if that was enough or made it all right.

Her tears started then, letting her know how surprised and hurt she felt. He could have at least called. Or stopped by. Even if he hadn't been able to reach her, he could have left a message on her cell phone or answering machine.

She studied the note again. There wasn't a soft word in it. Only the assumption she'd come to bring dinner and read the note. He'd left her instructions to contact Hobart, Deke, and Bud Jenkins at the store—like he might a private secretary. As if it meant nothing that he'd left abruptly to race to out west to an old flame.

She remembered his leg then. What was he thinking—taking off while recovering from that snakebite? Granted, the doctors suggested one day of rest probably enough, but they advised him to ease back into work responsibilities. And now this.

Alice, continuing to feel stunned, looked up to see Hobart's battered, farm truck drive up. He eased out of the front seat, his old beagle hopping down after him.

"Is Harrison here?" he asked her, starting up the porch. "Bud Jenkins called me to say he saw Harrison drive by the market. I figured I'd better come by and see why he tried getting out and about this soon."

Alice simply handed him the note.

He scanned it and then dropped into the nearest rocker. "Well, I'll be double dad-blamed," he said, shaking his head. "I've known that boy since the day the doctor gave him the first whomp on his butt at the hospital, but I'd never have predicted this one. Whatever do you figure got into him?"

Hobart looked up from the note, noticing Alice's tear-streaked face for the first time. He also saw the dinner plate sitting on the table by the door.

"Dinner for Harrison?" he gestured toward it.

She nodded.

"I gather, then, he expected you." He scratched his chin. "So that's why the note's addressed to you."

She nodded again.

"Looks like right good food to go to waste," he hinted, with a sideways grin.

"Help yourself." She tried to offer a smile.

Hobart got up to get the plate, sat down, and started to dig into the dinner.

"I was getting ready to cook fer myself when I got the call from Bud," Hobart told her between bites. "I planned to read Harrison the riot act for getting out and about too quick. It weren't like Deke and I didn't tell him all day we'd go out and get him anything he needed. Seemed sneaky like to me that he'd take off without phoning or anything. Sort of got me riled up to think on it."

"I know the feeling," Alice replied flatly.

"I guess you do, having brought dinner over to him and all."

They sat quietly for a few minutes.

"You hurt over this, girl?" Hobart asked candidly.

"Yes." Alice answered him honestly. "I haven't had time to think through logically whether I should be or not."

"Always hurts to get stood up without a warning," Hobart observed.

"I guess it does." Alice shrugged. "Hasn't happened to me often; I wasn't very prepared for it."

Hobart snorted. "Who is?" He jabbed his fork in the air. "Can't figure out what that dad-blamed boy is thinking. No one can get the man to take a vacation or take no time off for himself. Always worrying about the stables, the rentals, the store, or the orchard. Afraid something will need to be doing that no one else can do just like him. And, then, on a dad-blamed whim he off and flies out to Colorado. A day after he's been snake bit and might have ended up dead on a shingle. Don't even tell us where he's going in any detail. Or leave us a phone number or nothing. And hardly any kind of explanation that makes sense for why he took off."

Alice reached over to pat his knee. "Thanks, Hobart."

"Thanks for what, girl?" he asked, confused.

"For coming by when you did. For getting mad. For making me feel less emotional and stupid for being upset myself."

"I reckon you've got more a right to be upset than I am in some ways." He picked up a fried chicken leg with his fingers to eat it. "I guess you're aware Ava was an old girlfriend of Harrison's. Since he's sparked around you these last months, it can't make you feel any too good to have him take off to Colorado on a dang whim like this."

"You're right about that." She bit her lip. "Why do you think he went, Hobart?"

"Well, that's curious, it is." He scratched his head. "I can't rightly say I know. But now that I think on it, Harrison acted peculiar the last couple of days. Had his mind kind of divided. Didn't seem as focused as usual. Even took off up to Pinnacle Point. That's where he went yesterday before he rode back on Bishop and got bit by the snake."

Alice felt confused. "Where's Pinnacle Point and what does that have to do with this, Hobart?"

"I guess you wouldn't rightly know about that." He forked up a bite of mashed potatoes before continuing. "It's an old rocky peak up on the Greenbrier Pinnacle. Rough trail leads to it. Used to be a special place Harrison and Ava Reagan went to as kids. Gave them a thrill getting up there, being on top of the world. You know, teenagers like that risk stuff. They used to go there a lot, those two. But I don't think Harrison has been there once since the day Ava left. Too many memories, I guess. Right odd he should go there yesterday and then that she'd call him and he'd take off."

"How do you know he didn't call her?" Alice looked at him in surprise.

"Uh, just a gut feeling." He looked toward the barn thoughtfully. "Harrison might mull and stew on thoughts of Ava if he got her on his mind for some reason, but I don't reckon he'd call her. He hasn't called her once since she married fifteen years ago. Nor seen or talked to her since he learned about it."

"Then why would he go now?" Alice searched for answers. "Because her husband might be dying? Because he thinks he might get back with her?"

"It's too much for me to figure on," Hobart said confusedly. "I can't tell you, Alice. But it was my sense he'd started getting real feelings for you."

Alice nodded. "Mine, too," she admitted. She blinked to keep from crying again.

"You know," Hobart said thoughtfully. "I do remember this one odd aspect about the relationship of those two. Ava used to talk about it. She called it messaging. Said she and Harrison could message each other, that they were connected in some way. Girl had a lot of Indian blood in her so I always credited her talk to that factor. She said she could message to Harrison when she needed him. That he'd know."

"What did Harrison think of that?" Alice raised an eyebrow.

Hobart picked at the last scraps on the dinner plate. "You know Harrison's a right practical man in most ways. But living up here in the mountains, we come to know there's a lot we don't understand about the ways of things. Sort of humbling. But Harrison's always been keen to pick up on strong emotional feelings, pulls, and stuff like that. Gets a sense about things. Doesn't dispute or argue with what comes in that way much either. Usually just acts on it and often impulsively."

"I've seen that," Alice agreed, thinking about how they were drawn together from the first day they saw each other and how impulsively Harrison responded.

Hobart continued. "I guess what I'm remembering is how Harrison got to thinking on Ava right before she called him. Maybe picking up on her and her troubles but not knowing what it was yet."

"You think that's why he went to her?" Alice yearned to make logical sense of it.

"Could be part of it. Danged if I know the rest," he replied, scratching his chin again. "Woman's married, been settled on a resort ranch her husband's family owns and that he's managed for nigh on fifteen years now. Heard tell she birthed two boys. It don't make sense she'd pine for Harrison after all these years."

"But her husband may be dying," Alice offered. "Some women are afraid to not be married. To be alone and on their own."

"Yeah, I've met them clingy types. But that's not Ava." He shook his head. "She's a strong-natured girl. Tough and sure of herself.

Not one of them weak, flimsy types of women." Hobart sat his empty plate on the floor. "No, there's a story here somewhere for why Harrison's gone out to Colorado, that's for sure. But I guess we'll have to hang around in the dark wondering about it until he shows back up to explain it. Irritating, ain't it?"

Alice grinned in spite of herself. "Yes, Hobart, it certainly is."

He got up and patted her on the head like a child. "You don't worry none about this," he said. "Won't do you no good worrying and won't answer nothing, anyway. You just trust it on up to the good Lord and go on with your life raising those kids and doing your work."

"You're right in that, Hobart," she said, getting up to leave. "I'd better be getting on back home to those children now."

"You know, Alice," Hobart stopped her with a hand before she could leave. "Deke's always said Harrison don't have no gift or finesse with women. It's real likely he wasn't thinking at all about how this would strike you when he took off."

"I think that's obvious enough." Alice picked up Hobart's plate to carry home with her.

"If you'll pardon an old man's presumption, I'd like to say I think you and Harrison make a real good pair." He grinned. "Deke and me have put our betting money on the two of you getting together for a right good time now."

Alice shook her head, not open to consider his words right now.

"This here that's happened may be something. And it may be nothin'," he added. "But being the scrapper I am, I'm gonna offer the suggestion that you fight fire with fire."

"Whatever does that mean, Hobart?"

"That you get to messaging him right on back where he belongs." He chuckled at his own idea. "Birds fly both ways, you know. I've seen you and Harrison to have a right good connection of your own. If an old flame can call him out west after all these years, I reckon some new one can call him right on back home more powerfully. After all, it's your taste he's got uppermost on his mind right now."

Alice blushed. "I'll think about it, Hobart. I'd better get on back now." She walked down the steps and started toward Meadowbrook.

"If you think on it," he called after her. "You'll know the power place and where to do your messaging and praying. Everybody's got a place, you know. Some spot of meaning. Them things ain't easily understood. But they're even in the Bible."

"Maybe I don't want to message him," she called back.

"Nah, that's only your anger a speakin'." He sent her a toothy grin. "After that settles down, you think about what I said. My daddy always told me a woman's got a lot of mysterious power she can exercise on a man if she's a mind to."

Alice walked off, shrugging. These people in the mountains certainly had peculiar ideas. As far as she was concerned, the facts spoke clearer than all of Hobart's superstitious talk—that Harrison Ramsey had gone off on a whim after his old love while recovering from a rattlesnake bite. Alice figured that tantalizing story would be all over the valley by tomorrow.

She sighed. She'd better go home and prepare the kids before they started to hear the gossip from someone else.

Over the next few days, Alice found herself the subject of even more tittering speculation and gossip than before. It began to almost feel normal to be talked about and quizzed wherever she went. No one had heard anything further from Harrison. He faxed a few emergency phone numbers to Bud Jenkins the morning after he left, but he asked that no one call unless a serious emergency occurred. Surprisingly, everyone left it at that and respected his privacy.

By Saturday, Alice—totally ready for a break from it all—decided to load up the children and go to Gatlinburg for the day. They could eat lunch in one of the cute restaurants like all the other tourists, poke through the gift shops, and ride the Sky Lift on cut-rate passes Alice found in a local circular. She needed to get away from the house and all the reminders of Harrison, if only for a day.

The break proved a pleasure. They rode to the top of Crockett Mountain on the Sky Lift, which thrilled the children as they dangled their legs from the high two-seater chairs. They bought souvenir photos and drank sodas at the shiny, blue picnic tables by the gift shop while enjoying the views high above Gatlinburg.

Forsaking healthy eating for the day, they wolfed down foot-long corn dogs at Fannie's for lunch, shared pieces of homemade fudge after, and sampled fresh, warm, sticky taffy they watched being pulled and wrapped at the Ole Smoky Candy Kitchen. In The Village mall behind the candy kitchen, they explored the old world shops and boutiques, wandering in and out of the colorful stores, sniffing homemade candles at The Candle Cottage, trying on hats and buying a hiking guide in The Day Hiker, enjoying the tantalizing aromas of fresh-baked donuts in The Donut Friar, and laughing over the "Tennessee Popguns" in the Cartoons and Toys store.

Wandering up the parkway afterwards, they watched a weaving demonstration in the Arrowcraft Store, looked at the beautiful photography in Beneath The Smoke, and then explored some of the shops packed with tourist treasures. The girls now wore colorful, beaded Indian necklaces they purchased with their allowance while the twins proudly wore Indian headbands with a feather in the back.

The group split briefly as Alice took the twins into a small toy store while the older girls walked next door to a feminine gift boutique. As Alice herded the twins toward the gift shop a short time later, she could see Stacey in a confrontation with the store clerk.

"You know, I don't think you're a very nice person," she heard Stacey say loudly as she let herself in the shop door. "You ran off and left our friend Harrison standing at the alter in our church. Our housekeeper said, at the least, you should have left before Harrison got to the alter and the bridal music started to play. Did you even think about how he probably *felt* standing up there and learning you simply took off?"

The clerk, a pretty, petite brunette, about Alice's own age, leaned over the counter to shake her finger at Stacey. "Little girl, you're making a scene in here and causing my customers to leave."

The last of the remaining customers slipped out the door as she spoke.

Rachel walked quietly up behind Stacey. "It really wasn't very nice what you did," she said softly, backing Stacey up.

Scanning the store, Alice located Hannah and Megan keeping at a safe distance and smirking beside a shelf of colorful pocketbooks.

Alice marched over to the counter and took Stacey's arm. "Stacey Marian Stuart, for heavens sake! Mind your manners."

The clerk looked up and glared at Alice. "It's about time someone got in here to see about this. Don't you think these girls are too young to be traipsing around on their own without supervision?"

Standing closer now, Alice saw the clerk looked somewhat overdone, as Grandmother Beryl would say—her hair teased and lacquered with hair spray, her face heavily made up, and her cologne overpowering.

Alice pasted on an apologetic smile. "I was next door with the little ones in the toy store." She gestured toward it. "I could see the girls through the glass partition between the stores."

"Hummph," scoffed the clerk.

Alice turned to Stacey, her face angry and set. "Stacey, I think you owe this lady an apology, don't you?"

"No," Stacey answered back smartly. "Do you know who she is? She's that Patsy Ogle lady who stood Harrison up at the church. It says so on her nametag. I asked if she was the lady that almost married Harrison, and she said yes."

Alice's eyes moved to the clerk's nametag. "You're Patsy Ogle?" she asked in surprise, without thinking.

"I'm Patsy Ogle *Rimmer*, if you will note." Patsy taped her nametag with a long red nail. "I own this store, and I can't see why whatever happened with Harrison Ramsey and me years ago is any business of yours or your girls."

Alice began to feel embarrassed. "You're right, it's not, and I'm very sorry. We're neighbors of Harrison Ramsey, and I guess the girls heard the story of how you almost married Harrison from our neighbors. The children are fond of Harrison, you see, but that doesn't give them license to speak to you rudely or pass judgment on what they know very little about."

She gave Stacey and the other girls a pointed look after this. The older girls and Rachel had the grace to drop their eyes and look guilty, but Stacey held her stony expression firm.

Patsy rearranged bottles of cologne on the counter. "You'd think that old story would have lost its appeal for the gossips by now. I'm glad I live down in Gatlinburg now and away from all that priddle-praddle."

Alice began gathering up the girls for a quick exit.

Patsy cleared her throat. "Since your children ran all my customers out, the least you can do is tell me who you are before you leave."

"I'm Alice Graham." Alice offered her hand. "We live in the old Newland place."

She shook Alice's hand and then looked thoughtful. "I heard someone with a lot of children bought Meadowbrook. I guess that makes you next door neighbors to Harrison."

The twins sidled up beside Alice now.

"Are you really the lady that walked out on Harrison?" Tildy asked, wide-eyed and fascinated.

"Tildy!" Alice shook a finger at her.

Patsy rolled her eyes "Geese-Louise, they're making me feel like a seven-day wonder here. You know, I might have had *good* reason for not marrying Harrison Ramsey. I might have reasons not fit to discuss in front of your children, too."

Stacey stomped back toward the counter. "There's *no* reason good enough for what you did to Harrison. It was just mean."

Thomas jumped into the fray before Alice could intervene again. "Yeah, you did a mean thing, and you should say you're sorry."

Alice began pushing the children toward the door. "Stuart children, I don't want to hear you say another rude word. You go outside this door right now and wait for me until I come out." She gave Hannah a pointed look. "Hannah is in charge."

She turned back to Patsy. "I truly apologize. I had no idea the children had overheard so much gossip about Harrison's or your past. I regret their bad manners in criticizing you. They're usually much better behaved."

"Now there's a nice little apology." Patsy picked at a red nail. "I kind of figured after all this time, that old story would have died down." She leaned over the counter. "Let me ask you something. Has Harrison ever said why I left the church like I did?"

Alice paused before answering. "No, and it's probably that mystery aspect that's kept the old story alive for so long."

"Perhaps," said Patsy thoughtfully. "It's like Harrison to keep his own counsel about it all this time, too."

She looked out the window at the children huddled by the door. "You know, that smart-mouthed one reminds me of myself at about the same age. Pretty, spunky and sure of herself. You better watch out for her, you hear?" Patsy leaned over the counter toward Alice. "Listen, I'd say come back real soon, but I'm not sure I'd mean it." She laughed heartily at her own words.

"I certainly don't blame you for that," Alice muttered, as she left.

She silently directed the children down the street, back into The Village, an enclave of old world shops, and into a quaint ice cream parlor called the Village Café and Creamery. She ushered them to a table in the back of the store before she confronted them.

"Whatever brought all that behavior on?" she asked, frowning. "It was extremely rude of you to criticize that woman the way you did."

"Megan and I didn't do anything," Hannah said innocently.

"Silent accessories to a crime get arrested in the same way the criminals do, Hannah." Alice 's eyes flashed. "I saw both of you smirking over there by the pocketbooks."

Hannah rolled her eyes dramatically and shifted the subject a few degrees. "Isn't it unreal that we actually went in Patsy Ogle's shop? What were the chances that could even happen?"

Megan leaned forward. "Stacey noticed her nametag or we might not have known." Her eyes found Stacey's. "That was sharp of you Stacey."

Alice interrupted. "I don't think Stacey needs compliments."

Rachel lifted her chin. "I thought Stacey acted brave. She stood up for Harrison."

"I stood up for Harrison, too," piped in Thomas. "I told her she should 'pologize."

Alice shook her head. "Don't any of you understand why what you did is wrong? Even if you disapprove of what happened between Harrison and Patsy in the past, it wasn't your place to criticize it openly to an adult you don't even know. Especially in her public place of business. That was rude and inappropriate. I'm very disappointed in all of you."

Stacey put her hands on her hips. "Aren't *you* mad at her for what she did to Harrison?"

"Patsy claimed she had a good reason, Stacey," Alice said. "Perhaps she did."

"Pooh, you're only saying that because you're mad at Harrison for going off to Colorado to Ava's," bit back Stacey.

Hannah jumped on this new subject. "Why *did* Harrison go off to see Ava like that?" she asked. "Everybody's talking about it, and I don't understand. Odell says Ava was Harrison's old girlfriend way back in high school and that she's been married and gone from Greenbrier for over fifteen years. Why would Harrison want to go see her?"

"I told you," Alice explained. "Ava's husband is real sick and may be dying. Harrison went to help and support her right now."

"That's weird." Megan scowled. "Rhoda's mother said Harrison hasn't even seen or talked to Ava for all this time. Why would he go out there now?"

Hannah's eyes grew wide. "Do you think he still loves her and went hoping her husband might die so he can marry her now? DeeDee said he wanted to marry her once."

Rachel began to cry. "I don't want Harrison to marry anyone else except us."

Alice sighed. "Stop it, Rachel," she ordered. "I've had about all I can take today, and a scene in the ice cream parlor would be about one too many scenes for me, do you understand?"

Rachel made an effort to stop sniffling.

Thomas jutted out his bottom lip. "I thought Harrison was going to marry us." He turned to Alice. "Harrison won't really marry that Ava lady, will he?"

"There is no point in speculating about what Harrison Ramsey will or won't do," Alice replied. "That includes speculating about whether he'll marry us—or more precisely, marry me. If you recall, I didn't tell him yes when he asked me. I'm not sure yet if Harrison and I should even get married at all."

Thomas looked confused. "But you and Harrison kissed and hugged and did all that love stuff."

Hannah rolled her eyes. "People can kiss and hug without getting married. You know that, Thomas. You're hoping Alice will marry Harrison because you like him, but it's more important that Alice likes him enough."

"She has to love him and he has to love her back if they get married," pronounced Stacey. "That's the way it's supposed to be."

"That's very true, Stacey." Alice felt glad to see the child settling down. "Thank you for saying it. It takes time for a couple to know clearly they love each other and to be sure. Marriage is an important decision."

"You know," observed Megan, grinning. "The store clerk over there is starting to look at us funny because we've sat here so long and haven't ordered any ice cream. Perhaps we'd better get some?"

"Could we?" chimed in Tildy, easily diverted at the thought. "I want bubble gum flavor if they've got it!"

"I want chocolate with nuts," cried Thomas, already jumping up to go look at all the flavors in the ice cream cartons behind the glass.

Glad to change the subject, Alice readily gave in and ordered everyone ice cream, instructing the children to take them outside to eat. Typical of young children, they soon chattered and laughed over ice cream, skimming their hands in the mall fountain and talking about the shopping they wanted to finish in Gatlinburg, serious subjects forgotten for the time.

While the Stuarts slept soundly later that night, tired from the long day in Gatlinburg, Alice lay awake troubled and thinking. She wondered why Patsy Ogle Rimmer decided not to marry Harrison and walked out on him at the last minute, and then worried fretfully over why Harrison flew impulsively to Colorado to be with Ava Reagan Cawood. Most of all, Alice wondered how she could keep missing a man who'd walk out on her the way he did. Who hadn't even called her once since he left.

Unable to fall sleep, Alice pulled clothes over her pajamas, slipped into a pair of canvas shoes, and let herself out the back door of the house. She walked through the chill October night across the yard to the little bridge across Timothy Creek. A full moon rode high overhead and the stars twinkled brightly in the clear sky. Alice turned her eyes toward the high ridgeline where she'd first seen Harrison that snowy day. She couldn't see the mountain clearly in the dark, but she knew the ridgeline in her mind.

Alice remembered the strong drawing and pull she'd felt toward Harrison from that first time she saw him on the ridge, sitting on his dark horse, the snow falling all around him. He said he'd felt the same drawing toward her. It seemed to Alice, looking back, that from the very first they both tried to fight that draw. Tried to fight the attraction between them and the powerful magnetism they found so hard to understand.

What had he said to her once: "My response to you affected me strongly but I didn't want to acknowledge it."

As Alice stood on the bridge now, she thought it silly how they'd both battled acknowledging their attraction and feelings for one another. Even now, with Harrison staying out west with another woman from his past, Alice felt that draw toward him deep within her. It made her shiver.

She remembered Hobart saying Ava and Harrison messaged each other. He'd said with Alice's connection being so strong with Harrison that she ought to message him back. Draw him home. She felt tempted with the idea right now. Instead, she decided to pray. If any messaging was possible, she'd rather let God carry the message. She'd rather trust God to carry the call to Harrison's heart that she wanted him to come back. Needed him to come back. She hoped it God's will that he would. Because, no matter what had happened, she still loved him. She hated to admit it just now, with her heart raw and hurting, but she knew it was true. She didn't know why Harrison had left as he did, but she loved him. The children loved him, too. If, as Grandma Beryl said, God's plan called them together, then it would need to be God's plan that called Harrison back home.

"Send him a message, God," she prayed. "Let him feel me pulling him back. Let him know I'm calling him. That I'm messaging him in a righteous way."

She smiled at that idea and then grinned a bit maliciously at her next thought. "And let him toss and turn with the message, that insufferable man. Let him be tormented for how he's tormented me. That only seems fair, God."

After praying out all the rest of her thoughts, Alice made her way on back to her own bed. This time she slept peacefully.

CHAPTER 22

Friday evening, almost a week later, Harrison turned up the familiar side road onto his property. He unlocked the closed gates of the Ramsey Stable, noting with satisfaction that the weeds beside the sign and around the mailboxes had been trimmed neatly back. He smiled; it felt good to be home. If he hurried, he might make game night at Meadowbrook. He had business to take care of with Alice. And he hoped to heaven that she would understand the change in his feelings.

When he strode through the back screen door and into the kitchen at Meadowbrook a half hour later, the children erupted in a riot. The twins ran to sling themselves at his knees in delight, and he threw them up into the air in welcome, making them both giggle and laugh.

He arrived exactly in time for dinner, as the children settled into their places to eat. All the makings for tacos sat on the table, along with a bowl of fruit salad, and some sort of refried bean casserole.

Thomas kept his hand in Harrison's, pulling him toward the table. "We're having Mexican night." He pointed. "We have decorations."

Looking around, Harrison noted the homemade place mats and the array of colorful paper decorations draped over the chairs and hanging from the light fixture.

"You can help us do our piñata in the back yard after dinner." Tildy almost jumped up and down in excitement. "It has treats inside it."

Thomas interrupted. "We get to take turns trying to whack it with a stick." He demonstrated the whacking procedure for Harrison.

"But we have to be blindfolded when it's our turn," Tildy explained. "Like with pin the tail on the donkey. It will be fun."

"I'm sure it will be," Harrison said.

He hung his hat by the door, noticing the older girls pass speculative looks between them. Alice hadn't spoken to him yet. She'd glanced from the kitchen with a surprised look when he came in, but then promptly turned her back to him to finish preparing drinks for the children. He hardly blamed her for the less than enthusiastic response, he thought. This wasn't going to be easy.

"Did you marry that Ava woman?" Stacey asked in her usual direct fashion.

Alice turned around with shocked eyes, ready to offer a rebuke, but Harrison waved her back.

"No, I didn't, Stacey," he replied easily, settling down into his usual place at the table. "Ava already has a husband."

"But we heard he might be dying," Megan said.

"Well, he didn't die," Harrison told her. "After a good long season of rest and some physical therapy, I think he's going to have a full recovery."

Hannah caught his eyes. "What happened to him?" she asked, while she put plates and silverware out for him.

"His small airplane crashed in the mountains." Harrison's jaw clenched at the memory. "Fortunately rescuers found him before it was too late."

"Like Tildy got found when she fell out of the tree," put in Thomas.

"Yes, sort of like that." Harrison reached for a napkin.

"Would you have married Ava if her husband had died?" asked Stacey candidly.

"Stacey!" Alice's temper flared. "That's too personal a question to ask Mr. Ramsey or anyone."

"I think Alice may be right about that one." He kept his tone casual. "And I think maybe we ought to all have our dinner now."

It was Rachel's turn to say the blessing. After she said thanks, blessed everyone, and blessed the food, she added, "Thank you, God, that Harrison is back safe." She hesitated and then continued in a rush. "And that he didn't marry that Ava lady or the mean Patsy woman either."

After the amen, Harrison raised his eyebrows at Alice over that last remark.

"Don't even ask," she threatened softly, as she leaned over his shoulder to give him a glass of iced tea.

They shared dinner then. All the children soon began to lighten up with Harrison and tell him about the happenings of the week he'd missed. He listened and talked with them but noticed Alice stayed unusually silent. At one point, he looked across the table, caught her eye, and saw her flush before her eyes slid away from his. He also saw a hurt and pained expression in her eyes when she glanced his way and thought he wasn't watching. He hated that. He'd never set out to hurt her.

When the children raced outside later to try their luck with the piñata, Harrison tried to corner Alice alone out of the children's hearing.

"I think you and I need to talk," he told her quietly.

She turned to him stiffly "I delivered your messages like you asked in your note. You don't owe me any explanation for your life or actions, Harrison Ramsey. After all, you're only my neighbor and our friend. Your personal life is your own."

A thread of anger seethed through his blood at her words. He grabbed Alice's arm and hissed at her. "You don't know what you're saying."

"I think I do and you're hurting me." She flinched and looked pointedly at his hand on her arm.

He pulled his hand back, banking his anger.

"I'm going down to check on Bishop and the other horses," he said abruptly, his eyes flashing. "I didn't have time before I came over to the house."

With that, he strode off toward the barn, reining in his emotions along the way.

As he passed Stacey crossing the lawn, she cocked her head and said sarcastically, "That didn't look very romantical to me, Harrison."

He didn't answer her, but continued his course toward the horse barn. He needed to try to explain things to Alice, but she wasn't making the task easy. Her words lashed more coldly at him than he'd expected.

A short while later, he rode up through the back yard mounted on Bishop. Alice's mouth dropped open in surprise to see him riding his horse across her neat lawn, but before she could offer a complaint, he reached down, scooped her up, and pulled her onto the saddle in front of him. She struggled and spluttered, but his strength was greater than hers, and he pinned her against his chest with one arm, managing to keep her from getting back down off the horse with the other.

The children stopped their game in astonishment, Hannah moving immediately toward Harrison in preparatory defense of Alice.

Harrison spoke to her firmly. "Hannah, I don't plan to hurt Alice, but I need to talk to her privately. Do you think you and Megan can look after these children for a while so I can do that?"

"Maybe," said Hannah thoughtfully. "Where are you taking Alice?"

"Some place quiet where we can talk for a little while." He struggled to hold Alice steady in front of him. "Will you trust me about this?"

She studied him for a minute or two before replying. "I guess."

"I do not want to go anywhere with you!" Alice declared, grappling again to break free and get down.

"That's too bad," Harrison replied, and he kneed Bishop off across the yard into a brisk canter.

About twenty minutes later, Harrison made his way thru the falling darkness to the old Ramsey cabin in the mountains, the same cabin where he'd found Tildy and Thomas the day Tildy fell out of the tree. After struggling and arguing with Harrison for a long while, Alice had finally gone stiff and quiet, simply riding through the gathering darkness with him, not saying another word.

Reining in, Harrison slipped down from Bishop's back and then pulled Alice down after him, taking her hand and leading her in the door of the cabin.

"Don't try to run away," he told her curtly, going over to start a fire in the fireplace. "I'll just come after you."

She crossed her arms in irritation. "I certainly don't think any of this cowboy drama was necessary in order to have a talk with me. What insanity is going on in your mind to act like this, Harrison Ramsey?"

He didn't answer her until he started a fire to ward off the chill of the cabin and stacked a few good logs on the fire from the woodpile.

Then he turned. "This is going on in my mind, Alice." He swept her into his arms and kissed her with a passion almost as hot as the flames he'd just kindled. She struggled at first, pushing against his chest, but then he felt her yield as that powerful attraction kicked in between them. He knew exactly when she felt it, too, because he heard the catch her breath and felt her sigh with resignation when it engulfed them.

"Alice, I've missed you so much," he murmured, burying his mouth against her neck and tasting the flavor of her skin. Her subtle scent of lilacs invaded his nostrils like an aphrodisiac, and he searched for her mouth once again.

A thick, hook-rug lay in front of the fireplace, and Harrison pulled Alice down on top of it, gathering her into his arms again. It was dark in the cabin, but in the light of the fire Harrison could see all he needed to see – Alice's soft face, her expression when he held her and kissed her, the way her eyes clouded when his hands wandered over her and slipped under her shirt to find her bare skin. After trying to hold back, she yielded to him, pulling his shirttail out of his jeans, letting her own hands play over his back.

They kissed and enjoyed the glorious feel of each other until both breathed heavily and until Alice pulled back. "Enough," she whispered.

He drew back then, too, getting his heartbeat back in control, working hard to put a clamp on his passions. He framed her face with his hands. "You're very beautiful," he told her. "I love to look at you, to look in your eyes, to see you smile that warm smile that washes your whole face in happiness. I love your hair, the way it feels like silk and smells, like flowers—the way those little wisps are always escaping and drifting around your neck." He touched one. "Do you know there's never been a time I've seen you that I haven't wanted to touch you? You've gotten to me in a way no other woman ever has, Alice Graham."

"What about Ava?" She bit her lip and dropped her eyes. "You took off and went to Ava. I don't understand that, Harrison."

"I needed to do that." He stroked her cheek. "Ava needed me."

"I needed you, too, Harrison." Alice answered him on a hurt tone. "Didn't you think about how I'd feel when you disappeared like that? When you didn't call me or explain why you left at all?"

He ran a hand through his hair. "I'm a man that follows my impulses sometimes, Alice. I hadn't seen or talked to Ava in all those years, but I knew I needed to go to her only a few minutes after she called me."

Her eyes lifted to his. "Hobart said he felt sure Ava called you after all these years and not the other way around."

"Hobart knows me well," Harrison chuckled, thinking of the old man. He looked across at Alice, savoring being alone with her. They sat Indian fashion on the hook rug, knees against knees where they could keep physical contact and look directly into each other's eyes.

"I felt deeply hurt," Alice admitted now, tears starting in the corners of her eyes.

Harrison reached across to wipe them away with his thumbs.

"Don't be hurt, Alice. It worked for the best what happened. I needed that visit out west to see Ava. It released something in me locked up for a long time."

"Tell me." She reached over to lay a hand over his.

He paused to gather his thoughts. "I grew up a rather lonely child in many ways," he said. "My mother and I didn't have the best of relationships, and my relationships with my sisters weren't much better. Ava became the first woman I ever related to in a strong way—except possibly Aunt Dora in an affectionate way. Like a soul friend to me, Ava and I shared everything together. I loved her, and I felt devastated when she left. I think I simply locked off my heart after that and shut it away."

"But there was Patsy later," Alice said.

Harrison shook his head. "Patsy was what Deke would call a skirt, a girl to fill time and make me feel manly again after being dumped by Ava. Patsy didn't love me and I didn't love her."

"You did plan to marry her." Alice's voice sounded confused.

"There are a lot of reasons why people decide to get married besides being in love, Alice." He took a deep breath.

"Was she going to have a child?" Alice hesitated over the words.

"Yes." He gritted his teeth.

"Was it yours?"

Harrison met her eyes. "She said so, and I believed her right up until our wedding day. Then Carter told me in the parking lot at the church that he'd hung out in a bar in Cosby the night before and heard a guy crying in his beer about Patsy Ogle. The guy said he loved her, knocked her up to get her to marry him, but that she planned to marry some dumb sucker her daddy liked better. Laughed bragging the poor guy even thought the kid was his." He scowled. "Carter looked closer, recognized the guy, and thought I had a right to know."

Alice's mouth dropped open. "Oh, my heavens. What did you do?"

"I asked Patsy if all of it was true, right there in the parking lot before our wedding. She cried and admitted it all. Told me she'd dated me that year mainly so her daddy wouldn't be suspicious and find out she'd been seeing Cleton Spangler on the sly. Her daddy didn't approve of Cleton or of his family."

Harrison shifted slightly. "Good reason for that actually. You'd have to know the Spanglers to understand why. I felt furious, of course, that she lied to me and used me, but Patsy claimed angrily I'd used her, too, to get over Ava. I knew her words rang true, so I told her I'd marry her anyway. Heck, everyone already sat in the church with me due to take my place up front in a few minutes."

He sought Alice's eyes before finishing. "It seemed like a bitter punishment. Like being framed might feel. I admit, I didn't walk to the alter a very happy man."

"Then she didn't go through with it." Alice spoke quietly.

"No." He shook his head. "She bolted. Climbed right out the church window, got in her car, and ran off and married Cleton Spangler."

Alice's blue eyes studied his in the firelight. "If you hadn't found out the baby wasn't yours, do you think she'd have married you without telling you?"

"That appeared to be her plan." Harrison shrugged. "However, when I found out the truth, Patsy told me candidly she loved Cleton and not me."

Alice looked thoughtful. "What happened with that marriage?"

"Cleton was a drinker and an abuser like his father." Harrison winced. "I gather that fact became apparent to Patsy after she ran off and married him. Later, after she had enough, she called her daddy to come get her and bring her home again."

A small frown crossed her face. "What about the child?"

"I've never known exactly what happened there." Harrison scratched his head. "Patsy and I never talked about it since that day at the church. All I know is she came home without a baby. I heard Cleton roughed her up and she lost it. A year after she came back to Tennessee, she married one of her daddy's young business executives, named Daryl Rimmer. As far as anyone knows, it seems to be a good match."

Alice fell quiet for a minute, thinking about it all. Harrison took advantage of the quiet to pull her over to him for another kiss. It felt good to hold her again.

"What a story," she said against his chest.

He pulled her back to look into her face with one of his half smiles. "Speaking of stories, what brought on that prayer request about mean ole Patsy Ogle I heard tonight?"

Alice giggled and told him about their encounter with Patsy in Gatlinburg earlier in the week. It made for a light moment amidst all their serious talk.

"I want to know about Ava now," she told him, sitting back to face him once more. "About what happened when you went to Colorado."

"It's true, I'd never seen or talked to Ava since the day she left Gatlinburg." He answered her honestly. "I'd kept my old image of her in tact and kept the concept of how I felt about her as a kid pretty much enshrined. The first thing I realized when I saw her was that we'd both grown up. She'd become a woman and not a girl anymore—a wife and a mother, with a wife's and a mother's worries about the family she loved."

"How did that make you feel?" Alice asked softly.

"Peculiar at first." He grinned a little. "But there's an easy comfort that comes back quickly when old friends get together. They know each other in a special way. Do you know what I mean?"

"I do." Alice smiled. "It's always warm and comfortable getting together with old childhood friends."

"I found that so, too," he admitted. "We caught up on the years and I offered friendship and comfort to her at a very hard time. I owed her that for all the rejections I sent her way when she tried to make her peace with me over the years." He found Alice's eyes, hoping she would understand. "The time proved healing for both of us, Alice. Ava needed my strength for the days when she didn't know if her husband would live or not, and I needed her good counsel about my own problems, too – once we learned Drew would pull through and be all right."

"What problems did you talk about with Ava?" She dropped her gaze from his.

Hearing the edge of hurt and jealousy in her voice, Harrison took her hands in his and tilted her face until he could look into her eyes. "After I spent time with Ava, and realized my young love for her had turned into a warm friendship, I realized I held a big passion for someone else."

"You talked to Ava about me?" Alice asked in wonder.

"I did." He reached out to stroke her arm gently. "I told her all about you and about the kids, and she told me all about Drew and her boys and her life on their resort ranch. She took me on a tour, too, showed me the place before I left. I want you to know, without a doubt Alice, that I've got that old section of my life all in place now. I needed that to happen."

"You don't love Ava any more?" Alice asked in a whisper.

"Like a sister, I do." A flicker of a smile touched his face. "But someone else has invaded my life and heart now as a lover. I didn't realize that fully before my trip out west. I'd started to deal with that realization after the snakebite, I guess, but I fought my feelings because of fear. Afraid to trust again."

She turned her blue eyes to his gently and put a soft hand on his chest.

"I love you, Alice Graham." He framed her face again with his hands, letting his thumbs move softly under her chin, touching her lips with his fingertips. "Please say you'll have me and don't make me ask you again."

He reached into his pocket to take out the ring box he'd presented to her before.

"I hoped to have candlelight, soft music, and flowers this time when I asked." He chuckled. "The children told me I wasn't romantical enough the first time I proposed."

"The only thing missing were the right words," Alice replied softly, tears starting to trickle down her face. "All I wanted to hear was that you loved me, Harrison Ramsey. I love you, too, you know. I don't know why we both fought so hard loving each other."

"Both stubborn, I guess," he murmured, leaning over to catch her left hand and slip his ring onto it.

"Does this mean you're saying yes this time, Alice?" he kissed her fingers.

She nodded tearfully.

"Glory, I'm glad," he said, wrapping her up in another embrace, enjoying the feel of her heartbeat against his.

"I can't tell you how much I'm looking forward to seeing how all this attraction between us explodes when we consummate this marriage." He drawled this in a whisper against her neck. "I don't suppose you'd like to find out right now, would you?"

"No," she answered very softly. "I want to do this right and get married in the church first." She pulled back to smile at him teasingly.

"Witch." He growled under his breath. "You want me to sweat out standing at the alter waiting to see if you'll actually come down the aisle."

"Oh, I'll come, Harrison. You can count on it." She leaned forward to kiss him again and her kiss proved no chaste and gentle one this time. Soon, they lay stretched out on the rug in front of the fire, their breathing ragged, Harrison lying across her and touching her in places he had no right to yet.

He rolled away from her at last, while he could, curling beside her to cuddle her against his chest.

After a space of precious silence, Harrison kissed her on the neck, and broke the quiet of the moment, shifting their position until he could look at her again.

"Alice, you messaged me, didn't you?" His eyes searched her face. "From off the bridge."

Her eyes widened in surprise. "Why do you think that?"

"I had a dream." He let his fingers thread through her honeyed hair. "I could see you there, looking up toward the mountain and thinking about me."

"What was I wearing?" She gave him a mischievous look.

He grinned. "It was dark and hard to see you. Perhaps something dark. Not red like the first time. But I knew it was you, and I could feel the pull. I knew you wanted me to come back. You prayed for it. It gave me confidence to ask you to marry me again, to take the chance to tell you I loved you." He paused to trace a finger down her cheek. "You did go to the bridge, didn't you?"

"I did." She spoke quietly, her heart in her eyes. "And I prayed there."

"You know I agonized about whether you'd have me. Whether you'd forgive me for taking off to Ava's like I did. Ava told me I handled that badly."

He saw her eyes twinkle at that. "Funny how prayers get answered," she said. "Did you tell Ava I messaged you?"

"Yeah." He chuckled. "She said I'd better get back home and claim you soon before some other man found you. That thought scared me."

Alice smiled at him, touching her finger to the dimple in his chin. "I love that dimple in your chin. I noticed it the first time I saw you at the barn and I wanted to touch that dimple even then."

"I'd have gotten down off my horse and kissed you right then if Odell hadn't come along." He pulled her into his arms to kiss her again with warmth, glad he could do so now without needing to hold back.

Alice drew back reluctantly at last. "I suppose we'd better go back and check on the children. I don't like the idea of them being alone for too long."

"You're right," he said, standing and pulling her to her feet.

She gave him an amused smile. "You know, they're going to ask us a million questions when we get back," she informed him. "Like when we're going to get married and whether at the church. Where we're going to live. You'd better get ready."

"My answers are that we'll get married soon, the sooner the better, and in the church, like you want. I hope your family will come. I'd like to meet them."

"They'll come and they'll be happy for me." A smile played over her lips. "Especially Grandma Beryl. I've already told her about you."

He scratched his head. "As for where we'll live, I guess it will need to be Meadowbrook. The farmhouse doesn't have enough bedrooms for all of us."

"Will that upset you to leave your family home?" She reached up to touch his cheek.

"Nope." He turned his face to kiss her palm. "I have better memories attached to Meadowbrook, anyway. It was like my second home, you know. I'll be happy there. In fact, I'd be happy anywhere as long as I'm with you." He kissed her nose after saying that and then let his mouth stray on down to her mouth again.

"Ummm," she whispered against his lips.

Harrison broke the embrace regretfully, standing up to put out the fire before they left. "You know, Alice." He turned to look at her. "I think Deke's wanting to get married, too, and he's worried about having a nice enough place to offer this girl Julie he's so crazy about. I think I'll let Deke move into to the farmhouse if you don't mind. I know he'd take good care of the old place."

"That sounds wonderful." Alice stood up and wrapped her arm around his waist. "You've been thinking all of this through, haven't you?"

Harrison led Alice back out into the night and shut the cabin door behind him. "I had a lot of time to think in those Colorado motels and on the flight back, Alice." He gave Alice a leg up on Bishop and paused to look at her before he mounted. "You know, Ava wants to come over to the wedding and bring her husband Drew if he's strong enough. I hope that's okay with you."

She grinned down at him and then laughed. "It would be fine with me even if Patsy came."

"That might be a little too much." He smirked at the idea as he climbed up behind her and wrapped his arms around her to take the reins.

They rode back down the mountain, Alice happily giggling and making plans along the way and Harrison loving the feel of Alice's body against him. He found he looked forward to the future now with a lighter heart than he'd known in a very long time. Alice had brought him the peace and love he'd yearned for, even when he didn't realize he needed either.

Her voice interrupted his thoughts. "You do understand you're not becoming only a husband in this venture." He heard the humor in her voice. "You're going to be taking on fatherhood, too. You'd better think about that very seriously before we get down this mountain and tell those children."

"Good try on getting out of this marriage, Alice." He wrapped his arms closer around her. "I'm marrying you even if you drag home four more children."

"That's an interesting thought." She leaned back against him provocatively in the saddle. "Thomas always wished for another boy in the family."

Harrison sucked in a deep breath at that, watching a silky vision of Alice carrying his child flit through his mind. The idea hadn't crossed his mind before, but the thought pleased him.

Seeing the barn at Meadowbrook coming into view, Harrison said, "Now, listen, Alice, you let me handle talking to the children about this."

"With pleasure." She nuzzled her head against his shoulder. "I'll be happy to have you handle a lot of things with the children from now on. To use all those fine leadership skills of yours to your heart's content."

He whistled. "Whew, there's a change of tune," he said in surprise.

"Not really," Alice answered. "My concern was always that the children would grow too fond of you, get too involved with you, and then be hurt when you later paid us less interest. Or found someone else to love and marry."

He considered this. "Is that why you got prickly about me putting my oar into their lives?"

"Mostly." He heard her hesitate. "It's a big responsibility to have six children to care for, Harrison. Are you sure you're up to it?" She turned in the saddle to look at him.

"You know me," he replied, giving her one of his half grins. "I love a challenge."

"I can promise you'll certainly have one." She smiled at him. "And I think your challenge group has been watching for us to come back." She pointed to the children, heading across the back yard to meet them.

"Give me a kiss while they're looking." He laced his fingers with hers. "I want them to know I've been romantical this time."

She giggled and gladly obliged him.

CHAPTER 23

They planned the wedding for the first Saturday in November and Alice could hardly believe how quickly the day arrived. She stood now, in the lounge of the women's bathroom at the Beech Grove Baptist Church, waiting to walk down the aisle.

"Everything looks beautiful," her sister Margaret said, peeping out the door. "There's a big crowd in this little church—and a lot of family and guests."

"Yes. Harrison wanted to schedule the wedding earlier, but we had to coordinate with family." She grinned. "And, of course, we couldn't plan the wedding on Halloween weekend because of the children. Harrison drove them all around the valley in his truck, letting them hop out at every house he knew to trick or treat."

"He's good with them." Margaret propped on the corner of a sofa and smiled at her. "Good with you. I like him."

"I'm glad." Alice reached out a hand to squeeze Margaret's, glad to have her present.

Alice chose Margaret as her matron-of-honor and only attendant, and Harrison's cousin, Carter Newland, drove from Nashville to be his best man. Alice and Harrison wanted to keep the wedding simple. Margaret wore a wine red dress, and Alice had decided on an ivory cream wedding dress for this second wedding, instead of a pure white gown as at her first. It seemed appropriate.

She and Harrison chose crimson red, like the color of the sassafras trees and scarlet oaks on the mountainside, mixed with ivory white for the wedding color scheme. Red and white roses decorated the wedding cake, and lush flower arrangements spilled over with vibrant red mums, creamy white roses, and sweet-smelling tuberoses. Thomas suggested carved Halloween pumpkins for a further decoration, but Alice quickly vetoed that idea, even though Harrison teasingly encouraged him.

Reverend Campbell agreed to conduct the service, and Alice insisted—against some grousing from Harrison—that his mother play the wedding music. Vick Nichols, along with his hotel caterer, Revelta Kizer, created the wedding cake and planned the food for the reception after the wedding. White tents fluttered now on the church lawn where the reception would be held. The November day, after a chilly morning, had turned warm and shirtsleeve sunny, and it promised to be a fine afternoon.

Margaret picked at a nail while they waited. She looked wonderful in her simple wine red dress, her red hair a glory of waves with a broad matching hat above it.

"Nice thing that Harrison had those cabins for most of the guests and nice accommodations for the rest in Gatlinburg." Margaret straightened her broad-brimmed hat. "It's lucky, too, that the children's grandfather could come for the wedding and stay afterwards to visit so you and Harrison could go on a honeymoon. Where are you going?"

Alice gave herself a small hug. "To some wonderful little resort on a Georgia coastal island Harrison found. We'll have a whole week alone—and lovely days to walk on the beach and explore the area."

She sighed just thinking about it as she shook out her dress. "You know, Margaret, it seems like the days simply whizzed by since we started our first plans for the wedding, and I'm eager for a break. Along with planning the wedding, we had to integrate Harrison's things into the Meadowbrook house."

Alice settled the short veil and hair garland over her head as she talked. "Harrison needed a room and office of his own. We cleaned out the furniture in the front parlor and made it into a den and study Harrison can call his own. He brought his desk and favorite furnishings. It turned out very mannish and Harrison." She grinned. "He can work or relax there whenever he wants some privacy."

Margaret came over to help Alice arrange the veil. "I don't think you had much trouble integrating him into the bedroom. That room is huge and has several closets."

"No, I didn't." Alice blushed to think about Harrison's continual presence soon to be in her bedroom every day and night. "The room had a whole, unused closet for him to take over and we moved a second chest of drawers in. He brought most of his things to the house already, and the rest he'll move after the honeymoon."

Alice bit her lip remembering some of the things Harrison whispered to her about what those honeymoon nights would be like—glad the time would soon be here. On several heated occasions in the barn and in the mountains, they'd found waiting until November to be extremely difficult.

Alice's mother slipped into the lounge now, coming to fuss with Alice's hair and to slip a rose into her chignon before the wedding march began.

She looked toward the window of the lounge with annoyance. "I can't believe Harrison nailed boards over this window, even as a joke, as he explained, to keep you from bolting. Everyone's tittering about it. Harrison's mother is especially displeased."

Alice hid a smirk. She'd arrived at the church to find boards over the window and it didn't take an explanation for her to know who'd put them there or why.

Her mother smiled at her in the mirror. "It's truly wonderful that someone chose to marry you, Alice, and take on all those children." She fluffed the short veil around Alice's shoulders. "It's hard enough to find a second partner, you know, once you've been married before. It worried me when you chose to foster those six children. I didn't think you'd ever find anyone else to marry after that."

Margaret cleared her throat from across the room. "Nice compliment, Mother," she remarked sarcastically. "You make it sound like Alice is some sort of conciliatory prize and that you're glad she could be foisted off on someone."

"Margaret Ruth!" She raised her chin. "You know very well that's not what I meant."

Margaret rolled her eyes and walked over to kiss her sister on the cheek. "I think it Harrison who is lucky and has gotten the prize, Mother."

Ignoring her, Alice's mother sent a worried frown to Alice in the mirror. "You don't think Harrison will wear his cowboy hat down the aisle, do you? Or those dreadful boots? He wore both when he arrived at the church today."

Margaret's laughter broke out infectiously and Alice started to giggle, too.

"Honestly, Mother," Margaret chastised. "You've only met Harrison twice—once once at the airport and then, again, at the stables yesterday. Granted, he did wear jeans, a cowboy hat and boots both times, but that outfit is occupationally correct for him."

Alice's mother tossed her head. "I know that, dear, but some men carry all that a little too far, you know."

Margaret slipped out of the women's lounge for a minute and then reappeared. "Okay. I checked, Mother," she said, laughing. "I can see Harrison standing with Dad outside the men's lounge wearing a tux and without either cowboy hat or boots. You can rest easy now."

"That's good." She adjusted her dress and patted her hair a last time. "Now I think it's time for your brother to walk me down the aisle."

She gave Alice a kiss on the cheek. "Be happy, darling, and make a sweet bouquet of memories to recall this day."

When she slipped out, Margaret looked after her. "That last bit sounded nice." She grinned. "Mother actually does say the right thing now and then."

She came over to straighten Alice's dress. "You look like a dream, Alice. Harrison is a lucky man."

"You do like him, don't you Margaret?" Alice bit her lip.

"I like him very much." Margaret reached out to take Alice's hand. "He is certainly a take charge man, but he has a comfortable method in the way he does it, and possesses that wonderful, sly sense of humor, too. I watched him marshal those children into their wedding clothes and over to the church this morning with incredible skill. Especially with them so excited. I was totally impressed." She grinned. "The man's not bad to look at, either."

Alice smiled at her. She cared very much what Margaret thought, had always respected and looked up to her.

Margaret squeezed her hand. "But my favorite thing about Harrison is how he looks at you, Nooney," she added, calling Alice by an old pet name. "The man has a fervent love for you. I like him best of all for that. I think he'll be good to you."

Alice hugged her big sister with affection. "Margaret, I'm so glad you could come, and you look very beautiful today, too."

Margaret looked down at her dress in pleasure. "That's partly in thanks to you for not picking some insipid pastel color for me to wear. You know what ruffles and pastels do for me with my height and red hair." She swirled around. "But this color and style is nice."

She peeked out the door again then. "I've gotta go now, Alice. It's nearly my time to walk. Dad's waiting for you to come out to him next. I'll leave the door open so you can watch for your signal."

In a few minutes, Alice heard the first chords of the traditional wedding march. She smiled as she came into the church entry to take her father's arm. She'd always loved the wedding march. To her, it didn't seem like a proper wedding without it. After a kiss from her father, she drifted slowly down the aisle, her ivory satin skirts brushing the floor behind her. Down front, she could see Harrison waiting—looking incredibly handsome in his black tux, his friend Carter smiling beside him.

Across the front row of the church, beside their grandfather Lloyd, sat the Stuart children, dressed in crisp new clothes bought just for the wedding, young faces shining with joy and excitement. Their happiness about this marriage made Alice's heart especially glad.

Stopping at the front of the church, she listened to first the minister's and then her father's response, presenting her to Harrison to be married. Then her hand lay in Harrison's and they were nearly ready to take their vows. As the minister finished droning out those familiar words about whether anybody had any objections to the wedding taking place, a stir suddenly began at the back of the church. A woman had stood up. Alice peeked over her shoulder and saw Patsy Ogle Rimmer.

She said loudly, "Everybody's been staring at me and whispering about me ever since I walked into this church before the wedding started, so I figured it couldn't get much worse if I stood up to say why I'm here."

After a collected gasp, you could have heard a pin drop around the church.

Patsy looked around her. "To be truthful, a smart-mouthed girl came in my shop a month or two ago, blessed me out and told me I needed to apologize to Harrison Ramsey for bolting from the church before we almost married here a long time ago. She called it a mean thing I did, and her brother and sisters vocally agreed."

She put a hand on her hip and looked around. "I came to do that, to apologize to Harrison and wish him the best on this day. He did a fine thing agreeing to marry me a long time ago when I didn't deserve it. Most of you had your own ideas about why I planned a wedding in such a hurry, and you guessed right as to why. The mean thing was I let Harrison believe himself the responsible party when he wasn't."

She pointed toward the front of the church. "His good friend up there, Carter Newland, told him about the other man in the picture right before our wedding. I confirmed the truth of it to Harrison in the church parking lot, and he agreed decently and uprightly to marry me anyway. It's one of the few times I ever felt humbled. However, when I got to thinking about it more, I decided he deserved better than the deal I offered him. So I bolted and married the real father, if you know what I mean."

Patsy scanned the audience with her chin held high. "Those

children up there let me know Harrison never told all of you the truth about that time. Gentlemanly of him, for sure, but I figured I owed it to him—now that he was marrying again—to come forward and tell you the real truth."

Reverend Campbell cleared his throat nervously and asked, "Well, ummm … you don't have an objection to Harrison and Alice being wed?"

"Of course not, Pastor. I came to set things straight." She sat down primly then as if it wasn't a totally unconventional thing she'd done at all.

A gasp and a rustle of whispers ran around the church while Reverend Campbell fumbled to find his place again in the service book.

A dark haired woman stood up on the other side of the room during the pause. "Since honesty is on the agenda, I'd like to do the same and set some things straight myself."

Alice heard Harrison groan.

"I'm Ava Reagan Cawood, in case any of you don't remember me. I know there's been a lot of negative talk for years about why I ran out on my engagement to Harrison fifteen years ago. Like Patsy, I'd like to say my reasons had nothing to do with Harrison. I simply fell blindly in love with someone else and handled the breakup of our relationship poorly. Recently, Harrison and I had an opportunity to talk all that out in good friendship, and I traveled all the way from Colorado today with my husband, Drew Cawood, so we could wish Harrison and Alice our very best."

Reverend Campbell, almost sweating now, searched for words. "So, you are, ummm … placing no objections either, Mrs. Cawood, to this marriage?"

"Certainly not," Ava said, sitting down. "They both deserve only joy and happiness."

"Well, ah, ahem … uh … I guess we can proceed with the service now," mumbled Reverend Campbell, looking around nervously, and pulling on his collar, hoping no one else planned to step forward.

"I think you can get on with it now, Reverend," Harrison said to him softly, the hint of a grin playing around his mouth now.

"Uh, hmmm, yes …Let's do get on with it," he boomed then, too loudly perhaps, bringing a low chuckle from around the room and a critical scowl from Mozella.

"Dearly beloved," he began at last, moving into the traditional wedding promises. Harrison and Alice pledged their vows and exchanged their rings—the ceremony slipping by all too soon. Then Harrison kissed her and Reverend Campbell presented them to the congregation as husband and wife.

To Alice's surprise, Harrison held up a hand as the congregation rose and started to applaud.

"I'd like to say a word before Alice and I walk down the aisle," Harrison announced, startling Alice with his words. "I've committed myself to Alice today, but I want to commit myself to the children Alice and I plan to raise together. Would Hannah, Megan, Stacey, Rachel, Thomas, and Tildy Stuart please come up to the front for a minute?"

He gestured to the space before them at the base of the alter steps, and the Stuart children walked up, wide-eyed, to stand in a row in front of Harrison and Alice.

"Alice told me you children and she made commitment vows to each other before you moved to Greenbrier," he said to them. "I'd like for us to make commitment vows here as a family today, too. Would that be all right with each of you?"

The children nodded solemnly.

Harrison proceeded to gather them together in a group, their right hands placed hand over hand together. Then he led them in repeating commitment vows he'd created that echoed the wedding vows he and Alice made.

He walked back to whisper a few words to Reverend Campbell then, returning to her side as the minister said, "May I present to you, not only Alice and Harrison Ramsey, but the new Ramsey-Stuart family."

The applause sounded deafening in the small church, and hardly a dry eye could be seen in the whole place as Alice, Harrison, and the children made their way down the aisle of the Beech Grove Baptist Church.

Outside the church in the receiving line, Alice and Harrison greeted their friends and guests. The outdoor reception Vick and the caterer planned couldn't have turned out better. The food looked exceptional, the cake stunning, and the music by the Parton Boys proved fun for all. Most of the valley turned out for Harrison and Alice's wedding, and everyone took pleasure in greeting the new bride and groom and lingering at the reception, enjoying the food, fellowship, and dancing. As the day wore on, Alice felt glad she'd worn old shoes dyed to match her wedding gown rather than brand new ones. She and Harrison led off several waltzes in the dance tent and later participated in hearty rounds of lively square dances.

The photographer had taken pictures of the bridal party before the wedding, but he snapped many more shots at the afternoon reception. Alice looked forward to seeing them all later.

As Alice stood watching the dancing, Margaret appeared at her elbow. "Alice, it's time for you to change your clothes and for you and Harrison to leave," she said. "Harrison has already left to change, and then we'll line everyone up to wish you both happy, throw rice, and tell you goodbye."

She took Alice's hand and led her toward the church. "Your bags are already loaded in Harrison's car and Carter told me you planned to head for the beach tonight. You'll want to get started on your way. Don't worry about anything, Alice. There's a whole crew to clean up, and I plan to go home with Lloyd to help with the children tonight. Tomorrow, when we leave, Odell will come to help Lloyd every day while you're gone." She gave Alice a hug. "Promise me you won't worry. Okay?"

Alice nodded, and allowed Margaret to scoot her into the church and back to the ladies lounge where she'd dressed earlier in the day. A few minutes later, Alice, clad only in her slip, sank wearily into a chair, thinking how beautifully the day had gone. Just as she closed her eyes a moment, she began to hear shrieks, screams, and crashes from outside the church. Worried, she scrambled into her clothes—distressed over the commotion going on. She'd just started to put on her shoes, when she heard a tap on the window behind her.

"Pssst!" said Harrison. "It's me. Open the window. There's a latch on the inside."

Alice searched for it, and then opened the window to him. Already out of his wedding clothes, he was taking down the boards he'd nailed in jest across the lounge window earlier.

"What's happened?" Alice asked him, hearing more crashes and raucous noises now that the window stood open.

He pulled the last of the boards away. "A stray dog sneaked into the reception tent and pulled a tablecloth off the table trying to get at some of Vick's gourmet food. Mozella saw him, started shrieking, and scared the poor dog so much he started running around frantically inside the tent with people chasing him. Naturally Thomas and Tildy soon led the pack trying to catch the dog and save the day, but somehow they ran into a row of chairs that fell and then dominoed against one of the tent pegs."

He grinned at Alice. "The whole side of the tent fell down on everyone, and as they struggled and panicked, they pulled out the other tent pegs on the other side of the tent." He shook his head. "You should see the mess out there, Alice. There's a mill of people shrieking and bouncing around under that fallen tent, and, of course, the food tables were under there, and they are an absolute mess now. The people who are crawling out from under the tent have cake and gourmet gravy all down their clothes and grass stains on their knees. And get this, the Parton Boys kept playing right on, through everything, in the tent next door. It's the funniest spectacle I ever saw in my life. I thought Carter and I would laugh our guts out."

"Oh, Harrison, this is awful!" exclaimed Alice. "Let me get my shoes on so I can go out and see about the children and make some apologies. I bet your mother is terribly upset over this."

"The kids are fine, Alice. They're with Margaret and she has them neatly in hand. As for my mother, she is already past redemption, shrieking about a smashed corsage and the giant mess everyone's made on the church grounds."

He laughed then, surprising her. "We're bolting, Alice. We're out of here. It's been a wonderful wedding and a wonderful day. As Carter says, between Patsy and Ava giving their wedding speeches and the tent falling in, the people of this valley will have something to talk about for weeks and weeks to come."

He climbed in the window and knelt to help her into her shoes. "Come on, Cinderella." He slipped her last shoe onto her foot after giving her toes an intimate kiss. "Let's make out exit. It's time to honeymoon."

Her foot still in his hands, Harrison began to rain a series of soft kisses all the way up her bare leg to her knee. As their eyes met, he gave her one of those rare smiles of his that lit his eyes and made his dimple stand out.

"What's your answer, Alice?" He pressed his lips against the bare skin on the inside of her knee. "Ready to bolt?"

Alice felt that old drawing starting between them, spinning her softly into its vortex and making the sounds outside fade away from her consciousness.

"I love that dimple of yours," she whispered to Harrison, leaning over to kiss his chin and then his mouth.

"You know," he said in a slow-as-honey drawl. "Babies born with dimples in their chins often have dimples on their bottoms, too." He gave her a roughish look. "I'll let you check mine out later on if you'll bolt with me now."

"Harrison Ramsey!" Alice gasped in shock. Then, despite herself, she leaned over and whispered to him softly, "Do you actually have them there, Harrison?"

He offered her a slow grin. "It's an absolute promise."

"Then let's go," she told him, with a mischievous smile. "You'd better not be lying about that only to get me to leave, either."

He stood up, turning to climb out the window.

She stared after him. "You know, probably everyone will think we're rude and inconsiderate for cutting out like this."

He held out a hand to her. "They'll never even notice we're gone with everything that's going on." He laughed. "And Carter said he'd get my car and hide it down the hill for our escape."

"Come on, Alice," he urged her, grinning. "All we need to do is sneak around the back of the church and cut down through the trees to the car."

She put her hand in his and pushed up her skirt to climb out the window.

"Somehow, Harrison, I have a feeling my life is never going to be boring between you and the children." She gasped as he dragged her around the back of the church and down a short, wooded slope toward their car.

"Not for one second," he told her huskily as he helped Alice into the car and kissed her soundly. "And this is only the beginning, Mrs. Ramsey."

As they drove away, they could hear Mozella's voice shrilling out over the air, "Someone get that dog out of that church pond! He's ruining the lilies and he'll be soaked and shaking water over everyone if you don't get him out of there right now! No, no! Wait, Thomas, don't go in the pond after him! ...."

Her voice faded away gradually as Alice and Harrison sped down the country road. They both howled with laughter by then—Harrison's arm draped companionably across Alice's shoulder.

"We're going to have a good life, Alice." He glanced away from the road to give her a loving look.

"You know, I think we truly will, Harrison Ramsey." She smiled back at him. "And I can think of six very good reasons that might make our lives even richer in the years to come."

He chuckled at her remark. "Perhaps while we're at the beach, Alice, we might consider your idea of increasing that number. Discuss it while you're checking out those dimples of mine."

Harrison leaned over to give Alice a quick kiss and then another longer one. She kissed him back with joy, her heart light and happy.

Suddenly she forgot to wonder whether Thomas dragged the dog out of the pond or got soaked in the process. If Mozella still shrieked or if the other children had fallen into the skirmish—or even whether the reception continued at all. She'd think about it all later, she thought. Much later.

EPILOGUE

Almost a year later to the day, Hobart Rayfield drove his old truck up to the Ramsey Stable and screeched it to a quick halt.

"We've got ourselves a boy!" he called out to Deke Olds. "And a fine boy, too."

"Well, I'll be danged if that ain't good news," Deke exclaimed, getting up from the barn bench to welcome Hobart. "How's our little mother?"

"Alice is doin' jest fine, Deke, and Harrison's about fit to be tied, he's so proud of that little boy of his."

Hobart reached down to scratch the ears of his old beagle, Skeeter, before he plopped himself down in his battered cane chair by the stable door.

"You been busy at the stable?" he asked Deke.

"Not much," Deke answered. "I let Josh ride up the trail with the three girls that came a while ago. He's gettin' real good with takin' the riders around since he's worked so many summers and weekends now. Besides, I hoped you'd be getting' on back soon with some news."

"Yeah, I'm glad not to have missed being there when Harrison's little boy got born," said Hobart. "You know I was there, too, at Harrison's birth, Deke. Took his ma to the hospital to have him."

"No kidding?" Deke thought about that and then asked another question. "Did those little Stuart kids all go to the hospital with you today, Hobart?"

"Yep, every blame one of them and they were about tickled to death over that new baby." Hobart grinned. "It made for a real pile of us in the waiting room, and then, later on, when we was all looking at the new baby in the nursery we about filled up the hospital hallway." He chuckled in remembrance.

Deke rubbed his chin thoughtfully. "Funny, I never figured Harrison would get married after all that happened to him. For sure, I never figured he'd marry himself into a big ready-made family."

"It was no surprise to me," asserted Hobart. "The man has been hungry for a real, happy family to belong to since only a tyke. I figure it just took a while for the good Lord to send the right family along his way."

"Yeah, maybe." Deke considered this.

They sat in silence for a while, mulling that idea over.

Then Deke asked, "You heard any word on that girl of Sissy's that went missing? She's your brother Ben's grandchild, ain't she?"

"Yeah, Hallie Walker. She's my great-niece, and it's about to worry me to death that she's gone off. She recently graduated high school, but she ain't even eighteen yet."

Deke picked up a handful of stones and began to toss them toward an old can. "Hallie used to come to the stable all the time when she was growing up and lived over acrost from you at your brother's place. I liked that kid."

Hobart nodded. "Yeah, and she proved a real comfort to her Grammie, Etta Mae, when Ben died. It about broke Etta Mae's heart when Sissy came traipsing back home and said she wanted her daughter to come live with her now—the girl nearly grown at that point. There weren't no real love developed between them neither. It was Grammie that raised her."

Another of Deke's stones found its way into the can. "If Grammie Rayfield hadn't died this spring, I bet Hallie might have come back to the farm to stay with her if she got unhappy or something."

"Maybe." Hobart scratched his chin. "Sissy had married herself again—and to another bad 'un from what I heard. I know Grammie worried about it some for Hallie's sake even before she died. I'm sure there's a story there."

Deke, finished with the stone toss, dropped his hands to his lap. "Perhaps it'll all turn right. I only mentioned it because a call came for you about it while you were gone. Wondering if you'd heard anything from the girl." He sent an apologetic look Hobart's way. "Didn't mean to spoil your moment of practically becoming another grandpappy today with bad news."

"Speaking of which." Deke went around the corner of the barn and came back with a sack in his hand. "Julie and I got Harrison's new boy his first little cowboy hat for a baby gift. I reckon we'll go up to the hospital tonight and take it to him. See how the boy's doing." He pulled out the little blue hat for Hobart to see.

"What if it had been a girl?" Hobart asked teasingly, noting the color.

Deke shook his head. "Nah. God had to even things out for little Thomas some. The kid needed a break with all those sisters. Some things are just destined to work out."

To learn what happened to Hobart's niece, Hallie Walker—and to find out what brings Hallie's Virginia cousin, Delia Walker, down south to her Aunt Dee's old cottage in Gatlinburg, watch for the next book in the Smoky Mountain series entitled *Delia's Place*. After that, travel back to Wears Valley for another wonderful family story called *Second Hand Rose*.

FOR SIX GOOD REASONS

Lin Stepp

About This Guide

The questions on the following pages are included
to enhance your group's reading of
Lin Stepp's *For Six Good Reasons*

DISCUSSION QUESTIONS

1. When Alice Graham considers buying a country home in Greenbrier in the Smokies, she remembers an earlier visit there in the winter. What unusual event happened at that visit? When does Alice first officially meet her neighbor Harrison Ramsey?

2. Why does Alice need a big country home at this time in her life? Why did she take in six foster children when she is single and a social worker? See if you can name the six Stuart children in her care and tell something unique you remember about each of them.

3. What is Harrison's Ramsey's occupation? What do you remember about Hobart and Deke, who both work for Harrison at the stable? How long has Harrison known these men? Were you ever "horse crazy" when younger?

4. What is Harrison Ramsey's relationship like with his mother Mozella? How do Harrison and his mother come to a better understanding of each other later in the book? Do you have any Mozellas in your life?

5. Did you like Odell McKee? How was she a help to Alice, Harrison, and the Stuart children? What was her past link to Meadowbrook?

6. After a happy summer, the Stuart children begin to develop problems when they begin school. What are some of these problems? How does Harrison try to resolve them? Why does this cause a quarrel with Alice?

7. Why do you think both Alice and Harrison fight against the attraction they feel for each other? What are some of their differences that cause friction between them? How does their ride together up the mountain help their relationship?

8. Thomas and Tildy Stuart seem to attract disasters. How does Thomas get kicked by a horse? What is Harrison's reaction? What is Alice's?

9. Several times in the book Harrison is drawn into unexpected spiritual discussions. What does he advise Hannah to do when people cause her trouble or hurt her? How does he explain salvation to Thomas in the hospital waiting room?

10. What happens when Alice and the children visit Beech Grove Church that makes them not want to return? Is the church's response what it should be after this event? What persuades the family to visit again? Do you think events like these often make people pull away from attending church?

11. What events have caused Harrison to distrust women and want to avoid future relationships? Why do you think Harrison never explained to people what happened to end his past relationships? What was unique in his relationship with Ava?

12. Alice worries that she might not be a good parent to the Stuart children, might try to push them into a pattern not right for them. How have both Alice and Harrison experienced negative parental pressure, not feeling loved or affirmed for who they were, in their earlier childhood? Have you ever felt negative parental pressures in your own family?

13. How are Harrison and Alice's methods in handling the children different? Do you think both authoritarian and democratic methods can work well in parenting? Which do you think is best? Which did you experience most in your childhood?

14. When Thomas and Tildy are lost, who does Alice reluctantly yearn for? When Harrison is snake bit, who helps and rescues him? How did these two events help bring Harrison and Alice closer? Can you remember a time when a hard situation helped you realize who was most important to you?

15. In the hospital after Harrison was snake bit, Stacey criticizes Harrison's courtship skills with Alice. What does she tell him? Has Harrison and Alice's courtship followed traditional patterns? How does Harrison try to improve on this later?

16. What happened on the overnight trail ride that caused a scandal for Harrison and Alice in Greenbrier? How did they respond to it? How did others respond?

17. Why did Harrison go immediately to Colorado to Ava when she called long distance? What did you think about this and about how Harrison handled leaving? What did others think about his actions—Alice, Hobart, the children, and others in the valley? How did this trip bring resolution to Alice and Harrison's relationship?

18. The wedding of Harrison Ramsey and Alice Graham proved eventful. What happened? Did you enjoy this ending? What did you like most about this book?

About the Author

Lin Stepp

Dr. Lin Stepp is a *New York Times*, *USA Today*, and *Publishers Weekly* Best-Selling international author. A native Tenessean, she has also worked as a businesswoman and educator. A previous faculty member at Tusculum College, Stepp taught research and a variety of psychology and counseling courses for almost twenty years. Her business background includes over twenty-five years in marketing, sales, production art, and regional publishing.

Stepp writes engaging, heart-warming contemporary Southern fiction with a strong sense of place and has sixteen published novels set in different locations around the Smoky Mountains and the South Carolina coast. Her coastal novels in the Edisto Trilogy are *Return to Edisto* (2020) and *Claire at Edisto* (2019). The latest Tennessee and North Carolina mountain novels are *Happy Valley* (2020), *The Interlude* (2019), *Lost Inheritance* (2018) and *Daddy's Girl* (2017), with previous novels including *Welcome Back* (2016), *Saving Laurel Springs* (2015), *Makin' Miracles* (2015), *Down by the River* (2014) and a novella *A Smoky Mountain Gift* in the Christmas anthology *When The Snow Falls* (2014) published by Kensington of New York. Other earlier titles include: *Second Hand Rose* (2013), *Delia's Place* (2012), *For Six Good Reasons* (2011), *Tell Me About Orchard Hollow* (2010), and *The Foster Girls* (2009). In addition Stepp and her husband J.L. Stepp have co-authored a Smoky Mountains hiking guidebook titled *The Afternoon Hiker* (2014) and a Tennessee state parks guidebook *Discovering Tennessee State Parks* (2018).

For more about Stepp's work and to keep up with her monthly blog, newsletter, and ongoing appearances and signing events, see: *www.linstepp.com*.